THE WAY WE GET BY

THE WAY WE GET BY

CHRIS DRABICK

For information contact:
Unsolicited Press
Portland, Oregon
www.unsolicitedpress.com
orders@unsolicitedpress.com
619-354-8005

Cover Design: Joseph Popa
Author Photograph: Tim Fitzwater
Editor: S.R. Stewart

ISBN: 978-1-950730-37-7

For Bob: The Truest Person I Ever Knew

CONTENTS

DREW & AARON

I went to college to get smarter, which now seemed stupid. My Bachelor's in American Studies didn't present a single marketable job skill, unless I could figure out a way to turn my talents in party conversation into a career. I had things all lined up to start graduate school that fall, but after I came home to my apartment one afternoon a few weeks before graduation and walked in on my girlfriend fucking my roommate, there was an abrupt change of plans. With no other viable options, I put my tail between my legs and headed for my mom's basement back in Flint.

At first, it was nice to be home. I had some wounds to lick, and there's nothing like a doting empty nester to help accomplish that. I could only spend so many weeks eating Kathy's pot roasts and having her do my laundry while I moped in my room listening to *Stranger's Almanac*. It wasn't healthy for me to never shower before noon. Boredom, a lack of disposable income, and a bit of gentle prodding from Kathy sent me out of the house in search of some sort of employment.

The best I could do at that moment was twenty-five hours a week at Home Theater Video, a small chain that was hanging on against the Blockbuster encroachment through a wide selection of foreign and independent titles, as well as a healthy-sized backroom of porn. After a few weeks of getting shouted at because all of the copies of *Twister* had been rented and helping weird dudes find nurse videos, I had enough superfluous cash to start spending on pints at Bob's. It was essentially the only thing I really looked forward to when coming back to Flint, and I was hopeful that the novelty wouldn't wear off.

***

My first trip to Bob's had been just a little more than a year earlier, although it seemed like a hell of a lot more time had passed.

I don't think I'd ever been on that block before, a little south of the Flint River, just west of Saginaw Street. I was pretty sure we were near St. Matthew's, where my family went for Midnight Mass on every Christmas Eve until my Dad's parents died, but that was pretty much the only time we ever came to this part of town. The area was pretty deserted, being a Friday night at around ten p.m. Most folks had the good sense to hightail it out of downtown Flint once the sun had set.

My friend Aaron had been coming to the bar since the previous summer, while I was hanging around in East Lansing with my girlfriend, Megan. That summer, instead of another few months of faux connubial bliss, she'd taken an internship in the attempt to firm up her med school application. I figured I'd spend the break at home, keeping my mom company and trying to prevent Aaron from making a mess.

We'd had to park a couple of blocks away from the bar, which made me nervous. "Remind me how you found out about this place?" Aaron was walking faster than I was, so I had to raise my voice to be heard.

He stopped, finally noticing I was a few steps behind him. "From Curt McCoy."

Curt McCoy was several years older than us, one of those lovable losers who was great to party with, but going nowhere. Aaron once told me that Curt hadn't been the same since a high school LSD binge had caused him to become obsessed with Prince's *LoveSexy* album. He'd spent days on end skipping school listening to it over and over, staring at the cover and tracing Prince's image with his index finger. When he finally got it together enough to return to classes, he demanded that all of his teachers address him as 'Spooky Electric'. He'd progressed enough to find work bagging groceries at Farmer Jack, where Aaron had worked in High School, but that was probably about the best Curt would ever manage. He was a sure-fire bet to score beer for us back in the day though, and

I assumed that, even with his mental capacity diminished by the hundreds of hours spent listening to "Alphabet Street", he'd be able to recommend a cool bar.

"I remember Curt. Or should I say 'Spooky?'"

Aaron shook his head. "He still tries to get people to call him that."

As we crossed the street, I could see the three-story red brick building that housed the bar in front of us. It wasn't much to look at, not anything more than an average storefront with apartments or office space on the top two floors. The weathered sign hanging over the entrance read "Robert's Grill" in faded black script.

I pointed to the sign. "Grill? They serve food?"

"Maybe once upon a time, I don't know."

As we got closer, I could hear the din coming through the open doors. There were dozens of voices in loud conversation mixed with a jukebox that may have maxed out its volume, pumping out "Percolator" from the most recent Stereolab record.

I took a few big strides to catch up and then poked Aaron in the ribs. "Stereolab?"

He nodded. "You won't believe the jukebox. I told you."

The bars in East Lansing usually filled their air with Candlebox or Stone Temple Pilots or whatever rape-rock the frat boys were into that week. Those places were also not surrounded by seemingly abandoned properties with overgrown weeds and an almost sinister darkness. I might have been a little scared.

We walked into the side door, but couldn't get very far due to the crush of humanity. It was unbelievable; a sea of young faces, goateed and otherwise, all manner of thrift store dress, polyester shirts and dresses: dead people's clothes, so uncool that they were cool again. People were crowded four, five and six deep in conversation, words that swelled and ebbed in unintelligible, overwhelming waves, but I could tell were frantic, almost frenzied, talking loud and saying nothing, like James Brown sang. Every cool kid in Genesee County had found their way into these four walls, holding unfamiliar microbrews and not quieting down one bit when "Percolator" ended and the jukebox clicked and whirred and came back to life with the menacing one-note bass intro of Pere Ubu's "Final Solution". I felt at once at home and completely out of my element.

Aaron wedged his way through the crowd to an open space at the bar and I stuck close behind him. The bartender held up a finger in a just-a-moment gesture, and Aaron nodded. He turned to me. "Pretty cool, right?"

"Pere Ubu?" It was equally surprising to me that there'd be a bar in Flint with Pere Ubu on the jukebox and that there was someone in the bar who'd played Pere Ubu.

Aaron gave me a quizzical look. "How do you know this song?"

We'd been engaged in this dance since Junior High; who was into this band or band before the other. The answer was almost always me, but through his insistence and my lack of desire to argue with him, I often deferred credit for discoveries. "I picked up a used copy of this record last year at Flat, Black and Circular."

This satisfied him, and we were saved from further discussion by the arrival of the bartender, a tall, thin guy who looked sallow and unhappy, which may have been caused by his need of a nap.

"Hey Charlie, how's it going tonight?"

"Good, busy. What can I get you two?" He nodded in my direction as an acknowledgment of my presence, and although he didn't smile, I got the sense he liked Aaron despite the bad body language.

"Two pints of Anchor and a bag of Better Mades." Aaron put down a twenty.

I looked over the back bar, which was exposed brick covered with mirrored beer signs for more brands I didn't know, some shelves covered in pint glasses and a small selection of liquor bottles, as well as a couple of racks of chips and nuts. The ceiling was tin, with some exposed ductwork running along the expanse. There was a smoke-stained amateur painting of JFK on the wall, and someone had framed bottle-cap art that spelled "Bob's" in vertical capital letters.

The bartender came back with our beers and chips and Aaron's change.

Aaron left a couple of dollars on the bar, and then held out a ten and asked for singles for the jukebox.

Charlie put his hands up. "Sorry, I'm really short."

Aaron put the ten in his pocket and grabbed the beers. "That's cool." He turned and gave me a pint, then muttered something about being short on his tip next round.

I reached into my pocket and pulled out several one-dollar bills. "I can hit the jukebox."

He frowned and shook his head. "C'mon, Drew. Hand 'em over. My bar, my tunes."

Technically it was Spooky Electric's bar, but I doubted they had *LoveSexy* among the discs in their machine. "We can't team up on this? Let me choose some and then I'll leave the rest for you."

Aaron shrugged. "Whatever. Don't play a bunch of bullshit."

I was one more dig from suggesting Aaron find alternate transportation back to the suburbs. "Bunch of bullshit coming up."

I moved over to the jukebox and fiddled with the bills and the slot for a moment, then started going over the selections. It was impressive. There was some of the usual: the Stones, Velvet Underground, *Dookie*. But there was also Yo La Tengo, Hank Williams, Guided By Voices. The first Cars record. Tindersticks and Cornershop and some alt-country, and I didn't even know of any bars in East Lansing with Whiskeytown or *Too Far to Care* in the mix. It was an embarrassment of digital riches. As I got to the end of the selections, it dawned on me that Grand Funk Railroad was nowhere to be found. I'd always assumed that it was a local ordinance that they be on every Flint-area jukebox. Knowing no one could bring me down by punching up "Bad Time" or "Shinin' On" was a cool comfort.

I was having trouble making up my mind when "Final Solution" ended and the ensuing moment of no music made me realize that my first selection would be the next song everyone would hear. That was a lot of pressure. It felt like everyone's eyes were on me. I'd never been so unsure of what to play on any jukebox, ever. I settled on "Love Will Tear Us Apart", and the opening guitar strum was the sound of sweet relief. I picked a few more songs and noticed Aaron lucked into a booth that had been vacated seconds before.

I sat across from him. "I could've very easily used all those credits."

"But you left some?"

I nodded. Aaron slid out of the bar and punched up some selections. I sipped my beer, which was a touch on the warm side for my taste. For whatever reason, a couple of groups had left the bar since we arrived, and it made it easier to look around. The place wasn't really all that special. It was a dive bar in downtown Flint. I couldn't know what had attracted all these like-minded young people, but I guessed that obscure beers and the eclectic jukebox were both good starters.

Aaron finished at the jukebox and stopped at the bar. I watched him down the rest of his beer and then place an order. The bartender brought him beers and a shot of Bushmill's, which he downed with a flick of the wrist at the bar before turning around and making his way back to the booth. I figured he didn't want me to see him drink that whiskey.

"Round two." He slid one of the beers across the table to me. My first was still two-thirds full.

I pulled the pack of Parliaments from my shirt pocket and took two out, handing one to Aaron. He rarely had any.

He lit his with a pack of matches the previous booth tenants had left behind, took a drag and then studied the cigarette. "What's with the filter on these things?"

I finished a large swallow of my beer, trying to catch up before the new pint got any warmer. "I don't know. I like it."

"Why can't you smoke a normal brand? Everything's got to be an affectation with you."

I'd really had enough of Aaron's attitude toward me, but I didn't want to make any sort of scene. "What exactly do you think I'm trying to affect?"

He looked me up and down. "Cool kid, hipster, suede Pumas, polyester shirt." He gestured with his cigarette around the bar. "You look just like these kids."

"I couldn't have possibly known how people would be dressed here, could I?"

"Let's just drop it." Aaron took another drag from the cigarette.

"I wasn't the one who brought it up."

"How's Kathy? She happy you're home?"

I nodded. "I think so." Everyone, including me, called my mom Kathy. I don't know how it started. She pretended to hate it, but I could sense that she always believed it meant my friends and I thought she was secretly cool, which she wasn't. But it was nice to be home, even at the expense of another summer with Megan, because I worried about Kathy some, all alone in that house that was now way too big for her.

"Is she ready to admit Clinton banged that girl yet?"

I shook my head. "Of course not. She blames it all on Kenneth Starr."

Aaron smiled, the first one since we'd gotten to the bar. "Kathy's cute."

"How are your folks?"

Aaron finished most of his second beer with a gulp. "You need to catch up." He pointed at my beer.

"I'm not in this race."

I hadn't enjoyed drinking with Aaron much over the last couple of years. In high school, his crazier tendencies seemed harmless and made for good stories. Since we'd turned twenty-one, he'd shifted toward the surly once more than a few drinks were involved, and I'd spent more time than I'd like getting him out of scraps. Over the previous Christmas break, I'd watched him get sucker punched in the eye at a party, puke on the table at Senor Smoke's Grill and get a drink thrown in his face by a woman who he'd inappropriately propositioned. At some point, history becomes just that, and if the present involved more dragging him out of places and cleaning up after him and getting ice for his eye, then it was time to let the past be the past.

Aaron drank the rest of his beer. "No race. I'm just trying to get up the liquid courage to talk to flowered dress over there." He gestured with his head at a pretty brunette sitting with an equally pretty friend at the bar.

I looked at her through my peripheral vision. "I like that dress." She might have been a little out of Aaron's league. "You had any success in this place?"

He nodded. "Just last week, in fact. Went back to her place and rolled around for a few hours."

"Nice."

He looked over at the brunette and her friend again. "Maybe you go with me and talk to her friend?"

I took a last drag from my cigarette and put it out in the black plastic ashtray on the table. "C'mon. You don't need my help."

Aaron glared at me. "Just talking to some girl at a bar doesn't constitute cheating on your girlfriend."

Probably not, but that didn't mean I'd appreciate Megan talking to some dude when she was out without me. Do unto others and all that. "That girl's been flirting with the bartender since we got here."

He glanced over in time to see her flipping her hair behind her left ear and smiling demurely at Charlie, who looked like he may have preferred her friend. "Fuck you, Drew."

I drank from my beer and followed it with a deep breath. "Sure. Makes sense. Fuck me." I took out another cigarette and lit it. Isaac Brock was singing about convenient parking on the jukebox.

"You've been giving me shit all night, Aaron. I don't know what the fuck your problem is, but it isn't me."

Aaron spun his empty pint glass around in his hands on the table. "I flunked two classes this semester. My dad said they won't pay for my senior year unless I move back into the dorms."

I swallowed a sip of beer. "So move back into the dorms."

"I'll figure out a way to pay." He reached into the Parliament pack on the table and took out a cigarette. "Fuck that hypocrite."

I could've pointed out that one of us at the table might've liked to have a hypocritical dad, but I kept my mouth shut. "What's so bad about living in the dorms for one more year?"

"I'm not at school to be a social pariah."

No, you're in school to get an education. "I don't know what you want me to tell you."

"You don't have to tell me anything." He stood. He looked over at the brunette again. She hadn't even noticed him. Isaac Brock sang about the malls being the soon-to-be ghost towns. "I'll tell you that I'm glad you drove because I'm about to get all shitty." Without waiting for me to respond, Aaron turned on his heel and headed to the bar, where he ordered and downed another shot, then brought another beer with him back to the booth.

I looked down at my second beer, which was still mostly full. Aaron was too angry at the world for some sort of speech about how his drinking was to blame for his year of dormitory exile. But I also didn't want to have to drag his ass out of that place the first time I'd come there. I've never liked being a spectacle. "Is it too much to ask for you to maintain some semblance of control tonight?"

Aaron flashed a devious smile and then emptied his full pint in one giant gulp. It was an impressive party trick in high school, and everyone would gather around to watch him drain beers like this when we were teens. The past was the past.

He belched a little before he said, "Control is overrated."

17

***

The last hour of my shift at Home Theater Video was crawling by, so I was attempting to move the clock by doing some re-shelving when a customer commandeered me. She was a middle-aged woman with a toddler who either was a late-life surprise or made her a somewhat young grandmother. She was holding a copy of *Flubber* in her left hand and *Men in Black* in her right. She invaded my personal space and held them up before me.

"Which of these is better for kids?" She smelled of dried milk and sweat.

"Well, I think *Flubber* was made for children, and the other is a slightly more adult film. Truthfully, I haven't seen either of them, so it's possible they're both fine."

The woman continued to hold the movies up, waiting for me to say something else. After a few uncomfortable beats, she gave up and turned to walk away. "Thanks, I guess."

Monty, the store manager, heard the exchange and hustled over. He was a tall guy, mid-thirties, with a paunch that was growing faster than his two kids. He'd been working for the small chain of video stores since they opened ten years prior, and acted more like an owner than an employee. "*Flubber* is definitely the right choice for kids, ma'am." He smiled at her. "It's a cute movie. My son loved it."

The woman smiled at Monty and then glared at me. "Thank you for answering my question."

Monty nodded. "Anytime."

She walked towards the counter to rent the tape.

Monty waited until she was out of earshot. "Why couldn't you just tell her *Flubber* was the better kids' movie, Drew?"

"Because I haven't seen it. For all I know, it's got content she might find offensive." It could also be a brain-numbing pile of shit, which I assumed it was. But I didn't say that.

"Just answer the question. You don't want to sound like an idiot to the customers."

"Not having seen *Flubber* makes me an idiot?"

Monty took a deep breath. "That's not what I meant. But you're smart enough to make the judgment for her. Didn't you tell me you took some film courses at State?"

Flubber wasn't screened in *Film Noir* or *Italian Neo-Realism*. If someone were deciding between *Out of the Past* and *Double Indemnity*, then the choice would have been in my wheelhouse. "I did, yes."

"Then just tell her which movie to rent. It isn't rocket science."

"Got it. I'll do that, Monty."

Monty was holding a clipboard in his right hand, which he then looked at. "While I've got you, I wanted to talk to you about your 'Staff Picks' selections."

I nodded. I'd pored over those choices for days, deciding at the last minute which Truffaut to select, and I had to dig *The King of Comedy* out of a bin in the back room.

"Well, since you put your picks up, no one has rented any of the titles. Do you think that you could choose a few more mainstream movies?" He tapped his thumb on the clipboard.

"I'll change it up after I finish this restock."

"Thanks. Just remember, sometimes we have to keep it simple. We can stay ahead of the competition by providing good customer service. Stocking your picks with a bunch of obscure French films doesn't really qualify." Monty shifted his weight between his feet, then looked down at his polo shirt and picked off a piece of crusted peanut butter that had fallen near the buttons.

Scorsese directed *King of Comedy*, and he's certainly not fucking French. But I didn't say that. "Keep it simple. I'll remember that."

***

19

I was hanging out at Bob's a few days a week, enjoying the bar and getting to know Charlie and Ralph, who were the primary bartenders. Kathy was starting to wonder why I was spending so much time in the city, and I had some trouble explaining it to her. She wasn't being over-protective; it was mostly just her curiosity getting the better of her. I might've tried to bring her to the bar so she could see for herself, but I wasn't sure that would even clear anything up. Bob's had become both a refuge from Kathy's basement and a place to feel connected rather than sit around and feel sorry for myself. Self-pity was becoming something of a specialty.

On a Wednesday off from the video store, I'd spent a couple of evening hours chatting with Ralph and feeding dollars into the jukebox.

The bar was empty. I'd learned there was a sort of no-man's land between the crowd that had an after-work drink or two and the night rush when the bar was quiet.

Ralph was washing some glasses, bent over the sink. "I forgot to tell you I was in Home Theater earlier today."

I looked up from my pint. "Oh yeah?"

"I asked some dude if you were there. He said you had the day off."

"Was it Monty?" I stubbed a Parliament out in the ashtray.

"Maybe. I don't quite remember. I was a little high." Ralph finished his task and walked over to the end of the bar while drying his hands on a bar towel.

I chuckled. I'd gotten the impression Ralph was a stoner, but it could've just been the fact that he smokes cloves. I always assumed that anyone past the age of seventeen who still smokes those probably gets high.

Ralph sat on the stool that the bartender usually used for a quick break and shook a Sampoerna out of his pack. "You like that job?"

20

I took a drink from my beer. "It's alright for now. The customers can be annoying."

He lit his clove with a match and exhaled the sweet smoke over the bar. "Customers here can get under my skin. A lot of the suburban kids that come in to slum it on the weekends rub me the wrong way."

I wasn't sure if Ralph knew I was one of those suburban kids. "I can see how that might be a drag."

"Right? But you're from the 'burbs, aren't you?"

"I am." I grabbed the Parliaments out of my shirt pocket and took one out.

"You don't act like it."

I took this as a compliment, even though I didn't know what made me different. I nodded at Ralph and lit my cigarette. "It's always nice to know you're not an asshole."

The side door to the bar opened and I looked over my shoulder to see Aaron standing in the doorway. He spotted me and shook his head a little. He walked over towards where I was seated and took the stool next to me.

He slapped me on the back a little harder than necessary. "Drew, Drew, Drew." He took a pack of Camel Lights out of his shirt pocket and tossed them on the bar. "How's the single life treating you?"

Ralph sighed audibly as he put his hands on the bar. "You two know each other?"

I nodded. "Since sixth grade."

Aaron took a cigarette out of his pack and lit it with matches from the bar. "That's right. Drew here was Mr. Popularity in High School; did you know that? Prom King, Most Likely to Succeed. I was Class Clown, of course."

Ralph didn't smile. "Yeah, you're fucking hilarious, Aaron." He looked at me for a brief second, and I thought he might have given a slight roll of his eyes. "Are you going to behave if I let you drink here?"

Aaron blew smoke over the back bar. "Let me? What the fuck does that mean?"

"Do you even remember grabbing that girl's tits last week?"

Aaron looked at me with his devious smile, but I was sure what Ralph was talking about hadn't been at all funny. He threw his palms up. "I was kidding around."

Ralph shook his head. "It's not funny, Aaron." He paused and thought for a few seconds. "You can have a couple of beers. Drink them slow."

Aaron gave an exaggerated bow of thanks. "Most gracious, Sir. May I humbly request a Leiny Red?" He placed his hands together in mock sublimation.

Ralph was not amused. "I'm serious. I'm not in the mood."

"Alright, goddamn, Ralph." Aaron reached into the front pocket of his jeans and took out a wrinkled ten. "And one for my old friend here."

"Are you ready for one, Drew?"

I nodded.

Ralph walked to the taps to pour our beers.

Aaron took a deep drag from his cigarette and fixed me with a glance. "What's his problem anyway?" He gestured with a head nod at Ralph.

I shrugged.

"Come to think of it, what's your problem? I've heard fuck-all from you for a couple of weeks."

The last time I was supposed to have gone out with Aaron was a few nights earlier. I'd closed the video store, ran through a drive-thru for a quick bite and met him out at Rolando's in Burton. By the time I got there, Aaron was already completely wasted and sloppily making out with an overweight thirty-five-year-old with Tammy Faye Bakker makeup in a back booth. I sat at the bar and drank a couple of beers, waiting for Aaron and Tammy Faye to come up for air. They left the bar together as I was nursing a third, walking right past me on their way out. He was too drunk to notice me or the fact that his conquest smelled like farts.

Aaron was still waiting for a reply. "Cat got your tongue?"

I reached for my pack of Parliaments on the bar. "Rolando's? Monday night?"

Aaron paused as he tried to suss out what I was referring to, followed by a nod of recognition and a smile that split the difference between pride and embarrassment. "Oh, yeah."

"Yeah. I hope Tammy Faye's apartment smelled better than her ass."

Ralph returned with our beers. "Six bucks, Aaron."

Aaron slid the ten over the bar. "Ralph, let me ask you. Is it acceptable to bang a fat old mom provided she's got bigger than a D-cup?"

Ralph shook his head. "You lost me at fat and old."

I got up from my stool, grabbing a few singles from the stack of bills I'd left in front of me. "I'm gonna hit the jukebox."

Ralph pointed at me. "Just nothing from *Odelay*."

Aaron threw up his palms and looked from me to Ralph and back again. "Is no one gonna answer my question?"

✳✳✳

The video monitors throughout the store were blasting *Beaches*, one of Monty's favorites, which had been causing me to zone out most of the morning. Although I'd intended to only have a couple of pints at Bob's the previous evening, I'd gotten into a conversation about the Tigers with a couple of people at the bar, and I spent a few hours attempting to convince them that On-Base Percentage was the better statistic than Batting Average. Two pints turned into seven, and though I'd sobered up by the time the bar closed, I didn't get back to Kathy's until nearly three a.m. My shift at the store started at eight-thirty, so I was functioning on a less than ideal amount of sleep.

The morning was mostly slow and uneventful, and I was staring blankly ahead and thinking about lunch when a woman came to the counter and interrupted my slow-moving train of thought.

She was sloppy, in her thirties with her hair in curlers, wearing sweatpants and a too-large, faded Michigan t-shirt. She placed a tape in front of me. "There's something wrong with this."

I looked down at the item in question and saw right away that it had been left in a hot car, warping the plastic and rendering it completely useless. "I'll say."

She didn't think my comment was funny and started to raise her voice. "What kind of goddamned place is this that rents tapes you can't even watch?"

I looked across the store at the office door, but it was closed with Monty safely ensconced behind. The doorbell chimed and I looked over at Ralph walking in. He smiled at me, gave a little wave, and started walking towards the counter.

I picked up the tape. "Ma'am, I understand your frustration, but the only way this happens to a tape is if it's left on the dashboard of a car in the sunlight."

She fixed me with a stare. "Are you saying I did this?"

"I'm not saying that you did it purposefully, but we'd never rent a tape in this condition."

"That's how it was when I got it home."

I looked over the warped case. What had once been a copy of *Turner and Hooch* now looked more like *Trn and Hooch*, with the two "o's" in the middle stretched out to three times their original size. It was cooked.

Ralph stood at the side of the counter and smiled.

The woman crossed her arms and tapped her right foot on the worn carpet. "I want a different movie."

I set the tape down and sighed a little. "Well, the bad news is that, under these circumstances, we'd need to be reimbursed the cost of a replacement before you can rent anything else."

"Maybe you're not hearing me? I said the tape was like this when I got it home."

In its present state, the destroyed copy of *Turner and Hooch* wouldn't have been able to even fit on the shelf. There was exactly zero chance that she'd been rented the tape in its present condition. "I'm sorry, ma'am, but the damage had to have been done since you've had it."

She looked at me with wide eyes and her face turned red. "Are you calling me a fucking liar?"

I took a deep breath. "I didn't say that."

She uncrossed her arms and put a hand on each hip. "Well then, what the fuck are you saying, smart guy?"

I looked over at Ralph, who was attempting to stifle a giggle. "I'm saying you can't rent any more movies until you pay for this one."

She picked up the tape and threw it on the ground, smashing the case and the tape into pieces, one of which hit Ralph in the leg

Ralph lifted his leg off of the floor and glared at the woman. "Take it easy." He brushed off the leg of his jeans to drive home the point that he'd caught some VHS shrapnel.

"You can shove this store up your ass." She pointed at Ralph and made an audible hiss. "You can fuck off too, you prick." She turned around and stomped out, cursing under her breath the whole way.

Ralph moved towards the counter, shaking his head. "Unbelievable."

"I've had worse." I moved around to where Ralph stood and began picking up the pieces of the tape and case that had splintered around the floor.

Ralph bent down to help me, and after a moment, we'd gathered up the detritus in a pile on the counter. Ralph chuckled. "What an idiot. Did she really expect to get away with that?"

"I don't know, man. People are fucking crazy."

"How could you not just go off on her? I wouldn't have been able to hold back."

I grabbed the biggest pieces of the now twice-destroyed copy of *Turner and Hooch* and threw them into the trash. "It's not worth getting upset about. I don't take it personally."

"You have a lot more patience than me."

"I don't know. It's weird, I guess. I mean, people are in here pursuing a leisure time activity. You'd expect them to be in a better mood. I'd hate to see how some of them act at their jobs."

Ralph laughed a little. "That's a good one."

I nodded. "What brings you in?"

"Some guy at the bar was telling me *Amazon Women on the Moon* is pretty funny to watch when you're stoned."

I walked around the counter. "It's got its moments. Arsenio Hall has a funny bit in it. It's over here in Cult Comedies." I led Ralph over to the section, found the case, and then headed back to the counter to grab the tape. I punched up Ralph's account in the computer and noticed he'd racked up about eight dollars in late fees. I erased them and rang up his rental.

Ralph put his hands in the back pockets of his jeans as he followed me to the counter. "Do I have any late charges?"

I smiled. "I got rid of them for you."

"Thanks, Drew. I owe you a beer for having saved me the trouble of cursing you out."

I laughed and handed Ralph his movie. "Please note that the tape is in good condition. Don't leave that shit in your car."

***

I walked into Rolando's and saw Aaron sitting at the bar. At least he wasn't motorboating the local PTA treasurer this time. I'm not sure why I'd agreed to come out with him, as his behavior was deteriorating to the point that I was actively wishing for a rapid end to the summer so that he'd be back at school and out of my hair. Even Kathy knew something was amiss as I waved off several of Aaron's phone calls over the previous couple of weeks. But he was a persistent son of a bitch. Or possibly had so completely torched every other bridge in town that I was his only option left. Charlie had confided in me that he was nearing a lifetime ban at Bob's. I was sort of surprised he'd gone this far without one.

As I got closer, I noticed that he had neither a beer nor a rocks glass in front of him; instead, the red plastic cups that Rolando's used for soda was in his right hand.

I sat on the stool next to him. "What's goin' on, A-Ron?"

Before he could answer, the bartender noticed me and walked over to take my drink order. I'd been told that Budweiser is the most polite drink order in a bar, as it's always handy and in ready supply.

"Bud? A little bourgeois, no?" Aaron smiled.

The bartender returned with my beer and set it in front of me. "Trying to reconnect with the little people." I took a sip. It was lukewarm. "Can't help but notice the soda."

Aaron nodded.

"Something happen?"

He reached for his cigarettes on the bar, pulled one out and lit it. "I really fucked up this semester. Incompletes in every class. My folks are pissed."

"I'd expect so."

He took a deep drag from his cigarette and then looked down at his sneakers. "I need an extra year, obviously. They won't pay."

I couldn't blame them. Aaron was like me in the sense that his major in English provided little in the way of career preparation.

Unlike me, he didn't take school at all seriously, joking that he wanted to be the first English Literature major in U.S. history to never read any Faulkner, Hemingway or Melville. Based on his increasingly aberrant behavior over last summer and this, I didn't think it was at all surprising he was flaming out. "Bummer. What are you gonna do?"

"It's too late to transfer. I'll take out some loans, get a job. Cut back on the partying." He raised his red cup of soda.

I could have asked why he wasn't going to completely quit drinking, but I didn't want to scare him off of confiding. I did wonder if he had me meet him at the bar in the hopes that I'd buy him some drinks. I wasn't interested in spending the few dollars I earned getting berated at the video store on beer for Aaron. I grabbed a bar menu from the edge of the bar and looked for what sounded good to eat.

Aaron took another drag from his Camel Light. "You've got nothing to say?"

"What do you want from me? Go to class, what can I tell you?"

He shook his head, scowling a little. "I just thought maybe you'd be a little more sympathetic."

I wasn't sure what about this situation called for sympathy. Aaron was a fuck-up whose drinking and lack of seriousness cost him an extra year in undergrad and several thousand dollars in student loans that he'd otherwise not have to take out. "Why's that?"

"The best laid plans and all that. You had your ducks in a row, Megan blows that up, so you've been moping around town all summer."

I saw no parallel. I also didn't think I'd been moping. "I'm not unsympathetic. I'm sorry your folks took away their support."

Aaron shrugged as he ground out his cigarette in a black plastic ashtray on the bar. "Maybe it's for the best. Force me to get serious."

I nodded. "There's the optimist I know and love."

"Suck my balls."

The bartender came back around and I ordered some buffalo wings and a burger. My resolve was crumbling, as I figured to share the wings with Aaron, who didn't order any food.

I took a Parliament from my pack and lit it. "Haven't seen you in Bob's in a bit."

Aaron shook his head. "Charlie's all pissed off at me."

This was the second least surprising piece of news that night. "Why's that?"

"I got pretty hammered in there recently and I guess I was creeping out some chick that he wanted to bang. You know how Charlie is."

I nodded. "Yeah. Who was the girl?"

He raised his hands off the bar, palms up. "I don't really remember too much about the night, honestly. Bushmill's."

"Maybe your folks taking the money away is the best thing for several reasons."

He nodded. "What about you, man? How's the video store? How's Kathy?"

"Kathy's a goof, the video store is awful."

Aaron reached for another cigarette. "You working on a plan?"

I shrugged, took a drag from my smoke. "Something will come up."

Aaron reached for my Bic to light his Camel. "You were always the most driven of us, Drew. Remember in Mrs. Krakow's class? The rest of us figured out how to cheat on those vocab exercises, but you always did the whole thing yourself."

I took the last sip out of the by now totally warm Bud, and pushed it across the bar with a head nod toward the bartender for a fresh one. "High school was a long time ago."

"No, it wasn't." Aaron pointed at me with his Camel Light. "Don't get sucked in by that bar."

The bartender returned with the new beer and I thanked him. "What do you mean?"

Aaron shook his head. "That place is like a vortex or something. Look at how every twentysomething who consider themselves cool or whatever wind up there. But they're stuck, stuck in Flint for God knows what reasons. You need to get the fuck out."

"Flint's not so bad." I sipped my Bud.

"Oh yeah? And where's Carl Solomon right now?"

"Chicago."

"Right. Gibbs is there too. Symanski's in New York. Winkler moved to Austin, Jonesie stayed in Columbus for grad school. Do you see a pattern here? The best and the brightest do not return."

"I'm not sucked in."

Aaron dragged from his cigarette and then took a sip of his soda through the straw. It was an odd mixture of adult and childlike gestures. "How many nights a week are you in there?"

"One or two."

He gave me a sideways glance but didn't say anything.

"What?"

"You can't bullshit me."

I shrugged. "What's the difference?"

"How many nights a week are you in there, Drew?"

"I told you."

"You think those people are your friends. They're not. Ralph and Charlie want your money. The customers are lost, lonely, whatever. They'll make no difference in your life, in any real way, in the long run." He took another drag from his cigarette. "How many nights a week?"

I didn't appreciate getting a speech from Aaron, of all people. "Three."

He looked at me and shook his head slowly.

"Sometimes four."

PHIL & BOB'S

Ten thousand dollars commission in one month sounds like a lot, and I suppose it is. Luckily though, the month in question was October and the brand-new ninety-four models were arriving in earnest. The shiny Accords and Civics and Passports were rolling off the trucks and onto the lot practically every other day. I was practically jumping over my fellow salesman to get at the customers not unlike the overgrown carp in an amusement park lake leaping over one another with mouths agape for a nickel's worth of fish feed.

I wanted out. I needed nine thousand more dollars to buy the bar, with a thousand extra to float the necessary capital for the first month or two.

I probably wouldn't have been taking the opportunity very seriously were it not for the blessing from my wife, Pam. She and I met at Bob's a few years prior, after I'd dropped out of Ball State and she was in her first year as a tax attorney at Knight-Ridge, the biggest remaining firm in downtown Flint. She and some of the other younger lawyers had started to stop in for an after-work drink or three a few times a week. I started going to the bar years earlier, and I'd resumed my love affair with the place's Depression-era ambiance and ultra-cheap beers and jukebox. I guess the young lawyers liked the place for the same reasons. Pam and I initially bonded over my selection of a classic Faron Young tune on the Wurlitzer, and even though she was a couple of years older, we went from zero to sixty in the relationship lane in what felt like under ten seconds. Our friends thought we were crazy, but it's pretty difficult to reason with a couple of kids in their mid-twenties who are blinded by raging endorphins. But it wasn't just that -- we understood each other.

When I found out the bar was for sale, I expected her to put a quick kibosh on the possibility and that I'd shortly move on to my next escape route from car sales. We were living pretty high on the hog between what I was pulling down at Schneeberger Honda and her lawyer pay, and I didn't figure that she'd want to see one of those dual gravy trains derailed. To my surprise, she thought it sounded like a great idea, although of course, it's possible that she was mostly just sick of hearing me complain about selling cars. I started the ball rolling, agreeing on a purchase price with Rob Roberts, the bar's current owner, and spent most of that summer getting ducks in a row.

I scrambled around to get the paperwork in order with the help of one of Pam's colleagues, but the money was a different matter. Neither of us wanted to go into debt in order to finance the purchase, and my savings account was about fifteen grand short. I powered through and had a good September and got six thousand closer to the purchase price, but time was running out. I needed to make up the difference by the end of the month, or the deal was off.

I might not have been the most well-liked employee at Schneeberger prior to the autumn of 1993, but there was little good-will left as October progressed. I caught Tom Shevlin getting ready to piss in my gas tank one afternoon, Marty Brown slathered Vaseline all over my desk phone, and I'm pretty sure that one or more people put things in my food at various points. I didn't really care. I took a lot of cues from *Glengarry Glenn Ross*. It takes brass balls to sell real estate and cars. Second prize in this contest was a set of steak knives, and I wasn't interested in those metaphorical Henckels.

✳✳✳

I'd started coming to Bob's when I was a senior in high school. My friend, Sal Boccutti, heard about a downtown bar that didn't card and didn't ask questions. He said it was kind of a sad old man bar, but the beer was cold and there were a lot of cool old country 45s on the jukebox, and the spins were still two for a quarter. He was right.

Robert's Grill, as it was called on the big, lighted sign out front, was down on its luck, and Sal and I seemed like its first new customers in three or four decades. The first time we went in, during that other gloaming in between school letting out and your folks coming home after work, it felt like midnight inside. There were a few wrinkled old crocodiles sitting at the bar, barely speaking to one another, and we were clearly out of place. The interior hadn't been redecorated in any substantive way for a generation, and apart from the Dukakis/Bentsen sticker near the old, ornate NCR cash register on the back bar, everything was tainted yellow with nicotine.

Although I didn't have a lot of experience going to bars, it didn't take a genius to see that it was out of time. Behind the bar, the exposed brick walls held faded framed photographs of some ancient Tigers like Willie Horton and Norm Cash, and a pretty amateurish painting of JFK. There was an old English phone booth at the end of the bar, although I could see it no longer held a phone. The jukebox Sal had told me about faced the bar from between a couple of booths, and I wanted to plug in some coins and break the silence, but Sal confidently sauntered to the bar and sat on a stool, so I figured I should follow his lead.

Sal and I drank a couple of Stroh's and shared a few Camel's out of a communal pack we'd bought earlier that week. We were there for maybe an hour and a half, but no new customers came in. We repeated the trip several times over the next two months or so, but there were never any more than three or four other customers, always really old guys. I wondered how the bar was still in business, but even as a naïve high school kid, I could tell it had some hidden charm. It was in a shitty neighborhood that was getting even shittier, but I didn't feel unsafe parking my car on the block or going in to the place. It was like this weird oasis, some kind of invisible shield surrounding it that kept the nastiness at bay. The rest of the block was littered with empty fast food containers, broken glass, empty potato chip bags, all sorts of trash, really, but the building housing the bar was clean. There was graffiti on lots of walls up and down the block, but Bob's red brick was clear of paint. Even the weeds that grew over lots of the storefronts and apartment buildings in the vicinity seemed to know that there was something special about this structure.

After going there for a while with Sal, I'd worked up the nerve to head in by myself on a Wednesday after school. It was a typical Bob's afternoon, meaning the place was practically empty, and I pulled up a stool and ordered a Stroh's. The bartender that was normally there was absent, and the new guy, if it's fair to use the term for someone in his sixties, seemed to feel some sort of need to entertain me.

He was a grizzled dude, tall but a little hunched over, long, liver-spotted arms. He put my beer in front of me and slid over a clean ashtray. "Off work early today?" He waited for an answer.

"Something like that." I grinned and caught sight of myself in the mirror behind the bar. The glass might have been in desperate need of a wash, but it wasn't so dark or streaked with nicotine that I couldn't see that my round baby face wasn't fooling anyone, even as I tried to cover it with a goatee and some muttonchops.

"Where do you work?"

Now I was afraid this guy was going to bust me. I hesitated, probably way too long, but I'm not a good liar under pressure and he wasn't leaving without some sort of answer. "At the high school." I felt somewhat confident in this, as it wasn't exactly a lie.

"Oh yeah?" He reached into the pocket of his yellow polyester shirt and took out a pack of Kent Golden Lights. He shook one up, took it out of the pack the rest of the way with his teeth. "What do you teach?"

I started to get the sense that these questions were genuine. "Uh, well, sometimes I feel like I'm the one getting an education, you know?" I took a sip of my beer and chuckled nervously.

He nodded and smiled. "I sure do." He reached out his hand. "My name's Bob, nice to meet you."

I shook his hand, trying to remember to keep my grip firm and my eyes on his, like my dad taught me. "Bob, like the bar?"

He nodded as he lit his Kent with a white Bic with a Tigers logo on the front. "And my father before me. It was his place."

"Wow." By my math, that meant the place probably opened sometime in the thirties. "I'm Phil, by the way."

"Pleasure, Phil." He walked back towards his other customer, the cigarette trailing smoke from his left hand.

I felt as though I'd dodged a bullet. It seemed like he believed I was a teacher at a high school. I sat quietly with my beer and was thinking about putting a few quarters in the jukebox, maybe fill the dead air with some Buck Owens or Lefty Frizzell. I pulled a couple of coins from the left front pocket of my Levi's and was putting them on the bar when I felt eyes on me from the other end of the bar.

I looked over to see the only other customer in the place staring at me. I kept my eyes on him through my periphery, but I couldn't tell if the look he was giving me was aggressive or quizzical. He looked to be at least as old as the bartender -- jowly, nearly bald. I thought he was wearing a Members Only jacket, but I wasn't certain from out of the corner of my eye. What I was sure about was that this guy was way too old to beat me in a fistfight. He still hadn't stopped staring at me. The uncomfortable seconds stretched to less comfortable minutes.

I swiveled around on my stool to the left and faced him. "Why are you staring at me? Am I that pretty?"

The man was as old as I thought, and it was definitely a Member's Only jacket. It was tan or sandalwood, whatever the fuck they call it. He was still staring at me. "What's your name?"

"What's the difference?" I wasn't completely sure why I would be scared, but my heart was beating fast. I would have preferred to be at the jukebox, punching up "Walking the Floor Over You."

"You look like someone I know." The old man grabbed a pack of cigarillos that were sitting in front of him on the bar.

I was forever being told this. I had one of those faces when I was younger, I guess. I had a couple of friends who called me Pills, short for the Pillsbury Doughboy, for whom they insisted I was the mirror image. Assholes. Whatever the case, I wanted the old man to speed up this interaction a little so I could get to my tunes. "Oh yeah? Who's that?"

He lit one of his miniature cigars with a match and exhaled a cloud of dirty smoke. "Herb Franklin."

My dad.

"You look just like him."

I nodded and then took a sip of my beer. I was busted. I just hoped they wouldn't call the cops and get me hauled in for underage consumption.

"Do you know him?"

I looked up and down that bar, trying to think of a way out of this, but I was coming up empty. I nearly whispered when I spoke. "He's my father."

"Your dad?" The old man got up from his stool and walked over towards me. "Hey, Bob. This guy says he's Herb Franklin's kid."

Bob looked up toward me from the beer cooler where he'd been moving bottles around. He had the lit cigarette dangling from his lips. "Is that right?"

I nodded and smiled. "Yeah, he's my dad."

Ray sat on the stool next to me, smiling all the while. "Bob, I'd swear that Herb told me his oldest son is a senior in high school this year."

Bob closed the cooler door and then grinned while screwing out his cigarette in an ashtray on the bar. "A senior? Well, unless he's been held back a few times, I'd say young Phil here isn't of age. And he definitely isn't a teacher."

I fought the urge to run out of the place. "I never said I was a teacher."

"Didn't you hear him say he was a teacher, Ray?" Bob grabbed Ray's pint glass and headed towards the taps to pour him a fresh draft.

Ray shook his head. "Come to think of it, I don't believe he did."

Bob finished pouring the beer and brought the glass back to Ray. "Sure he did. Remember all that malarkey about the kids teaching him?"

Ray took a sip from his pint. "I do. But I'm about one hundred percent certain that he only said he worked at the school and you made the inference that he was a teacher."

Bob shook his head. "It doesn't help that I can't tell how the hell old anyone is anymore. He could've passed for thirty for all I knew."

I beamed inside at that comment, but I fought to keep my face from betraying my cool.

Ray tapped his cigarillo into the ashtray. "Does your dad know you're here, kid?"

I shook my head.

"I think I know Herb well enough to say that he'd be alright with it as long as you stay in control and you're not here every day of the week."

I nodded. "How do you know my dad?"

"I own the Tick Tock Bar. I'm Ray Schmidt." He reached out his hand for me to shake.

I repeated the firm grip and eye contact drill that I'd used with Bob a few minutes earlier. "And my dad goes to your bar?"

"Since around the time you were born. He's a good guy. One of the few I still let carry a tab."

I knew my dad went for a beer or two after his shift, but I never knew he went to the same bar every time. There was a lot I didn't know about him, and I felt kind of funny finding this sort of stuff out second hand.

Bob walked back towards Ray and me, waggling his finger at me as he shuffled. "Just don't go telling all your little friends about this place and we won't have a problem. I don't need Liquor Control up my ass. Got it?"

I nodded. "Thanks."

Bob waved me off. "Thanks, nothing. You're a good kid. Ray and I have known your dad for a long time."

Ray stabbed out his smoke in the ashtray. He reached into his pocket and put a five on the bar. "His next one's on me."

✳✳✳

It would seem that selling GM cars in Flint would be like taking candy from a baby. That assertion would be overlooking a significant amount of complexities. First, most of the customers in Genesee County are GM employees, and their laundry lists of discounts and savings might add up to slam-dunk sales, but they sure as hell eat into the salesman's cut. Too many times to count, I'd bust my ass getting some mark into a Cutlass or an Eighty-Eight, tricking the thing out with features they'd never even know the car had, and they'd pull out that goddamned employee discount card and I'd kiss a few hundred bucks goodbye.

There was also the not-small matter of the vehicles' steady decline in reliability and value. Sure, there were plenty of folks willing to insist on blind loyalty and delude themselves into believing GM cars were of comparable quality to their competitors. But I was on the front lines, trying to sell Pontiac Sunbirds in the early nineties. I'm pretty sure there's no such thing as a Sunbird to begin with. That's a problem. Then there's the indisputable fact that the cars were terrible, ugly, underperforming messes in a market dominated by stronger, faster and cheaper models from Detroit and overseas. The roll tops might have looked a little nicer, but this was really just polish on a turd. The Sunbird did not burn bright. It didn't take a genius to see the handwriting on the wall, and I got out. Straight to Honda.

Selling Hondas in Michigan during this era was not without its own unique challenges. During those years, I was physically threatened, had my Accord vandalized with patriotic graffiti, and was nearly run off the road on no fewer than nine occasions. Past that though, it was easy as hell. Those cars were selling themselves. If a customer came on the lot, they were there because of reputation. Once they got behind the wheel, they could see and feel that there was no real comparison between those cars and what the Americans were building.

I wasn't selling cars because I loved doing it; I only loved the money. I was good at it. It was kind of a game, really. I could have kept selling those Sunfires, sure as shit, but why go in and make one-third on a vehicle against what Honda would pay me? I'll say this: if a good salesman is really behind the product, watch out. Sky's the limit. You walk in thinking you're just looking, but you're driving off that lot in a Civic LX with power everything and rust proofing that may or may not have been actually applied. Like Blake said in *Glengarry*, "a guy don't walk on the lot lest he wants to buy." It's true. No one has time to just idle around a car lot. I wouldn't want to know anyone who'd choose to spend their free time checking out the new selection at Schneeberger. That'd be fucking weird.

I knew I had my work cut out for me as the calendar flipped from September to October. There were a couple of other salesmen who wanted most weekends off to head to Ann Arbor or East Lansing for football Saturdays, plus some other guys trying to get their boats out of the water up north. Covering for all of these shifts meant I was working six days a week for the entire month, but that's exactly what I'd have to do if I was going to get near the ten grand.

The ink wasn't yet dry on some contracts for an Accord LX when my boss, Gary Danko, peeked into my office door. Gary was a timid guy and continuously allowed his sales staff to run roughshod over even the most minor of requests. He engendered little respect, and when someone got hold of the fact that he'd fought off testicular cancer a couple of years prior but lost a nut in the process, most of the guys tore him up behind his back. I stayed out of it and most of the jokes weren't very clever anyway. It isn't funny to call a guy Hitler just because he's only got one ball. He generally left me alone, so I was surprised to see him.

"Phil, nice job on the Accord."

I looked up from the paperwork and smiled. "Thanks, Gary."

"Do you have a second?"

"For you, Gary, I've got nine. But that's all, then I've got to fuckin' sell."

My boss gave a slight chuckle and sat in a plush chair on the other side of my shiny pine desk. "I've been getting a few complaints lately, Phil."

I leaned back in my chair and put my hands behind my head. "Is that right? What about?"

Gary leaned forward. He mumbled. "Well, some of the other salesmen think you've been stepping over them for sales lately."

I smiled. "They're right. Anything else?"

"There is, yes. I'm going to have to split your commission on the blue Civic from yesterday with McLaughlin." He looked at the floor as he said this.

"Horseshit, Gary. You don't have to do anything. Because McLaughlin would rather go to lunch for two hours than sell a car, he deserves half that pay?" I took my hands from behind my head and leaned forward. I tried to look Danko in the eyes, but he was still staring at his shoe tops. "Don't do it. He doesn't deserve it."

"I'm between a rock and a hard place. I know you're going for big numbers this month. You're kicking ass. We're doing great because of it."

"Then why are you taking food out of my mouth and giving it to McLaughlin?"

He got up and walked over to close the door. "I know McLaughlin isn't half the salesman as you are. But he's going to be working here next month."

I couldn't argue that point. It set a horrible precedent for me though, as it left the door wide open for just about anyone to try and horn in on my sales after the fact. I could predict Dan Garvey, that toothless fuck, would be next. "I could sue you."

Gary nodded. "If anyone else had heard what I just said, you probably could."

Perhaps Gary Danko was more devious than I had realized in his eight months running this shop. "You don't have the ball to really do this, Gary."

His faced turned red and he stared at me. "I'll do more than that." He didn't wait for my response, and instead stomped toward the door, opened it and left without closing it.

***

His real name was Charlie, but around the lot he was known almost exclusively as Snarly, as his upper lip was perpetually curled in a foul mood sneer. It looked almost like Elvis Presley's expression, but I assume the King was of a sunnier disposition than ol' Snarly. I never let it scare me off, and Charlie and I became pretty fast friends around the lot. Besides, most of the other salesmen didn't want anything to do with me, so if I wanted a work friend, the pickings were slim. Eventually, I started inviting him to Bob's, and he fell in love with the place.

Charlie was a bit adrift, having dropped out of UM-Flint a couple of years before. He was working at Schneeberger as a detailer, getting used cars ready for sale and touching up newer models as needed. It was shit work and certainly beneath someone with Charlie's intelligence, but he seemed to prefer a job with as little real responsibility as possible.

The evening following my confrontation with Gary Danko, Charlie and I were at Bob's. I was playing my potential purchase of the bar close to the vest; I didn't want anyone to know what was happening in case the deal fell apart. With the Uniball's threats from earlier that day, this seemed like an increasingly likely outcome.

Charlie was leaning forward with his elbows on the bar, right hand on his pint glass. Although he'd just worked a nine-hour shift cleaning crud out of the nooks and crannies of trade-ins, he looked as though he'd just stepped out of the shower. Charlie favored somewhat outdated clothes, often looking like he'd stepped out of some fifties teen movie with solid-color tee shirts, rockabilly jeans and a collection of various colored Chuck Taylors. "I should probably make this the last one. Colleen's going to wonder where I am."

I nodded. "Same here." I drank the rest of my beer and motioned to Russ, the only other bartender besides Bob, for a refill. "You know, Pam's been after me to get the four of us together again soon."

Charlie finished his beer and then took a Marlboro Red out of the pack he'd left in front of him on the bar. "Colleen's been doing the same thing." He lit the cigarette with a match from the bar. "Why are women so in love with the idea of double dating?"

I shrugged my shoulders. "Because they're secretly sick to death of spending time alone with us?"

"That's as possible as anything else."

Russ stopped over with our fresh pints and I left a five for him. He thanked us and walked to the other end of the bar.

I moved on my stool to face Charlie. "I want to get your advice about something." I took a sip from my Stroh's.

"I can't imagine any scenario in which that's a good idea."

"I'm serious, Charlie." I grabbed his pack of cigarettes and stole one for myself. "Here's the quick version. I'm buying this bar."

His eyes went wide. "You're shitting me."

I shook my head. "Problem is, I need to make ten grand commission this month before I have enough cash to finalize the deal."

"Man, that would be awesome. There's so much you could do with this place. It's like *Field of Dreams*. They will come, Phil. They will come." He chuckled. "Good jukebox, update the beer selection, and leave pretty much everything else exactly as it is." Charlie was talking faster than I'd ever heard him.

"I'm glad you're excited, but there's more to this. I have to make ten fucking grand this month."

"I heard you. You can do that." Charlie took a deep drag from his smoke.

"Thanks for the confidence. But Danko threatened me today with halving some of my commissions."

"Danko? Fuck him. What's the line, 'you can't think on your feet, you ought to keep your mouth closed?' That's Danko." Charlie stubbed out his cigarette and drank half his beer in one gulp.

"True as that may be, he's still got the authority to dip into my commissions, and with McLaughlin and Garvey and whoever the fuck else lining up to grab what they can't get on their own, he's got the numbers." I took a sip from my Stroh's. "Who's going to defend me in this instance? Those guys hate me."

Charlie shook his head. "They don't hate you; they fear you." He lit another Red. "Big difference. Danko's afraid of you, too."

"Danko's afraid of his own shadow."

Charlie chuckled. "Seriously dude, I can see the Sierra Nevada and Anchor Steam taps right there." He pointed down the bar. "People will come, Phil. People will most definitely come."

"That's great. It's not going to happen unless I can get the money."

The side door opened and Edgar, a friend of the bartender's who I'd come to know over the years, ambled in. I nodded at him as he walked past.

Charlie leaned in and whispered. "I've got some money saved."

I was surprised at this. I couldn't imagine Charlie made more than eight dollars an hour cleaning the cars at Schneeberger. "I don't know."

"I've been ready to move on from the lot for a while now, Phil."

"I would expect so." I took a sip from my beer and then ground out the borrowed cigarette in the ashtray. Down the bar, I could hear Edgar complaining about his litany of health issues. I needed to figure out how to gently get rid of some of these crocs when Bob's was mine. "I'm not sure. I might need to talk to Pam first."

"It's perfect. You can't run the place on your own. I've always wanted to be a bartender."

I worried to myself that Charlie's alter ego, Snarly, was not the best candidate for being behind the bar, but I figured it was possible that a fair amount of Charlie's bad attitude at work was due to his being unhappy at Schneeberger, which I think just about everyone was.

"How much did you say you need?" Charlie drained the rest of his pint and motioned to Russ for another.

"I thought you said Colleen was going to wonder after you?"

"I'm all fired up now."

I nodded. "I need ten grand. Well, probably minus about three based on what I've made so far this month."

Charlie paused. "I've only got about five."

I leaned forward on the bar and rested my chin on my folded hands. "I'm worried that Danko's got me over a barrel, too."

"I think we can handle Danko."

Russ brought Charlie his beer.

"Fuck it, can I get another, Russ?" I drained my glass and slid it to the bartender.

He nodded and went down the bar to pour our drafts.

"Pam's going to be pissed." I stole another cigarette from Charlie's pack.

"She'll be fine."

Russ returned with our beers. It was Charlie's round, so he counted out some singles from a wad in his pocket and slid them across the bar.

"Thanks, Russ." Charlie turned towards me. "Here's what we do. When I get a new car sale clean-up, if it's McLaughlin or Garvey's, I'll fuck with it."

"What do you mean 'fuck with it'?"

"I've got some ideas."

"Such as?" I took a sip of my beer and looked at my watch. I'd promised Pam I'd be home an hour before.

"I'll bring in chicken gizzards, put them in a plastic bag and then hide them somewhere in the spare well."

I brought my beer to my lips, but stopped short as I thought about the stench of rotting chicken parts combining with new car smell. "That's disgusting."

"Yes, it is. But they're sure to bring the cars back. You let McLaughlin or Garvey or whoever know that they need to back off or this happens to every car they sell."

"You'll get fired."

Charlie looked up and down the bar, gestured with his right arm like Vanna White. "Doesn't matter. I work here now."

***

I was waiting for an eleven o'clock appointment to show when Gary ambled over toward me. It was unseasonably warm for late October and he was wearing a short-sleeved white shirt with a skinny black tie. He looked like a Mormon missionary.

"Garvey's going to take this appointment, Phil." He reached out for the Accord keys that I had in my hand. "We need to talk."

I smiled, my eyes hidden behind a pair of mirrored sunglasses. I assumed Danko could see the fire-red tips of his ears in the lenses as he tried to meet my gaze. I handed him the keys.

"Let's go."

We walked past the showroom and into Gary's office, which was decked out in all manner of pennants, posters, and a giant flag from his alma mater, Bemidji State University. Why he was so proud of some second-rate state school in dumbfuck Minnesota was beyond me, but I didn't really have room to poke fun, seeing as how I didn't even graduate.

Once we were both inside, Gary motioned for me to sit down. He stayed on his feet, his ears getting even redder, and he was shaking a bit. "How long did you think you could get away with this?" His voice cracked on the last word, turning it into two syllables.

"You expected me to take your bullshit lying down?"

"You're not even going to deny it?"

I shook my head. "I don't give a fuck. You don't have the foresight to have HR in here to document this? It's your word against mine."

He looked confused. Gary pulled out his desk chair and sat on its edge. "What was I supposed to do, Phil?"

"The right thing. Pay me my money. If McLaughlin and Garvey and whoever didn't like it, tell them commission is for closers. If they can't close, fire them."

"I had to keep them happy. You can understand that." He grabbed a stress ball from the corner of his desk and started squeezing.

"I understand that you're gutless in addition to nutless."

"Why are you talking to me like that, Phil? I thought we always got on well."

"You got the memory of a fucking fly. I never liked you, anyway. I told you I'm buying a bar. I made enough to close the deal over a week ago."

"I already fired your buddy Charlie this morning. I've got to fire you, too."

I stood. "Good. Let's move it along. Get HR in here, fill out the fucking paperwork. It'll be a pleasure to collect unemployment while I get the bar going, you dumb shit."

"You were a good salesman. It's a shame it has to end like this."

"You're right, Gary. It is a shame. It's a shame you stole from me and rewarded your shittiest salesmen by paying them money that was rightfully mine. Did you notice that Robertson, Luntz, and Smitty never asked for a cut? You ever wonder why? Because they can fucking sell cars on their own."

"I don't have time for this." Gary stood and moved toward the door.

Neither did I. First, I needed to get to Knight-Ridge Attorneys-at-Law to sign some final papers. After that, I was meeting Charlie, Pam, Bob and others for a celebration at the bar. On the following Monday, ownership would transfer to me. Bob would get to retire. Pam would be our primary breadwinner. We'd all see if Snarly only existed at Schneeberger Honda.

And if Gary Danko ever walked in looking for a drink, I'd happily point to the sign allowing me the right to refuse to service anyone.

CHARLIE & CINDY

I woke up in my clothes, which was odd because I was pretty sure I took Cindy home from the bar the night before. I blinked my eyes and turned to my right, and sure enough, there she was. A skinny little thing, barely any tits to speak of, even wore braces. She sort of reminded me of a shorter Fiona Apple, if Fiona Apple had a boyish haircut and a mouthful of metal and rubber bands. I'm not sure what I initially found attractive about her, but goddamned if she wasn't a fucking wildcat in the sack. Uninhibited. A little crazy, obviously, as the best fucks almost always are. She scared me some, but if I knew anything, it was how to get rid of them, no matter how crazy.

She was still asleep, which gave me a chance to get to the bathroom and take care of business before she woke up. I liked to joke with people that I hadn't taken a solid shit in years, and it'd be much funnier if it weren't the truth. There's nothing all that funny about your ass exploding most mornings.

Somebody once told me that a "Jersey Salute" was spraying ass water all over a public toilet, but I'm not sure what to call it when the victim is your own throne. Wretched nastiness, that's for sure. But I exorcised some demons there, hopped in a quick shower, and got back into bed like nothing happened.

She was stirring a bit when I got under the covers. The bedclothes needed a wash, as per usual, but I was comfortable, so why should I give a fuck if some Bob's groupie might not be? Cindy rolled over and smiled that metallic smile that I sure as hell didn't want wrapped around my cock, no matter how much she begged to let her blow me. "You won't feel them," she promised. Fucking right I won't, because you're not getting that chance, ever.

"Good morning." She reached over with her tiny left hand and touched my arm. Her breath smelled like she devoured a bag of assholes for breakfast while I was taking my shit and shower.

"Hey." I looked at the ceiling, which was turning decidedly yellow around the popcorn edges from my years of smoking.

"You smell all cleaned up. Big day today?"

"Not really."

She sighed, rolled over on the bed, turning her back to me, thankfully blowing that dragon breath in the opposite direction. "Do you want to go get some breakfast with me?"

I didn't. "I don't. No."

"You don't know?"

"I said I don't. I don't want to get breakfast with you."

"Why not?" She stretched her back, and her neck gave a series of somewhat sickening popping sounds like a Coke can being smashed.

I gave a heavy sigh. "I don't need to see you eat."

Her eyes were wide, mouth agape. It was not unlike her "fuck me harder" look. She put her hand in front of her mouth to cover the braces. "What the hell does that mean, you don't need to see me eat?"

I hadn't thought about her taking that comment as a dig at her metal mouth, but now that I could see that's what she thought it was, I didn't really give a shit. It was easier to just go with it than to explain that watching women eat was pretty much a prelude to watching them take a dump in my mind. I grinned. "The thought of egg yolks all caught up in that metal is pretty gross, Cindy."

She sat up, put her feet on the floor, looked over her shoulder at me. "You're a dickhead."

It was probable that this would not be the only time such an epithet was hurled my way that day. "And this is a surprise to you?"

She shook her head. "It shouldn't be. Everyone knows about you." She made her way to the bedroom door, pulled it open in a huff. "Don't bother calling me."

The thought hadn't even occurred to me. "That won't be a problem."

***

Although he was perpetually at least fifteen minutes late to every shift, I thought Ralph was proving himself to be a fairly reliable addition to the Bob's stable of bartenders. Doug, on the other hand, was pissing me off. I had been lining up participants for a card game that night when he called to see if I could cover his double. Some shit about needing to drive to Pinckney to help his girlfriend's mom move some furniture. I'm sure the fuckhead could've let me know weeks ago, but he had to wait until I'd put some plans in motion for my day off. This was the third or fourth time I'd covered for him over the past six months, and I think Ralph had done the same once or twice.

I'd purposefully pushed Doug into working the double on Tuesdays so that I didn't have to hang around with Phil as often. Tuesdays had been Phil's weeknight to hang out in the bar for the last couple of years, and the bar was usually filled with his fan club of dilettantes and sycophants -- people trying to kiss his ass. I got tired of it. But that wasn't all. It's hard to explain without sounding like an ungrateful dick, but I was sick of Phil's happiness. That's really the only way to put it. Phil's not the type to rub things into anybody's face, let alone one of his oldest friends, someone who'd been with him from the beginning. It's not as though he'd come bounding into the bar, giant grin splitting his face, shouting, "Look at this happy motherfucker, you miserable prick, Charlie. Why, the divergent trajectories of our lives are shocking in every conceivable way."

I wasn't in the mood for an afternoon of Phil's happy tales. I knew that Ray rarely came down when Doug worked on Tuesdays, so I slipped a few dollars into the jukebox and played *Superjudge* from start to finish, which I knew would annoy Phil. After I finished pulling down the stools and wiping down the bar, I poured a pint glass of water and then sat and lit a cigarette, which burned my lips a little, probably because they were still raw from making out with Metal Mouth the previous night.

Just as the title track moved in to "Cage Around the Sun", Phil came through the side door, sat in the stool closest to the end of the bar and greeted me with a somewhat puzzled expression. "What are you doing here?"

I exhaled my drag in Phil's general direction. "Nice to see you, too."

"I didn't mean it like that." He got up and opened the cooler door just to my right, and then reached in for a Labatt. He pulled off the cap on the opener fixed to the front of the cooler and sat back down. "Where's Doug?"

I shrugged my shoulders. "His girlfriend's mom's? Something like that. Pinckney."

Phil shuddered a little. "You know they still have active KKK there?"

"Whatever."

Phil took a big drink from his beer. "What's up your ass?"

I dragged on my cigarette, and then rested it in a plastic ashtray on the bar. I took a drink of water. "Nothing. I'm fine."

"The fuck you are. You've got goddamned Monster Magnet cranked up, which you only play when you're pissed off. Don't think I haven't noticed that. You're acting all pissy; you're sub-verbal, what's the deal?"

Phil had been overly concerned with my mental well being since Colleen had split on me about a year before. I have to admit that Phil helped a lot. I was pretty adrift for a little while there, maybe because I'd set up so much of my life to revolve around Colleen. If I had to be on point to make sure she was happy at all times, then there really wasn't any mental space left over to consider my own happiness, or lack thereof. Colleen and I had spent over seven years together, and when she abruptly announced that she was going to law school in Chicago, it hit me pretty hard. Especially considering that I didn't even know she'd taken the LSAT. I didn't quite know what to do with myself and Phil looked after me for some time. He and Pam kept me fed for weeks, and Phil was hanging out at the bar with more frequency when I was working, making sure things went okay. It got to be fun, hanging out so much felt like old times. But eventually, Phil assumed I was improving and stopped coming around so much.

Probably within a week, I started filling the space left by Colleen and Phil with a steady string of at-times dubious conquests, like Cindy. Phil didn't like it; he was concerned that sleeping with women who came to the bar was bad for business, some old crocodile code that Ray was always on about too. But fuck both of them; I'd spent almost my entire twenties with the same woman who, in the end, couldn't even be bothered to have an adult conversation with me about her changing plans. I was making up for lost time because, I'll tell you what: there's nothing in this world like that split second when you slip your hard cock into a new, wet and waiting pussy. You never feel more alive and I was tired of wishing I was dead.

Phil was waiting for an answer about what was bothering me. "I'm not happy that Doug called off again. That's it."

"So let's get rid of him." Phil finished his beer, threw it into the empty trashcan under the bar with a dull glass-on-plastic thump. He looked at his watch. "You know Ray won't come down when Doug's opening. I don't like that."

Ever since Ray sold his bar and then moved into one of the upstairs apartments, he'd come down to have a few beers right after opening. I loved Ray, but I was mildly happy not to have to hear his entreaties into my sex life today. I'm not sure why Ray avoided Doug, because Ray was mum on the subject. But actions speak louder than words anyway, and Ray wasn't in his stool drinking a Stroh's and smoking a cigarillo, so that was that. Phil was right: we needed to get a replacement in here for Doug, but even though lots of people theoretically wanted to work at Bob's, the realities of being paid under the table always narrowed the applicant pool. At that moment, the pool was dry.

I shook my head. "It's not the right time. I've got no back up right now."

Phil reached into the cooler and grabbed a fresh beer. "No one?

"I'd tell you if there was."

"Hm. Could you work a skeleton crew for a while?"

Fucking Phil. It was just like him to suggest that Ralph and I cover the extra shifts without once thinking of helping out himself. He hadn't been behind the bar since he got his realtor's license about eighteen months earlier, unless you counted the ten seconds it took to pry his fat ass off the stool and reach into the cooler for a Labatt. Even before he started selling houses, he worked maybe once a month to cover an emergency or a super busy night. "I was hoping to hit more shows, try and get more bands in here."

"I know. The problem is—"

"There's no fucking problem, Phil. Everything's covered. I've got one band that's ready and we could start next week."

"Who is this band?"

"They're called God, I Love Pie!"

Phil nearly did a spit take with his beer. "What?"

"God, I Love Pie!"

"The fuck kind of name is that?"

"It's ninety-eight. Long, quirky names are all the rage. Like Today's My Super Spaceout Day or ...And You Will Know Us by the Trail of Dead."

"You're making these up."

"Godspeed You Black Emperor? System of a Down?"

"Bush?"

"Please let them never release another record."

"I liked that one song."

I glared at Phil.

"You know more about this shit than I do."

That was putting it mildly. Bob's wouldn't be Bob's without the jukebox and Phil knew that even if he never acknowledged it. I was the one with the taste and the knowledge to put together a hundred discs that would draw Flint's cool kids downtown. Phil had never even heard of Nick Cave or Creeper Lagoon. He had the money and the connections, but it was my music that created the community, and we both knew it. My ten-percent cash equity in the bar should have been bumped to fifty-fifty after all my input. But here I was battling the absentee owner who liked that one Bush song to let me run this place the way I knew it needed to be run. Live music was the next step in the bar's evolution.

I pretended that I hadn't heard Phil. "What did you say?"

"I said you know more about the music stuff than me."

I smiled, maybe for the first time that day. "That's gotta be worth something."

***

The night was winding down. I surmised that Doug wasn't proving to be a rousing success on Tuesdays, as it stayed pretty quiet. If I cover for Ralph, there are a bunch of schmoes asking after him all night, but no one made a peep looking for Doug.

I was down to just a handful of drinkers with no prospects for pulling a one-nighter out when my old card buddy, Jason Young, popped in. Jason was a good guy; he'd been part of the regular game I had on Wednesdays for a few years. It was a competitive game that got pretty intense some weeks, and there were nights the winner was walking out with a couple of Gs. Jason was a pretty good player, but he'd knocked up his girlfriend a while back, so he married her and settled down. He was an assistant manager at the Circuit City in Beecher, and between the wife and the kid and running the store, he'd bowed out of the Wednesday game forever ago, and he was just the first domino. Dudes were dropping out every couple of months until it was no longer a regular game, leaving me scrambling most weeks unless I wanted to join a mobbed-up game, which I didn't. I probably hadn't seen Jason in six months or so.

"Youngster. What're you drinking?"

"I'll take an Anchor." He tossed a five on the bar and sat on a stool close to the end of the bar. The few people left at that hour were concentrated at the other side. "Mind if I play a few tunes? Anything new on there I haven't heard?"

"I put the newest Grant Lee Buffalo in there since the last time you were here. That's a good one."

Jason nodded and then walked over to the jukebox. I watched him slide in a dollar and punch up a few tracks. Soon the quiet in the bar was replaced with the rootsy pop of "Testimony."

I finished Jason's Anchor draft and met him at the end of the bar with it. I tapped out the last cigarette from a pack of Reds and lit it. "What brings you in so late on a Tuesday?"

Jason took a sip of the Anchor. "I got your message about the game being canceled, thought I'd stop in and say hello."

"Right on. It's been tough getting a regular game together. It gets frustrating."

"I can imagine." Jason took a sip from his beer.

I took a drag from my cigarette. "How's the family?"

Jason smiled. "Melissa's pregnant. Totally unexpected."

"That's great, Dude. Mazel tov." I had no beer with which to toast.

"It's pretty exciting. Life is funny, you know?" Jason took another sip from his beer.

The only thing funny about my life was my complete refusal to accept any of the trappings of becoming a typical adult, although most people probably thought this more pathetic than funny. "I'm not sure I'm following you."

"Well, it wasn't so long ago we had a regular card game, and I was in here four or five nights a week, cooking at Chili's. Having fun, being young. It feels like a different lifetime."

55

He might have been smiling as he said this, but I thought Jason sounded like he'd rather be dead.

"Remember the night that Kip Healey got pissed off when I bluffed the inside straight and took the biggest pot of the night? He ran into the kitchen and grabbed that rusty steak knife and started jumping around with it?"

I waved him off. "Of course. You don't need to do a blow-by-blow replay. I was there."

"You were more than there, Charlie. You disarmed him."

"He wasn't gonna do anything." That was a lie. Kip Healey was a crazy motherfucker. I'm pretty sure he was going to cut Jason for real. What was I supposed to do, let that happen in my fucking kitchen? The cops would be there, then there'd be all sorts of questions about the game that was happening, and I couldn't have that. So I jumped up, grabbed Kip Healey's wrist and twisted his arm up behind his back until he settled down. Truthfully, I couldn't blame him for being pissed. Jason's bluff cost Kip Healey over eight hundred bucks that night.

"Even if he wasn't, I haven't forgotten what you did for me that night."

I did it to protect my game, but whatever. "It's cool."

Jason took a sip of his beer as "Testimony" segued into some David Bowie. "I've always wanted to pay you back somehow, but I didn't have any way to do that until now."

I took a last drag from the Red and stubbed it out. "Go ahead."

"There's a friend of mine who has an in on some point-shaving. I can't give you any other details about who he is."

This was the sort of thing I'd heard before. Anytime someone found out I did some gambling, they'd try and buddy up with insider knowledge. I hadn't fallen for it since I lost a few hundred on a Boston College basketball fix someone told me about a few years earlier. "Okay."

"I know you're probably thinking this sounds like bullshit, but it isn't. I know the whos and whens and whats of this thing, Charlie.

There are less than a dozen people who know what I'm telling you. It's the real deal. Money has been paid to the players who are in. This is happening."

Jason sure sounded convinced, which intrigued me. "I'm not asking who's behind this, but what can you tell me?"

He looked over his shoulders as though he was about to tell a racist joke. He leaned in. "It's the October 24th Toledo at Akron football game."

"What makes this game so special?"

"Nothing special at all. That's why it's so perfect. My friend went to high school with a couple of the Toledo players, who are acting as the go-betweens. Like I said, the key players have their money. The spread should go off at between eighteen and twenty-two because Akron's gonna be pretty bad this year. They're not going to lose, just keep the final score under the spread. It's gold, Charlie."

The more Jason talked about it, the more intriguing it became. There were rumors about Mid-American Conference football teams shaving points in the recent past, so it seemed within the realm of possibility to me. I also thought it was interesting that the Toledo players weren't throwing the game, they were only agreeing to not cover the spread. I always had a hard time seeing how it'd be possible to get guys to lay down and lose the game, but that wasn't what was happening here. They just weren't going to run up the score. I could see easily how it might be done with payoffs to just a handful of players; maybe a linebacker to miss a few tackles, a cornerback to get burned on a key play and a receiver to drop a couple of passes. Maybe an O-lineman to miss a block.

Jason took a sip of his beer and then tapped on the bar. "You're awful quiet."

I shook my head to snap out of my reverie. "Yeah, sorry. I just wonder if it isn't one of those things that's too good to be true, you know? I've been burned before. I'm not accusing you of not having the best intentions."

Jason shook his head. "Don't apologize, Charlie. I understand. I just felt like I owed you after that near-knifing."

It was best that I not let Jason know that I believed him. If he didn't know that I was going to place a bet, and who I'd place it with, then what he didn't know literally couldn't hurt him. If he did really know the principals involved in this shave, then the less he knew about my bet, the better, especially considering I was going to lay down the bulk of the ten grand I'd saved over the last five years.

Jason finished his beer and then slid the empty pint glass across the bar. "Too bad I couldn't convince you."

I grabbed the glass off the bar and then walked it over to the sink, which was pretty full of glasses, as I hadn't felt like washing them most of the night. I moved back over to the end of the bar, wiping my hands on the rag in my front pocket. "Don't sweat it, Dude. Consider us even."

***

It had been a couple of weeks since that last night with Cindy, which meant I was working on my longest dry spell since Colleen left. I wasn't above looking a gift horse in the mouth, as was evident by hooking up with Brace Face anyway. It was a pretty busy Wednesday night, but the bar cleared out somewhat suddenly around half past midnight, and things were really winding down as the hour slid past one. The pickings were slim, but I settled for an attentive audience with this girl named Marie, who was maybe a little fatter than I'd have picked out willingly, but this was slump buster time. If I were to get myself out of the dry spell, she'd have to do.

She went all moony over me after I'd tossed a guy from the bar a couple of hours before. I felt a little bad because it was this kid named Aaron who'd been coming in pretty regularly for a year or two. I liked him okay. He was a good tipper and tonight he'd brought a new friend who seemed like a cool enough guy. But Aaron has been getting increasingly out of control, and he'd followed suit tonight. I had my eye on a girl wearing a flowered dress at the bar, but as Aaron got drunker, he kept creeping up on her and got a little too grabby. She stormed out all disgusted, and I didn't have any choice but to give him the heave-ho at that point. His friend collected him and was all apologies, but I told him to keep Aaron out for at least a week.

Marie propped one of her elbows on the bar, resting her head in her hand. She wasn't too drunk, but she did seem tired. I'd probably just have to say "bed" a few times as I closed up and she'd be in mine. "Did anyone ever physically attack you when you threw them out of the bar?"

I shook my head as I wiped down a glass. "One time some dude said he had a knife and was going to wait for me outside, but a couple of guys heard him and followed him out and made sure he left."

She may have actually fluttered her eyelashes. "Were you scared?"

No, I wanted to get fucking stabbed. Always wanted to feel a hot blade enter my body. "Not really."

"I would've been scared." She sipped at her drink, a Maker's and water on ice that had shifted to largely water as she nursed it and the ice melted.

There were a couple of guys I didn't really know at the end of the bar who'd been hanging around since about ten, getting slightly sloshed on pitchers of Bell's Amber. I was headed down to get them a refill when the side door opened and Cindy walked in. She wasn't alone. Somehow, she'd found the only person in Flint skinnier than she was, a dude with close-cropped blonde hair and a small Clash t-shirt that still hung off his shoulders as though they were a wire hanger. She flashed a metallic grin at me and sat near the taps with her new beau.

"What's up, Dickface?" She slapped her small leather backpack onto the bar. "This is Marcus. Marcus, this is Dickface, but some people call him Charlie. Marcus and I would like a pitcher of Stroh's."

I laughed inside at Cindy's attempt to make me jealous. She told me not to call, I hadn't called. Clearly, she wanted the opposite, and imposed upon Hanger Shoulders here to accompany her and make it look like she was in demand. "First, I'm going to pour a pitcher for these gentlemen." I gestured with a nod of my head at the two dudes at the end of the bar. "Then I'll need to see Marcus' driver's license."

She huffed a little, but Marcus did as he was told. I finished pouring the Bell's for the two dudes at the end of the bar and came back to pour the Stroh's for Metal Mouth and her boy toy.

I slid the pitcher around the taps and grabbed two pint glasses. "Six bucks for the pitcher."

"Pay him, Marcus." Cindy took the pitcher by the handle and poured herself a quick half-pint and then drank it in one gulp. She then poured a full pint and set the pitcher down without pouring any for Hanger Shoulders. She got up to put a few singles in the jukebox, presumably to play a bunch of songs from *Exile in Guyville*. Sure enough, "Divorce Song" soon filled the empty spaces of the bar.

I walked back towards Marie, shaking a Red out of the pack in my shirt pocket. "How are you fixed for a drink down here?" I tried to sound affable, but it probably came out more ineffable. Ray was right about one thing: I needed to smile more often.

Marie looked down at her glass. "I'm fine for now."

I sat on the stool closest to the end of the bar and lit my cigarette. "I'm not sure you told me where you live." If possible, I liked to try and get them back to their place, as they were usually more comfortable that way and, perhaps more important, didn't know where I live. Of course, it left me at the mercy of someone else's music collection, and it was never pleasant to be balls deep in some broad while being forced to listen to the Dave Matthews Band. Sometimes, I had no choice, though. Cindy lived with her folks in Beecher, so that one was unavoidable unless I wanted to say hi to Mr. and Mrs. Metal Mouth before I violated their daughter amongst her stuffed animals, high school play photos, and New Kids trifles and trinkets.

"I have a place in Eastside. In the States."

They'd once been Flint's nicest area of rental properties, but the state streets were quickly turning rough. The novelty of living on a series of streets named for various states was not cute enough to protect residents from break-ins and the occasional shooting. Not really a place for a single lady.

I nodded. "There are some nice places over there."

"I'm pretty close to Mott. It's not so bad. Things are getting worse a little farther north."

The area near the Community College was probably safer, as she said, but I wouldn't want to live there. I took a drag from my cigarette. I looked down the bar and Cindy was staring at me, giving me the finger.

Marie's eyes followed mine to Cindy's middle finger. Cindy sat perfectly still, not bothering to hide the fact that she was flicking me off.

"Do you know her?"

I wasn't sure how to answer that one. Yes, biblically? That didn't seem to be the way to get me into Ms. Chunky-but-Funky's pants. "She comes in from time to time."

"Why is she giving you the finger?"

I shrugged my shoulders. "I can only speculate."

Marie looked over at Cindy again, who was still giving me the bird. "Do you always let customers sit there giving you rude finger gestures?"

Actually, I didn't. I walked over to Cindy and Hanger Shoulders, whose real name I had already forgotten. Marcus -- that was it. I looked straight at the kid, but he didn't want to meet my gaze. This was more than he'd probably bargained for when he agreed to step out for a late-night beverage with Metal Mouth.

She kept her middle finger up as I approached. "What can I do for you, Dickface?"

I smirked. "I was wondering the same thing. What can I do for you?"

"For starters, you can act like you know me instead of sitting down there trying to fuck that heifer."

"That isn't any of your business."

Hanger Shoulders stood. "I think we should just go."

Cindy snapped at him. "Sit the fuck down, Marcus." She looked at me, finally putting the middle finger away. "It's a free country. I can observe whatever I want; say whatever I want."

I pointed to the sign near the cash register that read "Management Reserves the Right to Refuse Service to Anyone at Anytime for Little or No Reason."

She read it over. "You're management in this scenario?"

I nodded.

"You can't even manage your fucking apartment. That place was a sty, and it smelled."

I smirked. "That was your pussy."

She looked at me with wide eyes and an open mouth.

I took a last drag from my cigarette and stubbed it out in an ashtray. "Get the fuck out of here. Don't come back. Take this fucking beanpole with you."

Marcus rose from his stool. He looked at me with sort of pleading eyes. "Does this mean I can't come back too?"

I laughed. "Whatever, Dude. Show some better judgment about who you come in here with next time."

Cindy reached for her pint glass. I knew she was going to throw it at me, so I grabbed her wrist to stop it.

She glared at me. "Let go of my goddamned wrist, you piece of shit."

I shook my head. "Just get out of here. Don't make this worse." My tone was calm.

She pulled her arm from my grasp and narrowed her eyes. "You haven't seen the last of me."

Marcus called her name from the doorway and she turned to storm out. She yelled out "Fucking cocksucker," as she pushed the door open. Marcus trailed behind her.

Her songs were still queued on the jukebox and had cycled through more of *Exile*. I reached for the "Skip" button near the sink, but not before Liz Phair sang, "You said things I wouldn't say, straight to my face, boy." At least it hadn't gotten to "Fuck and Run" yet. I needed to get that disc out of there.

The two dudes at the end of the bar sat there as if nothing had happened, their pitcher nearly empty. I pointed to it as a gesture to see if they wanted a refill. They both slowly shook their heads, eyes down at the bar.

I walked back over towards Marie. On the way, I reached into the cooler for a Sam Adams. I popped the cap on the opener fastened to the cooler and sat on my barstool.

Marie didn't look at me. "Remind me not to give you the finger."

I smiled.

"I think I'm going to get going." Marie stood and grabbed her small purse from off the bar.

I nodded. "I'll walk you to your car."

She shook her head and waved me off at the same time. "That isn't necessary, really."

This went from a sure thing to a no thing with one middle finger. Fucking Brace Face.

✳✳✳

63

I would be lying if I said I wasn't looking over my shoulder fairly frequently in response to Cindy's threat. I'm pretty sure no woman had ever said anything to me like, "You haven't seen the last of me." In fact, I was really used to the opposite; I'd piss them off, usually intentionally, and they'd storm out and declare I'd never see them again or some shit like that. This was new. But a week turned into two and two into four, and the next thing I knew, I had wasted a couple of months in fear of a retaliation that apparently wasn't going to come.

It seemed like autumn was early that year, but it felt like football weather, so I didn't mind. I would normally have around a thousand bucks out in bets on Saturdays, but I was taking it a little easier than normal. I wanted to be sure I had a serious chunk to lay down on the Toledo game that Jason Young had told me about over the summer. I hadn't seen him since that night, which was just as well.

The October sun was strong, but it still felt cold inside the bar as I unlocked the doors to the bar and Ray shuffled in. I greeted him, poured him a beer and sat on the stool nearest his at the end of the bar.

"How are you this afternoon, Charlie?" Ray tapped out one of his cigarillos from a pack he'd put on the bar.

"I'm good. Not much of a game last night." I was referring to game one of the American League Championship Series, in which the Yankees had crushed the Cleveland Indians.

Ray shook his head. "I didn't figure the Indians had much of a shot after the five runs in the first."

I nodded.

"What are the big games this weekend on the college slate, Charlie?" Ray took a small drag from his cigar and blew it out. It was still a little cool in the bar and he'd yet to remove his tan Members Only jacket as a consequence.

I couldn't explain that Akron at Kent State was the game I was watching closely this weekend, even though Ray knew I liked to wager on college football. "Nothing much in the Big Ten. Ohio

State always finds a way to collapse against Michigan. I'm sure they will again this year."

Ray took a sip from his beer. "I thought you'd say Nebraska at A&M for sure."

Under normal circumstances, he'd be right. I thought Nebraska was overrated and a road loss wasn't out of the question. It'd be a solid bet if I were taking more chances. "That's a good one, no doubt, but I'm not sure I know enough about either team to pick."

Ray lifted his beer as if to take a drink and then set it back down. "I almost forgot to ask how your show went last night."

After a few more weeks of kissing Phil's absentee ass, I finally cajoled him into agreeing to book God, I Love Pie! I thought a Tuesday would be a good choice, as Doug was still having trouble bringing anybody in and there wouldn't be much else happening around town to compete. The band had played a couple of shows in Ann Arbor and one in Pontiac by then, but this was to be their first Flint show. I helped the band print a ton of fliers and we pasted them everywhere we could think, and I had Doug and Ralph talking up the show to everyone who came into the bar.

About ten people showed up, which was why I was able to watch game one of the American League Championship Series.

It was a real drag. The band still worked hard; played their guts out. They had a bunch of new songs that sounded like a post-rock band playing power pop. The few people that were there really liked the band, pogoing around at the front of the bar. A couple of people were even asking if the band had CDs to sell, which they didn't yet.

None of this prevented me from having to pay three-quarters of the two hundred dollars I'd guaranteed the band out of my own pocket. The only thing keeping me from getting shitty drunk was adding to my expenses for the night. Instead, I mostly just sat at the end of the bar, pouting and watching the Yankees rout the Indians.

"It didn't go that well, Ray."

He took another drag from his cigar. It smelled like burnt peach peels. "I'm sorry about that. I thought I heard a lot of people coming and going while I was watching the game."

I reached into my shirt pocket for my pack of Reds and shook one out. "Maybe that was just the band loading and unloading equipment."

"I hadn't thought of that."

Before I had to defend the God, I Love Pie! debacle to Ray, I was saved by the bar's phone ringing.

I picked it up. "Bob's." Over the years, I'd honed my bar phone answering technique to a truncated version of that one syllable that hardly sounded like a word.

"Charlie, this is Colleen."

I hadn't heard from my ex in several months, the last time being to complain that she was getting collection calls because I had let the phone get disconnected, and it was still in her name. I'd taken care of that since, but she still sounded annoyed. "Hey. How are you?"

"I'm fine. Busy."

"Sure." I took a drag from my Red. "What's up?"

"Who is Cindy Glaser?"

I didn't even know Brace Face's last name, but I instantly knew that's who Colleen was talking about. "Why?"

"Why, Charlie? I'll tell you why. This crazy person has called me a dozen or more times over the last few days, threatening me, telling me to stay away from you."

"I'm sorry." I wanted to kill that little bitch. My ears turned red.

"I'm sure you are. I don't know what's going on there. You have your new life going on, I guess banging every skank that comes into that place. It makes me feel really special, Charlie, let me tell you."

I didn't see how any of this was Colleen's business, seeing as how she'd left me with absolutely no warning and didn't seem to care what happened in her wake. "I said I was sorry."

"Get your shit together, Charlie. You're nearly thirty years old. How old was this girl? Eighteen?"

"She's not eighteen."

Ray looked up from his beer. I needed to lower my voice.

I turned my back and cupped my hand over the receiver. "This is none of your concern anyway. You're in Chicago, you made your choice. I can do whatever I want."

"You don't get it." Colleen was yelling now. It hurt my ear a little. "Of course you can do whatever you want, but what should you do, Charlie? Indiscriminately put your dick wherever the fuck so that I have to hear about it three hundred miles away?"

"It was a mistake. I'll take care of it." I was whispering.

"Why are you being so quiet? Ray's there?"

"Yes, he is."

"What does he have to say about your behavior, Charlie?"

"None of this is your business. None of it."

"You should listen to Ray. He loves you. He cares."

Truthfully, I felt bad that Cindy had harassed Colleen. I know enough Freud to know what he said about accidents, but I really didn't intend for her to get involved this way. "Maybe you're right. Again, I'm sorry."

"Okay, Charlie." Colleen sounded as though she was a little disappointed that I wasn't fighting. "Hang in there, alright?"

If I'd been in a different mood, I'd have flown off the handle at that one. Hang in there? What am I, that kitten in the poster? Don't patronize me. "Yeah. Talk to you later."

"Bye."

I hung up the phone, and then took a drag from my cigarette as I walked back over towards Ray. The theme from *Kids in The Hall* played through the TV speakers. I normally watched that show for the first hour that I was open and Ray never complained, although I don't recall him ever laughing at it. Not once.

"That sounded like a serious conversation." Ray took a sip of his beer, which was almost empty. "Not to intrude."

"No, that's alright." I then told Ray everything that had happened with Cindy. I didn't hold back, I told him she was too young to legally drink in the bar, that I took her home one night and had pretty much the best sex of my life with her and got a little hooked. I told him that we fucked every night for a couple of weeks, but that I'd grown tired of her and tried to get rid of her. I told him about the night that she came in with Hanger Shoulders, that she'd call my number sometimes ten or fifteen times in a day, and that she tried to hit on both Ralph and Doug, but they each knew about her and gave her a wide berth. I told him that it was Colleen who had called, and that Cindy had tracked her down and was harassing her. I told him I was ready to call in Doug or Ralph to replace me so I could find her and beat the shit out of her.

Ray was quiet for a moment and then he finished the last drink from his pint. "Could I get another, Charlie?"

"Of course." I stood, grabbed his glass and went to the taps to pour a fresh pint of Stroh's for Ray. I watched him tap out another cigarillo and light it. I walked back over with his beer, and then sat it in front of him.

"The first thing is that you can't contact this girl." He took a sip of the beer. "This Cindy. That's exactly what she's trying to get you to do."

In my anger, this hadn't occurred to me. "I'm glad you said that."

Ray nodded. "She's trying desperately to get you to interact with her. You're going to have to do that, but in a way that isn't what she wants."

I couldn't imagine that she wanted me to punch her in the face, but I could be wrong. "I'm not sure I understand."

68

"What she wants is for you to come running to her, to confront her, so that you'll physically see her. I'm guessing that she thinks she still has a chance to be with you if she can just get you in a room with her. The funny thing is, Charlie, I suspect she might be right about that." Ray smirked and then took a sip of his beer.

I didn't think that was true, but I wasn't going to argue. "Then what do you think I should do?"

"First things first, you should stop sleeping with customers."

This was well-covered territory with Ray. He was forever telling me that taking women home from the bar was bad for business. I didn't think he was right, but I also hadn't foreseen the potential danger with someone like Cindy. "I get it, Ray. It's a problem."

"As far as Cindy is concerned, you told me she lives with her parents, correct?"

"That's right."

Ray took a shallow drag from his mini cigar. "Tell on her."

"Say what?" I don't know the last time I said that.

"Call her parents and tell them what she's been doing. She's an overgrown brat, she's used to getting what she wants all the time. I'm sure her parents still treat her like a child. If you align yourself with her parents, then she won't see you as an object of affection any longer."

This sounded brilliant, but also too easy. "You don't mean about us sleeping together, though? I don't want to tell her folks that."

Ray shook his head. "Tell them about the phone calls, the threats. It probably won't be the first they'd heard of this sort of behavior."

Cindy was more than I'd bargained for. She seemed a little unbalanced, but I never expected all this craziness. What Ray was proposing sounded unpleasant, but I couldn't think of any alternative on my own. I couldn't imagine a less pleasant phone call, but I had to do something. She'd gone far enough.

It was a good thing that Colleen had inadvertently informed me of Cindy's last name. That saved me some sleuthing.

I'd never called her before. I didn't know her number. I'd need to call Information.

I rose from my stool and walked toward the bar phone.

"No time like the present."

✳✳✳

There was no broadcast of the Toledo-Akron game, so I was stuck keeping an eye on the scrolling score ticker for updates while I half-watched Nebraska at Texas A&M. If I won the bet, one of the first things I thought I'd buy would be a desktop computer so that I could avoid exactly these annoyances. Those new iMacs were pretty sweet. I was tired of hearing everyone at the bar talk about various websites and exchanging email addresses while I was living like a Luddite.

I had put together a small card game the night before, and the apartment still smelled like cigar smoke and French onion dip. I needed to clean up, but I was tired and, for some reason, my leg muscles were sore even though I didn't do much all evening. It wasn't a huge game, but it was competitive and it felt good to get some players in my apartment again. I managed to lose over three hundred bucks, mostly to Eric Cooper, who bluffed his way through most of the night.

Toledo was coming into the game at 4-3, but their losses were not surprising, especially a shellacking in Columbus. Akron's performance had been less predictable; they were playing better than expected, although they did get skunked at Pitt a few weeks back. Going into the season, the line on the game probably would've been upwards of seventeen points, but the teams were proving to be a bit more evenly matched than previously thought. Toledo was giving ten points, which meant that a margin of victory of more than that was a loser for me.

I flipped back and forth between the Nebraska game and Indiana at Michigan, but for obvious reasons, neither of them were interesting me. I'd placed a bet on one other game so that Dugan, my bookie, didn't get too suspicious, but I didn't know anyone else well enough to scatter the Toledo-Akron wagers around, so he had to figure something was going on. I'd watched the line all week, but the needle never moved so if Jason Young was absolutely correct and this fix was in, they had successfully kept it quiet. I hoped so; I had eight grand out. Antonio Randal-El was almost enough to get me to keep more than half an eye on the Michigan-Indiana game, but not quite. I was mostly studying that ticker, waiting impatiently as the scores cycled all the way through the dregs of I-AA before catching the updates.

It was not easy to concentrate. The Toledo game seemed like it was tied at zero for the longest time, but it was also possible they weren't sending the score out, which happened from time to time at the smaller schools. Sometimes I'd have to switch over to Headline News, as they often moved through the scores quicker than ESPN, but this only resulted in me missing the score on each channel, as well as missing a touchdown in the Nebraska game. Even though I was predictably anxious, I still managed to nod off at least twice and miss the score that way. The second time I fell asleep, I awoke to the switch of post-game sounds on ESPN. Michigan had defeated Indiana. The Toledo game would more than likely be finished by now as well.

I watch and wait for the score. My head hurts. I should stop drinking canned beer. Vandy beat South Carolina. Ole Miss over Arkansas State. Clemson lost to Duke, which was the only other game I put money on. I lost. Thought Clemson could handle them. That was only two hundred, though. Still, fuck Clemson. That'll probably be all she wrote for Tommy West. I'm hungry, but I ate the rest of the pizza from last night for breakfast. I'll have to order something after I see the score. Maybe I'll treat myself. Night on the town, paint the town. There are the rest of the ACC scores. I hate the ACC. Maryland has a fucking turtle for a mascot. North Carolina is a foot. Seems easy to defeat a foot. Here we go.

Cincinnati over Miami of Ohio. The MAC scores should be right behind. Goddamnit, they're cycling through the Big East again. Tulane over Rutgers. Virginia over UAB. Why does the entire Big East seem to be playing out of conference today? It's late October. My heart feels like it's in my stomach. I'm fighting the urge to shit. I really don't want to shit my pants, but it'll have to wait until after I see this motherfucking score. The sink in the kitchen is dripping onto the dirty dishes piled inside. I'd get up to turn it off, but the score has to be coming up soon. Okay, here comes the MAC. Shit, they're previewing the late games in the Big West first? Jesus, is it more important to know that Nevada plays Idaho at 8pm than to end this misery? I haven't showered. My scalp itches and even I know that I smell pretty bad. I reach onto the coffee table for my pack of Reds and light one, but that only makes my head pound worse. That's it, that has to be it. The drip-drip-drip in the kitchen is driving me fucking crazy. Now the MAC scores are starting. Here it is. Bowling Green all over Kent State. Central over Western. In all the anticipation, I'd totally forgotten that the Victory Cannon game was being played today. Marshall crushes Ball State. No surprise.

And here it is.

Toledo over Akron.

Twenty-four to seventeen.

Seven points.

I win. They beat the spread. I'm eight thousand dollars richer.

I was alone in the apartment, so there was no one to hug or high-five or even smile at. I didn't really know what to do with myself, so I took an extremely languorous and scalding hot shower. I cleaned up the apartment, bagging a lot of the trash and emptying the ashtrays and collecting the cans and bottles for the deposit. I might have lost three hundred on the game, but it looked like I'd get about five of it back from the empties. It was pretty warm for late October, so after spending nearly two hours cleaning myself and the apartment, I opened the window that overlooked the parking lot to try and clean the air.

I was looking outside, enjoying the autumn sun and the euphoria of my windfall when I noticed a familiar pink Ford Escort pulling into the lot. I didn't see a lot of those around town, and even fewer of them pulled into my apartment's parking spaces, so I knew who it had to be.

Cindy.

I watched her get out of her car. My heart started racing, trying to imagine what she was going to do. Slash my tires? Vandalize my car in some way? That seemed overly obvious, and besides, it had been nearly a month since I talked to her parents, so this would seem a little late for such a poorly constructed response. She wasn't carrying anything besides a small purse, so unless the tools of malfeasance were located within that small bag, maybe she came in peace. I wondered if she might be there to see a neighbor of mine, but there were only six units in the building and although I wasn't very neighborly, I thought that the majority of my fellow tenants were either married couples or older people.

She moved toward the front door and pulled it open. I listened for her footsteps on the stairs, which followed about thirty seconds later. Soon, she'd be at my door, I assumed, and I had no idea what I'd do when she gets here. I thought I could just ignore her and pretend not to be home, but I figured she'd seen my car.

When she knocked, I jumped out of my skin with a start, even though I'd been anticipating the sound. My heart was pounding. Her skinny little knuckles rapped on the door, somewhat aggressively. I looked around my apartment, ostensibly for a way out. If I really wanted, I could take out the screen in my bedroom window, climb out and jump down. I lived on the second floor. The landing would hurt, but I put the chances of a broken ankle or two at fifty-fifty. Was it worth it just to avoid whatever Cindy had planned on the other side of that door? I looked around again, this time thinking about grabbing a weapon with which to defend myself because it seemed possible that she'd shown up intending to do some sort of physical harm. Her pounding grew more insistent.

73

I pulled the door open. There she was. Such a little thing; it was almost hard to believe I had allowed myself to become so intimidated by her. She had a great big grin on her face, metal flashing and reflecting the sunlight that was coming through the building's front windows. A stray ray caught me in the eye and I had to turn my head quickly to the left in an attempt to avoid one of those annoying flash spots that you get when someone snaps a picture. I was too late. I'd be chasing that thing for an hour.

Her smile stayed wide. I had no idea what she was thinking. "Aren't you going to invite me in?"

I furrowed my brow. "Why would I do that?"

"Charlie." She sighed. "It's time we got past this little tiff."

I wouldn't classify harassing me at work and stalking my ex-girlfriend a little tiff, but I stepped aside and let her in. There was something about her casual tone that disarmed me. Plus, there was the small matter of the essentially animalistic attraction between us. It was something I could feel just under my skin, an electricity to the promise that if we fucked, it would be the sort of in-the-moment sex where you'd cringe if you could later see and hear yourself, where the things you're saying and the noises you're making are only possible if you've completely given yourself over to what's happening.

She walked over and plopped down on the couch as though she lived there. "You cleaned."

I closed the door, but I didn't move away from the entrance area. "What are you doing here?" I tried to sound unfriendly and impatient.

Cindy reached into her purse and pulled out a pack of Virginia Slims. She lit one. "I thought you might be in the mood for a celebration."

I couldn't imagine that she knew about my bet, but she had tracked down Colleen in Chicago. I probably should stop underestimating her. "What are you talking about? Celebrate what?"

She exhaled a drag from her cigarette and gave me a sideways glance. "You mean you're not in the mood to celebrate the big Toledo win?"

My head started spinning. I couldn't pull down a single clear thought. They raced around, chasing each other's ends and beginnings and I felt a little light-headed. I'm not sure I had remembered to breathe, so I collected myself as best I could and filled my lungs, although the place was full of Virginia Slims smoke and the breath was at least half smoke instead of all air which is what I needed at the moment and those Virginia Slims were gross and were totally deserving of the name 'Vagina Slimes' and their tagline was 'You've Come a Long Way, Baby,' and I think the temperature outside has dropped at least ten degrees since I opened those windows; it feels a little cold in here, and damnit just take a breath, a deep breath. "How?" I swallowed. "How do you know about that?"

"Charlie." Her voice had the same almost condescending tone that she took before I let her into the apartment. "Jason Young is my cousin. My mom's maiden name is Young? You might know this sort of thing if you'd taken the time to get to know me."

So much for keeping the fix quiet. Jason had told me that less than a dozen people knew about this fix, but one of these was your fucking cousin? I should've let Kip Healey cut you, you fucking dipshit. "Did you place a bet, too?" It occurred to me that I'd done nothing but ask questions of Cindy since I opened the door. She was about fifty steps ahead of me.

She nodded. "I did. With Dugan. You know Dugan, right?"

It couldn't be. I think my mouth was hanging open.

"Charlie?" Cindy snapped her fingers. "You're going all Cameron in *Ferris Bueller* there."

I couldn't see anything but Cindy; on her back with her legs spread wide on my dirty sheets, my hips driving into hers; bent over the edge of the bed while I buried my cock deep in her asshole; standing against the wall of the shower, my arm under her left thigh, propping it up, facing her; shoulders pinned to the ground, hips in the air while I thrust into her from above.

I knew I didn't have any money.

She took another deep drag from her cigarette, then stood and headed towards the kitchen. "I'm going to get a beer. Do you want anything?"

I may or may not have answered. I probably didn't.

She came back into the kitchen with two cans of Black Label and handed me one. "Drink this." She took a sip from hers. "You'll feel better."

I drained the can in one gulp and then crushed it in my hand. "You canceled my bet with Dugan, didn't you?" Still nothing but questions. My head was still pounding.

"Your Clemson bet?" She smiled. "No."

My legs felt funny. I sat on the couch next to Cindy. I reached onto the coffee table for my Reds, shook one out of the pack and lit it.

Cindy took a sip from the can in her left hand. "You're awfully quiet."

The nicotine was calming me down, but I still couldn't really take hold of any of the thoughts swirling around my brain. I ran my hand through my hair, tugged on it just enough to hurt a little. I suppose you can't miss what you never had. It's not as though Cindy walked in here and took eight thousand dollars out of my hand. Without Jason's tip, I'd have never bet on that game; it had probably been two seasons since I bet on a MAC game, anyway. Easy come, easy go. I couldn't see anything but Cindy.

"You said something about a celebration?" I took a drag from my cigarette and then exhaled. "What did you have in mind?"

RALPH & RAY

I put my aging 626 in park, surprised that Ray wasn't already waiting for me, considering I was on what my friends affectionately refer to as "Ralph Time" by being twenty minutes late. Come to think of it, maybe they don't call me that out of affection after all. I rang the ghetto doorbell, too lazy to climb the stairs and knock on the door. Ray lived in one of the six apartments upstairs from the bar. The way I understood it, he'd been there since he sold his bar and retired, as he and Phil's family go way back. Ray was there rent-free, as far as I knew, re-paying many kindnesses he'd shown Phil's dad over the years.

It wasn't the norm for me to be at the bar earlier than two in the afternoon and the decrepit block that housed Robert's Grill had a different look in the morning. The adjacent abandoned lot was full of overgrown weeds, the hulky browns and greens masking what was almost certainly a lot of garbage beneath. A few weeks earlier, one of the local gangs had made an aborted attempt to tag the rear of Bob's building, but were probably scared off by one of the routine patrols that Phil's friendships with several local officers afforded him. Their full name was "Saginaw Swagger", but they'd only been able to get as far as the first three letters of the second word, so it read "Saginaw Swa". Bob's was always teetering on the edge in this way, as the surrounding neighborhood swayed back and forth between gentrification and annihilation. It might have been this danger that attracted some of the bar's more decidedly upper middle-class clientele that came from Grand Blanc and Burton in order to slum it. The struggle was far less romantic to me, and I knew that "Swa" would inevitably turn into "Swagger."

As I was lost in thought, Ray opened the passenger door of the car and moved in with great effort and a groan. I considered getting out to assist him, but I knew he was already accepting more help than he was comfortable with by taking the ride. He slid into the seat, his left leg twitching violently, as though he had put pressure on the wrong nerve. His tan polyester slacks pulled up enough to reveal an inch of liver-spotted skin between the pants and his wrinkled black socks. I figured it might be time to offer to help with Ray's laundry as well, but he'd be as likely to resist that as he initially did this little trip.

"Good morning, Ralph." Ray pulled the door shut with an almost defiant slam. "It's good to see you."

"Same here." I put the car in gear and pulled a quick u-turn to head back onto Saginaw. "This will be interesting. I haven't been in the library for years. Probably since high school."

"That's unfortunate. It's a great resource."

"I did go fairly regularly at Ferris. I'm not averse." My car radio, which notoriously had bad reception, lost the signal, so I switched off the power to stop the white noise.

"I didn't figure you had a moral objection to libraries." He chuckled.

We rode in silence for a few blocks and Ray looked out of the window at the struggling city. "How many years did you spend at Ferris, Ralph?"

"Three semesters. I didn't go back after winter break sophomore year."

Ray stroked his chin with his right hand. "What were you studying?"

"I was undecided. My advisor was trying to push me toward Advertising."

"And you disagreed?"

I stopped for a red light and then picked up my sunglasses from the center console, sliding them on with my right hand to fend off the morning sun. "Not exactly. I took an introductory course and I liked it, but I liked lots of other things too."

"That's good. It does raise the question about why you didn't continue."

78

I tapped my right index finger on the steering wheel and thought about turning the radio back on. "I'm not sure I have a very good answer for that. I know I was tired of being broke all the time. I applied for a job at Michigan Electric Supply on a whim and then I got it. I thought I'd join the real world for a while and see what happened."

Ray sighed and picked at his left thumbnail. "And you're in your late twenties now?"

"That's right."

"So it's been almost a decade since you quit school?"

"Yep." I decided to give the radio another shot, hoping the wire coat hanger I used as an antenna would be able to pull in enough of a song to interrupt this line of questioning. I didn't feel like Ray was being intrusive, he was just naturally curious and we'd never talked about this area of my life. The radio's white noise continued, however, and my respite was not granted.

"I hope my questions aren't bothering you, Ralph."

"It's not that. I guess I'm a little embarrassed is all."

"There's nothing to be ashamed of. I didn't take an undergraduate degree either."

This seemed hard to believe, since I only needed to talk with Ray for about five minutes before it became obvious he was the smartest person I ever met. I imagined Ray was the sort who was just a dissertation shy of a doctorate in some exotic, unknowable field. "You didn't? What happened?"

"My father got stomach cancer during my sophomore year, coincidentally. I had been studying English Literature in Ann Arbor." Ray coughed into his balled up right hand. He continued. "My father was too weak to return to work, so it became necessary for me to go back to Detroit to get a job and help my family."

Somehow, this didn't make me feel less ashamed for flaking out at Ferris eight years prior. "That's too bad."

"It's trite to say it, but that's life, isn't it?" Ray coughed into his fist again, and it was productive and troublesome.

"Do you have regrets about not returning to school?" I took my eyes off of the road for a second and looked at Ray.

"One thing turned into another, which is a fact of life I'm guessing you've learned quite well yourself."

He was right about that. I had only intended to take a year or two off of school, and I thought I could use my job at MES to stockpile some cash and make the financial part of college life easier to deal with. Two years turned into eight before I knew what had happened, and by then, it just seemed too late to go back. By the time I got laid off, my roots in Flint had taken hold, and it didn't feel like the right time to try and pull them up.

"Yeah." Any further discussion was preempted by our arrival at the Flint Public Library. I'd driven by the place many times without notice, as it looked like a late-60s elementary school rather than a book depository.

We climbed out of the car, with Ray taking an extra minute to make the escape. We walked around the 626 towards the front doors.

"What are you looking for here today, Ray?"

"The same thing as always. Something to read."

***

I starting smoking clove cigarettes when I was a junior in high school. My friends, who were cultivating their habits with more manly brands such as Marlboros and Newports, made fun of me for smoking what tasted like, according to my pal Carl Johnson, "one of those purple gumdrops my grandma kept at the bottom of her purse." It might have been this constant assault that made me stubbornly stick to my trusted and delicious Sampoernas, but whatever the reason, here I am over a decade years later, still puffing away at the purple gumdrops.

It seems as though there's something about clove smokers that leads others around them to assume they're potheads. At least that's been the case in my experience. When I first started bartending at Bob's, it was an almost daily occurrence that someone would offer me weed damn near immediately after I lit up a smoke. Their nostrils would flair after that sweet kretek scent in the air, and once traced back to me as its source, they'd accost with some variant on the question "Dude, you like to get high?" It's not as if I didn't. But there was something about the presumptuousness that rubbed me the wrong way, so I usually shrugged off the inquiry with an "Eh, not really."

In truth, I always enjoyed smoking pot, sort of a carryover from my aborted stint at college. But in my early days behind the bar, I tried to be mindful of the advice Phil gave when he hired me, that it was often best not to share too much about your personal life with your customers. I was finding that an air of mystery might have been great in theory, but wasn't always easy for someone of my disposition.

When The Man started coming into Bob's for an afternoon Newcastle or two about six months after I began working behind the bar, I could tell he was high every time. He was one of those smokers who didn't feel the need to hide the fact, and he'd even leave the bar from time to time, obviously going to his car to pack a one-hitter or finish off a roach. He was several years older than me, his close-cropped hair showing a bit of gray, but he carried himself with a pretty youthful attitude and a lot of confidence.

One Wednesday night before the ten p.m. crowd made its way in, The Man fixed me with a glance after I'd lit a clove.
"Ralph, do you get high?"

Internally, I gave him a sarcastic eye-roll because of the predictable question. "I usually don't say no if it's offered, but I don't carry any."

"Do you want to get high now?"

I wasn't as taken aback by the question as perhaps I should have been or normally was. There was no one else in the bar and I hadn't smoked any weed for a few weeks, so I didn't see the harm. "Why not? Let's head to the basement, though. I'll hear the door down there if anyone comes in."

"Lead the way." The Man took a drink of his beer and rose from the stool.

I waited for him to come around the bar and then propped open the ancient access door to the cellar. The blast of moldy mustiness was thick in the air and The Man reacted with a somewhat troubled look.

"Don't worry," I said. "Phil has the place checked for black mold and whatnot fairly regularly."

With a shrug of his shoulders, The Man followed me down the creaky stairs and into the de facto storage area of the basement where all the old, useless beer signs and tap pulls had gone to die.

He handed me a short glass pipe packed with buds that didn't really look like anything I'd seen before. They were almost mint green and covered in sugary white crystals that had a pungent, skunky scent.

"What is this shit?" I asked as I reached for the pipe.

"A specialty."

I flicked the lighter over the bowl with my index finger on the carb and took a tentative drag. It tasted like it smelled, piney and sweet at the same time. Even though I'd taken a pretty small hit, I started to violently cough up a lung almost instantaneously. My chest felt hot.

"Nice." The Man reached for the bowl. "You cough, you get off."

I nodded in between hacks, feeling my face turn red.

After taking a much larger hit than I had, The Man passed the bowl back to me. Even more cautious than before, I took as small a puff from the bowl as I could manage and handed it back.

"That's probably all you need. I'll finish it and we can head back up." The Man cleaned out the bowl with an astonishing show of lung capacity. The cloud of smoke he exhaled seemed to engulf my entire body.

As we turned and climbed the stairs, the buzz hit me much faster than I had expected. I felt as though I was somehow simultaneously the marionette and puppeteer. I could control my arms and legs, but it took some focus to accomplish a simple task like shutting the cellar door.

The Man took his stool and smiled. "How are you feeling?"

I gave this some thought. "Good." This seemed to be all I could get out. I was having difficulty concentrating. Between scrunched up eyes, I was able to pull myself together long enough to pour a pint of Stroh's that would hopefully quench the desert in my mouth.

How I'd be able to manage fetching beers, mixing drinks, and counting change for the next several hours was a mystery.

***

A week after my first encounter with The Man's weed, which I affectionately termed "The Crippler", he was back on his regular stool.

"How was the rest of your night last Wednesday?"

"Jesus. Great but terrible." I finished wiping out an ashtray and placed it on the bar.

"I know what you mean. Not for amateurs. No offense." He grinned.

"None taken. The usual?"

He nodded.

I turned around to fetch The Man a Newcastle. I placed it in front of him, leaned against the back bar and grabbed my right earlobe between my thumb and forefinger. "I might enjoy that stuff more in the comfort of my apartment."

The Man drained half of his bottle in one swig, then looked over each shoulder. "I can spare some for you. But it isn't cheap."

"I figured as much."

"Fifty for an eighth. But that should last awhile as you're smart about it."

"That sounds fair. Do you want me to come to your house or what?"

"Can you get the money tonight?"

I thought for a second. I'd easily triple the fifty required for the purchase in tips before closing, but I was about that much short for the rent that was already a few days overdue. "Yeah, I can do that."

"How about I come back around after you close?"

It was Wednesday, which meant there'd be fewer of Phil's cop buddies hanging around. I realized I had no idea what The Man did for a living, but it was obviously something that allowed him to drive around downtown Flint at all hours of the night. "That's cool."

He drained the remaining half of the bottle of beer, set it on the bar and nodded. "See you around two." He left a single on the bar and turned around to leave.

I pocketed the bill. Forty-nine to go.

***

I'd spent most of the following Saturday and Sunday in a Crippler-induced torpor, and I had to use a lot of focused mental power in order to do simple tasks like showering and pouring milk over my Cap'n Crunch. There were several hours devoted to delving into the nooks and crannies of Morphine's *Cure for Pain*, figuring that my own search for the record's titular relief was over. It was really great.

Tully had been one of my Monday afternoon regulars since I started working at Bob's. He was one of those guys who straddled the line between customer and friend, and if I had to choose one category to place him in, it'd be the latter. Even though we were cool, Tully was smart enough to know which side of his bread was buttered, and he generally didn't pester me for free drinks and friend treatment when I worked. In the afternoon dark of the bar, he was nursing a Budweiser and half-watching the Cubs and Phillies game on one of the TVs, his head slumped in between the balled-up fists that were propping it up. He looked bored.

"Tully, what's going on over there?"

"Just hating life at the moment. Thinking about going back to work tomorrow makes me want to poke my own eye out."

"Then don't think about it." Tully managed a greeting card store in the Genessee Valley Mall. Their main business had become selling Beanie Babies over the previous few months. Now it seemed he was forever getting screamed at by otherwise kindly grandmothers in regard to shipments and stock levels. He even fended off bribes to hold a few Blackie the black bears in flagrant disregard of the rules. Ty, Inc. had made Tully one miserable guy. "I've got something that might take those blues away. For a few hours, at least."

"A hooker?" He fixed me with a slightly hopeful smile.

"Yeah, Tully. A hooker. I'm a fucking pimp now?"

"I was kidding. What are you talking about?"

Even though the only other person in the bar was at the other end, I still looked over both shoulders before I spoke. "I've got some of the craziest weed I've ever smoked. This shit had me paralyzed most of the weekend." I emptied an ashtray and replaced it with a fresh one.

"Oh yeah? Where did you get it?"

"Can't tell you that. But I can get you high if you want to hang at my place after Charlie relieves me."

Tully's smile changed from hopeful to satisfied. "That might be just what the doctor ordered."

"Don't start calling me Dr. Feelgood." I laughed. "But this stuff is a real cure for pain."

I had *A Picture of Nectar* cued on my stereo and although the sun had set about an hour earlier, it had nicely warmed my living room. The brand-new two-foot glass Graffix bong sat sparkling on my coffee table. The devilish jester logo smiled at me as I finished packing the first bowl and handed it over to Tully.

"Be careful on your first few hits." I leaned back, put my Pumas on the ottoman and watched as Tully flicked his lighter over the slide tube.

He filled the pipe about halfway, pulled the tube and quickly inhaled the grayish smoke.

"Nice, huh?" I smiled.

He nodded as he struggled to keep the hit in his lungs. Trey was singing about Guelah Papyrus on the stereo, whatever the fuck that meant. Tully handed the bong back to me as he exhaled, filling the room with the sickly-sweet remnants of the Crippler.

Tully coughed a little, covering his mouth with his right fist. "This shit's crazy, Ralph. I've never tasted anything like that. It's like smoking a pine cone."

"After another hit or two and about five minutes to settle in, you'll be saying you've never felt a buzz like it, either." I approximated that jester's smile and leaned in for the day's first bowl.

Tully started poking around the stack of CDs piled on the coffee table in front of him. He held up *OK Computer*. "I didn't know you like Radiohead."

My cheeks puffed out as I held in my hit and nodded.

"Mind if I put this in?"

I shook my head, still holding my breath.

Tully walked over towards the stereo at the front of the room, an old Sony rack system that had seen better days but was still serving me well. He swiped out discs and pressed play. The swooping guitar chords of "Airbag" poured out of the speakers. "I guess it sort of makes sense, now that I think about it. You like a lot of classic rock and Radiohead is classic rock in a weird sort of way. You could play this in between Pink Floyd and Led Zeppelin on a radio show and it wouldn't sound out of place."

I exhaled the hit slowly through my nose. It seemed like I'd never held my breath for so long. "You're already high."

***

As I made the left off of Saginaw to park in the alley next to the bar, I noticed Phil's Explorer in my usual parking spot. He usually made his Sam's Club run for supplies on Friday, so I wasn't entirely sure why he'd be at the bar at this hour on a Wednesday. My heart sunk into my stomach, as The Man would be showing up in less than half an hour with what had become my bi-weekly supply of the Crippler.

As I got out of my car, Phil came out of the bar's side door to fetch another armload from the open hatch of his SUV. He was wearing the de facto uniform of the aging frat boy: baggy khaki shorts, rugby shirt, and faded Lake Superior '92 NCAA Hockey Camps hat. He waved me over. "Ralph, give me a hand."

"Of course." I stomped out a half-smoked Sampoerna under my sneaker. I was sure Phil would easily be able to tell how high I was. This wasn't the first time I'd shown up for an afternoon shift after a few pulls of the Graffix tube, but there usually wasn't anyone to deal with for the first hour or so. I didn't have the requisite time to sober up a bit and I was feeling pretty paranoid.

"Looks like it was busy last night. The trashcans are full. I think Charlie did a lot of re-stock for you, though." He handed me a case of grapefruit juice.

"Cool." I cleared my throat and wished I had a breath mint. "What are you doing here on a Wednesday?"

"Nice to see you too, prick." He grabbed a box of paper towels and turned toward the side door. "Pam and I are going up to her folks' place in Petoskey Thursday night, so I won't be around to drop this stuff off."

We walked into the bar where the smelly combination of spilled beer, unventilated cigarette smoke, and urine was thick despite the open door. As I looked over the back bar, I was surprised to see that the rack of nuts was full. It was empty when I left on Tuesday evening, and the Nut Man usually rolled in later on Wednesday afternoons.

"Was the Nut Man here already?" I grabbed the beat-up corn broom from the utility closet and started sweeping.

"You just missed him. He was asking after you." Phil pulled down a bar stool, sat and took the tin of Copenhagen from his pocket. "I thought he hated everyone who works here. Seems to like you."

"I guess I've cracked the Nut Man's hard shell." I was flashing more stoned wit than I might have thought possible. Maybe Phil wouldn't be able to tell after all.

"Give me a fucking break." He reached into the cooler and pulled out a Labatt.

I smiled and went behind the bar to grab the dustpan. Through the open side door, I could see The Man pull up in his well-kept late-80s Olds Ninety-Eight. I had a miniature panic attack as he got out of the driver's side and headed toward the door.

He peeked his head inside. "Hey man, are you open yet?"

What a beautiful improvisation, I thought. "Not yet. I'll be open at three."

He nodded. "I'll be back." He turned around and got in his car. I wiped away the flop sweat from my brow and stared into space.

Phil drained his Labatt and tossed the empty into the trashcan with a clank. "Ralph, are you high?"

I brushed the bottle caps, labels, and ashes into the dustpan and then walked over towards the bar to empty it.

Phil hadn't moved his glance from me. "Are you?"

I set the dustpan against the bar and looked at my boss. "Maybe a little."

He shook his head, then turned around with a huff and muttered what sounded like curses as he stomped out of the door. I heard him slam his hatch shut, get in the car and start it. Then he peeled out into the alley with an exaggerated tire squeal.

"Only a little," I yelled at the open door.

***

Ray exited the front doors of the Standard Federal Bank and walked toward the car. He didn't bother to look before crossing the parking lot, and his interminable shuffle disrupted the flow of drive-thru traffic for a minute or two. Ray clearly didn't care about this sort of inconvenience, as I suppose is the right of all the aged. They've put in their time, now we have to wait on and for them from time to time. It was only fair.

Ray was moving ever slower and I got out of the car to offer him a hand getting in. He waved me off with a bit of annoyance, so I got back into my seat and waited.

"Thanks again, Ralph." Ray sat in the passenger's seat and collected his breath for a time before pulling the door closed. "Here." He held out a few bills in his shaky left hand for me to take.

"Keep your money, Ray." I started the car.

"Ralph, I insist." He waved his hand.

"And I insist on not taking that. I'm not doing this to get paid." The clutch, which had been on its last legs for several weeks, struggled to find reverse as I backed out of the parking space.

Ray sighed and put the bills into his pocket. "I know you're not doing it to get paid, but you've been dropping off groceries lately, too. I wish you'd at least let me pay you back for those."

"What goes around comes around. If I need a favor from you, I won't hesitate to ask." I gave the car enough gas to ease the clutch into first.

"You didn't need to take care of any business at the branch?"

I hesitated, as it was always an awkward discussion if I tried to explain to anyone that I didn't have a bank account, and I didn't figure it'd be any less awkward telling Ray. "Well, I don't actually use this bank."

"Oh, I see. You're a Comerica guy?"

"Not exactly. I had an account at the MES credit union when I worked there, but I haven't had an account since I was laid off."

"You have no bank account at all?"

I could feel Ray's quizzical stare even though my eyes were on the road. "No, I don't have a bank account."

Ray and I sat in silence. I assumed he was trying to either work out how best to digest this information or how to gently lecture me about how irresponsible this was.

"I understand. It's harder for the government to track under the table income if you can keep it out of the bank." Ray reached into his shirt pocket for one of his mini cigars.

I shouldn't have been surprised that Ray knew how Phil operated the bar, especially considering how far back they went. But I assumed that my boss didn't go around bragging about it; avoiding payroll taxes and keeping a lawyer on retainer to help dodge music royalties didn't seem like anything to be proud of. I was taken aback that Ray attributed my lack of a bank account to something so cunning, as in reality it was almost entirely due to laziness. The party store closest to my house accepted payments for most of the utilities and provided a money order service, so that was all I really needed. Knowing that keeping the money out of the bank made it easier to hide was actually a bit of good news.

"You know how Phil runs things at Bob's?" I took the turn onto Saginaw and headed toward the bar.

"I've known Phil a long time. He hasn't kept any of it a secret from me." He made several attempts at starting his lighter before he successfully lit his cigarillo. "I can't say that I approve, but it's his business. I do feel it puts his employees in an unnecessarily bad position."

A Ford Taurus slowed down in front of us, forcing me to ride the clutch to keep my car in second gear without slipping. "We all knew the deal when we took the job."

"That's true, but what do you do at tax time? You have no income to declare."

I hadn't thought that far ahead. Because the pay at Bob's was under the table, I was able to collect unemployment from my MES layoff. I knew I'd have income to show, but the fact that it wouldn't last forever hit me at precisely that moment. Charlie had been working for Phil since he bought the bar, and I wondered how he handled this situation. "I guess I didn't think that through."

"It might be time that you do." Ray inhaled on his cigar and then blew the smoke out the window.

I made the turn into the alley next to Bob's and took the car out of gear. I'd spent so much of the last few months reacting to changes that there was a lot I hadn't considered. It felt like I was living in a sort of movie, watching all of these things happen to someone else rather than actually living my life. It wasn't a very entertaining film, to be sure, but I still felt like I had ceded control to some unseen director and his staff of gaffers and best boys.

"You're right, Ray. You're always right."

Ray opened the car door and then swung his legs out onto the ground. "I'm just old, Ralph. If I haven't gained any wisdom at this point in my life, then I just haven't been paying attention." He smiled. "I'll see you later."

***

Tully set the Graffix onto the coffee table and exhaled his hit. Over the ensuing months, the uncleaned glass had turned a cloudy brown with resin build-up. He fixed his glance on the TV where I had the VCR playing my used copy of *Pulp Fiction* for the second time that afternoon.

"When they show this on regular television, how do you think they'll dub all the swear words?" He leaned forward on the couch and grabbed his half-empty bottle of Miller High Life.

"That's a good question." I pulled my right earlobe between my thumb and forefinger. "I'm not sure. Maybe they'll use the *Do the Right Thing* strategy of replacing motherfucker with 'mickeyfickey.'"

"I hope not. I've seen that. Too distracting." Tully drained the rest of his beer.

"Yeah." I rose from the couch to go to the kitchen. "Do you want anything?" I asked Tully over my shoulder.

"I'll take another High Life, thanks."

I grabbed the beers out of my otherwise empty fridge and crossed the kitchen, stepping in something squishy with the ball of my left foot. I rubbed it onto the floor mat, but all that accomplished was attaching bits of cereal, ash, and whatever else to the stickiness. I hopped back in to the living room with the beers, then handed one to Tully.

He reached for it. "Thanks, dude. Why are you hopping?"

"It doesn't matter." I eased into the loveseat and looked over my dirty foot.

"I'm still thinking about how they'll dub this movie." He pointed at the screen with his beer.

I picked the largest chunks off and threw them onto the floor. "Maybe they'll use mammajamma for motherfucker."

"That's a good one." Tully opened his beer and sort of stared at the bottle for a moment, almost as if he was unsure of what to do with it.

"My favorite is the edited version of *Repo Man*. Ever seen it?"

He shook his head. "With Emilio Estevez, right?" Tully seemed to remember that the beer was for drinking and took a sip.

"Yeah. And Harry Dean Stanton. Anyway, there's like this hold-up scene in a convenience store, and the cops bust in and yell 'Hold it right there, motherfucker.' They dubbed in melonfarmer for the TV version. 'Hold it right there, melonfarmer.'"

Tully laughed. "Melonfarmer? Holy shit. That's classic."

The movie grabbed my attention for a minute as Jules interrogated Brett. I kept hearing mickeyfickey and mammajamma and melonfarmer as the scene progressed.

Tully reached into his pocket and pulled out the sad remnants of what had recently been his healthy eighth-ounce of Crippler. "My shit's almost cashed."

"I can get some tomorrow." I pulled the slide out of the bong and tapped the ashes into an empty can of Coke on the coffee table.

"That's cool. Do you think you can get me an extra eighth?"

"I guess so. Why?" I put the slide back in its tube and handed the contraption to Tully.

"Don't be mad, but I smoked Sailor out a few days ago and he wants it."

I fixed Tully with a somewhat stern glance. "You didn't tell him where you got it, did you?"

"Of course not." Tully pinched a bit of what remained in his baggie and placed it in the pipe, then handed it to me. I took it as a sort of peace offering.

I lit the pipe and drained all of the green out of the load in one giant hit, which I exhaled with a bit of a huff all over Tully. "Alright. I'll get you an extra eighth. But I want sixty bucks for both."

✳✳✳

"You have got the sexiest eyes." The drunk girl leaned over the bar and tried to tongue the stir straw in her nearly empty Beefeater and tonic. I assumed she was trying to be flirtatious, but it was more comical than enticing.

"Thanks." I moved down the bar to take a drink order from Aaron, one of the few tolerable Grand Blanc kids who came into the bar.

"Hey, Ralph. Busy tonight." Aaron looked up and down the bar, which was full and noisy.

"Yeah, it's great. What are you drinking?"

"I'll have a Dewar's on the rocks."

"Goin' heavy, huh?"

Aaron chuckled. "Trying to get some liquid courage to talk to that brunette over there." He nodded his head in the direction of Jenny, a weekend regular who I knew Charlie had a fling with a month or two prior.

I turned around, scooped the ice and poured a double shot for Aaron because he was a good tipper. "Good luck, dude. She's a cool girl." I pushed the drink across the bar. "It's two fifty."

He handed me a five. "Keep it, thanks."

"Thanks, Aaron." I opened the register and put the change in my quickly filling tip jar, and then looked over the bar for thirsty customers. Out of the corner of my eye, I could see Beefeater and tonic trying to get my attention with what she probably thought was a subtle wave. I took a drink from what had turned into a lukewarm pint of water that I kept on the back bar and walked over towards her.

"Have I told you that you have sexy eyes?" She had enough of a slur going that the "x" in sexy came out as more of a "sh" sound. It wasn't attractive.

"You did, yes." She was cute and it was probably best for her that Charlie wasn't behind the bar tonight. She'd be easy prey.

"Can I get another drink?" She drained the remainder of her rocks glass.

"Why don't I get you some water instead?" I turned around to get a pint glass before she could argue. I placed the full drink in front of her. "You'll thank me later."

Somebody had been playing too much Beck on the jukebox tonight, and as the third trip through "Devil's Haircut" cued up, I decided it was more than I could bear at that moment. I walked over to the sink where our clandestine skip button was located and gave it an angry push.

"What gives?" Someone yelled from one of the booths.

I ignored the complaint and shook a Sampoerna out of my pack. I lit it and let the nicotine calm me for a moment. My Friday nights had gotten very busy of late and it was nice to have even the shortest of breaks.

"Hey, Ralph."

I turned toward the left to follow the voice. It was Tully, who had elbowed his way up to the bar. I walked over to him. "What's up?"

"Fuckin' crazy in here tonight."

The jukebox moved to the next track, which was another song from *Odelay*. Fucking Beck. I really wanted to get that thing out of there, but Charlie controlled the contents of the jukebox with an iron fist.

"Yeah, it's busy. Are you drinking?"

"No, I just wanted to stop in and see if you'd met up with The Man yet." Tully gave me a hopeful look.

I shook my head. "I don't have time for this shit now. I'll let you know."

He waved his hands in front of him. "Sorry, man. It was a rough night at the store and I was just looking for a buzz."

I blew a drag of my cigarette at him. "Then have a fucking beer."

"Alright. Give me a Bud."

"Give you? You're paying, Tully."

He reached into his pocket and pulled out a crinkled five. He tossed it on the bar. "Happy?"

I grabbed the bill and made an exaggerated show out of straightening it out to put it in the register. "I'll be back with your beer after I make sure that my less bothersome customers are taken care of. Why don't you go to the jukebox and play a few Pixies songs for me?"

Tully nodded and headed toward the Rowe machine.

Ray had warned me about making friends with people who came into the bar, but it was difficult for me to draw distinctions sometimes. People like Tully seemed genuine, but everyone who came in here looked up to the bartenders in a weird way. I guess it was coolness by association; the bar was cool, the patrons were cool, so the bartenders were cool as well. I didn't feel cool, though. I'd probably like Beck if I were.

I walked over to get Tully his beer. On the way there, a girl I'd never seen before got my attention.

"Hi. Can I get some drinks?" She was short but curvy, with wavy dishwater blond hair cut into an unflattering bob. She seemed unaffected, which was increasingly a rarity in this place.

"Yeah, of course. I'm sorry I didn't see you there. What can I get you?" I smiled at her, but realized too late that I was actually smiling directly at her chest. I tried to recover, but she'd clearly caught me and I blushed.

She smiled. "I'd like a Bell's Amber and my friend will have a Budweiser."

"Coming right up." I turned around to get the beers, making sure to get Tully's Bud while I was at it. I felt like an idiot for staring at her tits. It really wasn't cool. I put the beers in front of her. "Three for the Bell's, two for the Bud is five."

She slid a ten across the bar. "Can I get singles back?" She smiled again.

"No problem." I put the ten in the register and counted out five singles. I put them on the bar in front of her.

She took out three and pushed the remaining two across the bar at me. "One dollar for each of those roving eyes of yours." She laughed.

"I'm sorry, that's so embarrassing. You must think I'm a real asshole."

She took a sip of her beer. "Not at all. If I didn't want anyone to notice, I would have tried to hide them in a sweater." She looked down at the objects in question. "I'm Molly, by the way." She stuck out her right hand.

"Ralph. Nice meeting you." I shook her hand, which was tiny but had a confident grip.

"Same here." She grabbed her beers and looked over toward the jukebox, which Tully was fumbling over as he searched for *Doolittle* or *Bossanova*. "Please tell me there's some Pixies on that thing."

***

My living room windows were open to take advantage of the late October heat wave. Airing out the apartment after another Wednesday after-hours was a welcome relief. I heard the Ninety-Eight pull into the drive and The Man approached my side door.

"Come on in, it's open," I called out of the window.

The Man walked in and tossed the goods next to me on the couch. I hadn't wanted him coming around the bar for sales after the near miss with Phil. "We need to talk."

"Okay. Can I get you a beer or anything?"

"No, I'm fine, thanks. May I sit?"

"Sure." I cleared a Wize Guys' pizza box off of the loveseat.

"You've been buying a whole lot of extra dope lately, Ralph. You're up to over two ounces almost every week. I assume you're selling a lot of it."

He sounded more matter-of-fact rather than pissed, but I was still a little afraid. It would make sense that he'd be wary about me selling his stuff, since he didn't even want anyone to know he was providing it. "I have, yeah, but not to make money. It just sort of happened."

"I'm not trying to give you a hard time. Relax."

I reached into my shirt pocket for my Sampoernas, shook one out and lit it. I offered one to The Man with a nod.

He reached for the pack. He took one and sat back without lighting it. "These things are terrible, cloves." He turned it over in his fingers. "They're like smoking an entire pack of cigarettes at once, health wise."

"So I've been told."

He continued twirling the cigarette in his right hand. "I'll get to the point. I think you're trustworthy, especially since you work in that above-the-law bar."

Evidently, Phil's business strategies were much more common knowledge than I had been led to believe. "How do you know that?"

"Doesn't matter. But if you can keep those secrets, I figure you'll keep mine." He rummaged through the mess on the coffee table for a Bic and then lit the clove.

"You don't need to worry about anything like that."

"I know. But I think we can come to a more beneficial arrangement." He took a shallow drag. "Let's cut out this weekly shit. I'll be here once a month from here on out. For now, I'll set you up with a half-pound each trip. At the old price that'd be thirty-two hundred, but I'll let you have it for twenty-five. Does that work for you?"

My head was spinning a bit. I'd really only been selling to some friends in order to get free weed. At the prices he was quoting, I'd be making about a grand per month. I was already hiding all sorts of income from Uncle Sam, so I didn't see the harm in a little more. "Yeah. That works."

"Good. We'll start next week. I know I can trust you, but I'd still rather get the twenty-five up front. Nothing personal." He stubbed out the Sampoerna in an overfull ashtray that clung precariously to the side table.

"No problem. I'll have it."

"Alright. See you Wednesday." He stood to leave.

"Same bat time, same bat channel." Completely different bat arrangement, however.

***

I was trying to stay on top of my apartment's trash situation, tossing the detritus from the previous night's gathering into a wheeled trash barrel that my old neighbors left behind. Just cleaning out the kitchen and living room had filled the thirty-gallon receptacle almost to its brim.

Tully was going through packages of cigarettes, looking for anything that might contain a few strays. "Score." He held up a half-empty pack of Basic Lights.

"I'm not sure Basics constitute a score, Tully." Although he may have been helping himself more than he was helping me, I still appreciated the company. No one ever seemed to want to stick around at the end of my after-hours nights and help clean. Even the minimal contribution from Tully was welcome.

He sat down on the now-cleared sofa and lit one of the Basics. "I don't want to go back to work tomorrow. It's fucking shipment day, man. Do you know what that means?"

I'd been hearing Tully complain about the state of affairs at his shop for several months, so I knew exactly what he meant. I was tired of hearing about it. "Why don't you just look for another job?"

"I would, but the pay's pretty good. I had an interview for assistant manager at Circuit City and they were offering five thousand less a year."

I tossed a wet peach pit into the trashcan, wiping my hand on a paper towel. Why the fuck anyone would eat a peach at a party was beyond me. "Five thousand sounds like a good trade for a little more peace of mind, if you ask me." I walked over to the hall closet and took out the vacuum.

"Do you mind not running that until after I leave? I've got a pretty serious stress headache." Tully took another deep drag from his cigarette.

"I'm sure the Basics are helping with that." I sat on the loveseat and reached for the bong, which still had a few hits remaining on a partially smoked bowl.

Tully lightly rubbed his temple with his right hand. "I don't understand how this happened with these Beanie Babies, Ralph. They're just fucking stuffed animals. Wish I could've seen into the future, bought stock in Ty. I'd be retiring right about now."

"Yeah, I know."

"First thing tomorrow, I'll have to deal with Margaret. She'll be waiting outside the gate, even though she knows full well we don't open until ten, and that shipment doesn't get there until one. Then she'll argue with me about holding back some new goddamn Baby. I'll explain to her for the hundredth time, 'We can't hold Beanie Babies for any customers, Margaret.' And she'll look at me over the top of those Elton John, coke-bottle bottom glasses of hers and say, 'I think you can.' That shit drives me crazy. 'I think you can.' If I've heard it once, I've heard it a hundred times." Tully stubbed out the cigarette butt in a recently emptied ashtray.

If he'd heard it a hundred times, that must've made it ninety-nine for me. I lit the bong and cleared a thick tube of smoke. Through held breath and clenched teeth, I told Tully, "Sorry, dude."

"Yeah. I'm sorry I keep complaining about it."

I exhaled, filling the living room with a healthy cloud. I leaned over toward the side table to go through a stack of CDs piled there, and was surprised to find a copy of *Nothing's Shocking*, as someone stole mine a few years prior. What goes around comes around. I rose to put it in the stereo.

Tully got up at the same time. "I think I'm just going to head home and turn in early. Maybe I'll be able to deal with Margaret and her pals with a solid night's sleep."

"That's cool." I pressed play and waited for "Up the Beach."

"I have a favor to ask, though. Could you spare me a couple of nugs to smoke at home?"

I didn't mind smoking Tully out when he came around, but the to-go packages were annoying me almost as much as his job complaints. I knew I had a full three ounces left in my hiding place, but enough was enough.

"Sorry, man. Maybe later."

***

I was finishing mopping under the rear booths when Phil's Explorer pulled up to the side door. The scent of Pine-Sol now permeated the bar, although it struggled to mask the cacophony of equally noxious smells that had greeted me when I opened up the side door just an hour earlier.

I assumed that Phil was there for another oddball Wednesday supply run, but he strode into the bar empty handed. "How's it going, Ralph?" He pulled down his bar stool, grabbed a Labatt and sat.

"Just getting ready for Ray." I wheeled the mop bucket toward the men's room.

"Before you dump that out, I need to ask you something."

I stopped short of the bathroom and stood beside Phil. "Fire away."

"Did you take Beth Death home from here Sunday night?" Phil took a large drink from his beer.

My mind ran through the permutations, especially as I was unsure of how this tidbit could have gotten back to Phil so quickly. Beth, who earned the derogatory sobriquet based on her daily bath of patchouli and goth tendencies, was not one to fuck and tell. Also, we were the only two people left in the bar for about the last hour that night. "Yeah, I took her home."

"Goddamnit, Ralph. How many times do I have to tell you guys not to shit where you eat? It's bad for business."

"What's the big deal? It's just Beth. She's not the type to get hung up."

"That may be the case, but she's a Bob's rat. You don't need to encourage groupies." He drained his beer and tossed it in the empty trashcan behind the bar, then reached into the cooler for a second.

"How did you even find out about it?" I abandoned the mop bucket and started pulling down the stools. Ray would be down in a few minutes.

"Don't worry about that. Just be smart about it."

What Phil didn't know was the primary reason for my dalliance with Beth was to sell her a quarter-ounce of Crippler. The fucking had just sort of happened after we'd gotten high. I nodded at Phil and pulled down the last stool. "Sorry."

"Look, I understand. A lot of girls throw themselves at you guys here. But I've never been able to teach this lesson to Charlie, and look how his business has been suffering. I don't want the same thing to happen to you."

And, by extension, to his bar and his bottom-line. "I understand."

Ray ambled through the door; his Member's Only jacket zipped up against the mid-December chill.

"Gentlemen, good afternoon." Ray pulled out the stool next to Phil and sat.

I poured him his Stroh's and sat it in front of him. "Good to see you, Ray. I got a few things for you when I was at the grocery.

They're in the cooler. Remind me to get them when you're ready to leave."

"Thank you, Ralph, I appreciate it, as always." He took a drink from his beer. "If I didn't know better, I'd say I sense a bit of tension in the room."

Phil and I exchanged glances.

"You're not wrong, Ray. I was just having a discussion with our young charge here about the importance of refraining from taking women home out of this bar." Phil finished his second beer, tossed the empty, and reached for a third. I'd only seen him drink this quickly when he was pissed off about something. In this case, it was obviously me. At least he wasn't storming out and peeling away in that yuppie mobile.

"Female customers present an ages-old dilemma." Ray nodded at me. "Alcohol lowers their inhibitions and you're the trustworthy working man in the room who they feel they already know intimately. It can be hard to resist." He took a sip of his beer.

"So maybe you can explain to him why it's a bad idea. I can't seem to get through to these guys." Phil motioned toward the cooler. "Get yourself a beer, Ralph. On me."

I reached in for a Sam Adams. "Thanks."

"It's business, Ralph," began Ray. "It's important for you to be available. Approachable. If your favorite female customers know who you're sleeping with, and, worse yet, that woman is in the bar, the others might stay away. They like to think they have a chance with you."

"And you think this is why Charlie's nights are slowing down?" I looked at Phil.

"I know it is. Tell him, Ray."

"Just the other afternoon I was having a similar discussion with your co-worker. I used the same reasoning to explain to him that it wasn't wise to dip your pen in the company ink." He sipped his beer. "So to speak. Charlie took the opposing position, but I've been here when various paramours stop in to moon over him. It would be ignoring the obvious to think there's not a deleterious effect on the other female customers."

I went to the sink and turned on the tap to fill the wash water. "That makes plenty of theoretical sense, Ray. But couldn't the matter be considered on a case-by-case basis?"

"I'm sure there are exceptions to the rule."

"Sorry to interrupt, Ray." Phil shifted on his stool. "If you're trying to suggest that Beth Death isn't one to screw-and-tell, then you should ask yourself how I found out about it, Ralph."

I put my right hand under the running water to check its temperature, then pulled back quickly as is scalded me. I turned down the hot water by half and put the plug in the sink. "I get it. It won't happen again."

Ray finished his beer and I walked over to grab the empty. "Don't be shortsighted, Ralph. Remember that delayed gratification can be a key to your success as a bartender. You take your time cultivating your clientele. It can be a slow process, but it's one that eventually pays off. It's a bad idea to let one night tear down what you're building."

Phil finished his third beer, threw the empty away and got up to leave. "One night with Beth Death hardly seems worth it, man."

Phil clearly had no idea of my ulterior motives or my new source of income. Contrary to what he was saying, Beth was actually pretty fun in bed, but this didn't seem to be the proper venue for me to explain that. I placed a fresh draft in front of Ray. "I hear you."

***

Tully counted out ten twenties and handed them to me. "Thanks for giving me the friend price, Ralph."

I handed him the half-ounce and nodded. I turned down "Jerry Was a Race Car Driver" and placed the remote atop the trash on the coffee table. I paused a moment to think about how I got to that point. Over the months, I'd turned the business into more of a mini-distribution system, selling half-ounces to Tully, Beth, and a select few others that I trusted for them to break off and sell. It was clean and easy, and still had the bonus of the occasional roll in the hay with Kelly. I'd even gotten her to agree to forego the patchouli before she came to see me by feigning an allergy.

"No problem, Tully." I put the money in my pocket and leaned back on the couch.

"You got some time to smoke up and hang a bit? I brought that Tricky CD that I was telling you about at Bob's the other night."

I looked at the clock on the VCR. It flashed twelve.

"Sorry, man. Maybe later."

***

I'd been selling to this dude they called Spider for a few weeks. He was pretty creepy, as might be expected of a guy called Spider, and I always found a way to make the deal someplace other than my apartment. I didn't want him in there. I'd arranged to meet him outside the bar about ten minutes before I was to pick up Ray to take him to the library.

Spider was already waiting when I pulled up beside the bar. He got out of his ratty old Escort, wearing an Army surplus jacket that was far too light for the cold December day. Young dudes wearing military surplus had always freaked me out. It made them seem like they were practicing for their eventual homelessness.

Spider walked over to my car, hair wild and unkempt with a three or four-day beard. He smiled and revealed teeth in desperate need of a visit to the hygienist. "Hey, Ralph."

I rolled down my window but didn't shut off the engine. "How ya doin', Spider?"

He nodded. "Same shit, different day."

105

That was not my favorite phrase. If your life is shit, make a change, then every day doesn't have to be the same. Start by washing your hair and clothes and teeth. "I hear ya." I reached into the center console and pulled out his sack, a quarter ounce of Crippler. "One-twenty, like before."

He reached into one of the pockets of his jacket and pulled out a bunch of bills of various denominations. Most of my customers paid with fresh twenties straight out of the ATM. "Do you want to count it?"

I shook my head. I wanted to speed this along. "I trust you, Spider." That was obviously a lie. I handed him the plastic baggie and he handed me the cash.

He gave a sort of salute with his left hand, still carrying the sack in his right. "You're doing God's work." He smiled and turned on a dime, giving me a back-handed wave with his left hand, then got in his car and drove away. I'd have loved for Spider to find someone else to buy from.

I rolled my window up and reached into my coat pocket for my Sampoernas. I looked over at the glass door that led up to the apartments over the bar and saw Ray inside. I waved him over. He waved back at me, motioning for me to come inside.

I killed the engine and put the clove back in the pack. I got out of the car, walked across the street, and Ray pushed open the door from inside.

He looked confused. "What was all that about, Ralph?"

The inside hallway was dark. The walls were water stained. I didn't think it would kill Phil to spruce things up in this entryway. "What was all what about?"

Ray shook his head. His winter coat had seen better days. There was a small hole in the left chest where a few feathers were poking through. "You know what I'm talking about."

It hadn't occurred to me that Ray might see the transaction. "Just saying hello to a friend."

"Ralph, I don't appreciate you treating me as though I'm stupid."

I shrugged. "The less you know, the better."

Ray balled up his fists. If he were younger, I had no doubt he'd have struck me. "You'll excuse me if I don't feel like making our scheduled trip today." He turned to walk up the stairs.

I reached out and gently grabbed his coat. "C'mon, Ray. Don't turn this into something it's not."

He turned to face me. "And what is it?"

I pinched my right earlobe between my thumb and forefinger. "I'm just making a little extra money."

"By putting your friends in harm's way."

It wasn't like I was selling crack or heroin or something dangerous. It was just weed. This may have been a distinction lost on Ray. "That's why I said the less you know, the better."

Ray nodded. "I wish I didn't know. But I can't ride in your car when a simple traffic stop could put me in jail."

"There's nothing in my car, Ray."

He held up his hand. "I said don't insult me. I've seen other customers of yours come into the bar in the afternoon. I couldn't be sure, until now."

It hurt to see how disappointed Ray was with me. I wish he didn't know, too. "You won't tell Phil, will you?"

He shook his head. "It's not my place."

"I'll keep it out of the bar from now on, Ray. I promise."

Ray turned to move up the stairs. He walked up two or three and turned back around. "I'd say I trusted you, Ralph, if that were still possible."

***

On Tuesdays, I normally stopped by the grocery store on my way in to pick up a few essentials for Ray. Milk, bread, eggs, cheese, lunch meat, a few other odds and ends. I'd been doing it for months. He'd always try and pay me more than the items cost, and I'd always refuse. It really was no trouble. I was happy to do it.

I put the bags from Farmer Jack into the cooler and set about cleaning the place up. Charlie hadn't bothered to restock so I made that my first task. I replenished the cooler with Sierra Nevada, some Geary's, Corona, a few others. There was a lot of Sam Adams missing, which meant Charlie probably had more than a few.

I turned on the television closest to the sink. I put the news on. It was all about the International Space Station. The very thought of being trapped inside that thing for months on end made me feel claustrophobic. I suppose it's not all that insightful to say I don't like feeling trapped but, well, I don't.

I moved on to the bathrooms and then the floor, and it felt nice in a way, to do all of the opening tasks without a lingering Crippler buzz. I'd told Ray I would keep it out of the bar and that would include in my lungs and head. It was my first clean morning and afternoon in several months.

I was about fifteen minutes ahead of schedule, so I pulled down a stool and poured myself a Coke and then lit a Sampoerna. I looked around the bar and realized how much I take for granted, how living in a marijuana fog might have been at least partially responsible for my lack of gratitude. Working behind the bar, this bar, was pretty great. Every day was different, it was hardly ever dull, and I met all sorts of interesting people. I took a short drag from the clove and let the sweet taste linger on my tongue, numbing it a little. I liked it at Bob's, and I was grateful.

I finished my cigarette while half-watching the news. There was a story about a riot over the weekend in Reno, Nevada. It made me think about mob mentality, getting pushed along by forces greater than yourself, not bothering to make rational decisions, getting swept up. In a way, going into business with The Man had been exactly like that. It was something I didn't really think through; I'd let myself get swept up. By that point, the money was too good to turn back. I was entrenched. But I thought from then on, all decisions would be mine. I wouldn't get trapped. I wouldn't get swept up. I had too much to be thankful for to keep taking it all for granted.

I got up and pulled the stools down, one by one, right to left. The bar smelled like Pine-Sol. I went to the sink and grabbed a bar rag, soaked it in the hot water, and then wiped the bar down. I pulled out ashtrays and set them up, one between every other stool. I dumped the mop bucket in the men's room toilet. I pulled the switches on the neon signs, slid the jukebox out and flipped it on. It came to life with a whirl, the lights flashing, the ornamental CDs near the top spinning, spinning. I went behind the bar and drained the sinks, then filled them again with fresh water.

I went to the front door and unlocked it, then moved down the bar to the side door and opened it as well. I checked my watch. Right on time. Ray would amble in any minute.

I sat. I watched the news. I looked again at my watch. No Ray. I lit another clove. This one hurt my chest a little. I should have waited a bit longer to smoke again. I got up to change the channel. Comedy Central. *Kids in the Hall.* I sat on the bar stool. "Chicken Lady." I laughed. I sipped my Coke. I checked my watch. No Ray.

I thought about the groceries in the cooler. Ray would need the food sooner or later, probably sooner. "Cathy and Kathy." I laughed again. I put out the cigarette, half-finished. I'd smoke the rest later. Episode over.

No Ray.

A half-hour turned into an hour. No Ray. A couple came in, ordered a beer and a CC and Coke. They chatted about Christmas shopping. I didn't really listen.

No Ray.

An hour turned into two. I changed the station again. I don't remember what I put on. The couple ordered another round. Two dudes came in and got a pitcher. Anchor. They smoked and talked about something I didn't bother to listen to.

No Ray.

Two hours turned to three.

No Ray.

The food was still in the cooler. The couple left. They tipped me a dollar for two rounds. Assholes. The two dudes put some singles in the jukebox. They played some Bowie, a Sebadoh song, Yo La Tengo. Butt Crack Larry came in and bugged me for a little while before I pretended to be busy with something on the back bar. The two dudes left. They tipped me five, which almost made up for getting stiffed earlier. I continued to ignore Butt Crack Larry. He got the hint, left his customary quarter behind on the bar. Butt Crack Larry was something for which I was not grateful.

No Ray. I might have been worried, if I didn't know why he hadn't come down. But I knew. I wish he didn't know, but it was too late.

No Ray.

RAY & MIRIAM

Ray walked towards the ticket counter fingering the two ten-dollar bills in his right pocket, ready to utilize some strategy that his dad taught him over a decade before. With the Yankees in town and only one game behind the Tigers for first place, Briggs Stadium was sure to be filled to capacity. On just such occasions, Ray's dad showed him a trick to get a crack at good seats. If he wanted to impress Miriam, he knew that sitting four hundred feet away in the grandstand wouldn't be sufficient.

It was about five minutes before nine in the morning, just before the ticket windows opened for business. Ray was nervous; the twenty dollars he was spending on their seats represented about two and a half days' pay he earned behind the meat counter at Fenwick's Grocery.

There was no one waiting in line before him, so Ray leaned his back against the brick façade. He looked up and down the block at the line of Buicks, Fords, and the occasional Hudson traveling south on Trumbull, turning onto Michigan Avenue on their way to the CPA Building or Michigan Central or the post office. Although Ray felt removed from the hustle and bustle as he waited for the ticket windows to open, it didn't mean he could relax. As the hot early August sun rose over Lake St. Clair, its light bounced off the cars' windshields and the Corktown streets. Ray took off his beige felt Resistol and fanned himself with it. Between the sun and his nerves, his brow was beginning to sweat freely.

The window closest to Ray opened with a shudder. Ray put his hat back on, pushed it away from his forehead, and collected himself.

"I need two seats for today please, best available." He pulled the tens out of his pocket, slid one forward with his right hand, waited a few seconds, and then held the second one out for the salesman.

He looked Ray over. Behind the salesman, it was dark. "What's this for?" He took the bill from Ray's hand.

He could almost hear his dad's voice as the words left his lips. "My eyes aren't so good. The closer I can sit, the better. If there's anything you can do."

The salesman thought for a moment and then nodded. "What's your name?"

"Ray Schmidt."

"Come back in a half hour." The cashier pocketed one of the bills and wrote something on a slip of paper.

Ray smiled and then turned to walk south on Trumbull. He poked his head inside a newsstand and looked over the selection of paperbacks. He kept his hands in his pockets, fiddling with a quarter on the right side that was getting slick with his palm sweat. He thought maybe the Gaelic League would be open for the third-shifters of Corktown, so he headed west on Michigan Avenue in search of a beer with which to calm his nerves.

He settled in on a stool with a Goebel, thinking how it was nice to have a break from grinding hamburger and wrapping steaks, even if it was just one day. It had been a tough six months; Ray was in his sophomore year at the University of Michigan when his father took ill, and he'd come back home to Bagley to help around the house and make some extra money. He took the job at Fenwick's shortly after returning to Detroit, and the only positive to burying his forearms into animal flesh five days a week was meeting Miriam Rosen.

She worked the bakery counter after school a few days a week. Ray asked his boss, Al Nickels, all about her before he'd even worked up the courage to say hello. Al Nickels had been working at Fenwick's for almost twenty years and knew everyone in the neighborhood; he was Bagley's Walter Winchell. Al told Ray that she was her family's middle child, an older sister and younger brother on either side, and she lived a few blocks from Fenwick's on Litchfield Road, just by the cemetery in Sherwood. Her dad worked for Ford. Al thought she was headed to the U of M in the fall.

What Ray didn't need Al Nickels to tell him was that Miriam was the prettiest girl north of Seven Mile. Ray assumed she had lots of callers from school and it was unlikely she'd be interested in dating a college dropout who worked the meat counter. He watched Miriam from afar, giving only an occasional shy smile or wave for what had to be weeks.

Everything changed when Ray happened upon Miriam in the break room. Ray said hello, then walked over to the table where workers left old magazines, searching for *The Sporting News*. When he couldn't find it, he looked over to where Miriam was sitting. She was going over box scores with the vigor of John Lardner. He poured a small cup of coffee and sat at the next table over from Miriam. It was an ideal situation for Ray to finally initiate a conversation with Miriam, but he found himself exceedingly nervous and frustratingly tongue-tied. This was unexpected, as Ray had a bit of a reputation as a ladies' man among his Ann Arbor friends. He'd even secured a couple of dates with Frannie Franklin, an otherwise unapproachable beauty who turned out to be far duller than Ray or his friends could've predicted.

Ray sipped his coffee and thought of things to say. He wrung his hands, which had become unnervingly sweaty with anticipation. Had he been alone, he might have splashed cold water on his face or even pinched the veiny flesh of his forearm to snap himself into reality.

They talked about baseball for the rest of her break and every day that they saw each other after that. She loved the Tigers, but not so much since they'd sold Hank Greenberg to the Pirates; Ray loved the Yankees since his dad had taken him to Briggs when he was seven and he first saw the great Joe DiMaggio play. It took some weeks before their baseball chitchat turned into talk about other things; first they gossiped a little about their co-workers, then they talked about school, and then they talked about television shows and books and movies. But mostly they still talked about baseball.

It took a few more weeks before Ray had the nerve to ask her out, but he finally did. To a baseball game, of course. She accepted.

Ray looked at the Hamilton on his wrist, a high school graduation gift from his dad in happier and healthier times. It was twenty-five after nine. It would be a five-minute walk back to Briggs Stadium, so Ray finished his beer, thanked the barman, and pushed the bar's swinging door open. The move from dark bar to bright sun made Ray noticeably wince.

As he approached the ticket windows, he noticed that business had picked up since he'd been there a half hour earlier. There were three people in front of him at the window of the salesman who was holding his tickets. The sun was getting warmer; Ray took off his hat and wiped his brow again. He watched and waited as those in front of him in the line bought their tickets and moved on. It was his turn.

"Hi. Ray Schmidt, I'm back for my tickets."

The ticket salesman fixed him with a humorless stare. "What tickets?"

"I was here when you opened? I've got bad eyes. I was looking for something close to the field?"

The salesman shook his head and frowned. "I don't know what you're talking about. Do you want to buy tickets or not?"

Ray knew he'd been had and there was no recourse. Screaming and hollering at this thief would do no good. He only had a couple of singles and a few bits left after the earlier bribe and the Goebel.

"What's it going to be, Ray Schmidt?" The salesman gave him a sly, knowing smile.

Sometimes, there's just a meanness in this world. Ray always tried to keep his wits about him. Losing his temper never changed anything.

He sighed. "What's left in the grandstand?"

✳✳✳

"It's a tough situation, but I'm sure glad you're back." Gene held out his glass of Stroh's in a sort of toast. When Ray didn't respond, he set it back on the bar dejectedly.

"Thanks." Ray was grateful for a friend like Gene, but the truth was that he'd barely thought about him or anything else about Detroit during his time in Ann Arbor. Even though it was only forty-five miles away, it felt like a different world to Ray. Gene had started coming to their current location, the Elmwood Bar, over the past few months and Ray thought that it was a nice enough spot; clean, quiet, somewhat friendly. But Ray knew that the chances of engaging in a discussion about Joyce or Yeats here in a neighborhood tavern were slim. It made him homesick in reverse.

Gene fiddled with a pretzel from the small bowl on the bar in front of him. "How's your dad?"

Ray fought the urge to grab Gene by the lapels and shake him. What a stupid question. His dad was very sick. Stomach cancer is a nasty business. "He's hanging in there."

Gene nodded and sipped his beer. "So, what was it like?"

"What was what like?"

"College." Gene tapped a Sano out of a pack and lit it with a match from the bar. He watched the match burn down to his fingertips before extinguishing it with a panicked wave.

"It was good." Ray stared at his beer. The Red Wings were facing off against the Rangers on the new television set perched behind the bar, but Ray wasn't interested in Gordie Howe or Ted Lindsay at the moment.

"What about the girls? I'll bet the girls were somethin'."

Ray had known Gene since they were in elementary school. He wasn't a bright kid, but he looked up to Ray almost as if he were a big brother, even though their birthdays were less than a month apart. Neither boy had a brother at home; Ray's only sibling was his older sister Gladys, and Gene was the lone boy child among four girls on either side of him in the birth order. As the smarter and stronger between the two, Ray had always felt a certain obligation to look out for the gullible, naïve Gene. The neighborhood kids were forever trying to trick him into drinking pee masquerading as lemonade, convincing him of terrible baseball card trades or once even tying him to a stake in the wooded area of Gemeiner Park and just leaving him there. Gene needed Ray to knock the cup out of his hands, tell him to hang on to his Jimmie Foxx card or sometimes just untie him.

Ray nodded. "The girls were something, alright."

"Yeah." Gene dragged from his cigarette and then sipped his beer. "Remember Nancy Holan? I took her out a few times last year, but I don't know."

Ray knew what "I don't know" meant without having to ask. Gene had gone to work for Ford like a lot of his classmates, starting out paying his third-shift dues like everyone else. Only Gene was scatterbrained, and he held things up a few too many times. The foreman ran out of patience, and they pulled him off the line and pushed him to broom duty. Even there, Gene couldn't keep his wits about him. A girl like Nancy Holan wasn't going to marry a broom pusher. "What do you mean, 'I don't know?'"

"I mean I don't know if she's the right girl for me. She's stacked and she's nice and I like her. But when I got put off the line, boy, she was mad."

Nancy Holan's temper got her in trouble more than a couple of times back in high school. She'd been dating Bobby Junkin: the big man on campus, football captain, basketball star. There were rumors that he'd knocked her up, someone claimed to have seen her leaving a clinic of ill repute in the Campus Martius. What wasn't a rumor is that Bobby started stepping out with Connie Rogers before having the courtesy to tell Nancy that he didn't want to go with her any longer. Nancy took her revenge on Bobby's Studebaker Champion in the school parking lot with his favorite baseball bat. No one knows how she got her mitts on the bat, but Bobby loved the stick and that car equally. When he ran out to try and stop her, she kicked him square in the balls and kept right on smashing that car. Ray knew a girl like Nancy was definitely not a fit for Gene. He'd only disappoint her, and then run the risk of incurring her wrath.

"She sure was mad." Gene shuddered and finished his Stroh's. He motioned to the bartender for a refill.

Ray looked into the mirror that hung over the back bar. On the opposite wall was one of those reverse clocks that read properly when looked at through the mirror. It was about half past seven. This was the first chance Ray had to leave his parents' house since he'd gotten back just over a week ago. He wanted the time to slow down, even if Gene was a bit of a dolt. Ray turned and looked at the clock over his shoulder so as to fool himself into thinking that it was actually five o'clock. It worked for a split second. He looked back into the mirror and saw that his tired eyes made him look twice as old as his actual twenty years. Over the past few mornings, he'd noticed a lot of extra hairs in his comb. His back hurt.

Their fresh beers arrived and Gene took a sip. "If you want, you can come with me to Highland Park tomorrow. I can introduce you to the foreman."

Ray sipped his beer and then shook his head. "No, thanks."

"What do you mean, 'no'? You're going to work in the plant, aren't you? What did you move home for?"

"I got a job at Fenwick's."

"Fenwick's? You can make twice as much at the plant. Why would you want to work there?"

This was just like Gene. Ray didn't want to work there, or at the plant, or to even be back in Detroit, running around Bagley with friends he'd outgrown, talking about Nancy Holan. He wanted his dad to be well, wanted to be finishing his semester's coursework, drinking at the Union Bar and maybe finally getting to third base with Joyce Pembroke. "It's only temporary."

"What about your folks? Aren't you here to help?"

"What's with all these questions, Gene? I said it's temporary. Once Dad..." Ray trailed off. "My dad's very sick."

"I thought you said he was hanging in there."

Ray didn't want to take his anger out on his friend. "I was being polite."

"He's not doing well?" Gene lit another Sano. He was a regular Martin Kane, Private Eye.

"No." Ray took a sip of his beer. On the television set, the Red Wings held off a Rangers power play. "I'll be back in Ann Arbor by the fall."

***

Miriam and Ray squeezed into their row in the upper grandstand. He was still angry with the ticket salesman who'd pocketed his twenty bucks, but it wasn't obvious to look at him, as Ray was all smiles for his date.

The trip from Seven Mile and Livernois had given Ray and Miriam their first chance to talk outside of Fenwick's. Sure, they chitchatted at work about baseball and the bakery counter and Al Nickels, but as they cruised down Woodward in Ray's dad's Mercury Eight, they moved past their tried and true topics. Miriam told Ray about her brother and sister, her parents that were still trying to figure out how to be Americans, her love of math and plans to major in Engineering at the U of M in the fall. Ray talked about his dad, how hard it was for him to leave school to come back to Detroit, but how he owed it to his mom and dad because his sister Gladys was married and lived in Pontiac with a new baby boy and couldn't lend a hand. He told her that he was taking courses in English, that he'd like to continue after completing his bachelor's degree, but to maybe find a school that went beyond Hemingway and Steinbeck. He wanted to study comic books. Miriam was incredulous; she told Ray that there'd never be a college where comic books would be part of the curriculum.

"What a crowd." Miriam looked over the ballpark, which seemed to have every seat full. On the field, the home team was

118

finishing their warm-ups while the visitors prepared for their first at-bat. "Don't these people have jobs?" She laughed. "The home stand flu, right?"

Ray smiled, although it was hard to tell because he essentially hadn't stopped since he had picked Miriam up outside of her house an hour earlier. He'd thought it was a little strange that Miriam hadn't dragged him inside to meet her parents, but when he asked, she waved him off and said something about her parents trusting her for a day game date. He tried not to stare at her, but she was easily the prettiest girl he'd ever been on a date with. She was taller than average, just an inch or so shorter than Ray's five feet eight inches, slim with dark brown shoulder length hair parted to one side and pinned back behind her right ear. The New Look suited her, and her parents clearly allowed her to spend at least some of her Fenwick's paychecks on clothes, as she was post-war from head to toe.

Johnny Groth and Hoot Evers tossed the ball back and forth from center to left in front of them; even before the game started, some of Evers' fans were already starting to holler "Ho-ooot" in his direction. The Tigers had come home after a road swing through Boston and Philly with the same fingernail hold on first place that they'd left with. The excitement of the hometown fans was palpable; now that the calendar had flipped to August, they could smell a pennant.

"What do you say to Carl's after the game?" Ray's voice sounded a full octave higher than normal in his ears.

"The game hasn't even started yet and already you've got us down the street with steaks in front of us?"

Ray chuckled. "Maybe I'm just thinking about the air conditioning." He wiped some sweat from his brow.

"It is a little hot." Miriam fanned herself with her scorecard. She hadn't complained until Ray did.

Ray watched as Dizzy Trout took the mound and Gene Woodling, the Yankees' left fielder, moved into the batter's box. "You said it's been awhile since you came to a game."

119

"Yes. My dad thought it was a shandeh when they sold Hammerin' Hank. He so far has refused to come back, but he'll give in eventually."

"A shandeh?"

"Oh, right. Sorry. It means a shame, but worse than that. A terrible shame."

Ray twisted his program between his sweaty hands. "Sure. It was. A shame, I mean. No one wanted him to finish his career in another team's uniform."

"I'm a little embarrassed, but I have to admit that I cried."

Ray looked at Miriam. He could tell she was being honest. "I'm not a Tigers fan, but I thought it was a rotten deal. Maybe if it was a trade and the team had gotten a player or two in return."

Miriam nodded. "It doesn't seem right, does it? That players have to go where the teams tell them?"

While they'd been talking, Dizzy Trout made quick work of the first three Yankee hitters and the game moved to the bottom half of the inning. Ray would have to wait until the second inning to see his hero at the plate.

He twisted in his seat. "The owners have all the power. It's the Reserve Clause. Players are effectively indentured servants."

"Maybe someday they'll form a union."

Ray nodded. "It's just a matter of time."

The Tigers loaded the bases in their half of the first, getting the crowd into a lather, but Johnny Groth's flyball to center didn't have the distance to blow the inning up. The long fly was so exciting that Ray forgot his Yankees allegiance for a brief moment and jumped to his feet with the rest of the crowd. It was just as well; Tiger fans were known to be not very accommodating to Yankee fans. Ray had learned to keep his love for the Bombers quiet when at Briggs. When he was eleven, an angry fan poured a beer over his dad's head after Ray had cheered a little too vociferously at a DiMaggio homer.

Miriam showed her baseball smarts throughout the inning. She correctly predicted that Tommy Byrne, the Yankees starter, would pitch carefully to Hoot Evers with two runners on, and this was borne out when Hoot drew the walk. She knew that Groth's drive to the outfield didn't have a chance to clear the fence, and pointed out that, rather than get swept up in what the crowd thinks they see, you should instead watch what the outfielder is doing. If he's moving in or staying put, then it's not going to be a homer, and DiMaggio was flat on his feet as he waited for the ball. Ray's dad had never taught him that one.

As DiMaggio took his warm up cuts between innings, Miriam asked Ray what was so appealing about the Yankee Clipper.

Ray looked over each shoulder and spoke quietly to his date. He didn't want a Stroh's dumped over his cap, and he didn't need to learn that lesson twice. "I don't think I'll see another player like Joe D in my lifetime. He can do everything; hit, run, throw, moves around center field like a deer. Look at that last play to end the first. He knew exactly where to put himself before that pitch. He didn't even have to move to catch the ball."

Miriam nodded, smiling.

Ray was just getting started. "One of the most curious things about Joe is that he hardly strikes out. Lots of players strike out one hundred or more times a season, but Joe D's never struck out more than forty times in a year. Forty."

Miriam laughed. "You seem so concerned with numbers, maybe you should give up the comic books and take courses in math and statistics."

Ray would have agreed, but it was really only baseball numbers that fascinated him because eventually they came alive with the activity on the field. All other numbers just sat there on a page. "I'll give you a number. Fifty-six."

"Of course. The hitting streak was an achievement. I was only eight years old that season, but I can remember all the attention. It must've been impossible to concentrate."

The inning break was over and the Yankee first baseman, Johnny Mize, lifted a deep fly to left-center, but Hoot caught it near the fence. It was Joltin' Joe's turn at bat.

Ray turned to Miriam and smiled. "Are you convinced yet?"

Miriam returned the grin. "He can convince me with this game. If he hits a home run, I'll be a Yankee fan with you for life." She reached over for Ray's hand, which was embarrassingly slick with sweat. She didn't seem to mind.

DiMaggio took ball one and then fouled off a few pitches, daring Dizzy Trout to throw him another fastball. He looked at another ball and then fouled off a pitch to the stands in deep left that would have been a homer had he straightened it out.

Trout gave DiMaggio the fastball he was waiting for, but Joe got a little on top of it and sent a liner to Hoot in left. Had he gotten under it just a fraction of an inch more, it would have been a home run for sure.

Ray shook his head and looked down at his feet. "They call it a game of inches for a reason."

✳✳✳

"It won't make any difference, Miriam. I would have had to register for the fall term. It's too late." Ray put his fork down. The schnitzel at Metzger's was one of his favorite dishes, but he hadn't had any appetite for weeks.

"But your father can't work. Couldn't you defer because of that?" Miriam had matured in her first year and a half in Ann Arbor, much as Ray felt he had. Not just physically, although she did look more grown-up; she was measured, considered, wise. Ray imagined if he was telling some other sort of girlfriend that he'd enlisted in the Navy, there'd be crying and pleading, maybe even hysterics that'd turn heads in the old German restaurant. Not from Miriam, though. Her voice showed no overly emotional or sentimental response and there were no tears in her eyes.

Ray shook his head. "It's better this way. If I enlist, I stand a better chance of staying out of combat."

"But the commitment is four years instead of two."

"Yes." Ray removed the napkin from his lap, wiped off his mouth and placed it on his plate. He'd eaten less than half of his dinner.

Miriam deliberately chewed a piece of Sauerbraten. "And when do you leave for basic training?"

"In three weeks." Miriam looked beautiful sitting across from him in the dark light of the restaurant. She had pinned her hair back and her long neck always reminded him of Lauren Bacall. Ray thought about the last time he and Miriam had made love. He'd driven to Ann Arbor and they strolled the Arboretum, had a nice dinner and saw *On Dangerous Ground* at the State Theater. They drove to the River Drive Motel towards Ypsilanti, checked in as Mr. and Mrs. Stein. Miriam was distracted, tense. It had been over six months since that night.

Miriam picked at another piece of her dinner, her eyes never leaving the plate.

Ray reached across the table for her hand. "I want you to marry me."

She eased her fork down onto the table. "That's not very reasonable."

"It is. If I don't make it back, you can collect the benefits."

"Don't talk like that."

Ray thought about his dad, still fighting his disease after two years, barely able to move from his bed, sicker from his treatments than the cancer. His mom, working as a seamstress to keep them afloat, the unfairness that a war half the world away was forcing him to leave his family who needed him and the woman he loved. Marriage was the only way he could think to keep Miriam close while he was away. "Don't you love me, Miriam?"

"Of course I do." She sipped her nearly empty glass of water, still looking at the table. "But I can't marry you."

Ray took a deep breath. His head spun. "Why?"

Miriam fixed him with a condescending look, as though he were an impertinent third-grader asking an unnecessary question. "I shouldn't have to tell you why."

"But I've met your parents. I thought they liked me."

Her expression hadn't changed. "They do like you, Ray. But they like you in practice, not in theory."

"I don't understand."

"You're too intelligent not to grasp this."

In Ray's view, their divergent backgrounds were not insurmountable. His parents were not fresh off the boat; they'd both been born in the States. They were horrified by the Nazis; they'd nearly changed their name when Hitler took power. Of course, he was Catholic and had been confirmed at St. Boniface like his mom and dad had wanted, but he hadn't been to Mass for years. God was God, as Ray saw it. He would convert, if that's what it would take for Miriam to see he was serious. Besides, she'd never presented their religious difference as a problem in the past; they'd been seeing each other for over a year and a half. He'd spent time with her parents, and although he was nervous at first, he found there was an easy camaraderie, especially with Miriam's father. They always had baseball.

Ray took a deep breath through his nose. "This isn't about your parents. It's about you."

Miriam fingered the green glass brooch she wore on the left lapel of her light cream jacket. "You're right."

"Your parents are fine with us seeing each other."

"My parents don't know about us, Ray." Miriam glared across the table and folded her arms. Now she appeared like the petulant child. "I told them we broke it off last year. They were happy."

Ray's back hurt. He stretched in his seat. "I see."

She picked up her fork again and pushed at the remaining beef on her plate. "I didn't want to tell you. We don't have to talk about this now. We can see each other when you return."

"If I return."

"I told you not to talk like that."

Ray propped his elbows on the edge of the table and folded his hands in front of his face. "Why would you want to see me when I come back anyway? To pass the time until the right Jew comes along?"

Miriam pursed her lips. "This isn't like you, Ray."

"You'll understand if I'm not myself at the moment."

***

Nancy wasn't too keen on letting Gene out of the house since the baby was born, but she made an exception for Ray, especially since he was due in North Chicago for training in just a few days.

Gene sipped his Stroh's and looked at the Elmwood's television set behind the bar where the Red Wings were flailing against an inferior Leafs squad. "Look at it this way, Ray. You're going off to Korea unattached. Maybe you can bring a Korean lady home."

Ray bristled a little at the thought. If there were problems with a girl from the neighborhood to the east, crossing a cultural divide thousands of miles wide struck him as unworkable. But if Gene could marry the former Nancy Holan, anything was possible. "You never know."

"I'll miss you all the time, Ray."

Ray sipped his beer. "Thanks. Me too."

"For what it's worth, that girl must not be thinking. You're the best guy I know." He held out his glass in a sort of toast. When Ray didn't respond, he set it back on the bar dejectedly.

Ray was still in shock from the fight with Miriam. He thought he'd be heading to training with a new bride, but instead was walking around stunned, asleep on his feet. Perhaps he should have seen something like this coming, given their distance over the preceding months, but he'd taken Miriam at her word that she was busy with school. He hadn't asked before he stormed out of Metzger's, letting his anger get the better of him, but he assumed she had also been seeing someone else. What he didn't know couldn't hurt him.

Ray nodded at his friend. "That boy of yours will be running around and talking up a storm by the time I get back."

"I hope he'll have a little brother or sister by then, too."

"That sounds great." Fatherhood had matured Gene, even though James was only six months old. He'd worked his way back onto the line, had bought a bungalow in Highland Park. Nancy, on the other hand, hadn't really calmed down at all. There'd been some sort of incident at the lunch counter Kresge's a few weeks back, but Ray didn't know all the details and he didn't want to ask Gene. "I hope so too. A girl this time, though."

"I'll check in on your mom and dad when I can."

"That'd be nice of you. I know you're busy."

"It's the least I can do, Ray, with you off fighting that war."

Ray nodded and sipped his beer. He reached across the bar for Gene's pack of Sano's. "Do you mind?"

"No." He fished in the pack for a cigarette and handed it to Ray, then lit it with his shiny brass Zippo. "Since when do you smoke?"

Ray shrugged. "Since now, I guess."

✳✳✳

The game remained scoreless until the bottom of the third, when baby-faced Vic Wertz clubbed a two-run homer over the right-center wall that got the home crowd really going. Ray fought the urge to plug his ears, the cheers were so loud.

The Yanks cut the lead in half on a Bob Swift error in the fifth, then took a three to two lead on a Mize homer that also scored Hank Bauer. The momentum shift quieted the crowd and Ray was silently pleased.

DiMaggio wasn't part of the scoring. He grounded out weakly to George Kell at third earlier in the inning.

As the game progressed, Ray moved from a theoretical infatuation with Miriam to something less esoteric. As she spoke, he was struck by her strength and her smarts. He'd always liked smart girls; Joyce Pembroke was easily the best-read person in his English classes, for example. But Miriam's smarts went past intelligence. There was worldliness to her, even though she'd barely left Detroit. Her parents had different expectations for her than he was used to. It was taken as a given that she would receive an education and that she'd study what interested her, even if the other students in her chosen discipline were overwhelmingly male. She wasn't like any other girl he'd known.

She kept her hand on his through most of the game. He barely moved as a consequence. Each DiMaggio at-bat found them each silent, sitting close to the edge of their green wooden seats, watching each ball and strike and foul with unwavering attention. Ray willed his hero to connect, to send a ball soaring over the fence, to give the Yankees the lead.

In the sixth, Joe flied out to center field on a zero and two count.

In the eighth, he sent a towering fly to Hoot in left that ended the inning.

The Tigers had broken the game open in the sixth with another Wertz homer and a Johnny Lipon single that scored Hoot and Don Kolloway. The Yankees went weakly in order in the ninth, and the final score was Tigers seven, Yanks three.

DiMaggio didn't get another shot at the bat.

As the crowd filed out around them, Ray and Miriam stayed in their seats. They watched as the ballpark's green seats revealed themselves and the crowd moved toward the aisles and the stairs and the concourse. Ray sat still and took it in. It's an amazing thing, he thought, these acres-wide patches of green in the middle of the city. All the concrete and steel surrounding them, the streets and the cars and nearly two million souls, a real city growing up and out and swelling until it feels like it could burst. Ray mostly felt that calling the site of the mythic first baseball game Elysian Fields was heavy-handed, until he took a moment to sit and wonder at how just such an expanse could be preserved in the middle of all that growth. Ray knew Miriam felt it too, even if they didn't vocalize it.

Ray fiddled with his program, which by now was somewhat torn and soaked with the sweat from his hands. "I'd like to get back to another game before the end of the year. What do
you think?"

"I'd love that."

"Mr. Briggs makes it hard, though, with all of these day games. He's a traditionalist."

Miriam nodded and smiled. "I'm sorry Joe didn't come through for you today."

Ray smacked the program into his open left palm. "Can't win 'em all."

Miriam stood, smoothed her skirt and reached for Ray's hand. "He's no Hank Greenberg."

DREW & BOB'S

Tuesday was new release day at the video store. Technically, I guess it's new release day at every video store, but I only worked at the one, so I don't really care what went down elsewhere.

There was a customer, John Allman, who showed up at opening every Tuesday ready to grab his limit of four new releases. John was a nice enough guy, I suppose, but I didn't dig too hard. I didn't want to ask too many questions about a man in his early thirties who had the sort of life in which his Tuesday routine was to select four new movie releases on videocassette, rent them and take them home, then proceed to spend eight to ten hours of his day — every week, don't forget — watching said movies. Perhaps most troubling is that he was arbitrary about which movies he rented. He was just as likely to rent some nameless, faceless direct-to-video tripe than the latest blockbuster. If it starred Eric Roberts or Dolph Lundgren, John Allman was renting it. It seemed what brought him the most pleasure was to be the first to take a tape home. Maybe it was a twisted psychosexual thing, like some sort of VHS virginity. The dull vapidity of the video store lent itself to labyrinthine theories like that.

As I walked out front, I could see that John Allman was in his usual Tuesday spot. I unlocked the swinging glass doors and let him in. I'd cued up *Say Anything* as I got ready to open and Diane Court's valedictorian speech was bouncing around the empty store, echoing and slapping off the walls. "When I think about the future, the truth is, I am really scared." No shit, Diane.

"Hey there, Drew." John Allman walked past me and made a beeline for the New Release racks near the counter. He smelled so strongly of Irish Spring that I wondered if he'd forgotten to rinse before he got out of the shower that morning.

"It's manly, yes, but I like it too." I'd taken to muttering weird things at customers in a nearly perceptible manner. Normally, they

129

were simple curses at people who were rude to me, but sometimes, I got creative.

John Allman stopped and gave me a quizzical look. "Did you say something?"

"Yeah, I was just saying hey there to you, too."

John Allman nodded and moved his gaze back to the new selections.

Just as I was turning toward the counter, the glass door opened and Charlie stepped into the store. Ralph was a fairly regular customer, but I hadn't seen Charlie in here before.

"Hey, Charlie."

He nodded at me. "Drew." He didn't smile. One had to work to elicit a smile from Charlie.

"Haven't seen you in here before."

"Ralph says you've got a lot of porn."

Based on the number of women who seemed to throw themselves at him in Bob's, I didn't figure Charlie for the porn-renting type. "I don't personally own a lot of porn, but the store has a good selection. I've just got a well-worn copy of *Edward Penishands.*"

Charlie cracked an almost imperceptible smile that seemed to hurt his face a little. "Funny. Through there?" He motioned with his head at the swinging doors that closed off the porn from the non-porn.

"A regular pornucopia awaits you on the other side there."

Charlie nodded and walked in the direction of the porn room. John Allman made quick work of his selections and was already waiting for me to check him out.

I moved behind the counter and reached for the cases he'd set down. "That was fast, John."

"Yeah, I'm excited to see this new Rutger Hauer movie."

I looked at the artwork for *New World Disorder.* I didn't even know such a movie was being released. John Allman would have been a much better video store employee than me. "Andrew McCarthy co-stars. Looks interesting." There was no way I could tell him what I really thought.

Charlie exited the swinging doors and stood behind John Allman impatiently. I rang up the Rutger Hauer movie and three others for my Tuesday morning regular.

"Your total is nine twenty-five, John."

He handed me a ten, I fetched his change, thanked him, and sent him off to deflower the new titles.

Charlie set the cases for a few nurse videos on the counter. "I like nurses."

"I can see that." I didn't tell him that I always thought dudes with a thing for nurses were a little creepy. It seemed like they might have some Oedipal issues, as both moms and nurses take care of us when we're sick. "Do you have a membership?"

"Nope. Can I use Ralph's?"

I shook my head. "We'll just sign you up. It takes two minutes. You get a fancy laminated card and everything."

"You're a real stickler for the rules."

I shrugged. "Can I see your license?"

Charlie dug into his wallet and slid his white Michigan license across the counter. I grabbed a membership form and a pen and started transferring the information. He looked more hungover in the picture than he did standing in front of me, but only slightly.

"Charlie, if you don't mind my asking, it seems like the number of women after you in that bar would negate any need for porn."

"Sometimes I'd rather jack off than to have to listen to them talk."

Yikes. It was pretty easy to tell that Charlie was fucked up, but I didn't think we knew each other well enough for him to say some hateful shit like that. "They do love to talk, don't they?" I slid Charlie's license back across the counter, skipping the phone

131

number slot on the membership form. For some reason, I really didn't want to ask for his phone number at that moment.

"You like working here?" Charlie's eyes moved around the store.

"It's okay for now." I printed out his new membership card and took it over to the small laminator.

"Do you meet a lot of girls in here?"

Not unless you counted the bored housewives and the fat, sloppy unemployed dudes and the smelly white-trash teenagers with chocolate all over their faces. Why did area redneck kids always seem to be hopped up on Hershey's? I shook my head in response to Charlie's question. "It's six thirty-five for the movies."

Charlie counted out seven ones and handed them to me. "Customer service blows."

I would have completely agreed, except that it occurred to me that I was often a customer of Charlie's. I handed him his change. "It has its ups and downs."

I slid the nurse tapes across the counter.

Charlie picked them up and then nodded his head as a thank you. "Maybe something better will come along soon."

It had to. "Hopefully you're right. See you for a pint later on."

Charlie nodded again and turned to leave.

Regrettably, I'd know all too well how he spent the late morning and early afternoon before I'd get to Bob's. Nurse videos. Gross. I'd rather hang out with Diane Court.

✵✵✵

A couple of weeks later on a Thursday, I was sitting near the end of the bar at Bob's, feeling sorry for myself while nursing a pint of Anchor and hoping that the cute brunette a few stools down would make eye contact with me. I wasn't having much luck. Maybe she wasn't into self-pitying skinny dudes wearing vintage Arrow polyester shirts.

The side door opened and in walked a heavy-set guy in a faded Lake Superior State cap and rugby shirt. He took the seat next to mine at the very end of the bar. This was odd, as in the few months that I'd been coming into the bar, it seemed that stool was always left open so that the bartender on duty could sit down for a moment when and if business allowed.

Charlie walked over and shook the new guy's hand. "Why are you in here on a Thursday?"

"Nice to see you too, you prick." The guy leaned behind the bar and opened the cooler door closest to him, took out a bottle Labatt and then closed the cooler.

From down the bar, a forties-ish dude that I'd seen in the bar a few times before, yelled at the new guy. "Hey, Phil. What's shakin'?"

"Hey Kirby, you fuck." Phil took a sip of his beer. "Hey Charlie, get that asshole a beer on me."

Right away, I made the connection. Phil was the bar owner who I'd not yet met. As I understood it, he bought the entire building for a song earlier in the decade, attracted by its status as one of the oldest bars still standing in the downtown area. Even though Flint, given its present state of decline, was a long shot for a successful youth-oriented bar, Phil had an idea. He guessed that there was a market among the suburban kids from Beecher and the other well-to-do towns that would be fascinated by the romance of a bar located in the heart of the city, especially if it had a great beer selection and a carefully curated jukebox. He let word of mouth prove his guess to be correct. After all, this was exactly how Curt "Spooky" McCoy got Aaron to come to Bob's, and, by extension, me.

Phil took a tin of Copenhagen out of his back pocket and placed it on the bar. "How's business?"

Charlie shrugged. "Alright. Too many dudes tonight."

Phil nodded. "It's nice to get out of the house. Nate's teething. I've been with him all day, so Pam relieved me after she got home." He took a sip of his beer. "Sorry to add to your sausage party."

I laughed.

Phil noticed and turned towards me. "How're you doing, I'm Phil Franklin." He reached out his hand. "I don't think I've seen you in here before."

"Nice meeting you." Phil's grip hurt my hand a little.

Charlie ambled over and stubbed out a cigarette in the ashtray nearest me. "You haven't met Drew yet? I know I've told you about him. Just graduated from State, big baseball buff."

A look of recognition spread over Phil's round face. He wore a pair of John Lennon specs that were rendered almost comically small in contrast to the size of his head. "Oh yeah, Drew. Great to finally meet you, Ralph and Charlie both mentioned you. Let me buy you a beer."

I couldn't imagine why Charlie or Ralph would be talking about me to their boss. "Thanks." I nervously tapped a Parliament out of my pack.

"Did you like State?" Phil grabbed a small bag of Better Made chips from behind the bar and opened it.

"A lot. I'm sorry it's over. I was supposed to be starting grad school there in a few weeks, but I had a change of plans."

Phil nodded. "I know what you mean. I always meant to go back and finish my architecture degree, but life kept catching up. Now I'm twenty-nine with a wife and baby at home. I'm not complaining. I've got this place." He gestured down the length of the ancient, ornate bar.

"I love it here. I'm not just saying that. There's nowhere like it. I spend five bucks every time I come here just on the jukebox."

"I can't really take credit for the jukebox, Charlie mostly set that up." He nodded at the bartender who was currently being ogled by three of the four women seated at the bar while he poured a Smirnoff on the rocks. "With the condition that there always had to be a few classic country discs on there as a tribute to the previous owner."

I smiled. "That explains it. Charlie's always pissed at me when I play George Jones."

"Glad to hear someone's still got taste amongst all these cooler-than-thous." Phil held up his bottle of beer.

I met his Labatt with a clink from my Pilsner Urquell, suddenly conscious that my down- home George Jones reference was probably made moot by the affected beer choice, not to mention my chartreuse polyester Arrow shirt with a wide collar. "What do you do for a living, Phil?"

"I'm a stay-at-home dad." He shoved some of the chips into his mouth and chewed loudly.

"Is that right? Not sure I've ever known anyone of that occupation."

He finished crunching and swallowed, then took a gulp of his beer. "I did have a real job, once upon a time. I sold cars." There was enough potato chip detritus left in his mouth to spray a bit on his S's. "Made enough money to buy this place and retire. So to speak."

"That's cool as hell." I nodded, then finished my beer and turned over the empty shot glass in front of me, which was the signal to Charlie that I was ready for my freebie. "If you don't mind my asking, why were Ralph and Charlie talking about me?"

Phil wiped the grease from the chips off onto his pants legs. "Well, the short version is that we're going to be looking for a new afternoon bartender a few days a week, and this isn't the sort of job we advertise in the Journal."

My curiosity was piqued. "I'm flattered. This seems like a cool place to work. People treat Charlie and Ralph like rock stars. I've never worked in a bar before, though."

Phil finished his first bottle, threw it in the garbage can under the bar with a loud clink, and reached into the cooler for a second. "There isn't much to it. Once you know how to restock and change a keg, that's really about it. This is a big shot-and-a-beer crowd, you wouldn't need to learn how to make a Manhattan."

I laughed a little as I looked down the bar at the succession of pint glasses and beer bottles. "Yeah, not a lot of martini drinkers here tonight."

"Or any other night." Phil took the tin of dip off the bar and started the wrist slap ritual to pack the tobacco. I've never known exactly what that accomplishes, apart from alerting a group of people that you're about to use chewing tobacco. "There's more to it, though." He pulled out some of the chew and stuck it in his mouth.

I bristled a little at the smell of the dip, which always turned my stomach a bit as a result of a junior-high baseball experiment with the stuff that went terribly awry. "Okay."

"The truth is that we need to know we can trust each other around here."

Charlie sauntered back to our end of the bar, still not smiling even though he'd been talking up the brunette I'd been eying earlier. He brought my fresh beer with him and put the shot glass behind the bar.

"Did you ask him yet?" Charlie opened a bottle of Sam for himself.

"We're getting there." Phil swiveled his stool back toward mine. "The issue is that I run this place according to my rules. That means I'm the only employee of record and everybody here gets paid under the table. Some people aren't comfortable with that, so I wanted to be upfront."

Anything was better than renting anal videos to the local degenerates. "I don't have a problem with that."

Phil grabbed an empty bottle of Bud off the bar and spit tobacco juice into it. "You also don't walk in and get the plum shifts. You're going to have to work only afternoons until we think you're ready to handle a night or two."

"That makes sense. I've seen it get pretty busy. I'd rather get my feet wet for a while first."

"That's good. If all goes well, you should be ready to take over a night shift from Charlie and Ralph after a few months or so. By that point, they'll be ready give one up, I'm sure."

Charlie grabbed the back of his neck and rolled his head from side to side. "I'm fucking ready now."

Phil spit into the bottle again. "I don't want to hear any labor pains." Phil turned back toward me. "You get five bucks an hour base, plus whatever tips you make. Charlie, what do you normally take home in tips for an open to eight shift?"

"Thirty or forty." Charlie walked down the bar to take a drink order.

"With the twenty in base, you're looking at fifty or sixty bucks a shift. You'd be opening on Monday, Tuesday, Friday and Saturday. On Saturdays we open at noon, so there's a little extra hourly."

I pictured giving Monty two-week's notice. Telling Kathy about working downtown would be thornier. "That all sounds pretty good."

"Great. There is one final hoop to jump through, though." Phil pulled out his dip, tossed it into the trashcan, and then took a drink from his beer. "We need to know you're a good fit for Ray."

☆☆☆

As I walked up from the basement, I could smell the fresh cut flowers my mom was arranging in a vase on the kitchen counter.

"Good morning, Drew." Her voice had a sing-songy quality I found endearing and unnerving at the same time.

"Hey, Kathy." I sat on one of the counter stools and rubbed my eyes.

There were still times her gut reaction was to become annoyed at my calling her by her first name, but it was quickly replaced by the realization it was futile. "What can I get you for breakfast?" She finished fussing with the flowers, put her hands on her hips and looked over the finished results with a cocked head. Even though it was only eight o'clock in the morning, she'd already gone out to the garden to pick the late-summer blooms that now graced the kitchen, showered and dressed herself in a pair of slacks and a Jones New York blouse that looked new.

I stretched my arms over my head and cracked my back. "I'll be fine with a little cereal. Is there still coffee?"

"There is. I'll get you a cup." I watched her reach into the cupboard for a mug, choosing an oversized green cup with the cartoonish face of Sparty painted on the side. If all had gone according to plan, I'd have been back in East Lansing by now, probably discussing Habermas or Foucalt in Theory and Methodology. Instead, I was heartsick and hung over in Flint, drinking coffee with my mom.

She poured a full cup of Folger's into the mug and brought it to me at the counter. She'd already had the cream at the ready, which I found necessary to overuse in order to be able to swallow the acidic swill she brewed every morning.

I stirred the concoction, turning it light beige. I took a small sip. "What do you have planned today?"

"Your Aunt Pam and I are taking your grandmother shoe shopping and then to lunch."

I was never sure why she insisted on affixing possession of those two to me, since they were her sister and mother well before I was born. "Grandma needs some new shoes, huh?" I feigned interest in this minutia.

"Of course she doesn't." Kathy poured herself a fresh cup of coffee and sat on the stool next to mine. "What about you?"

I steeled myself for the bit of news that I was about to break to my mom, something I'd been avoiding since I'd made my decision a week before. "I'm giving notice at the video store today." I looked down at the coffee mug.

"I see." She poured a bit of cream into her coffee and stirred with the spoon I'd left on the counter. "And then what do you plan to do?"

"Well, the owner of Bob's offered me a job. I'm going to bartend there."

She considered her response for what felt like five minutes, but was probably only about thirty seconds in reality. She didn't take her eyes from me. "You're going to work in downtown Flint? At night?"

"No nights at first, my shifts will end at eight." I was already hanging out in the bar until the wee small hours three or four nights a week, so I didn't really see why working there would make any difference.

She kept her eyes on me and pushed her hands and fingers together as if getting ready to pray, which she might have been. "Should I be worried about you?"

This question was as direct as my mother had been since I'd moved back to the house. There was a part of me that wanted to answer, "Yes, obviously. The girl I thought I'd marry broke my heart and is in Kansas City. I was supposed to be in grad school, postponing adulthood with another few years of school. Instead, I'm alone and lonely in your goddamned basement, nursing my wounds at a bar with pints of microbrews and in-depth conversations about Sonic Youth and sabermetrics. Even my fuckup drunk friend is telling me to get out of Flint." I didn't say any of that. Instead, I shook my head. "Why would you be worried?"

She shrugged her shoulders and took a sip from her coffee mug.

✻✻✻

"Alright." Ralph removed the gloves. "That's how it's done. It's all in the wrists. Push and twist in on the coupler at the same time." He handed the gloves and tap to me.

It was appropriately cold in the keg cooler and it was a little hard to navigate the footing in between the dull metal containers. I don't know if it was because I was cold and wanted out of there or if I had a natural, untapped talent, but I accomplished the task smoothly on my first try.

"That's some beginner's luck right there. Take it out and try again." Ralph kicked the empty keg.

I reversed the steps to remove the mechanism and then reattached it with even more ease.

"Now you're pissing me off." Ralph smiled. "That's impressive. It took me the better part of an afternoon to get that down."

I smirked and shrugged my shoulders. "I'm just surprised I wasn't overthinking it."

Ralph walked out of the cooler and motioned for me to follow. "At this point, I think I've showed you everything. I'll stick with you for this shift, but tomorrow, you're on your own."

I followed him out and slammed the heavy door behind me. "Sounds good."

I took off the gloves and followed Ralph up the narrow, creaky stairs to the bar.

Once at the top, I watched him disengage the locking mechanism that kept the trap door open, and then kick it shut. I made a mental note of the process so I wouldn't have to ask again how to open or shut the door.

Ralph and I started pulling down stools off of the bar at opposite ends. Ralph shouted down to me. "One thing about Ray is that he likes to dispense bar advice. Some people don't like it, but, you know, he owned a bar here in town for almost fifty years, so I don't mind. He knows what he's talking about."

I pulled down the last stool. "I don't think that'll bother me." My dad didn't pass much knowledge down to me before his car accident, but I remember him telling me you can always get smarter by listening to people who know more than you do.

Ralph sat on the corner stool and waited while I unlocked the two entrances. I went back behind the bar and poured myself a pint glass of water, feeling a little uneasy at the prospect of starting my first shift.

An old man in a tan Members Only jacket and brown slacks opened the side door and shuffled in. He had sagging jowls and a few wisps of gray hair that he'd grown long and combed over in an attempt to cover his otherwise bald pate. He sat on the stool nearest Ralph.

"Good afternoon, gentlemen." He reached into his jacket pocket and pulled out a package of Cigarillos, then set them on the bar. I hadn't seen those since my grandfather quit smoking them about a decade before, then promptly died of nephritis. He should've quit the aspirin instead.

Ralph nodded to the old man. "Hey, Ray. How was your morning?"

"Another day spent on this side of the ground at my age is a great one."

"Ray, I'd like you to meet Drew Nemec. He's our new afternoon guy a few days a week." Ralph nodded in my direction.

"Drew, it's a pleasure." Ray reached over the bar with an arthritic and wrinkled hand.

We shook. "Same here, Ray. Everyone around this place holds you in the highest regard."

"Always nice to hear. I appreciate you opening on time." He gave a glance over at Ralph.

"Yes, I know. I've been late more than twice." Ralph tapped on the bar. "Can you get Ray a Stroh's, Drew?"

I headed to the taps. "Of course."

I fiddled with the pint glass and taps a bit, pouring off more foam that I'd expected. After a couple of tries, I'd gotten a decent enough pour and walked down the bar.

Ray accepted his beer, took a small sip and tapped one of the cigars out of his pack. "Thank you, Drew," he said as he handed me a five-dollar bill. "The change is for your jar."

Ralph sat on the stool next to Ray. "Drew, can I get a Sam Adams?"

I looked over the labels on the coolers to figure out which one held the Sam Adams and then got Ralph his beer. "No afternoon ball games today. That's a drag."

Ralph shook his head. "Not sure I'd even want to watch the Tigers at this point in the season anyway."

"Hey, Dean Palmer is having a hell of a year." My life-long love of the Tigers caused me to search for the silver lining in the blackest of clouds.

Ray lit one of his cigarillos. "You two should take at a final trip down to Tiger Stadium before the end of the season, no matter how bad they are. It's your last chance to experience the history of that place."

I nodded in agreement. "Everyone wants the new parks. I understand that they need the increase in revenue to stay competitive, but it'd be nice to be one of the handful of teams left with an old treasure."

Ralph crinkled his nose. "I wouldn't call it a treasure these days."

Ray tapped the end of his miniature cigar into an ashtray. "It might need some upkeep, but Drew's right. There's no way to create the sort of history that comes with almost ninety years of baseball. No matter how nice the new park might turn out to be, Ty Cobb won't have played there. Nor Hank Greenberg or Al Kaline or Charlie Gehringer."

I felt encouraged that Ray had defended my point. I grabbed a few ashtrays to clean. "Did you see a lot of games at Tiger Stadium, Ray?"

"My dad took me to my first game when the place was still called Navin Field, if that's any indication." Ray smiled.

"Ray's a Yankees fan." Ralph sipped his beer.

"That's the worst news I've heard in a while." I smiled at Ray, although I did really hate the Yankees. I'd spent most of my life enjoying their slide to irrelevance, but now that they had righted the ship and returned to past glories, I really hated them again.

I was just about to ask Ray about his love for the Bombers when the front door bell alerted us to the presence of a second customer. A middle-aged man in a business suit sat at the other end of the bar. I walked over towards him.

"Can I get a drink down here?" he barked.

"Sure, what'll you have?" I laid a cocktail napkin down in front of him.

"Double Canadian Club on the rocks."

I poured his drink and served him. "That's five dollars, please."

He tossed a wrinkled Lincoln on the bar. "Thanks." I unrolled the bill before placing it in the register and headed back toward Ray and Ralph.

Ralph nodded down the bar. "Your first customer who's not Ray. Your cherry is busted."

"He wasn't the nicest guy in the world." I looked over my shoulder at the man in question, who was swirling his drink in the glass and glowering.

Ralph shrugged his shoulders. "Yeah, he's a lawyer who works at Knight-Ridge. Their office is pretty close by. We get some of the younger ones. Most of them are super nice, but that guy's a dick. His name is John something, but all the other lawyers call him Ham-Bone. I have no idea why."

I gave Ralph his bottle of beer and peered over at Ham-Bone. "That guy's a lawyer? What's he doing here so early in the afternoon?"

Ralph rubbed his right ear between his thumb and forefinger. "Not tipping you."

Ham-Bone answered a call on his cell phone and starting talking loudly into it.

Ralph lowered his voice to a whisper. "Jesus, at least Phil goes outside when his wife calls him. I hope those things really do give people brain tumors. At least in his case."

Ray cleared his throat. "Jokes aside, when you're behind the bar, you own the place. Ralph and I talked about this when he first started, so I'll tell you the same thing, Drew. The phrase 'the customer is always right' might be true elsewhere, but not here. It's your bar. If you've got a rude customer, it's not up to you to be overly nice to them. It's wiser to spend your time treating your good customers nicely. The jerks will always be jerks."

I gave Ray a flat smile and shrugged. "I'm not sure I have it in me to be rude to people."

Ham-Bone slammed his empty rocks glass down onto the bar with more force than necessary and then turned around to leave.

"You'll get the hang of it."

***

As the side door swung shut, Kirby was laughing and lightly slapping his right palm on the bar. "That was your first encounter with Butt Crack Larry, wasn't it?"

I nodded.

Kirby looked at Kent, and the two of them erupted in guffaws.

BCL, as his self-explanatory moniker was often abbreviated, might have felt like some sort of phantom hazing ritual had I not just seen him in the flesh. He was an odd bird; a middle-aged guy who clearly wore a toupee, fairly dirty clothes and a somewhat rotten smile, but fancied himself a sort of intellectual. He was insufferable to most of the bar's patrons as well as Charlie and Ralph, but there was something so oddly entertaining about him that they'd never bothered to ban him. He'd introduced himself to me by trying to talk my ear off about various conspiracy theories involving the Clintons and Vince Foster, running me around for beers, peanuts, and clean ashtrays, then tipping me all of two quarters for my trouble.

Kent stopped laughing and pointed at me. "Did he tip you?"

I held up the change between the thumb and forefinger of my right hand. "Two bits."

They exchanged glances and started cracking up again.

Kirby pounded his palm on the bar. "That's pretty generous from Butt Crack, Drew. He must like you."

The side door opened and Ham-Bone walked in. I'd had a couple more encounters with him and he hadn't gotten even marginally friendlier. I nodded in his direction.

"Double Canadian Club on the rocks down here," he said as he sat.

I reached for a clean rocks glass, filled it with ice, and then took the bottle off the shelf to pour his drink. I placed it in front of him. "That's five dollars, please."

Ham-Bone slammed a five down on the bar and took a sip from his drink. No tip yet again. I remembered that Charlie told me that the word tips was, in fact, an acronym that stood for "To Insure Proper Service." I argued that it should be "Ensure," which would make the acronym "teps", but his point was valid.

I stood near him and thought about saying something or using some gesture to let him know that I was getting increasingly annoyed at his refusal to tip as well as his attitude, but thought better of it. I headed over towards Kirby and Kent, who were still laughing about Butt Crack Larry's earlier appearance.

Kirby nodded at Ham-Bone. "At least Butt Crack is entertaining. This guy's just a turd."

Ham-Bone's cell phone rang and he answered it loudly.

"See what I mean?" said Kirby. "Take your calls out of the bar. We don't want to hear you get the grocery list from your wife."

I nodded. I didn't think cell phones were as annoying as some others did, but I found pretty much everything Ham-Bone did to be bothersome.

Kent finished the rest of his beer and slid the empty pint glass across the bar. "Hey Drew, can I get another?"

"Yes, sir." I grabbed the empty and put it in the sink, then reached for a fresh glass and started to pour Kent another Leinenkugel's Berry Weiss.

"Alright." Ham-Bone ended his call without a 'goodbye' and shouted down the bar while I was pouring the draft. "Get me another drink."

I put my head down and sighed, and then closed the tap and took the beer to Kent. I walked over to the back bar and then grabbed the bottle of Canadian Club, then ambled over to Ham-Bone. "Don't you think you could be a little nicer?" I poured the drink and looked at him. His brown suit was in need of a press and his ten-dollar haircut set him apart from the other Knight-Ridge attorneys who had a clear sense of style.

"What's the difference? My money's green either way." He took a drink from the rocks glass.

"That's true, I guess. I just think you could be more respectful."

"Is that right? I don't really give a rat's ass what you think. I'm out there in the real world while you and your dipshit buddies circle-jerk in this extended adolescence you've carved out for yourselves." He gestured around the bar with his left hand while keeping his drink aloft in his right.

I looked over at the dipshits in question, who were leafing through the pages of the bar copy of *Total Baseball*, probably trying to settle a disagreement they were having earlier about whether Zack

Wheat finished his career with Brooklyn. He played a season for the Philadelphia A's, but I didn't want to come across as a know-it-all.

Ham-Bone slapped another five on the bar. "Let me give you some advice. I say pour, you pour." He stood and finished the rest of his drink in a single gulp. "If I want to hear anything else out of you, I'll let you know. But I don't want to hear anything else out of you." He took his cell phone off of the bar and turned to leave.

"Have a good evening," I said to his back.

He muttered something under his breath and shoved the side door open.

Kirby shook his head. "I hate that guy. Total asshole."

***

Kathy's coffee tasted even worse when warmed up in the microwave, but I needed a pick up after a long night at the bar. Charlie had gotten really busy as I was hanging out after my shift, and he asked me for a little help. It was worth an extra fifty bucks, but my arms and legs were as sore as after the first day of basketball practice.

My mom had gone to run some errands before I'd gotten out of bed, so I was enjoying commandeering the living room stereo with some Elliott Smith without having to explain who he was. I'm pretty sure I'd told her that he was the nervous guy on the Oscars with the wrinkly suit at least a half dozen times.

I heard the garage door open, followed shortly after by Kathy pulling her Catera in. I listened to her shuffle around to the trunk and then shut it while I went into the living room to turn off *XO*.

Kathy opened the door that adjoined the attached garage into the kitchen. She walked in carrying a couple of bags from Lord & Taylor that she placed on the counter.

"Getting a jump on some Christmas shopping?" I walked into the kitchen.

"Not exactly. I did buy something for you." She reached into one of the bags and pulled out an oversized shoebox.

"The salesman said young people like these and that they're good if you're on your feet a lot." She set the box on the counter.

It was a Dr. Marten's AirWare box. I opened it to find a classically simple pair of Doc boots. "Jeez, thanks, Mom. That's really nice." Of course, I didn't have the heart to tell her that Doc's hit their peak five years earlier. It was the thought that counted, really, and it was nice to know that she was coming around to the idea of me working at Bob's.

"I'm glad you like them. They'll be more comfortable than those tennis shoes you're always wearing." She nodded over at the worn-out Vans near the door that had seen better days.

"You're probably right." I reached into the box and lifted out one of the boots. "Does this mean you've accepted that I'm now a bartender?"

She smiled at me and grabbed the boot from my hands. "I wouldn't go so far as to say that." She started to lace it. "Did you have any coffee?"

"I microwaved some that was left."

"Oh, that's no good. Let me make a fresh pot." She set the boot down on the floor and went to the coffee maker. She grabbed the carafe and went to the sink to rinse it out.

"Thanks a million, Kathy."

"Andrew." She looked over her shoulder at me and then shook her head. "Don't forget I'm leaving to visit Jeffrey in Tennessee on Monday."

"I haven't forgotten." I picked up the boot and began to finish the lacing job.

Kathy finished cleaning out the coffee pot and filled the filter with fresh Folger's. "I don't want this to sound wrong, but I'd appreciate it if you'd refrain from having female visitors while I'm gone."

I cracked up inside, but didn't want to make my mom feel stupid, so I only smiled at her. "I don't think you have anything to worry about there, Mom."

She reached into the shoebox for the other boot and set about fixing the laces on that one. "Well, you spend a lot of time in that bar, I imagine you're meeting some new women."

Meeting? Yes. Dating? No. I spent most of my female-centered mental energy on trying to will Megan to call me. It was truly pathetic. "It's not really that kind of place."

Kathy gave me a quizzical look. "It's not a gay bar, is it?"

This time I couldn't help but laugh. "It would be a problem if I were gay?"

"That's not what I meant." She blushed.

"I know." I finished laughing with a chuckle. "I just meant that Bob's isn't a meat market or anything like that."

She finished lacing the left boot, even though I was only about halfway done with the right. "Your sister-in-law hinted that I should stay in a hotel when I visit." She studied the laces intently before removing them to start the process over.

"Mom, I'm sure that's not true."

"She hates me."

"She doesn't hate you. Southern women are just different." The coffee maker had finished, so I walked over to get a fresh cup.

"I suppose." She pulled the lace through the first eyelet and then held up the ends to make certain they were even. "I just hope you find yourself a nice Michigander so I don't have to continue crossing a cultural divide with my son's wives."

I poured in some cream into the coffee and stirred. "Let's just start with 'nice', huh? Nice would be good."

"I don't see how you could meet a nice girl in a bar, Drew." She raised her eyebrows at me. "Why don't you ask out the Seiferts' daughter, the one who's always at Mass with them?"

"She's a high school senior, Mom." I took a sip of the coffee.

149

"Oh." She finished lacing the boot, and then set it on the floor next to the left one. The pair was ready for me to start breaking in when I started my shift in a couple of hours.

"I'll add 'of age' to the earlier requirement. 'Nice' and 'of age', then we'll go from there." I smiled at her.

She looked at the boots. "I hope these are comfortable."

"They're great. Thanks again, Mom."

"Of course. I can't you have you coming home with aching feet." She stood and went to the cupboard to pull out a coffee mug for herself. "I'm sorry I said that about you bringing girls here while I'm at Jeffrey's. Just ignore that."

"It's alright." I took another sip of coffee, and winked at my mom. "Only if I find a nice one."

"And of age." She laughed.

✳✳✳

I was wiping down one end of the bar after a group of messy drinkers had left on a Monday in the early evening. Ray had already gone upstairs, so I had a quiet moment to get cleaned up and maybe drink a beer. I'd only been behind the bar for a few weeks, but I was getting more comfortable and feeling as though I had a handle on the job.

The side door opened and I looked up to see Aaron walking in. I hadn't spent any time with him since I started working at the bar, as he had already gone back to Mount Pleasant.

"What's going on, A-Ron?" I wiped my hands off on the bar towel and came around to give my friend a hug.

"What's new, Drew?"

Aaron and I gave each other a warm, quick embrace.

"What are you drinking?" I walked behind the bar.

150

"Can I get a Goose Island?" Aaron sat on a stool and took some bills out of his pocket.

"Coming right up." I whirled around to grab the beer, stopping to get an Urquell for myself. I opened the beers and slid the Goose to Aaron. "What are you doing in town on a Monday, my favorite Fifth-year Senior?"

"I don't have any Tuesday classes until three, so I thought I might head down to St. Andrew's tonight to see Manic Street Preachers." Aaron took a drink from his beer. "Do you want to come with?"

"They're still together? Didn't one of the band members disappear or some shit?"

"Richey James, yeah. Just vanished. They still don't know what happened to him."

"That's crazy." I moved to the back bar to grab my pack of Parliaments.

Aaron reached into his shirt pocket for his own pack of smokes. "Do you want to go to the show?"

"Ralph doesn't come to relieve me until eight. Would that give us enough time?"

"Yeah, there's a couple of openers and doors are at eight, so we should be fine." Aaron lit his cigarette with a match from one of the matchbooks that were kept on the bar. "How's it going in here, anyway?"

"It's pretty great. There's this really cool old guy who lives upstairs, Ray. He's here every afternoon. I've enjoyed getting to know him. It's mostly quiet until work lets out, but I've been cultivating a few customers."

"That's great." Aaron tapped the cigarette on an ashtray. "I just hope you know how lucky you are. Don't take this for granted like you do everything else."

I wasn't sure what Aaron was referring to. He was one of my oldest friends and had been there for some of the roughest spots in my life, like my dad wrapping his car around a tree when we were in junior high, or Megan ripping out my heart and destroying my plans. I didn't see a whole lot in my life that I took for granted.

I furrowed my brow and lit my cigarette, figuring it was better to let Aaron's comment die on the vine than to start an unnecessary fight. I took a drink from my beer and stared straight ahead.

Aaron rose from his stool and pulled a few singles out of his pocket. "I'm going to hit the jukebox. Any requests?"

I shook my head. "Whatever you want to hear is cool with me."

Aaron slid his bills in, made some selections and downed his beer. When he finished, he came back and put his empty bottle on the bar. "Got a dead soldier here. Can I get another?"

"Of course." I walked over to the cooler to get the Goose.

"Want to do a shot with me?"

I looked at my watch. Ralph would be here to replace me in a little over an hour. "I don't think so. Someone's got to drive to St. Andrew's. What are you drinking?"

Aaron thought for a few seconds. "Make it a Crown Royal."

I grabbed another Goose, a shot glass, and the oddly shaped bottle of whiskey. I opened the beer and then poured Aaron his shot, which he instantaneously grabbed and drank with a flick of his wrist. "While you're still up?" He pushed the glass at me with his right forefinger.

I rolled my eyes. "Jesus, Aaron." I'd hoped that he turned the corner on his drinking. I wasn't expecting him to join AA or anything drastic, but his parents had pulled their financial support. It seemed like that'd be a wake-up call for most people. I filled the shot glass again.

Aaron smiled and then drank the whiskey. He shook his head quickly from side to side. "Damn, that burns."

I took his glass to the sink and put the bottle back on the shelf. I walked back near his stool and took my cigarette out of the ashtray.

"Maybe you ought to slow down a little. Why go to the show tonight if you're not going to remember any of it?"

"Maybe you ought to mind your own fucking business." He drank the rest of his beer in a single gulp. "Get me another."

I looked at my friend for a moment, trying not to let anger dictate my response. I went to the cooler to get Aaron his third beer. I opened it and put it in front of him. "This is the last beer I'm going to serve you tonight. You're more than welcome to see if Ralph will serve you when he gets here, but I'm done."

Aaron stared at me for a moment and then downed half of his beer. "You're fitting right in behind the bar here, Drew. Acting like a self-righteous asshole just like your co-workers."

I nodded and crossed my arms. I wasn't going to let Aaron get the best of me.

He downed the rest of the beer and slammed it on the bar. "Fuck you. Fuck your boy Ralph. Fuck this place." Aaron reached into the pocket of his jeans, pulled out a twenty-dollar bill, balled it in his fist and threw it at my chest. "What are you going to do now? Huh?" Aaron stumbled back a step and then steadied himself.

I shook my head at him, keeping my arms crossed.

Aaron turned and started towards the side door. "That's what I thought. You're a fucking coward, Drew."

Although I didn't think I deserved his miniature wrath, I'd witnessed this sort of drunken outburst from Aaron plenty of times. I'd just never seen it directed at me. I watched him stomp out of the side door and considered responding to his calling me a coward, but I didn't see any sort of positive outcome to doing so. He'd push, I'd shove. I'd shout, he'd yell. So I let him go.

I wondered if this wasn't how Richey James stumbled out into the ether.

***

153

Ray and I had spent the better part of a late-September Wednesday discussing the relative merits of some of the Tigers young players. It was difficult to find the positives in a lost season.

"I think Karim Garcia will be a hitter, Ray. He's only twenty-three, but he hit double-digit home runs. He's got some talent."

"Maybe. I'm sure his at-bats per homer were still well below league average. This is the era of offense."

Ray knew what he was talking about and wasn't viewing the Tigers with the same misguided hopefulness that I was. My love for the team forced me to see the plusses in guys like Deivi Cruz and Brian Moehler, even as most others saw them for the below-average players they were.

"I say Garcia's got a forty-homer season in him at some point."

Ray nodded at me. "It could happen."

I could tell he was humoring me. Out of the corner of my eye, I saw one of my customers at the other end of the bar trying to get my attention. I wandered over to the couple, a guy and girl about my age that didn't give the impression they were dating.

Charlie had tipped me to the idea on selling a potential couple shots; the guy will almost always say yes to the suggestion in order to impress his companion. "Are you two ready for some shots down here?"

They looked at each other for a second. The woman shook her head and the guy shrugged his shoulders.

"Just another round of beers," he said.

I nodded and turned around to get their drinks. I brought them their beers, then headed back to Ray. I sat on the stool at the end of the bar.

The side door opened and Phil bounded into the bar. "Out of my seat, Drew." He made a sweeping motion with his arms.

I rose and laughed, then made an exaggerated bow to present the stool to him. "Your throne, sir."

"Hey, Ray. They learn how to bust my balls pretty fast, don't they?"

Ray laughed and nodded. "It appears so."

"Drew, can you get Ray a beer on me? One for yourself, while you're at it." Phil reached into the cooler closest to the end of the bar to grab one of his strategically placed Labatt's. The way I saw it, this was equal parts kindness to the bartender and show of ownership.

"Coming up." I went down to the taps to pour Ray his Stroh's and got a Sierra Nevada Pale Ale for myself. "Thanks, Phil."

We drank in silence for a moment.

Phil took the tin of Copenhagen out of his back pocket and slapped it in his right hand. "So, Ray, how's our new guy doing?"

I looked at Phil, then Ray. "Should I go elsewhere while you have this discussion?" I smiled.

Phil chuckled. "This isn't exactly a formal performance review."

Ray took a sip from his beer. "He's doing great, Phil. Everyone likes him, he's got a good demeanor behind the bar. He knows a lot about baseball, even if he refuses to take off his rose-colored glasses when it comes to the Tigers." He laughed.

The guy at the other end of the bar waved me over. "I think we'll take those shots now."

Maybe it was a date after all. I walked down the bar, laughing a little inside that Charlie's strategy worked yet again. I guess Charlie's mild sociopathic tendencies gave him extra insight. "Sure thing. What are you drinking?"

He looked over at the woman and smiled. "I'll have a Southern Comfort; she'd like a chilled Citron."

I turned around to get the shot glasses and their drinks. I came back with the bottle of SoCo and the shaker I'd used to chill the vodka.

"Will you take a shot with us?" The girl smiled at me.

I looked over at the guy. I couldn't tell whether he approved, but I figured I'd be friendly. "Sure, happy to." I went to the back bar and grabbed a third shot glass, and then poured myself a SoCo to show some gender solidarity. I'd have rather had the Citron. I held my glass up. "Cheers."

The couple raised theirs as well and we downed our drinks. "Thanks, guys. Two-fifty each for those is seven-fifty."

The guy held out a ten. "Keep it."

"Thanks a bunch." I grabbed the shot glasses, deposited them in the sink, and headed back to Ray and Phil.

"See what I mean?" said Ray. "He's doing very well."

Phil smiled. "Charlie taught you how to sell shots, I see. Nice."

I took a drink of Sierra Nevada. "Like taking candy from a baby." I laughed.

Ray took out a Cigarillo and packed it on the bar. "There is one area in which Drew can improve, Phil." Ray looked at me. "He's got a little too much nice guy in him. He needs to learn how to be tough with customers who deserve it."

Phil looked at me. "The customer is always wrong, Drew."

I laughed.

Phil stayed serious. "It's true. This isn't the video store. You have my absolute permission to toss anyone from this bar for any reason. You wouldn't be here if I didn't trust your judgment. You have to stay in control when you work. That's one of the ways that we survive in this neighborhood."

I took a drink from my beer and leaned on my elbows on the back bar. "Anyone?"

"Well, within reason. I'll back you up." Phil finished his beer, threw the empty into the trashcan with a loud clink and grabbed a second.

Ray lit his miniature cigar. "He's a smart kid, Phil. He'll learn who should stay and who should go."

✳✳✳

Kirby and Kent were having what had become a weekly drunken discussion about sitcoms. They'd spent the last hour arguing over whether *Dharma & Greg* was better than *Frasier*. I was trying to stay out of it, as I had little to add seeing as how I thought they were both terrible.

Kirby was wagging his finger in the air. "I'm telling you, it doesn't matter. There's no difference. It's like, one's an apple and one's a pear, but they're both vegetables."

Kent sloppily shook his head from side to side and waited for Kirby to finish his sentence. "There's no actor on *Dharma* better than that David Hyde Park. No comparison."

Kirby waved me over.

"Drew, which show do you like better, *Dharma & Greg* or *Frasier*?"

I pretended to give it some thought. "*Mad About You*."

Kirby and Kent both laughed raucously.

Kent nodded. "Perfect answer. Perfect answer. I've got to take a piss." He slid off his stool and waited a moment to get his feet under him.

Kirby slapped his hand lightly on the bar. "Thanks for the update, Pissman." He continued laughing.

I shook my head as the door chime rang. I looked over to see Ham-Bone walk in. After the half-dozen or so encounters I'd had with him it was safe to say no one liked the guy, myself definitely included. I'd talked to both Charlie and Ralph about him, and they had never seen much tip money from him. Even his co-workers at the law firm were unafraid to dish about his sour disposition.

Ham-Bone sat at the bar near the taps and I ignored him for a moment as I pretended to be washing some glasses. It had been a slow afternoon, so there were only a couple, but I milked the task for a few minutes.

"Can I get a drink?" Ham-Bone's tone was impatient and he fixed me with an annoyed glance.

I looked over at him with my hands still in the sink. "I don't know, can you?"

"Is that supposed to be funny?" He put his hands on his hips.

"I can see how someone with absolutely no sense of humor might not find it amusing."

Kent returned from the restroom and took his seat next to Kirby. "Hey, Drew, can I get another draft?"

"Sure thing, Kent." I left the sink, dried my hands on the bar towel in my front pocket and got Kent his beer. As I walked over to place it in front of him, I could feel Ham-Bone's stare burning a hole in my back.

"What the fuck, you little shit? Get me a fucking drink." Now he stood and placed both palms on the bar.

I calmly walked over to him. "You're done. I'm not serving you."

"You can't do that. I've been coming here for years." Ham-Bone was turning red in the face.

"Just did. Get out. Take it up with Phil."

He was shaking. "Don't think I won't." He turned to leave the bar. "I don't know who the fuck you think you are." He pushed the door open with a shove and walked out.

Kirby and Kent were silent as they both stared at me.

Kent took a drink from his beer. "You just threw him out?"

I took my cigarettes out of my shirt pocket, removed one and lit it. "I did."

They looked at each other and chuckled.

Kirby nodded. "I hate that guy. Total asshole."

I took a deep drag off my smoke and smiled a little while I raised both my eyebrows.

I was getting the hang of it.

MOLLY & BOB'S

I did not go to Bob's with the intent of going home with Charlie.

Don't misunderstand me; I think Charlie's attractive and he's got the sort of mercurial hotheadedness that you might find in a poorly written romance novel. In other words, he seems really grumpy all the time. Plus, there's something of a challenge to scoring the bartender. Every woman in the place is after him, and to be the one to pull him out of there represents a certain power. Reality has a way of smacking you in the face though. Charlie was easily the lamest lay of my life. I once read something comparing inept men in bed to gorillas trying to play a violin, and that fit this guy to a T. All paws and claws and I'm not sure exactly what he was trying to do with that knuckle. Besides, his apartment smelled and frankly so did he, a little. Be careful what you wish for, I guess.

I went to Bob's with my roommate, Nicole, to hear God, I Love Pie!, who were having a small record release party at the bar. I've been watching the band develop over the past year or so since I moved back to town to finish school at UM-Flint. They've got a pretty polished sound for an area band and I've heard some rumors that a couple of bigger independent labels have been sniffing around. It wouldn't surprise me if they signed soon.

I'd been hanging out at Bob's for a while, actually since before my twenty-first birthday. They never bothered to card me, more than likely because of my tits. They've granted me access to all sorts of places since they grew so rapidly at puberty, but they meant murder on my back and would eventually need to be reduced a bit, as per Dr. Warner's orders. But even that old goat stared at them a lot. It'd probably cut him up to see them cut up. It can sometimes be difficult to get men to look me in the eyes, and if I'm telling the truth, it bothers me more than I let on. I remind myself that it's primal and men are simple but being treated like an object is never pleasant even if it is subconscious.

Charlie, for all his typical male-ness, is actually a bit warmer and more genuine than I expected. I felt a little sorry for him. He's got a lost puppy quality, something that makes you want to take care of him. It could all be an act, I suppose, but I thought he was sincere. At least he made an effort to look me in the eye now and then, which is more than I can say for my average date or the vast majority of my male customers at Hamilton's, the restaurant where I've waited tables for the past eight months.

I got way too drunk at the God, I Love Pie! show. Nicole and I had gone together, and she might have pointed out that I was drinking too much, but instead, she was pogoing around as the band played, strategically bumping into some kid with ironic Jeffrey Dahmer glasses and one of those bootleg t-shirts with the Black Flag logo turned into something else. I think it said 'Black Death', probably some band I hadn't heard of. Or else it was an actual reference to the plague, which isn't funny. Shortly after the set ended, she gave me the signal letting me know that he was coming back to the apartment with her, so I was on my own from that point on.

After the band tore down, I sat at the bar alone, feeling a little sorry for myself in the way that two too many beers can bring on with efficacy, for me anyway. I missed Muncie, I missed my Ball State friends, and I missed the opportunity that going away to college presents us for reinvention. Being back in Flint made me feel like life was less full of possibilities. Flint's a sad place and it makes me a sad person.

Maybe it was something about the melancholy that attracted Charlie that night, I'm not sure. I hadn't even really been watching him, but when he started talking to me, I perked up a bit and looked around. I took notice of at least three other women vying for his attention; a redhead with out-of-date fluff chick hair, a really hot girl who'd ruined her look by shaving her head and an overweight goth. Had it been my night to choose, I think I'd have taken the shaver, but my friend Stu in Muncie once told me that guys don't want to fuck women with shaved heads because it makes them feel like there's an outside shot that they'd just as soon fuck a dude.

160

Seems a little paranoid to me, but I guess I understand the sentiment. Whether or not Charlie agreed with Stu's short-hair thesis I can't say, but I do know that he parked himself near me and didn't leave except to fill drink orders. Maybe it should've lifted my mood, the attention from the cute bartender who could've given his attention elsewhere, but I'm not sure what could've gotten me out of those doldrums. I went home with Charlie partially to avoid the scene at my place with Nicole and the guy with the bootleg t-shirt, but also because at some point, you just make the commitment to an action and have to see it all the way through. When he asked me to stay behind after he closed up, I wasn't surprised and I was too tired and drunk and, sure, curious to say no.

As I said, I really didn't go to Bob's that night to go home with Charlie.

***

The following morning, I snuck out of Charlie's apartment before he woke and walked home. It was less than two blocks. I figured I'd conquer the problem of fetching my car after some more rest and a greasy breakfast.

When I got to our front door, I noticed our hookup signal, a worn-out Godfather's Pizza door hanger, was conspicuously absent. This meant Nicole was too drunk to put it out or something had gone wrong en route from Bob's to our duplex. It was a short trip, but that doesn't mean I'd put it past Nicole to fuck up a sure thing by talking about her ex-boyfriend. Although they'd split up over a year ago, Nicole was still totally hung up on Nick and drinking a few beers only exacerbated the verbal and emotional diarrhea that was always bubbling below the surface. Even at the most inopportune moments she'd start in about how handsome Nick is, how much she loved his family and they loved her, what a cute couple name they had because they were 'Nick and Nicole.' Without the yellow ad screaming for 'An Offer You Can't Refuse', I assumed that she effectively scared off the guy with the Dahmer glasses.

I opened the door and Nicole was already awake, sitting on the couch smoking cigarettes and reading from her Economics textbook. It was her second attempt at the class. She flamed out of a couple of courses last semester in her over-exaggerated blue period.

I closed the door behind me. "You're up early."

"Trying to catch up." She raised the book up to show what she was reading. "Where were you?"

I wasn't in the mood to share what happened with my roommate, but I had no lie at the ready. "I was at Charlie's."

Nicole's eyes went wide. "The bartender?"

I moved past the living room toward the bathroom. "No big deal. I just spent the night." She didn't need to know that I fucked him. Plausible deniability was the key. I figured she wouldn't think twice about me claiming that we didn't have sex. Maybe I could've added something about my period starting early, but I didn't feel the need to bludgeon the thing. I turned on the faucet, rinsed out my toothbrush and topped it off with twice as much Close-Up as necessary and started cleaning my teeth. It felt like heaven.

Nicole shut her book and walked over, stopping just outside the bathroom door. "Molly, I need details. Did you make out with him at least?"

I spat out some paste. "A little. I was pretty drunk and very tired. I'm sure I snored the whole time."

My roommate looked down at her feet. Her long brown hair was a mess and she hadn't bothered to remove the large amount of make-up she'd worn to Bob's before she fell asleep. "It still sounds better than my night."

I wasn't in the mood to comfort Nicole. Without hearing the story, I could assume that if things went awry, it was her fault. I spit out a glob of toothpaste, gagging a little in my dehydrated state. I filled my mouth with water to rinse, looked into the mirror at Nicole's reflection and gave her a look that told her to go on with her story.

"So Val drove me home. He's really nice, by the way."

I finished rinsing and spit into the sink. "That guy's name is Val?"

She nodded. "Why do you ask?"

I sat in front of these two girls in my Comm Research class last semester who were always swooning over some guy named Val, until one of them apparently took him home and got crabs. It wasn't a very common name, and I assumed the Comm girls weren't talking about Val Kilmer, so I thought it might be the same Val. Not knowing for sure, and figuring that he'd probably already defeated his minor STD, I didn't see the need to tell Nicole about it. "No reason."

"Anyway, he's driving and there's a moment of silence and I couldn't think of anything to say except to talk about Nick."

Cyndi Lauper's big hit album was *She's So Unusual*. Had it been Nicole's record, it would've been called *She's So Predictable*. "Jesus, Nicole. You've got to get over it."

"I know." Her voice cracked. "It's hard."

"What happened after you started talking about your ex?"

She wiped away a phantom tear from her right eye. "He pulled in front of the building and didn't even put the car in park."

"Ouch." No misreading that one. Maybe this Val wasn't the same as Comm-crab Val; seems like the crabbed-up Val would've fucked her anyway.

Nicole edged past me and sat on the toilet lid. "I need to make some changes."

Of course, this was putting it mildly. I put the water back on, warmer this time, and wetted my face. "Like what?"

"I feel like I can't move forward with things as they are."

I looked at my face in the mirror. My hair was a mess, as it had started to curl up overnight in the humidity that was arriving a little early in the spring for my liking. There were large bags under my eyes. "Spit it out, Nicole."

"I need to work harder in school."

"That sounds good."

Nicole rolled off a few sheets of toilet paper, balled them up and dabbed at the corners of her eyes. "My dad says I should quit my job."

She worked ten or fifteen hours a week as a cashier at Kohl's. It's possible that she'd get more studying in with those hours freed up. "Okay."

"He wants me to move home, Molly."

I couldn't afford this place without Nicole paying half the rent and utilities. I took a deep breath. My heart sped up anyway. "What did you say to him?"

She dabbed at her right eye again, although she wasn't actually crying. "What can I say? He's my dad. If he says move, I have to move. He's paying for my classes, the car, everything. If I say no, I'm fucked."

I wanted to shake her and remind her that if she says yes, then I'm fucked, but I knew there was no recourse. "You're on the lease, Nicole."

She nodded and then started crying for real. "I told him that. He said he'd pay my share through the end."

We were on a scholastic year lease, which was up at the end of May, with the option of going month-to-month over the summer. I had six weeks to figure out what was next. "Do you really think a few weeks of living at home is going to help you turn this semester around?"

She shrugged and choked back a deep sob that seemed real. "It doesn't matter what I think. My dad is pulling the strings here."

My mind began to run through the permutations. If Nicole was really leaving, and I couldn't find another roommate, I'd have to look for a cheaper place. Cheaper in Flint pretty much ensured that it'd be less safe, not that our duplex felt all that secure most of the time. I could take out more student loans, but one of my goals in coming back to Flint was to stop that train. I could try for a second job, but it felt like I was maxed out on hours as it was.

164

I couldn't move home. Repeat. Moving home: not an option.

"Nicole, I'm sure I don't have to tell you what sort of position this puts me in for next year."

Nicole threw her balled up toilet paper at the trashcan and missed. She unspooled a bit more. "I know, I'm sorry. The last thing I want is to leave you high and dry."

Then don't do it, I wanted to say. Stand up for yourself. I could feel my anger rising and I could visualize myself grabbing Nicole, shaking her until she really started crying, rearing back and striking her with the back of my right hand. I blinked my eyes for a moment and saw only black and then the vision was gone.

Nicole looked up at me. "Molly? Aren't you going to say anything?"

I looked down at my roommate. My soon to be ex-roommate. A girl I never liked very much, but needed more than I wanted to admit or deal with. She lacked the strength to make it on her own and she always would. She had used the words "pulling strings" to describe her father's actions. This was apt. Although she's half a foot taller than I am, she looked so small sitting on the toilet lid. I felt sorry for her. She'd always need a man to tell her what to do.

I really needed some eggs and greasy potatoes and toast and coffee. Maybe a pancake or two. "Do we have to talk about this in the bathroom? Let's go get some breakfast. You want to get some breakfast with me?"

**

I hadn't been in Bob's since the situation with Charlie. I wasn't ashamed or anything like that; in fact, Charlie didn't strike me as the locker-room type who bragged about his conquests. I didn't get the idea that he slept with a lot of women as an ego stroke. I didn't go in because school was ratcheting up a few notches and I was taking eighteen credit hours and working four nights a week at Hamilton's and trying to find a new roommate. I was mentally and physically drained.

Seeing as how waiting tables is one of the few jobs with enough flexibility to accommodate a student's schedule, I could have done worse than Hamilton's. It was a venerable place on the near east side of town, known for steaks and chops that were way better than the price might indicate. It was the sort of place with wood paneling and fixtures that were so out of fashion, they were almost cycling back to look cool, except they were filthy from the three decades of taking on beef grease and cigarette smoke. The clientele was mostly older, but there was a wave of people in their twenties who had caught on to the place, and it made for an interesting mixture, especially on weekend nights.

It was a Tuesday and the restaurant mercifully cut me early because it was pretty dead. I didn't bother to change out of my uniform, which was really just khakis and a Hamilton's t-shirt, before driving over to Bob's. It was one of the things that I liked about Bob's; although it was often packed with the cool kids of Flint, there was a large contingent of customers who didn't feel the need to put on any airs. After I parked my increasingly creaky Ford Tempo and walked towards the building, I could tell that it was a slow night, which suited me just fine. All I wanted was a couple of beers and a bag of Better Mades and maybe a few songs on the jukebox.

There were only a handful of people inside. They were mostly concentrated in a couple of booths and at the south end of the bar, so I sat on the opposite end. I had some twenties in the pocket of my khakis that I pulled out and set onto the bar. The bartender was chatting with the people at the other end. He noticed me and gave me one of those be-right-over nods. I didn't recognize him.

As he turned and started to walk towards me, I got a better look. He was cute; not too tall and not short either, with dark brown hair teased up with a bunch of gel or pomade into one of those "naughty boy" hairstyles. He could probably stand to trim the sideburns, which were bordering on muttonchops, but somehow

166

they suited his sort of roundish face. He was wearing a white shirt that read, "I Played With Whiskeytown and All I Got Was This Goddamned T-Shirt" in black lettering. As he walked closer, he paused to grab some cigarettes off of the back bar.

"Hi." He stopped in front of me. "What can I get you?"

"Anchor Steam draft?"

He looked at my face and then scrunched his forehead in thought with a fishhook in his left eyebrow. "I need to see your driver's license."

I was a little taken aback. I'd also left my ID in my car. "Really? I'm here all the time. I know Charlie and Ralph pretty well."

He shook his head. "I'm not trying to be a dick, really. But I just got a couple of night shifts and all I need is to find out that Phil sent you in here as some sort of test to see if I'm carding. Sorry." He paused to light his cigarette. "I can walk you to your car if you'd like."

I stood. "No, it's fine." I pointed to my twenties on the bar. "Watch those?"

He nodded.

I turned to leave, pushed open the door and walked towards my car. The sun hadn't set yet, so the block didn't feel as dangerous as it might in another hour or so. People who were unfamiliar with Bob's were always aghast that I'd ever consider wandering this neighborhood alone at night. It was hard to explain, but it was as though Bob's was an oasis in a desert of run-down or abandoned buildings in the vicinity. I never once felt threatened in the dozens of times I'd been there. In fact, I'd been harassed more inside the place than outside of it, although, to be fair, it was really only one time that some extremely drunk dude grabbed my boob and said "honk-a, honk-a", which was actually more comical than threatening.

As I opened the car door and then reached into the center console for my wallet, I stopped myself from getting annoyed at the new bartender. He was just being cautious. Getting a job behind the bar at Bob's was not an easy thing to do, and the turnover was minimal. I imagine he wanted to hang onto the gig with both hands. I decided not to be shitty to him when I got back in. I grabbed my wallet and flipped it open to make sure that my driver's license was, in fact, inside. My frizzy hair and soon-to-be-legally-drunk smile of six months prior stared back at me, making me glad I'd discovered the hair straightener.

As I closed my car door, I noticed a handshake drug deal a block or so away. It was really the first I'd seen anything like that happen in the immediate vicinity. I wasn't scared because it was sort of like crossing paths with a skunk. They were just as afraid of me as I was of them. Instead, it made me sort of sad. I pulled open the side door of Bob's and walked in.

I sat on the same stool I'd occupied earlier and made a mental note that my twenties were still on the bar. The cute bartender was chatting with his customers at the other end of the bar, but started over towards me as soon as he'd noticed I'd sat down.

I took my ID out of my wallet and handed it to him.

He looked at it and then me and handed it back. "I'm sorry again." He smiled. "Molly."

I might have blushed a little. "So that entire charade was just to find out my name?"

He shook his head. "Of course not." He held out his hand. "I'm Drew."

Someone had taught him how to shake a woman's hand; he didn't give one of those dead-fish grips like men generally did, as though they were afraid of damaging the delicate flower. His grip was gentle but firm and he gave me three pumps and broke away. Textbook. "It's nice meeting you, Drew. How about that beer?"

"Anchor? Draft?"

I nodded.

I thought about getting up to put a couple of dollars in the jukebox, but remembered I didn't have any singles. Someone had gotten there first and had chosen some Pavement, which was fine for the moment. Truth be told, I found the jukebox to be somewhat pedestrian, although it was still easily the best in town. But it didn't stop me wondering why they couldn't be a little more adventurous, maybe some Huggy Bear. Much as I loved the place, it broke my heart when someone carved out a chunk of Pearl Jam jams.

Drew came back with my beer. "That one's on me, for the ID thing."

"You didn't have to do that, but thanks." I took a sip and then nodded at the bills on the bar. "Can you break that for me?"

He nodded, grabbed one of the twenties off the bar and walked over to the cash register. As he walked back, the jukebox shifted to some Old 97s song that I'm not even sure how I recognized.

I took a sip of my beer as Drew put my change on the bar. "Is this your doing, all this alt-country on the jukebox?" I pointed to his t-shirt.

He looked down at his shirt and smiled. "It's a little too obvious, isn't it?"

"You're the new guy. It seems natural you'd want to put your mark on things."

"I guess. I worry that it's a little dorky."

I smiled. "Oh, you're a dork, no question."

"I'm pretty sure I haven't used the word dork since middle school." Drew reached onto the cooler for the ashtray that held his cigarette. It had gone out. He relit it. "You always come here alone?"

I shook my head. "Just got off work and felt like stopping in."

He pointed at my shirt. "Hamilton's? You like it there?"

I took a sip of my beer. "Yeah. It's alright."

"My dad used to take us there occasionally. Nice place."

"The food is good. Kitchen's cleaner than some other places I've worked."

Drew smiled. "Good to know."

"Your dad doesn't take you there anymore?"

Drew looked down at his shoes. "Can't. He's dead."

I felt like an idiot. "I'm sorry. That was stupid of me."

He waved me off with the cigarette in his left hand. "You couldn't have known. Besides, he died when I was sixteen. It was a shock, but I'm over it. I just don't go to Hamilton's anymore."

I didn't have any friends who'd lost a parent. My mind raced with questions to ask, but I didn't want to seem inappropriate. I'd just met this guy. "How'd you get into the alt-country thing?"

He perked up. "Some friends at State."

"You went to State? Did you graduate?"

He nodded. "Last year. American Studies. What about you?"

"I'm at Flint. I transferred from Ball State after my sophomore year."

"Beautiful Muncie, Indiana. David Letterman's alma mater."

I took a sip of my beer. "Yes, and home of the jars. Good stuff."

Drew dragged on his Camel Light. "That was stupid. Sorry. Why'd you transfer?"

"It got too expensive, out-of-state tuition and all that."

At the other end of the bar, one of the customers who was drinking in a booth had come to the bar for a refill. He was a short guy, like Prince-short, dressed in what seemed to be ironically conservative black Slate slacks and a crisp, long sleeved white dress shirt. It was either a fashion statement or he worked at Mario's.

Drew acknowledged him with a nod of his head. Then he looked back toward me. "Excuse me for a minute."

I got to thinking maybe he was interested in me as he walked over to get the guy's drink order. As I watched Drew pour a pitcher of Leinenkugel for the foursome at the booth, I wondered if he was just engaging in small talk because I was alone and new and he was building his clientele by being nice. I couldn't hear what he was saying to the short guy, but he smiled a lot and seemed amiable from afar. I wanted him to be sincere, but it wasn't as though I was unfamiliar with the necessity to plaster a Debbie Boone smile on my face for the sake of better tips.

The jukebox went quiet, so I got up and slid a couple of bills in. It was still hard for me to decide on seven choices, but I didn't want anyone to beat me to the punch. The bulk of the discs were overly obvious and way too dude-heavy. But I liked Smog, so I cued a couple of tracks from *Red Apple Falls,* and I liked The Sea and Cake so I played "Jacking the Ball." When I got back to my stool, Drew strolled over from the other end of the bar.

"Have you heard *Dongs of Sevotion* yet?" He pointed in the air, referring to the music, which was Smog's "Ex-Con." Their new record had come out a week or two before, but I was counting my pennies in preparation for Nicole's moving out.

I shook my head. "I haven't had a chance to pick it up. You?"

"Not yet." He took out a cigarette and lit it. "Didn't peg you for a Smog fan."

"Oh yeah? What did you peg me for?"

He stepped back and grinned, then took another drag from his smoke. "Dave Matthews?"

"Fuck off." It was a serious insult. I didn't even appreciate joking about it.

Drew's smirk shrank. "Jesus, I was just kidding."

"I didn't mean to bite your head off. But, you know, them's fightin' words. Dave Matthews is the devil."

He nodded. "Frat boy asshole music, for sure."

"Yeah. I'm not into the date rape scene."

Drew laughed. "Most of the frat guys I knew couldn't get laid without at least some coercion."

"They are a type, that's for sure." I took a sip of my beer and looked around the bar. The faded portrait of JFK on the wall had to be a holdover from the previous owner. I couldn't tell if its inclusion was ironic or not.

171

Drew took a last drag from his cigarette and then put it out in an ashtray on the bar. "I need to catch up on washing some glasses. Give me a holler if you need anything." He slapped a white bar towel over his shoulder and headed to the sink.

"Sure thing." I forgot my potato chips. I didn't want to ask, for some reason. I looked up at the TV. The Pistons were playing. I didn't care much about the NBA, but even I wished they'd ditch those god-awful teal uniforms.

The jukebox moved to my next selection, the title track from *Red Apple Falls.* It occurred to me these were not the peppiest of bar tunes. I wondered who chose this disc and why. It is what my friend Stu in Muncie would call "heroin music."

I watched Drew work a pint glass over the brushes in the sink. He noticed me watching him, looked over and smiled. This time I know I blushed, and tried to look away but it was too late and too obvious. I'd also somehow completely forgotten something.

I fucked his co-worker less than a month prior.

***

My co-worker Linda and I had just ushered out the last Friday night customer and were sitting down to do the rest of our side work. I hardly smoked, but Linda usually liked company in her post-shift cigarette, especially after a busy Friday, so I indulged her. Besides, I wanted a breather before rolling silverware, a mindless task that went a little quicker when done with a nicotine buzz.

Linda handed me one of her Salem Light's. "Found a roommate yet?"

I shook my head. "I talked to two girls last week. One was a complete spazz and the other said she didn't have the cash for a security deposit, so I figured that didn't portend good things." I lit the cigarette with Linda's ancient brass Zippo. It was one of the kind of annoying, smaller, lady-sized versions.

"Beggars can't be choosers." Linda took a deep drag from her Salem. She was one of those smokers who always stank; I'd been to her house to pick her up for a few shifts when her car was in the shop, and even her Lhasa Apso smelled like it smoked. It was rough.

"I disagree. Not in principle, but in this specific situation, I can choose. Letting some girl who can't even pay the deposit move in sounds like a recipe for disaster, don't you think?"

"I guess." Linda grabbed a napkin and spread it out over the table. "What are you going to do instead, move home?"

Linda had been my confidante at work for months. She was the wizened, hardened old waitress who'd had dozens of jobs in places ranging from diners to upscale eateries. She'd raised two sons by herself with the money she made waiting tables. She was exactly like my mom, if my mom were able to keep her nose clean and stop sleeping with any loser who'd have her out of a fear of being alone for longer than three minutes. I'd have been happy to swap the two of them. Anytime I felt tired or wanted to complain about coming in for a shift when I had a lot of class work hanging over my head, I reminded myself that I had it easier than Linda ever did. I respected the shit out of her.

I took a tentative drag off the cigarette. Holding one always made me feel a little funny, so I rested it in the glass ashtray that was sitting on the table. "I'll move home if I have to."

Linda stopped folding the silverware and stared at me. "Like hell. You'll come live with me before I let that happen."

I shuddered a little at the thought of going to class smelling like Linda's ranch house. "It's not going to come to that."

"What else are you going to do to try and find someone to live with?"

I finished wrapping a place setting and slammed it into the plastic tub that was still only about one-quarter full after the busy night. "Can we talk about something else, please? There really isn't anything I can do about this at the moment."

Linda looked at me with some annoyance. "Fine. Jesus. I was only trying to help."

I picked up the cigarette from the ashtray and inhaled. "I know. I'm sorry. I'm stressed."

"That temper's going to bite you in the ass if you're not careful. Devin's dad had a temper like that, he yelled at some guy in the Farmer Jack parking lot one time and the guy got out of his car and punched him right in the face. Knocked out four teeth. You want to lose some teeth?"

It was far more likely that my temper would cost me a job, but I didn't want to argue. I knew Linda was only looking out for me. "I don't."

"So, you don't want to talk about your apartment. What do you want to talk about?" Linda took a last drag from her cigarette and stubbed it out in the ashtray. Mine was only half gone.

"Why don't you come with me to Bob's for a drink tonight?"

She crinkled her face. "I told you I'm not going to that hellhole."

Napkin down, knife first, followed by spoon and then fork. Roll. Repeat. "And I told you it's not the same place. A young guy bought it a few years ago. Everybody who hangs out there is young now."

Linda held her arms out in a look-at-me gesture. "Is that supposed to sell me on going? So I can be the old broad?" She laughed.

I took another short drag from the cigarette and then put it out. It tasted stale, as though it were itself infused with the stale smell of smoke from Linda's house. "One day I'll get you in there. You'll see."

"I've been there."

My eyes went wide. "When? Why didn't you tell me?"

"It was years ago. I was going out with a guy who went there sometimes. It's a hellhole, and that neighborhood is full of crack heads."

I remembered the drug deal I saw the last time I was there. I shook my head. "The owner has a bunch of cop friends that patrol the area frequently."

"That's great for him. There's no way they could get the old man stink out of that place. I wouldn't be surprised if several of those old-timers died in that place."

"Alright I get it -- you don't want to go." I finished another silverware roll and put it in the bin. We were more than halfway done now.

Linda finished her roll and reached for her cigarettes. "We'll go sometime, I promise. Just not on a Friday."

Bob's was usually pretty packed on weekend nights. But Charlie didn't work Fridays, so it was safe for me to go. I was still avoiding him and his stinky knuckle. "Promise?"

Linda nodded as she lit her Salem. The air filled with the stale menthol. "And I promise that everything's going to work out."

"I know." Napkin down, knife first, followed by spoon and then fork.

"Look at me, Molly."

I paused and looked up. "I mean it. You need anything, you let me know. Anything." She took a drag. "You can't go back there."

I felt grateful. Linda was harsh to a lot of our co-workers, and she took little to no shit from the cooks who gave the rest of the wait staff a hard time from open to close. But she was so sweet to me. She wanted to protect me, and there was a part of me that wanted to let her.

Napkin down, knife first, followed by spoon and then fork. I put another roll in the plastic bin.

"Can I have another one of those Salem's, Linda?"

***

I made it a point to get cut from Hamilton's early the next couple of Tuesdays and hang out at Bob's while Drew was working. He was easy to talk to, and even though he got busier with each successive week, he still made time to chat with me about music and school and the service industry.

I guess I was waiting for him to ask me out. Truth be told, dating someone was a complication I didn't need at that moment, with Nicole already moved out and her dad's gravy train set to dry up in a few weeks. I'd put off signing the next lease with some dodging and parrying, and the realty company was losing patience with me. But no matter how I crunched the numbers, I'd be coming up a few hundred short every month if I stayed. I asked around and looked at a couple of places in the States, but there were some scraggly-looking hookers at the corner near one of the buildings and the other had extensive, unrepaired water damage that the leasing agent said happened when the prior tenant on the floor above passed out while running the bath and flooded the bathroom. He didn't say drugs were involved, but I wasn't sure how else one would pass out and flood their own apartment.

It wasn't looking good.

I was running out of options, not that I had very many to start with. It probably wasn't the best idea for me to waste ten bucks a couple of times a week on pints at Bob's, but getting to know Drew was a pleasant diversion.

Besides, there were some other women who'd begun to take notice of the new guy. I noticed a few girls making googly eyes at him, and there was even some graffiti about him in the women's room. My favorite was "Drew: The Cleanest Bartender at Bob's." I wondered if he noticed this stuff on the walls when he cleaned up the bathrooms, but I didn't ask. It would have been as embarrassing for me as it was for him, and I got the sense that Drew was easily embarrassed.

I normally cut myself off after two pints on Tuesdays, but on my third trip, I let the competition get the better of me. I was well into beer number four and I was starting to feel a little loose. Drew was down the bar a bit, chatting with a couple of what looked like swing dance chicks who kept giggling a lot and playing with their hair. Both of them. It looked to me like Drew was about to back his way into a threesome. I downed the rest of the beer in my glass and got his attention.

He walked down my way, smiling. I wasn't sure if it was for me or he was still grinning from talking to the Swing Out Sisters. "Hey, Miss Molly. Did you know the Old 97s wrote a song about you?"

I shook my head. "Nope." I pushed my empty glass across the bar. "Did you know those two are trying to get you into bed?" I pointed down the bar.

Drew followed my finger in the direction of the two women who were now both glaring at me. "Those two?" He shrugged. "I think I might have caught herpes just standing that close to them."

I laughed. "So you're not into the three-way scene?"

"No way." Drew grabbed my pint glass. "Sometimes, I can hardly keep up with one woman. What would I do with two?"

"You're just saying that."

"I'm not. I'm not saying that I would be unhappy with having two naked women in close proximity. Naked women are in my top three favorite things. Top two, really. But there's something totally implausible about attempting to satisfy both of these theoretical women."

I smiled. "Now you sound like you're doing a bit."

He grinned. "Maybe I am." He shook my glass in his right hand. "Are you having another?"

I nodded.

"You're way over your normal limit." He looked down at his shoes. "This is also the first time we've ever talked about sex. I was starting to think you were asexual or something."

I could feel how red my face was. "I'm not asexual." I rolled my eyes. "Would you just get that beer?"

Drew gave me a sort of salute. "Aye, aye."

I watched him head down the bar to pour my beer. He took another couple of drink orders as he was down there. I hadn't looked around much, but the bar was sort of filling up as the hour stretched past eleven, and the ratio of women to men was at least two-to-one. I watched him interact with the customers, and although a few more of the women were pretty clearly flirting with him, he seemed either blissfully or willfully unaware. He was friendly and amiable, but he had none of Charlie's predatory stance or Ralph's stoned charm. I'm pretty sure I'd never witnessed such a lack of guile in an attractive male bartender.

It took him several minutes to come back with my beer, and he was too busy to talk with me as I sipped from it. I slid a five across the bar, told him to keep it, and he smiled and thanked me. I knew that I should finish and head home, and maybe try and wake up early to work on some reading for my Advanced PR class. I'd already breached a gap that was between us by revealing my sexual interest in him. It was obvious he'd be thinking about that after I left, and probably even more so if I remained mysterious. But something kept me nursing that beer and glued to the stool.

As I waited and drank, a guy in a Western Michigan sweatshirt sat next to me and asked if he could buy me a drink. I didn't even look over at him before saying "No, thanks," and he slinked away to his table of bros. I wasn't sure if Drew noticed, but things calmed down for a few minutes and he quickly made his way back to my end of the bar. After my frat boy suitor moved on, I looked down the bar and noticed that the threesome girls had given up and moved on, probably to the swing dance bar whose name I could never remember and whose ability to stay in business I could hardly fathom.

With the fifth beer, I crossed the line from slightly brave to slightly sloppy. "Drew, where do you live?"

He lit a Camel Light, exhaled and smiled. "That's following a train of thought."

I looked down at the bar. "You don't want to tell me."

He shook his head. "I don't like to go around trumpeting the fact that I live with my mom in the suburbs."

The filter between brain and mouth had lost its interlocutor with my last sip of Anchor Steam. "You can stay with me."

Drew smiled in a way that might have been patronizing. "That's nice." He took a drag from his cigarette. "I think you've had a little too much to drink for that to be a good idea."

I felt like an idiot. I needed to save face. "I meant stay as in rent a room. My roommate's moving out. I'll have to find a new place if I can't find someone to share the rent."

He scrunched his brow in thought. He sort of stepped back and looked at me, as though he was trying to focus on something that he hadn't seen before. "That's intriguing. Where's your place?"

"Near campus. It's nice. An old colonial that was converted into a duplex. Wood floors, big living room."

Drew nodded. "And the rent?"

I was starting to feel a little excited, anticipating a solution to my biggest problem. "Three hundred and the utilities which average about fifty or seventy-five a month. Heat's included."

Down the bar, one of Drew's new female fans was trying to get his attention. He pointed at her as a signal that he'd be right over. "I want to talk more about this, but it's a little busy right now. Maybe I could come over tomorrow or the next day?"

I nodded and grabbed a cocktail napkin. "Got a pen back there? I'll give you my number."

"Yeah, hold on." He went toward the center of the back bar near the cash register, poked around and returned with a blue Bic and handed it to me.

I wrote my phone number on the napkin and slid it across the bar. I hoped it was legible.

Drew looked at the number and then shoved the napkin in his pocket. He smiled at me. "You've had a few tonight. How are you getting home?"

"I'm fine."

He stared at me.

"Really."

He didn't blink.

"I'll call my co-worker."

"Good. I'll call you tomorrow."

He moved down the bar towards the girl who was waiting to place a drink order. She was a cute brunette, sort of tall and thin, with cat's eye eyeglass frames and a too-small t-shirt. She looked over at me and glared a little.

I smiled and winked. No competition.

❉❉❉

Linda and I had just started in on what had become our Friday night ritual of cigarettes and silverware. She looked especially tired that night, and I'd noticed that she was wearing more makeup than usual. Linda was exactly my height, probably wore the same size bra, had frizzy hair that she kept bleached, which made it even frizzier. I imagined we looked like mother and daughter to the uninitiated, and it scared me a little. I didn't see myself as a younger Linda.

Linda lit her Salem, then reached over with her Zippo to light the cigarette hanging from my lips. "Look alive, Molly."

I sucked in on the flame and then pulled away, exhaling smoke. "Sorry. Lost in thought."

Linda took a drag from her cigarette and then placed it in the ashtray. "We didn't get a chance to dish on the details. When does he move in?"

"He's going to do it slowly over the next few weeks. He's already paid up."

Linda picked up her cigarette and took a long, slow drag. "And do you like him?"

"As in a crush?"

She nodded.

"I did. He's cute, smart. Funny. He's also hung up on an ex-girlfriend."

Linda pursed her lips and shook her head. "Of course. The good ones always get fucked over."

"It's fine. I think it's better that things remain uncomplicated." Napkin down, knife first, followed by spoon and then fork.

"Uncomplicated? Not likely."

I took a shallow drag from the cigarette, which made my head spin a little. "What are you saying?"

"Do you know how they get animals to procreate in captivity? They just put them in the same cage." Linda slammed a silverware roll into the tub.

"I'm an animal in this scenario?"

"That's not what I mean. Is he attracted to you?"

I shrugged. "He's hard to read."

"In my experience, men are pretty much attracted to anything with a pussy."

I was surprised to hear Linda speak this way. She'd always been more of a mother figure than someone who talks about pussy. "I can't disagree."

"And I read somewhere years ago, and it's always stuck with me, that women know within the first five seconds of meeting someone whether or not they'd fuck them."

I looked up from the silverware. First pussy, now fuck, and not as an exclamation when dousing sour cream on the front of her shirt.

This was rarified air. "What are you saying exactly? And don't dress it up with some shit from *Life* magazine."

"Okay." Linda grabbed her cigarette from the ashtray and held it. "How are you going to feel when and if he brings a girl back to your apartment and has sex with her?"

"I won't care."

She pointed the cigarette at me. "I don't believe you." She took a drag.

I laughed. "How am I going to win that argument? Ever? If I say it will bother me, then it will bother me. If I say it won't, you say it will bother me."

"They put 'em in the same cage, Molly."

Napkin down, knife first, followed by spoon and then fork. "Stop saying that."

"Okay. Let's say you bring a guy home. You won't feel awkward with him in the other bedroom? Listening? Knowing what's happening?"

"Linda, that's creepy regardless of gender." I took another shallow drag from the Salem. "I'll admit it isn't an ideal solution. But it is a solution nonetheless."

Linda smirked. "That's all I wanted to hear you say. You sounded like some sort of Pollyanna."

I'm pretty sure no one had ever called me a Pollyanna before. I wasn't a glass half full type, to put it mildly. It made me happy to think I was being subconsciously positive, even if it turned out to be misguided.

"That's me. Mollyanna."

✳✳✳

The following Wednesday, I stopped in at Bob's for a quick beer shortly after they opened. It was time to face the embarrassment of dealing with Charlie, something I'd been putting off for far too long.

I had never been to the bar in the afternoon before. As I opened the door, the scent of Pine-Sol was overwhelming. The place was almost empty; Charlie was at the end of the bar with two yokels and an old man. As I walked in, they didn't stop their conversation, and because the jukebox was silent, it was easy to overhear.

One of the yokels, a guy who looked to be in his mid-forties with a thick moustache and a logo-less green baseball cap, slapped his open palm on the bar. "Wait, Tom Hanks was on a TV show?"

"You don't remember *Bosom Buddies?*" The second yokel was about the same age, with a mop of unkempt light brown hair and those round frame glasses that looked good on Sting ten years earlier. "It was on ABC in the early eighties."

Charlie looked tired. "He and Peter Scolari played these two guys who dressed as women so they could live in an all-girls building in New York."

The mustachioed yokel looked confused. "Peter Scolari?"

Charlie was visibly annoyed. "He played Stephanie's boyfriend on *Newhart.*" He gave the yokels a hold-on gesture and walked towards the other end of the bar where I'd sat. "Hey there, Stranger. Can I get you a beer?"

I nodded. "Anchor draft."

"You got it." Charlie grabbed a pint glass off the back bar and moved to pour the beer. As he brought it back, he was smirking a little. "Sorry I didn't call."

I shook my head. "Don't think twice."

He pointed at the beer. "On me."

"I'll pay." I reached into my pocket and pulled out a five. "Is it always this busy in the afternoon?"

Charlie looked at the other end of the bar where the yokels were still talking about eighties sitcoms and the old man looked as though he might fall asleep. He shrugged. "Later in the afternoon, some lawyers and other downtown workers come in. But I think they've been coming in when Drew works lately."

I smirked a little at this. "Any idea why that is?"

Charlie turned to look at me. "He's the new guy. People always like the new guy. Same thing happened when Ralph started."

I wondered if self-awareness would come to Charlie all at once or in spurts. "Why no women bartenders?"

"Phil doesn't want that."

I took a sip of my beer. It tasted a little flat. "Aren't you part owner? You could throw your weight around."

He smiled. "I guess I don't want it either."

"Of course not."

At the other end of the bar, the conversation had stuck on *Perfect Strangers*. I wasn't here to listen to a couple of dimwits discuss Balki and Cousin Larry.

Charlie took the pack of Marlboro Reds out of his shirt pocket, removed a cigarette and lit it. "So why haven't I seen you for like a month anyway?"

I didn't feel like shattering his delusions by mentioning his stench and the knuckle. "No reason. Just busy."

Charlie dragged on his cigarette and nodded. "Right on."

"There is something I want to talk to you about."

Charlie put the cigarette in an ashtray and then leaned forward with his palms on the bar. "Fire away."

I felt my ears get hot. "You didn't tell anyone about that night last month, did you?"

He looked a little confused. "I'm not like that."

I took a sip of my beer. "Not even Drew?"

Charlie backed away from the bar and looked even more confused. He thought for a moment before speaking. "You're into Drew?"

I shook my head. "He's moving into my apartment."

His face looked as though he was trying to do long division without using scrap paper. "You two are together? When did this happen?"

"You're not listening, Charlie. We're not dating. He's just sharing rent. My roommate moved out; I needed a new one."

He took a deep drag from his cigarette. "So what difference would it make if he knew we slept together?"

I wasn't sure how to answer that. "None, I guess. I just don't want it to complicate things."

Charlie looked down the bar and then back at me. "What's it worth to you?"

"What are you talking about?"

He smiled. "Sleep with me again and I won't tell him."

It hadn't occurred to me that Charlie needed to resort to blackmail in order to get laid. "I'm not going to do that."

"All of a sudden you've got morals or something?"

I could feel my face turning red, my hands shaking a little. I took a sip of my beer and a breath. "You don't want me to lose my temper and embarrass you in front of your friends down there, do you?"

Charlie held out his hands in an "I surrender" gesture. "It was worth a shot to see those tits again." He pointed at my chest.

"You're a pig." I stood to leave. "And you fucking smell like one, too."

Charlie smiled and then took a drag from his cigarette. "I guess that makes you a pigfucker."

"I should have known better than to think you'd be decent."

He nodded. "Yes, you should have."

I looked around for something to throw at him, my nostrils flaring and my fists clenched tight. I remembered what Linda told me about her husband getting his teeth knocked out, and took a couple of deep breaths and realized I was giving Charlie exactly what he wanted.

I calmly sat and took another sip of my beer. "You can tell Drew whatever you want. And I'll be happy to tell whoever will listen that you're the worst lay of my life."

Charlie put out his cigarette and laughed. He looked at me and winked. "Right back at ya."

I sighed. "You win. Go talk to your backwoods fan club down there. Let me drink my beer in peace."

"No problem, Tits. Have a good one."

I wasn't sure what I'd ever found charming about Charlie. Maybe it was that he'd caught me on a night where I was feeling sad and lonely and disappointed to be in Flint.

But that was temporary. Flint was temporary. I'd get my degree and get the fuck out and never look back. Fuck this town and everyone in it. Fuck my mom's creepy boyfriend who climbed into bed with me and fuck my mom for not believing that it happened. Fuck the people I went to high school with for making my life hell. Fuck UM-Flint and the fact that it mostly held people I'd gone to high school with who'd made my life hell. Fuck Hamilton's and the under-tipping blue hairs who came in there and ran me around for water with vinegar and well-done filets. Fuck Bob's. Fuck Charlie.

Flint was only temporary.

KATHY & BOYD

My youngest son looked at me with a weary resignation. I suppose I should be used to that look by now, but somehow it still managed to make me sad. It stood to reason that he grew up a little too fast, which also made me sad. At these moments, I felt less like his mother and more like a clingy ex-girlfriend, which is creepy, I know. He dropped the garbage bag full of clothes he was carrying onto the couch next to where I was sitting. He sat on the other side.

"I need to feel like there's some movement in my life, Mom. I guess I want to feel a little more mature, responsible for myself." Drew slumped back into the cushions and moved to place his sneakers on the coffee table, but thought better of it and put them on the floor.

He called me Kathy at least ninety-nine percent of the time; he only called me Mom when he was being emotionally direct. Or patronizing me. I suppose this little speech could be some of each.

"I can understand that, Honey." I put my hand on his and looked at his face, which was a rounder version of his father's, with the same clipped nose and deep-set black eyes. Since he'd started bartending, his style has changed. He was favoring thrift-store polyester shirts over what I guess were band tee shirts. Today's was advertising something called Lambchop. I assumed it didn't have anything to do with Shari Lewis, unless the irony was running deeper than I'd been led to believe. "I'm not trying to make you feel guilty. It's been nice having you around. It's a little hard for me to be alone in this house."

Our cat Willie plodded into the room and rubbed his head on Drew's leg. Drew reached down and scratched him behind his left ear. "I'll be here a lot. You think I want to cook for myself every day?" He smiled.

"It's unfair of me to make you feel bad. I can't expect you to live here forever." Truthfully, I was also upset that Drew had decided to move to an apartment within Flint's city limits and with a woman his age who he claimed wasn't his girlfriend. We'd been lucky enough to be able to live in the safe and sound suburb of Grand Blanc, and I didn't understand my son's fascination with the failing city to our north. I also didn't understand members of the opposite sex sharing living quarters. *Three's Company* was a sitcom, not a guidebook for real life.

"Why don't you sell this place, Mom? Maybe move to Florida with Grandma?" Willie had jumped to Drew's lap and was pawing at the garbage bag that Drew had set next to the couch.

I gave Drew a sideways glance. "I would enjoy that about as much as you've liked living here."

"Fair enough. But if you sold the house, maybe you could do more traveling, visit Kevin and Jeff more often."

"Your brothers have enough on their plates as it is. They don't need me puttering around their houses, annoying their wives and children." I reached over to pet Willie, but he was a little overstimulated and swatted at my hand.

Drew played with a Band-Aid that covered a cut on his left thumb knuckle. "Well, if you're just going to disagree with every suggestion I have, then I don't know what else to say. But if staying in this house alone is too hard, then I think you should do something about that."

Willie jumped off of Drew's lap and ambled towards the kitchen.

I nodded.

***

"Kathy, everything will be fine. The severance will cover our planned expenses for the next eighteen months. Kevin won't have to withdraw. I'm sure in that time, I'll be able to find something else." Roger moved his unlit cigarette between his hands and wouldn't meet my gaze.

"But you and the team were fired, Roger. Don't you think your reputation will precede when you look for a job elsewhere?"

"In some ways. But there should also be a lot of understanding about the pressure the team was under. They pushed the platform through so quickly in order to compete with the Japanese. Without the proper amount of time for development, errors were inevitable. Everyone can understand that." Roger pulled a half-empty bottle of Crown Royal from the liquor curio, and then fetched a glass and some ice from the kitchen.

"We'll have to move. There's no way you'd be able to find a job in Flint." I pulled out one of the stools under the breakfast nook and sat. My mind was spinning with the permutations of selling the house, moving closer to Detroit, having Jeff and Drew change schools and seeing less of my mother and sister.

"Unfortunately, that might be true." Roger shook the ice in his glass to cool the whiskey. "I'm going to call John Weathers and see what he might have for me at Ford. If that were to come through, I could commute and we'd be able to stay."

"It would be hard for Jeff and Drew to start over in new schools." I looked out of the door wall at a hummingbird hovering at the feeder.

"I know. But we shouldn't jump to any conclusions about moving. There's still a chance we could stay here." Roger took a sip of his drink, keeping his eyes fixed on me over the lip of the upturned glass. I could tell he was scared. I was going to have to comfort him.

"I'm sorry, Roger." I reached for his hand. "There's a lot to consider right now, so much to digest. I haven't even asked how you're feeling."

"That's alright." He put his hand in mine with a relaxed sigh. "I'll be fine. The hardest part was saying goodbye to everyone. Jim Peterson took it especially hard. He was sobbing. That was hard to take."

This was a strange mental picture; the big, tough Swede we'd known for years was certainly not the crying kind.

Roger finished his drink with a large gulp and set about pouring himself another. "I feel like we were set up to fail, Kath. They knew this platform was going out with flaws and that once those were obvious, the whole team would be readymade sacrificial lambs. It's hard not to feel angry."

I looked back out at the feeder, but the hummingbird had moved on. The afternoon sun seemed incongruous with Roger in the kitchen. "How are we going to tell the boys?"

Roger finished his drink and shrugged. He looked at me as if to say something.

So many men to comfort.

***

My sister stood over the kitchen island, warming her hands on the coffee cup sitting on the breakfast nook in front of her. "With Drew moving out, I think you should consider dating. What have you got to lose? If you don't like Boyd, then what's the worst-case scenario? Free dinner."

Rose took a sip of her coffee and waited for me to respond.

I stared at her.

"The boys are grown. Roger's been dead almost a decade. When are you going to do something for yourself?"

My sister was right. I wasn't getting any younger. "Wouldn't doing this man Boyd be more for him than me?"

Rose gave me an I'm-not-amused look. "Hilarious. But I wouldn't try and set this up if I didn't think it could work. He's a very nice man, a strong Catholic. He's successful. I think he's handsome."

"You think?" I fixed a stare at Rose with a crooked eyebrow.

"What do you want me to tell you? He's not an Adonis, Kath. But he's tall and distinguished-looking. He's got a lot of style, too. Very well-dressed, nicely groomed."

"The natural question is why he hasn't been snatched up before now." I walked over to the coffee maker to freshen my cup.

"He's always been pretty career-focused. When his wife left, I think he let that part of his life carry him through the loneliness. I've worn him down about taking you out long enough that he might only be doing it in order to shut me up."

I stirred some cream into my coffee and then stuck my pinky in to test the temperature. "This sounds better by the minute, Rose. Before you dig the hole any deeper, why don't you just set something up for next weekend?"

Rose smiled.

***

Drew exited Holy Family first, pausing to cross himself before walking down the front stairs to wait for me. He turned around to face the front of the church, shielding his eyes from a quickly warming sun.

"Hi, Honey." I gave him a quick hug. "You should have come to sit with me. We would have made room for you."

"I know, but I was a little late so I snuck in back."

He was unshaven and looked extremely tired, but I was happy to see him. "Can I take you to breakfast?"

Drew looked at his watch and then at me. "Yeah, alright. Do you want to ride over together? I'll drive." He fished for his keys in his pocket. His Geo Prizm was parked within sight as we walked around the church.

He settled in behind the wheel and grabbed his Ray-Ban sunglasses from a clip on the visor. These were the same pair he'd bought for himself in high school. Unlike his older brothers, Drew took meticulous care of his possessions. He was like his father in this regard.

"Drew, I really wish you'd replace this car. I'd be happy to help you get something new." I looked around the spotless interior.

"No need, Mom." He started the engine. "This thing runs like a top. It's a ninety-one, it's not like it's ancient or anything. Plus, it's got Toyota guts, it'll run forever." He put the car in reverse and eased out of his parking spot, taking his place in the line of cars waiting to exit onto Saginaw Street.

"Well, if you change your mind, just let me know. We can always use Jeff's Toyota discount to get you a new Camry or even something fun like a 4Runner."

He shook his head. "Something that gets me from point A to point B is plenty."

Drew had always been practical. My efforts to spoil him after his father died had been met with resistance. When I tried to buy him a new computer for college, he told me he'd be fine using the labs on campus. I should have considered myself lucky.

I looked at the CDs that Drew kept in the center console. I didn't recognize any of the names. "I have something I want to tell you."

He stiffened in his seat, seemingly bracing himself for bad news. "I'm not sure I like the sound of that." He turned the car out of the church parking lot.

"Oh, I'm sorry, I didn't mean to make it sound like it's something bad." I paused, trying to decide on the correct word. "It's just different."

He took a pack of cigarettes out of his shirt pocket and pulled one out with his lips. Roger used to do the same thing. "Alright. I'm waiting."

"Your Aunt Rose has browbeat me into agreeing to go on a date."

"I think that's great." There was genuine excitement in his voice. "Who is this guy?"

192

"His name's Boyd Wesley. He was Rose's boss when she worked at the insurance agency."

Drew smiled at me. "Are you nervous? When are you going out?"

"Of course I'm nervous, Honey. I haven't been on a date with a man in over thirty-five years. He's picking me up Friday night."

"This is great. I can't believe Rose finally got through to you." He exhaled smoke out of his car window.

"It's just one blind date," I said with a smile.

"I know, but I think it's exciting. What made you agree to go out with him?" Drew took a right onto Fenton, toward the Venus Family Restaurant.

"I'm not sure. Rose said he's a nice man, a good Catholic. His wife left him a few years ago, and she said he's been very lonely since then."

"Wait a minute, you said his last name's Wesley? I wonder if he's Monica Wesley's dad. You remember her?" He flicked cigarette ash out the window.

"No, I don't think so."

"She was a year behind me in school. She went out with Aaron when we were juniors and she was a sophomore."

Aaron had always been a bad influence in my estimation. He was a charismatic little twerp, but he knew it. "Wasn't she the girl who was throwing up at our house all night at your prom after-party?"

"That's her. Last I heard, she'd gone to Marquette." Drew threw the butt of his cigarette out of the car and rolled up the window. "I wouldn't hold that episode against him as a parent, though. She was probably just acting out because of the divorce."

"Those in glass houses. There'd be plenty of opportunity to impugn my parenting skills if people held the high school drinking habits of my children against me."

Drew laughed. "Touché."

Rose placed another saucepan in the dishwasher and closed the door. She turned the knob to start the wash cycle and went back to the sink to begin rinsing out more of the accumulated piles of glasses, serving dishes and silverware.

I've never been certain why there is so much food involved when someone dies. Of course, life goes on, and the community assumes the aggrieved don't have the energy or drive to cook for themselves, but still. The mounds of detritus and dirty dishes in my kitchen suggested that my friends, family, and fellow parishioners were over for some grand celebration rather than to console me after my husband wrapped his car around a tree in Mundy Township last Friday night.

"Rose, give it a rest for a minute. Just come in here and sit for a while." Our mother was at the dining room table with an accordion-style folder in front of her. "The dishes will still be there in a half hour."

My sister wiped her hands on a dishtowel and joined us in the dining room. "I was just trying to make a dent in the mess in there."

"We need to help Kathy with some of the practical matters. Larry Meyer is handling the will, but we've got Roger's papers here. Since I've been through this twice before, I thought I could teach you what needs to be done while I show Kathy." My mother opened the folder that contained all of Roger's necessary paperwork. To Be Opened Only in Case of Death.

Rose looked at our mother. "This is pretty fucking morbid, Mom."

"How else do you think it is done, Rosemary?" snapped my mother. "Do you think a magical fairy flies in and makes all of the arrangements? Don't be such a child."

Rose unconsciously stuck out her bottom lip as she was scolded. My mother and Rose had some major difficulties transitioning into a more adult version of a parent/child relationship, to put it mildly.

"First and foremost, Kathleen, we need to find the life insurance policy. It's important we contact them and settle that claim." She began to rifle through the folder. "Here it is." She pulled a paper-clipped stack of papers out, removed the clip and then started leafing through them. "Oh my God," she exclaimed as she brought her left hand to her mouth.

"Mom, what is it?" I was afraid of the answer. Roger had been fairly inattentive when it came to keeping our affairs in order of late, and I envisioned a lapsed policy.

"Were you aware your husband's policy was for two million dollars?"

I was not.

***

"May I get you a drink before dinner?" Our waiter was impeccably dressed in a black shirt and pants that were so crisp, it looked as though he had them pressed in-between trips to his tables.

I closed the wine menu, which was filled with vintages and vineyards I couldn't begin to decipher. "I'd like a glass of the house Merlot."

"And I'll have a Dalwhinnie on the rocks, please." Boyd's manners, to this point in the evening, were as faultless as the waiter's clothes.

"I'll be right back with those." The waiter turned on a dime and headed towards the bar.

"That's an interesting drink choice. I have to admit that I don't know what a Dalwhinnie is." I reached to take a nervous sip from my water glass and then took another look around the restaurant. It was dark but nicely decorated, with lots of blood red accents livening up the mahogany wood tables. It was a new place that was highly regarded, with some sort of food called fusion. I wouldn't have chosen this place on my own, but didn't want to seem out of touch when Boyd suggested it.

"It's a single malt scotch. Frankly, I ordered it in an effort to impress you." Boyd laughed.

"Mission accomplished, then. It sounded very sophisticated."

"Yes, maybe. But now I'm stuck drinking a glass of pine needle juice. I'm not sure I really thought that through."

I gave this a genuine laugh. Boyd was charming, and he seemed at least as nervous as I was. He was exactly as Rose described him: he was dressed in a smart black suit with a simple blue tie. He appeared so natural in these clothes that they almost looked casual. Boyd was tall, well over six feet, with a sparkling head of gray hair that had enough length to it to be worn pushed back from his scalp. I always appreciate gray hair on a man, even though I've been dying mine since I was twenty-eight.

"Your sister tells me you're very involved in the parish at Holy Family. It's a nice parish. The church itself is very lovely."

Our waiter returned with our drinks and Boyd asked for a few more minutes to look over the menus, which we had forgotten to even open at this point.

Boyd sipped his drink and then winced as he placed the glass down on the table. "Oh, that's rough."

"You really don't need to force that down on my account."

"Oh, thank God. It's truly awful." He pushed the glass aside as though its very presence was troubling. "What is it you do at Holy Family?"

"I volunteer a couple of days a week to help with the bookkeeping. I've also been running the clothing drives for years."

Boyd nodded. "Bev and I joined St. Michael when we moved here in sixty-five. I've thought about switching parishes, but every Sunday, muscle memory forces me downtown. I'm a creature of habit, I guess."

The waiter came back for our dinner orders. We rushed through the menu and decided on entrees. Boyd also asked for a light beer, presumably to wash out the remaining pine taste.

"Are you still in touch with your ex-wife?" I took a sip of my wine.

"Monica, our youngest, is in her senior year at Marquette. Discussing her school expenses is about as deep as it goes. Once she graduates, I assume we won't speak until it comes time to plan her wedding."

"Monica went to school with my youngest, Drew." I remembered Drew's prom date holding Boyd's daughter's hair back as she hugged our downstairs toilet, but didn't see the need to relate the memory to my date. "How many other children do you have?"

"You didn't cover all of that with Rose? I must admit I'm a little surprised. Stephen, our oldest, is an attorney in Columbus. Laura is Monica's older sister; she's in graduate school at Emory. We quit at three."

"That's a weird coincidence. Roger and I had three, too. All boys, in our case."

"It's why I'm surprised Rose didn't mention my children, because she told me all about yours. Let's see what I can remember. The oldest is in Phoenix; he's a veterinarian? I can't remember his name, though."

"That's Kevin; very good."

The waiter returned with Boyd's replacement drink.

Boyd took a sip from the beer, which came in a tall, thin pilsner glass. "I remember Jeff's name, and that he's an engineer for Toyota in Atlanta. And Drew just recently graduated from State. What is he doing now?"

"Drew's a little lost at the moment. He took his father's death the hardest. He was still in high school, and they were never close." I fiddled with the napkin in my lap.

Boyd nodded. "The youngest always gets short shrift to some degree."

197

"I suppose you're right. Anyway, he's working as a bartender at a place downtown. Coincidentally, he just moved out of the house a few weeks ago."

"I wouldn't worry about him too much. He did get his Bachelor's, right?"

Drew had graduated cum laude with a degree in American Studies, but I really had no idea what that was. He was supposed to start graduate school, but he'd had a blow-up with his girlfriend and came sulking home. I was never able to find out exactly what happened with Megan, and I didn't try and press him for details. "He did get a degree, yes."

"I don't see anything wrong with a little breather after finishing school. Something will come along soon to shake him out of the malaise, I'm sure." He took a large drink from his pilsner glass.

We spent the next few minutes in child-related chitchat until our salads arrived. After nibbling at those for a bit, my mind wandered back to what had happened with Drew's girlfriend, Megan. She was a great girl, very different from the types that Drew brought around in high school. Megan was driven, and unless her plans had changed as well, then she was just about to start her second year in medical school.

"If this is too forward, then by all means tell me. But can I ask why you and Bev split up?"

Boyd put his fork down and finished chewing. "Well, to put it simply, she was having an affair with my ex-business partner, Charlie Greeson. After I found out, they moved in together and have been married since."

I felt like an asshole for asking. "I'm sorry. You must have been devastated."

"I was, truthfully. People told me I must have suspected something was going on, but the worst part is that I didn't. Well, maybe I shouldn't say that was the worst part." He laughed, and put his hand in front of his mouth. "It's taken me a hell of a long time to be able to laugh about any of it, that's for sure."

"I would expect so. When did this happen?" I pushed my half-eaten salad aside.

Boyd grabbed a slice of bread from the basket in the center of the table and started buttering it. "Four years ago, in March." He took a bite and chewed.

"What happened with your children?"

"Monica stayed with me until she went to college, and I've been alone in the house since then. They're forever telling me I should sell it and get something smaller. That seems like admitting a sort of defeat, for some reason."

"I know what you mean. The boys are always after me to sell, too." I finished my glass of wine, the second before dinner. I needed to slow down. "Boyd, I want to tell you something."

"What's that?" Boyd finished his bread and then washed it down with a sip of his beer.

I took a deep breath and looked over at our waiter, who appeared to be flirting with the busboy. I hadn't pegged him as gay. "When Roger had his accident, he was in the car with another woman. He was driving her home from a hotel. The receipt was in his jacket pocket. She was his secretary, twenty-four years old."

Boyd looked at me sympathetically. He reached for my hand, which I took out of my lap and placed in his.

"Kathy, I know. I settled Roger's life insurance claim."

***

Drew climbed off of the stepladder and reached into his small toolbox for a tape measure.

I handed him the pencil that I was keeping behind my ear. "These curtains are really going to change the room." Drew's apartment was looking a little lifeless, so I'd bought him some things to help add a little personality. Apparently, the woman he was sharing the apartment with had a roommate who'd moved out and taken much of the furniture with her. The new recliner and bookshelves were being delivered that afternoon, so I thought we'd hang the window treatments before they arrived.

"You're right." He climbed back up the ladder and made his measurements, marking his spots with the pencil. "It'll look nice. I know it was a little too dorm-y in here."

This neighborhood was one of the few remaining safe spots in the city. I'd rather he'd have chosen an apartment complex in one of the suburbs, but he insisted on staying close to his job. "It's time to leave the collegiate style behind."

He laughed a little and sat on the couch. "It's true, I'm not in college anymore." He put his sneakers up on the coffee table, maybe in a defiant show of what he could do without me around to nag him. "It's a nice Saturday. Why aren't you doing something with Boyd today? Antiquing or whatever you old folks do."

I sat at the other end of the couch and looked at Drew's shoes and then the floor. He didn't respond. "We've been on three dates. It isn't serious."

"I'm glad my nosiness was that obvious." He looked at the wall where he'd made and marked his measurements. "I'm a little worried about putting holes in the wall here. It seems so permanent."

"We can always spackle and paint before you move out."

"Yeah." He grabbed a screwdriver and stood from the couch. "I'm not very handy, you know? I'm not sure I even know what spackle is."

I nodded and then grabbed the package of screws that had come with the new drapery rod. "Your dad didn't get the chance to teach you very much."

Drew gave me a thin-lipped smile. "I wasn't trying to make you feel bad. I can figure things out."

"I know you can." I handed him the package of screws.

Drew tossed the screwdriver in the air. It flipped over several times before he caught it with the handle. He did this a few more times. "Three dates is a lot. When's the fourth?"

I could feel the tips of my ears turn red. "We're having dinner tonight."

"I'm going to need to meet this young man soon, Kathy."

I gave him a wry smile. "Maybe soon."

"Do we need to have a discussion about proper ways for a lady to behave on a date?" Drew tossed the screwdriver around again.

My smile turned to a small frown. "Don't push this bit, Drew."

✳✳✳

Boyd pulled his Cadillac into the driveway and put the car in park, but he didn't turn off the ignition. I guess the next move would have to be mine.

"Would you like to come in for a drink or some coffee?"

Boyd nodded. In the garage light, I thought I could see some sweat on his brow, but it was not at all warm in the car. "I'd like that."

Once inside the house, I went into the living room to turn on the stereo. Faith Hill came through the speakers, reminding me to just breathe, which seemed like sound advice. "I hope you don't mind a little music. Drew makes fun of my taste all the time. I guess it's not very hip."

Boyd followed me into the living room and stood near the door. He seemed unsure about what to do with himself. "It's nice. I'm a bit more of a classic rock fan, I guess. Stuck in my youth with Dylan and the Stones."

"I think I was old before my time. When all of that new rock music was taking over, I was still listening to the Four Freshmen."

Boyd laughed. "Should I fix us a drink?"

"Oh, jeez. Where are my manners? Sit down and let me get the drinks. What would you like?"

"A beer would be fine."

I didn't drink beer, so I knew all that was there was what Drew had left behind. "All I have is something Drew didn't take with him. There's a party store up the street if you'd prefer something else."

"I'm sure it will be fine." He sat on the sofa, taking a position in the center cushion.

I went to the kitchen and found one of Drew's remaining beers behind a jar of mayonnaise. It was something I'd never heard of, and I wasn't even entirely sure it was beer. It seemed willfully obscure that he couldn't just drink Budweiser. I found a bottle opener and poured the beer into one of Roger's old U of M mugs. Fuck you, Roger. Then I took the wine stopper out of the bottle of Merlot I had opened a few nights before and poured myself a glass, which would bring my total for the night to four. I needed to slow down.

As I came back into the living room, Boyd stood to accept his drink.

"Thanks for the beer." He took a sip, and then lifted the mug in a positive gesture. "It's very tasty. Do you know what this is?"

"I think it's called Sierra Nevada Pale Ale."

"I'll have to remember that, I really like it." He tilted the mug back for a larger sip, and then sat back onto the couch. He chose the center cushion again.

"Can I get you anything else?"

Boyd rubbed his chin. "This might seem like a strange request, but do you have any cigarettes in the house? I haven't smoked for over twenty years, but for some reason I have the urge."

"Actually, Drew left half a pack in the kitchen that I was just about to throw out. If you don't mind, let's go out to the porch for that."

"Not at all. It's still pretty warm out." He stood, carrying the mug in his right hand.

On the way to the door wall, I stopped in the kitchen to root through the junk drawer for a pack of matches. I walked over and unlocked the door, and flicked on the porch light.

"After you," I said to Boyd.

Boyd walked onto the porch and sat on the edge of the cushioned chaise closest to the lawn. "Thanks for indulging me. I don't know why I was overcome with wanting a cigarette all of a sudden. I must be nervous."

I handed the pack and matches to him. "You're nervous? What for?"

He took a cigarette from the pack. It was a little wrinkled. He struck a match on the concrete under his feet and lit the end, choking a little on the inhale. "I'm...a little...out of practice." He stuttered between hacks.

I wondered if there was a double meaning. "Give me those." I reached for the pack. "You're crazy." I smiled at Boyd and then took a cigarette out of the pack. It was even more wrinkled than Boyd's.

He shrugged and took another drag from the cigarette.

I lit mine. It tasted stale, far closer to the smell of an ashtray than the soothing, warm version of smoke that normally sprang out of the rare moments of nostalgia for my days as a smoker.

I sat next to Boyd on the chaise. He put his arm around my waist and smiled at me. I looked up into his face and gave him a small kiss on the lips.

"I like you, Boyd. This has been such a nice evening."

"I like you too, Kathy. I've enjoyed getting to know you."

I kissed him again, this time with a little more purpose. As I moved to put my right hand on his shoulder, I momentarily forgot about the cigarette. The lit end caught on Boyd's sleeve as I moved, knocking the hot ash onto my right leg. I jerked up with a start, knocking my head into Boyd's nose as I did.

"Oh my God, I am so sorry." I brushed the ash out of my lap.

Boyd cupped his nose in his hands, still keeping his cigarette between the index and middle fingers of his right hand. "It's okay, I'm fine."

"I'm so embarrassed." I stubbed my cigarette out in the grass. "Are you sure you're alright?"

Boyd stood and removed his hands from his face. He looked them over to check for blood, finding none. "No blood, no foul." He chuckled. He inhaled again on his cigarette, dropped it on the concrete and then crushed it beneath his left shoe.

"Let's go back inside." I opened the screen door.

Boyd followed me, and we moved into the kitchen where I went to the freezer to get some ice for my date's red nose.

"Kathy, really, I'm fine. I don't need any ice."

"If you say so." I moved closer to him to get a look at the damage in the light. It really did appear to be fine. I stood on my tiptoes to kiss the tip of his nose. He grabbed me around the waist and pulled me closer to him.

"Boyd, before we go too far, there's something I want to tell you."

"Yes?"

I looked into his eyes and steeled my nerve. "I haven't been with a man since Roger died."

He touched my face and looked at me warmly. "We don't have to move too fast if you feel like you're not ready."

"It's not that." Boyd leaned in and kissed me, and I was warm with want and wine. As I began to lose myself in the moment, Boyd broke away from me and took a step backward. He kept his hands on my waist. I smiled shyly. "Let's go back and sit in the living room, okay?"

He waited for me to sit first, which I did at my usual spot on the sofa near the end table. Boyd sat next to me. We both smelled a little like the stale tobacco we'd ostensibly enjoyed. In a way, I expected Boyd to tell me he'd been sexless since his wife left and was a little disappointed when he didn't. Boyd leaned in to kiss me again, but I backed away.

"I have something to ask you."

He smiled. "Anything."

I looked at Roger's U of M mug on the table. "It's just that, when I told you about my years without sex, I thought maybe you'd tell me something similar."

Boyd sighed. "I can't say that, because it wouldn't be the truth."

"This is stupid. It's none of my business. We've only just met."

"No, you were honest with me." Boyd reached over for the beer and took a sip. He took a deep breath and exhaled loudly. "This is difficult."

Boyd tapped his left loafer on the carpet and looked at his hands.

I was starting to feel less flush and more nervous. "What is it Boyd? You can tell me."

"I'm not sure how to explain it."

I looked at him a little sideways. "I'm a big girl, Boyd. I've raised three boys. I think I've heard it all before."

"Since Bev left, it's been rough on me." He trailed off. He took a drink from the beer and kept tapping his toe. "I lost so much confidence. Maybe if I'd seen it coming in some way, it would have been different. But I was blindsided. I didn't want to meet anyone new. For a long time, I told your sister I didn't even want to meet you, for crying out loud."

I smiled. "I'm glad you relented." I reached over and touched Boyd's hands.

He didn't look up at me. That left toe kept tapping. It was starting to piss me off.

"Anyway, I still had needs, I guess is how I could say it, but I wasn't ready to move on emotionally."

I took my hand away. Boyd still kept his gaze fixed on his hands, which he'd started wringing.

"What are you trying to tell me, Boyd?"

He finally took his eyes from his hands and fixed them on me. "For the last few years, I've been visiting prostitutes fairly regularly."

"You've got to be fucking kidding me." Rose's voice was a little loud for the quiet lunch crowd at Benson's, and her comment caused a few neighboring tables to stare. She was undeterred. "Boyd Wesley? Hookers?"

"I'm not kidding, Rosemary." I kept my voice down, hoping we could continue the conversation with less attention. "I can't begin to imagine why he'd make that up."

"My God. I never would've guessed it. That's so gross." Rose poked her fork around the Cobb salad in front of her. "What did you do?"

"I was dumbfounded. It was completely unexpected. I didn't know how to react."

"Kathy, what did you do?"

"First, I felt angry. I wanted to throw him out. But then I remembered how sweet he'd been to me over the past few weeks. You know he's sent me two separate, very elaborate floral arrangements?"

Rose talked with a mouthful of egg and salami. "He gives whores money and then puts his dick in them. Maybe he sends them flowers, too?"

Clearly I wouldn't be able to explain myself to Rose. I wouldn't be able to explain that, even though part of me was disgusted at what Boyd had said, there was another part that admired his honesty. I wouldn't be able to explain that while the very thought of paying women for sex was repugnant, the need for gratification was acute and was something I could relate to. I wouldn't be able to explain that I was ready to move on and let another man touch me and love me and caress me, even if that man was someone I wasn't sure I ever wanted to see again afterward.

It all made perfect sense to me.

Rose poked me in the arm. "Kathy? What did you do?"

I took a sip of my Sierra Nevada Pale Ale and shrugged. "What do you think, Rose? I threw him out and told him never to call me again."

My sister made a theatrical swipe of her brow. "That was a close one. I thought you were going to tell me that you fucked him anyway."

I took my fork and speared a cherry tomato out of Rose's salad. "You set me up with the pervert, don't forget."

DREW & RAY

Sometimes I get tired of talking and talking about things and prefer to just take action. It's one of the few things my dad taught me that I still carry around. He always said action speaks louder than words. I suppose lots of people say that, but it remains exactly the sort of talk they're trying to outsmart by saying "actions speak louder than words." My dad really meant it. He'd say that anyone can talk about wanting to do this or be that or fix this or go there, but unless you took actual, physical, real steps to do it or be it or fix it or go there, then shut the fuck up about it. I've found it to be true, time and time again.

Action speaking louder than words is somewhat antithetical to life as a bartender, since so much of the job involves talking and talking with people who are clearly never going to take any sort of action on damn near one hundred percent of what they talk about. Eventually, it's a trap that can be easy to fall into. But I didn't want Ray and I to talk and talk about heading to the new ballpark in Detroit to see the Tigers, so I took action. I bought us a pair of tickets down the first base line, slapped them on the bar a couple of weeks before the game, and said, "Ray, we're going to see your Yanks."

Ray was characteristically nonchalant, but I like to think he was excited. On a practical level, Ray's life would appear dreary to any outsider; he's a lonely retiree living above the bar, landlocked because he can't drive, with no family visits that any of us know about. When I slow down and think about it, it's pretty dreary to an insider as well. Even though Ray and I may have commiserated about the loss of our beloved Tiger Stadium, the chance of spending a day in a place other than his apartment or the bar had to be appealing.

Although they'd tried to put together a competitive team, the Tigers had had a terrible April. They sandwiched their only two-game winning streak with losing streaks of five and eight games. They'd traded half their farm system for former MVP Juan Gonzalez, who looked like he was waving a wet noodle at the plate. By mid-May, they were firmly entrenched in *la toilette*, which really didn't sound any better in French. I loved the Tigers no matter what, and I always did my best to remain optimistic, but even .500 was looking unrealistic.

There's always the hope of nice baseball weather in the early spring, but if wishes were horses, then Ray and I would have traveled to Detroit in the saddle. It was maybe fifty degrees out and felt much colder when the wind gusted to the mid-twenties. I overpaid to park close to the ballpark, figuring that it'd be a little much to ask Ray to hobble more than a block or two. We got there early, hoping to catch a bit of batting practice, so there was no crowd to speak of. We were close enough to hear the rumble of the People Mover, which was moving very few people as per usual. The future home of the Lions was taking shape next door. It was nice they'd be moving back from the exurbs, but the whole area had a scrubbed-up look that felt more than a little disingenuous. Besides, the corner of Brush and Adams could never have the same ring as Michigan and Trumbull. We were less than a mile from Tiger Stadium, as the crow flies, but among the Fox Theater and Grand Circus Park felt like a world away from hardscrabble Corktown and Nancy Whiskey.

Ray was looking around, hands shoved in his green Members Only jacket.

"What do you think?" I gestured with my right hand at the surroundings.

He shook his head a little. "It's exactly what I expected and nothing like it at the same time." He pointed straight ahead with his left index finger. "The Elwood was there. Detroit College of Law a little farther down. Stroh Brewery past that. All gone."

"The Elwood?"

Ray nodded. "It was a diner. Nothing special, neat little building. Miriam and I ate there after games now and then."

Ray hardly ever talked about the girlfriend he split up with before he left for Korea. I wasn't even sure who did the dumping, but because he didn't say much about it, I assumed he was the dumpee. Hearing this much was surprising. Ray didn't talk about his life much, and I didn't want to scare him away from it, so I kept my mouth shut.

We stopped walking and Ray took a short shallow breath and kept looking around. "I'm sorry. I haven't been down here in many years."

I put out my hands in a gesture meant to convey that I didn't mind standing. I reached into my jacket pocket for my Parliaments and took one out of the pack. I danced around a bit, cupping my hands in front of my face to shield my Bic from the wind. After what must have been a dozen tries, I got it lit. "How many years?"

"I'm not sure, to tell you the truth. At least ten, probably more like fifteen. Since my mother died."

I looked around. The ballpark looked great; it was clean and modern and it was certainly preferable that the Tigers had moved here rather than into the suburbs twenty years earlier like they'd often threatened. Pontiac Tigers doesn't have the same ring to it. I watched Ray, who was moving his eyes from here to there, up and down the block with a sort of confused look. I took a drag from my cigarette and exhaled. The wind dissipated the smoke with a rush. "It doesn't seem necessary, does it?"

Ray turned to look at me but didn't say anything.

"Why tear all of that stuff down? Tiger Stadium is a classic. It'd be different if this were Cleveland or Baltimore, where they needed new parks. We didn't."

Ray smiled. "Follow the money, Drew. There are luxury suites in this place that costs thousands of dollars to rent for one game."

I took a drag from my cigarette. Of course Ray was right, and maybe the extra revenue would help the team be more competitive financially, but the Red Sox and Cubs could make it work in their old parks. "I could use a beer. Are you ready to head in?"

"Sure." Ray turned and shuffled towards the entrance.

After entering and buying beers, we settled into our seats along the first base side, just a few rows off the field.

"Were the tickets expensive?" Ray sat and looked at the field.

I waved him off. "Someone at Bob's gave me a hook-up. Company seats."

Ray smirked. "We'd better be on our best behavior." He fiddled with the brim of his fading twill Yankees cap.

"Hey, he gave his seats to a couple of bartenders. What can he expect?" I lifted my beer and then took a sip.

Ray leafed through his program. "Have you heard an update on Jeter?"

"Abdominal strain. He's not going to play today, but I don't think they've put him on the DL." I hated Derek Jeter. Even though he was a Kalamazoo kid made good, Ray and I had plenty of arguments about his being overrated. I thought he was lucky to bat second in a loaded Yankee lineup, but Ray felt his speed and power combination would shine anywhere. In truth, I'd probably have felt differently about him had the Tigers had a higher pick in the 1992 draft and nabbed him instead of the non-entity they selected.

Although we'd planned to get to the park early, we'd missed BP. Ray fiddled with his lineup card, filling in the names to match the scoreboard. "Who the hell is Clay Bellinger?"

Jeter's replacement in the lineup was an unknown to me as well. I shook my head. "If Jeter goes on the DL, maybe they'll call up that Soriano kid to pay short."

Ray closed the program and set it on his lap. "I wanted to thank you for bringing me today, Drew. It's really very nice of you."

"Aw, c'mon. I'm happy to be here." I smiled. "Maybe not as happy as I'd be if we were sitting behind a pole a couple miles that way." I pointed toward Tiger Stadium.

"Still, you've gone above and beyond what's necessary lately."

211

I'd been picking up some staples at Farmer Jack for Ray over the last few weeks. It was something Charlie did occasionally as well, but never Ralph, although I hadn't asked why. All I knew was that Ray didn't come down to the bar when Ralph was working, but I didn't want to pry and neither of them had offered up any reason. "It's nothing. What comes around goes around, right?"

Ray nodded and then made a small gesture with his hand around the ballpark. "What do you think?"

I looked around the inside for a moment and tried to form into words what I felt about the place. A lot about it felt right; the view over the outfield walls was great, the dimensions were unique. From our seats, the scoreboard was dominant in the field of vision, but I didn't find that as disruptive as I might have predicted. I'd been to Jacob's Field in Cleveland and loved it, so it wasn't that I was averse to the new wave of retro ballparks. But I'd also been to Wrigley. Given a choice, I'd go see a game there versus the modern updated versions ten times out of ten.

I took a sip of my beer. The wind that blew in off of the field felt a little chilly. "I think it will never make me not miss Tiger Stadium."

***

It was the fifth inning, but my dad had doubled that in number of beers finished. I'd never seen him drink so much; he was normally a one-and-done after work imbiber from what I'd seen in my sixteen years. Remarkably though, I don't think he was slurring or acting wasted. His tongue was getting loose.

"What music are you listening to these days, Drew?"

"Jen has me delving into Van Morrison's catalog."

My dad nodded and smirked. "Brown-Eyed Girl?"

I looked over at my Dad. He was wearing a blue and white striped Polo shirt and a windbreaker that was a little flimsy against the chilly breeze blowing off of the field. His hair was bushy under his adjustable Tigers hat. His moustache was graying and in need of a trim, and his burgeoning belly was barely constrained under his shirt. He was aging fast. It made me glad that I bore a stronger physical resemblance to my mom. Kevin and Jeff were spitting images of my dad. I suppose that was a factor in what I always perceived as my dad's preference for the two of them.

I thought "Brown-Eyed Girl" was a little fluffy. I was more into *Saint Dominic's Preview* and *Moondance*. "Sure. That's a good one."

"It's about anal sex. You know that, right?" He took a sip of beer.

I'm pretty sure my dad had never uttered the word sex in front of me, never mind adding anal to the equation. He'd not even presented "The Talk" to me; my brothers took me aside and gave me the lowdown when I was twelve, although of course, I already knew most of it from what my best friend, Aaron, had gleaned from sneaking peaks at his dad's porn collection.

I squinted against the sun as Cecil popped up to Steve Buechele, who was manning third for the Rangers. "It sounds like a pretty innocent song to me."

He shook his head vehemently. "'Hey where did we go, days when the rains came?'"

I shrugged. Mickey Tettleton took ball one.

"She's got her period. Those are the rains."

I didn't know how to react. It was odd enough that my dad had brought me to this game without my brothers. We hardly ever did anything by ourselves. Add the ten beers and the talk of anal sex and I was out of my element on every level.

"Then he says, 'Down in the hollow, playing a new game.' The new game is anal sex. Down in the hollow." He took a satisfied drink from his plastic cup.

It occurred to me that the anus wasn't exactly hollow, but I wasn't about to sass my dad. "So what if it is about anal sex? There's been lots of clandestinely dirty songs. What about 'Afternoon Delight'?"

My dad clapped as Tettleton drew a walk and trotted to first. "The so what is that you'll meet a lot of women who love that song. They get all gooey when it comes on the radio or a jukebox." He mimicked a high-pitched, girly voice. "This song is about me, I have brown eyes. Hee-hee-hee." He rolled his eyes. "It's great fun to point out that the song is all about butt sex in those moments."

Rob Deer took a look at strike one.

I couldn't picture my dad telling Kathy about his theory of the hidden meaning behind "Brown-Eyed Girl". "I'll remember that, Dad."

" 'Going down the old mine.' He says that, too."

I nodded. Deer whiffed at strike two.

My dad put his arm on my shoulder. He gestured with his beer at the batter. "This guy's a bum. Strikes out too much."

Deer drew a ball.

"He walks a lot."

He shook his head. "Walks? This is the majors."

When I was in Little League, the refrain "a walk is as good as a hit" was chanted like a mantra. Aaron took it a step further and figured that if a walk was as good as a hit, then getting hit by a pitch was the same as a walk and required less time at the plate, so he was forever throwing his elbow into the strike zone. I don't remember my dad coming to very many of my games. He was usually working late. "But the object at the plate is to not make outs. It doesn't matter how you do that. A walk is literally as good as a hit." I took a sip of soda. "I like Rob Deer."

My dad looked at me and crinkled his brow. "No one pays to see walks."

"That's probably true, but mostly you pay to see wins. Not making outs helps the team win." Deer was ready to step back into the box. "And he was in the Top Ten in the league in homers last year."

The Rangers pitcher delivered a high and outside fastball. Deer guessed correctly, extended his arms and connected. He drove the ball high and deep down the left field line. The left fielder didn't even bother to turn around and give chase. Fair ball. Two-run homer.

My dad pushed the bill of my cap down, nudging it past my eyes. "You're a smart kid."

It was as close to a compliment as I was likely to get. "I don't think you're right about 'Brown-Eyed Girl' either."

✳✳✳

After the bottom of the fifth, with the Tigers ahead two to zero, Ray and I agreed to take a stroll around the park. He'd stopped keeping score after the middle of the second; his hand was shaky, but of course I didn't mention it.

We'd each taken it relatively easily as far as beer went, so we splurged on a couple of large drafts. We sat in the smoking section nearest our seats. I lit a Parliament and Ray unwrapped one of his cigarillos. We sat and smoked in silence for a moment.

Ray exhaled and coughed a little. "Drew, if you don't mind me asking, what are your plans?"

Ray and I usually kept it pretty light in the bar; we talked about baseball, mostly. Sometimes we discuss books, a little history, and, if no one else was around, politics. "I'm not really sure yet."

"You graduated two years ago?"

Almost to the day. I took a drag from my cigarette and nodded.

"I wouldn't guess you plan on bartending at Bob's forever. You don't strike me as a Charlie or Ralph, someone content to spend some years behind the bar."

I shrugged. "I still think about going to graduate school."

Ray picked a stray piece of tobacco off his tongue. He flicked it to the ground. "I know it seems like you've got all the time in the world, and in a way, you do." He took a sip of beer. "But time will speed up on you."

My dad used to say something similar, about time being relative. "Working at the bar is fun. It's easy to let days turn into weeks and then weeks into months, I guess."

Ray took a shallow drag from his mini cigar. "If you like the bar, that's great. If you want to stay in Flint, then plan on a way to make it home. Buy your own bar, a house. If not, then get the ball rolling on going back to school. It comes down to one word." Ray held his right index finger aloft.

I waited for him to speak. I took a couple of drags from my cigarette. "Do I have to guess?" I smiled.

"Commit." He kept the index finger raised. "You have to commit. Make your choice and then see it through. Don't look back."

I thought about it for a moment. I wasn't ready, at that point, to make a real choice about much of anything. If I had been, I wouldn't still be in Kathy's house, hung up on my college girlfriend, biding my time in some bar. What Ray said made sense, but I wasn't ready to hear it just then. I nodded at Ray. "Thanks for the wisdom."

Ray looked off into the distance. "I lost my dad young too, you know."

I took a sip of beer. "How old?"

"I was a sophomore in college. You were sixteen?"

I nodded. "A sophomore in high school, ironically."

Ray shook his head. "You mean coincidentally." He smiled.

I laughed. "More wisdom."

"It can be hard as a young man without your dad. I know I had a lot of questions no one could answer."

I wasn't sure, had he lived, that my dad could have provided what I needed to know anyway. I watched a couple about my age walk by. The woman looked familiar. I thought it may have been someone I knew from high school. I put my head down in an effort to hide. "I do appreciate you speaking frankly, Ray." I looked around. I didn't see the couple. "I'll figure things out soon."

Ray patted my arm and smiled. "Just don't let those days and weeks and months turn into more years than you intend." He took a drag from his cigarillo. "I know of which I speak."

I didn't doubt that at all. "Okay. I promise."

Ray stubbed out his cigar in an ashtray close to the table. He shook his head. "Don't promise, Drew." He held the index finger aloft again. "Commit."

***

"You've been dating Jen for a few months now."

It was now the bottom of the seventh. My dad had kept up his drinking pace. It was lucky for both of us that I'd gotten my driver's license in January. That event coincided with my first date with Jen Nowicki. She was a senior and probably out of my league, but in my naiveté, I didn't question why one of the most popular girls in the school wanted to go out with me. I didn't learn to look gift horses in their mouths until much later.

I took the last sip of my now flat soda and set the cup down. "Yep. She's great."

He slapped me on the arm, probably a bit harder than he intended. "She's very pretty. Nice girl. She's going to UM in the fall?"

I nodded.

"I assume you two have made love." He sort of stumbled over the last two words, seemingly caught up in what terminology he wanted to use in an awkward situation.

He couldn't have possibly known that it had only happened just a little over a week prior to this game. He didn't pay enough attention to what was happening in my life to have noticed anything. He wasn't even there when I got home after one a.m. that Friday. Kathy, on the other hand, was asleep on the couch, and huffed off to their bedroom when I came in. Maybe she'd told him, but considering they weren't exchanging more than unpleasantries for days at a stretch, I sort of doubted it.

I wished I had more soda to buy a brief moment to process his question. "What makes you think that?"

He smirked. "That wasn't a denial, Drew." He punched my arm, this time purposefully hard. "I think that because I was sixteen once too, you know?"

I really didn't want to get into this with my dad at all, never mind after a double-digit beer intake.

Mickey Tettleton struck out swinging on a curve ball in the dirt.

My dad pointed at the field. "Here's your guy Rob Deer again."

I shook my head. "I never said he was my guy, only that he's underrated because he strikes out a lot and people think that means you can't hit."

The Rangers' pitcher tried to fool Deer with the same bouncing curve he'd used to strike Tettleton out, but Deer watched it for ball one.

"Sex isn't anything to be ashamed of, no matter what your mom's church tells you."

I wasn't ashamed. I'd figured out around confirmation that I was going to be a cafeteria Catholic. I thought the church's stance on birth control and abortion was antiquated and not especially useful in the real world. I was also pretty sure Jesus said jack shit about sex in the Bible, and I didn't regard St. Francis of Assisi as an expert on modern sexual mores. I thought if I continued trying to ignore my dad, he'd get the hint.

Deer looked at a fastball outside. Ball two.

"If Deer hits a home run here, I'll take that as a sign that you have also crossed home plate with the lovely Jen."

Gerald Alexander tried another fastball, but this one caught too much of the plate. Deer teed off and sent it deep to left.

My dad leapt to his feet, spilling half a beer on me, screaming and shouting. The ball sailed over the fence. Home run. Tigers led eight to four.

He put the plastic beer cup between his teeth and clapped loudly. I stayed seated, feeling a little embarrassed by both his exuberance and his being correct about Jen.

As the stadium, which was only about one-quarter full, quieted down, my dad took his seat, a little out of breath.

"Rob Deer is now my favorite baseball player of all time." He beamed at me. "So how was it, Son?"

✵✵✵

It was the top of the seventh, and the Tigers' Dave Mlicki was still pitching over his head. He'd kept the Yankee bats silent all afternoon. The Tigers had eeked out a couple of runs and were ahead, but evidently most of the thirty-two thousand in attendance at Comerica had been hoping for more fireworks. The crowd was largely sitting on their hands.

Mlicki forced Jorge Posada into a weak groundout to third.

"We got ourselves an old-fashioned pitchers' duel." I nudged Ray.

He nodded and then pointed to home plate. "Spencer's due."

I thought Shane Spencer looked more like an adult-sized fetus than a ballplayer. "I can't believe how Mlicki's pitched today."

"He's looked good. Got that sinker working for him."

I nodded. Spencer drew ball one outside. "It's a shame we didn't get to see Jeter today." I pointed at the field. "The Yankees are like a completely different team without him."

Ray turned his head and smirked at me. "Did you just compliment Derek Jeter?"

I smiled. Shane Spencer was late on a fastball. "I guess I did."

"Will wonders never cease?" Spencer knocked a sinker that didn't sink to left-center for a strong single. Ray pointed at him. "I told you he was due."

"I was at a game with my dad and he called a Rob Deer homer in a similar fashion."

Ray nodded. "Do you miss him?"

My dad was a disappointment to all of us. Kathy rarely spoke of him anymore. "Is it terrible if I say I don't?"

"Not if it's the truth."

Ricky Ledee grounded out to Tony Clark at first. End of the top of the seventh.

"My dad was a fuck-up, Ray." I told him the whole story; how my dad crashed his car late one night driving from some hotel with his secretary in the car, and killed her too. How he was drunk and it was only by the grace of God he didn't kill anyone else. How he'd carried on this affair for many months, and others before it, as I found out later. How he hadn't been much of a father to me when he was alive, and his life insurance payout meant more to us than his presence ever had.

Ray took a deep breath. "You shouldn't be so hard on him."

People were forever telling me that. I generally considered it to be one of those annoying platitudes provided by people who've never been through something similar. "Why, because he's the only dad I'll ever have?" My tone may have been more hostile than I intended.

"No, because everyone makes mistakes. Everyone. Your dad happened to die in the course of making one of his, so he never got the chance to redeem himself."

I stood. "I'm going to use the restroom."

Ray got up as well. "I'll join you."

We left the row of seats and walked toward the concourse. One of the advantages of the new park was the proximity of nice, clean, and functional bathrooms. I got in line for a urinal and Ray walked into a stall.

While I pissed, I thought about what Ray had said. I'd allowed my dad's underwhelming capabilities as a father and ridiculous death to fuel my anger toward him for long enough. It wasn't getting me anywhere. There wasn't anything he could do to fix things anymore. Literally.

I zipped up and moved to the sink to wash my hands. Out of the corner of my eye, I saw Ray exit that stall and throw something somewhat bulky into the trashcan. I rinsed and hustled out of the bathroom without bothering to dry. My heart raced. I wished I hadn't seen that, and decided to pretend I hadn't.

Ray caught up to me outside the bathroom doors. "Would you want to grab another smoke before we head back to the seats?"

I nodded. We walked over to the tables we'd used earlier. We sat and lit up.

I took a deep drag from my Parliament. My mouth was dry. "What was your big mistake?"

Ray had been lost in thought. "I'm sorry?"

"When we were talking about my dad, you said everyone makes mistakes. I assume you have as well. Otherwise you'd have said most people, or something like that. Not everyone."

Ray shook his head. "That's a story for another day."

"I see."

Ray bit the tip of his cigar. "I'll tell you about it some afternoon in the bar. Just know that we all have something we'd like to take back, something we'd do differently. Maybe it was that way with your dad."

I wasn't sure why Ray was going so far out of his way to be an apologist for my dad, and it wasn't as interesting as what secret he was hiding. I'd have to wait, but eventually he did tell me.

I took a drag from my cigarette. It didn't taste good. I thought about quitting. I'm not sure I would've enjoyed watching my dad get old. It wasn't any fun seeing Ray go through it. "Maybe you're right, Ray." I stubbed out the cigarette. "He did take me to a ballgame a few weeks before he died. Maybe that would've been the first of many."

***

Mike Henneman was the Tigers' reliever. He gave up a flukey run in the eighth, but by the top of the ninth seemed to forget how to get anyone out at all. A couple of Punch and Judy singles and the lead was down to two runs.

Along with most of the remaining crowd, my dad's mood shifted to sour. "You know I love your mother, right?"

I couldn't predict where he was going with this. "I guess so."

"Well, I do. But marriage and family, it's hard. You'll find out. Balancing work and home, you forget who you are sometimes."

Kevin and Jeff sometimes spoke of this maudlin side of Dad's personality, but either I'd never actually witnessed it or was just too self-involved to notice. Both possibilities were equally likely.

Steve Buechele punched a line drive between Travis Fryman and Alan Trammell, scoring Gary Pettis. The lead was down to one.

My dad slapped his knee. "Goddamnit." He was shouting. "Get this bum out of the game. Get on the phone, Sparky." His tone was almost pleading. The few thousand fans remaining were so silent that the Tigers' manager probably heard his request. There were already a right and left-hander warming up, but it's possible my dad couldn't focus that far. It was well past time for Anderson to have brought one of them in anyway.

I pointed at the field. "Sort of the story of their season so far. Scoring plenty of runs but can't prevent them."

My dad shook his head. "Sparky's getting too old to manage."

Although he looked twenty years older, Anderson was only fifty-seven. I wanted to point out that he wasn't even the oldest manager in the American League, plus there were Zimmer, Lasorda and Roger Craig in the NL. Getting smarter than your dad is depressing, even if it only extends to baseball.

My dad grabbed my forearm and looked into my eyes. "Have you told your mother?" He looked equally drunk and crazed.

I furrowed my brow. I didn't know what he was talking about and I couldn't guess what caused the abrupt change in him. "Told her what?"

"Don't pretend. You're almost an adult. You're not dumb."

I shook my arm loose. "I don't know what you're talking about."

Denny Walling came to the plate. He'd doubled over Cecil's head his last time up.

"The phone calls, Drew?"

I shrugged. "What fucking phone calls?" My voice was shrill. It hurt my own ears a little. A couple of people turned around and glared at us.

My dad looked confused. He was quiet for a moment. I could see him working something out in his head. "Your mother has been so angry with me lately, I thought she'd gotten the wrong idea about me and Shelly: my secretary."

Ball one outside to Walling.

I shook my head. Maybe his secretary called, I didn't remember. If she did, I hadn't thought anything of it. I'd met her once; she was about Kevin's age. It never occurred to me that she'd be interested in my dad. She was young and fit and my dad was old and a little overweight and bald. I had no clue what women wanted, whether they were popular seniors at my high school or administrative assistants for automotive engineers. "I don't remember any phone calls, Dad."

He drunkenly winked at me. "That-a-boy."

Walling got under a fastball and lifted a high fly to center. Milt Cuyler settled under it, and then squeezed it in his glove. Tigers win.

My dad stood and clapped. "That-a-boy."

We hung around in our seats awhile after the game ended. My dad said he liked to do it that way, and avoid the crush of people all trying to leave at the same time. I could've pointed out that it wasn't exactly a crush, as the park had already pretty much emptied out, but I didn't mind sitting and soaking up the ballpark for a while longer.

My dad turned to face me. He looked exhausted. "I didn't mean to give you a hard time about Jen."

"It's okay."

He shook his head. "No, I mean it. I remember what it was like." He smiled. "I'm not that old, you know."

"I know, Dad."

"There's still lots of years for us to do this again. Eventually we'll bring your kids here. Fathers and sons. That's what a place like this is about. Generations." He smiled. Maybe he meant it. Maybe he believed it.

Of course, none of it mattered. Words are just words in the first place. Even my dad knew that. And even if he could've gone to a ballgame with me and my future son, it would have been elsewhere. It might have seemed like they'd play ball at the corner of Michigan and Trumbull forever, because it seemed like they'd already been doing it that long. But like Ray and my dad both said, time is relative, and like they both proved, nothing lasts forever.

RAY & ELLSWORTH

Ray was relieved that Flint at large had mostly dodged the bullet, but his stomach was still in knots. On Friday morning, the worst was over and the National Guard was withdrawing. As Detroit picked through its rubble and squelched the burning embers of five nights of unrest, Flint breathed easy as the spillover was contained to a few blocks near Buick City. Schmitty's Lounge, however, was perilously close to the epicenter of Flint's comparatively small rioting.

It must've felt like a chance to start over, as though the city was spared the destruction so it might heal in a better, different, and faster way than their larger neighbor to the south, Ray's hometown. As Ray pulled his Rambler around the corner of Addison Street, he wondered how his old stomping grounds of Bagley had fared. He pictured fire and bricks and trucks with hoses turned on his childhood home, the destruction savage and nearly complete up and down the block that was used to hold his entire world. He pictured it reduced to the sort of waste a tornado might have caused, toppling the structures that had seemed invincible. A pile of bricks and wood and charred remains.

That was exactly what he found as Ray looked though his windshield at where his bar should have been.

***

If one could time travel and approach the much younger Ray Schmidt about his plans for the future, his hopes and dreams, it's unlikely he'd declare a desire to be the owner and operator of a shift bar in Flint, Michigan. Ray wanted to be a scholar, an academic, not someone slinging Goebel to the second-shifters who piled in from the nearby Buick plant. He wanted to study literature and write critical essays and teach undergraduates, not clean piss and puke and powder- coated dust out of the bathrooms and booths of the tavern on Industrial Avenue he'd backed into buying a couple of years after he got back from Korea. But there he was, closer to forty than thirty, feeling tired and unfulfilled and pushed through from one day to the next by little other than momentum and a stack of paperbacks he wanted to read before going to sleep near sun up.

It was July, which usually meant an increase in production at Buick City as they ramped things up to get the new model year fleet onto the lots. As a consequence, Ray had found himself in short supply of Canadian Club and Jim Beam, and needed to make a run to his liquor supplier in order to replenish. He pulled up to the bar, opened his trunk and grabbed the first box.

Ellsworth was behind the bar, tall and lean in a white t-shirt and unselfconsciously anachronistic greaser hair, talking to a couple of younger neighborhood guys with bottles of Budweiser in front of them. Ellsworth had been working at Schmitty's since he'd lost his first-shift job at the plant for balling a woman from payroll while they were both supposed to be on the clock. It probably didn't help his case that said young woman was his shift supervisor's eldest daughter. Ellsworth had been a loyal customer when he was still at the plant, and his dismissal coincided with Ray losing a bartender, so it seemed like a natural fit. His Buick Wildcat was outside parked in front of Ray's Rambler and was rapidly deteriorating, looking ever more like a symbol of Ellsworth's fading class mobility. He was reliable though, and working a shift bar meant there were significantly fewer women customers with whom to behave inappropriately. He still often managed to find trouble, although in the ten months he'd been working for Ray, it had been generally minor.

Ray put the first box on the bar. "Hi there, Ell."

He nodded at his boss. "Ray."

"CC, Black Velvet, a couple of others here. I'll be right back with the second box."

Ray pushed through the side door and onto the sidewalk. He squinted a bit against the sun. He was especially tired that afternoon, after having been kept awake by the snoring of his girlfriend Ruby, who'd found a way to procure a head cold even though it was a warm July and her last day of teaching fifth-graders had been several weeks earlier. He'd used the sleeplessness to keep tearing through *At Play in the Fields of the Lord.* He grabbed the second box of bottles out of the trunk and then shut the door with his elbow.

Inside the bar, one of the young guys was dropping quarters into the jukebox and playing Rolling Stones songs. "Mother's Little Helper" filled the air.

Ray put the second box next to the first one. He'd assumed Ellsworth would put the stock on the shelves, but he was still busy doing something close to nothing. Ray sighed and opened one of the boxes.

Ellsworth looked at Ray. "How's Ruby?"

"She's got a cold." Ray slid out a couple of bottles and moved toward the back bar and opened the cabinet. It was a mess even though Ray had asked Ellsworth to reorganize a couple of weeks ago.

"Again?" Ellsworth shook his head and then pointed to the boxes. "You want some help with those?"

"That's alright." Ray huffed past Ellsworth with a couple of bottles of Jim Beam.

Ellsworth leaned with his elbows on the bar. He was talking to the guy who'd played the Stones tunes. "I like the Rolling Stones and all, but Terry Knight and the Pack blew them off the stage at the IMA a couple of years ago."

One of his new friends nodded in agreement. "Their version of 'Lady Jane' was better, too."

Ellsworth smiled. "You got that right."

Ray didn't feel qualified to add anything to this conversation, so he kept his mouth shut and put away more bottles while Ellsworth entertained his fan club.

"Hey Ellsworth, did you ever go to the Hideout?" Ray didn't see which of the two kids asked.

227

He nodded. "Used to drive down all the time. Went to The Chatterbox some too. Saw The Underdogs, Henchmen, The Four of Us. Good stuff."

Ray was a few years too old to have enjoyed the so-called garage rock bands that popped up all over southeast Michigan in those days. Ellsworth was going on about Bob Seger & the Last Heard when Ray wondered to himself if his employee was this inattentive when the bar was busy.

Ray knew that Ruby was waiting for him to bring her some chicken soup from the deli, but it had been a little while since he'd hung around for a bit in an afternoon to witness first hand how Ellsworth behaved behind the bar. He grabbed a bottle of Schlitz from the cooler and then moved around the bar to take a stool near Ell's new pals.

The one sitting closest to the bar looked underage to Ray, but he found as he got older, it became more difficult to judge. The longer hair favored by some guys under twenty-five wasn't helping matters. Truth be told though, Ray didn't see much of those types in his bar, making this pair a bit of an anomaly. His hair was well past his collar, but his buddy was keeping his a little shorter. They both had somewhat tight trousers with polyester shirts tucked in at the waist, spit-shined penny loafers and black socks. To Ray, the entire ensemble looked a little uncomfortable and a bit like a uniform.

The one with the longer hair spoke. "Ellsworth. What sort of name is that? I don't think I've ever heard it before."

Ray knew the story by heart. Ell here was the third in his family with that name, his granddad and pa before him being Ellsworth Mayle. The Mayles were descended from old Scotch Irish stock and had patrolled West Virginia for generations until rumors of miscegenation forced them out. To hear Ellsworth tell it, he had a few cousins he claimed "came out of their mamas blurple — so black they's purple," but he only talked that way and with that twang when he'd had a few too many Wild Turkeys. The Mayles followed the hillbilly highway to Akron and Youngstown and Detroit and

Flint, figuring the Northerners would be more accepting. They weren't.

"Family name." Ellsworth spared them the full tale, or else couldn't be bothered.

The jukebox switched over to "We Can Work It Out."

"Ugh." The kid with the shorter hair fidgeted in his seat. "I can't stand the Beatles."

Ellsworth was incredulous. "What are you talking about? Have you listened to *Sgt. Pepper's?*"

Ray thought the Beatles move toward something decidedly more adult-sounding was calculated rather than artistic, and had already been done better by Bob Dylan. As a cultural phenomenon, Ray couldn't deny the new record was interesting — there were local listening sessions in school gymnasiums all over the city for weeks. Ray may have preferred Otis Redding or Sinatra, but he couldn't remember a gym full of kids gathered around a record player while *Only the Lonely* spun around.

The longer haired of the pair sided with Ellsworth. "I like the Beatles, too."

Short-hair shrugged. "I think they're still teenybopper music. Maybe I need to listen to it while smoking some grass." He pointed at Ellsworth. "You know where I can get any?"

Ray stood from his stool without skipping a beat. "What did you just ask?" He moved towards him.

The kid stood as well. He had six inches and probably thirty pounds on Ray. "What's it matter to you, Pops?"

Ray had learned long ago that unwavering authority was the key to winning any sort of challenge in the bar. Compared to some of the hulking Buick workers he'd tossed out of Schmitty's, this kid was a bug. "This is my goddamned bar and we don't solicit drug sales here." He pointed over the kid's shoulder. "There's the door. Use it. Now."

He stood there in front of Ray, staring. He was silent.

After an interminable thirty seconds, the song ended and left the bar in silence.

"Let's go, Curtis. We knew this place was for squares." He tapped his friend on the shoulder.

Short-hair turned around. "I didn't finish my beer."

Ray fished in his pocket, pulled out a single and tossed it at the kid. "Buy your friend a haircut."

He reached down and picked up the bill from the floor. He and his friend turned to leave. "Don't trust anyone over thirty, Ellsworth."

Ellsworth smiled. "I'm thirty-two."

The pair left the bar through the side door. The bar was empty.

Ray sat on the stool and took a drink from his Schlitz. "You're not thirty-two, Ell."

He shrugged. "I know. But it was funny, wasn't it?"

Ray nodded.

Ellsworth shook out a Lucky from his pack and lit it. "Why didn't you let me handle them?"

Ray wasn't sure how to answer. The truth was that he didn't know how much he trusted Ellsworth to keep the bar clean. "Force of habit, I guess."

Ellsworth shook his head. "We can't keep scaring away younger customers. We're going to need them."

It struck Ray a little funny to hear Ellsworth refer to the bar in the collective sense. He didn't think his charge had any sense of ownership. "Our friends in the Police Department wouldn't be friends for very long if we let drugs in here."

Ellsworth took a drag from his cigarette, and then tapped the end in a glass ashtray on the bar. "You're probably right." He took another drag. "Ever think about selling this place?"

Ray had been squirreling money away for the last eighteen months in order to make an offer on the Tick Tock Bar. Ray knew from his friend Bob, who owned a tavern downtown, that it was quietly on the market for the right buyer. The Tick Tock was near the Van Slyke engine plant, but also closer to downtown and the Grand Traverse district. It provided an opportunity to run something other than a strict shift bar, to expand his clientele and offer far more potential for growth. But Ellsworth couldn't possibly have known about Ray's plan. "I've thought about it."

"You should think hard." He looked around the bar. "This neighborhood's fucked, Ray."

Ray sipped his beer and nodded. "I've been here long enough to know which way the wind is blowing."

Ellsworth took a drag from his Lucky, which had burned down close to his fingers. He smoked them fast. "All's I know is it should be blowing us right out of here."

✳✳✳

Ray met Ruby the previous winter at a Christmas party thrown by one of his customers and his wife at their small house in Burton. It may have been a fix-up, but for whatever reason, neither of them bothered to find out. It didn't seem to matter. Ruby was in her mid-thirties like Ray was, widowed and childless. Her husband Tom was a casualty of the big presses at Fisher Body; Ray never thought to ask for any details because who'd want them? She'd graduated from Eastern Michigan when it was still known as Michigan State Normal College and only trained schoolteachers. She'd taught fifth grade at Pierce Elementary since then.

After Tom died, Ruby didn't date much. She was into her thirties by then, and things being like they were, the pickings were slim unless she wanted to scandalize herself by dating much younger men. She'd had a brief fling with the married principal at her school, but called it off out of guilt and fear. She weltered a few years in loneliness, spending most of her free time with her nose in a book, which was how it was so easy for her to bond with Ray.

At first, she and Ray were just friends, each of them too cautious to force anything romantic on the other. Ruby had resigned herself to staying alone, and Ray had essentially done the same after years of entanglements of varying degrees with women who he felt couldn't compare to his first love. As weeks turned into months and Winter into Spring, a switch turned in each of them and their friendship became physical.

By July, they were clinging to the honeymoon phase with all the strength they could muster. It had been nice to allow romance to make them feel younger and more vital, as though the world held a bit more possibility for each of them, but eventually Ray began to miss some of his independence and Ruby feared becoming too dependent on Ray. Her third cold in two months only exacerbated these feelings for each of them.

By the time Ray returned to his ranch house just off Atherton, he was about two hours later than he'd promised.

Ruby was planted on Ray's couch in pajamas and a housecoat, her nose red and swollen. The first time around, he'd thought sick Ruby was somewhat cute; this time, he'd have preferred she convalesced at her own house.

"I'm sorry I'm late with this." He held up the soup. "I'll run back to the kitchen and warm it up."

Ruby started a coughing fit, so rather than give a verbal response, she only shook her head.

"No? You must be hungry."

"I don't have much of an appetite." Ruby kept her voice low and shallow to avoid further hacking.

Ray sat in the chair closest to the couch. He looked at the coffee table and noticed the lack of a paperback. Ruby was almost never without a book. "Should we get you in to see a doctor?"

Ruby waved off the suggestion.

Ray felt equally concerned and annoyed. Her coughing was both deeper and more frequent, and she made it a point to ask for the chicken soup before he left for the bar. It was possible she was upset with him for being late, but Ruby was usually understanding about the unique demands of Ray's business. She was also a pretty direct person, something she claimed to have learned from her marriage, so unless she wasn't expressing herself out of fear of another coughing fit, then Ray figured she wasn't mad.

He looked down at the wax paper container in his hands. He'd been so busy looking over Ellsworth's shoulder and worrying about Ruby that he'd forgotten to feed himself. The soup smelled good; his stomach noisily churned. He turned towards the kitchen and put it in the refrigerator and then walked back to the living room where Ruby was spasming with a deep, painful cough.

Ray looked at Ruby with sympathy. "Is there anything I can get you? Maybe some tea?"

She gave a weak smile, "I'd like that."

He went back to the kitchen and pulled two cups and the Lipton bags out of the cupboard. The presence of the tea spoke to the increased presence of Ruby; Ray never kept any hot beverage in his place other than coffee. He put some tap water in the kettle and turned on the burner. He sat at the small dinette set and pulled open the crisp copy of the *Journal*, which he hadn't had a chance to read. He flipped to the sports section; although it was only the third week of July, it was safe to say his beloved Yankees were out of the running. They'd just lost their fifth in a row on Friday, in Detroit. Normally Ray would drive down to Briggs Stadium for a Sunday game, but between Ruby's illness and the Bombers' continued struggles, he wasn't even considering the trip.

The kettle whistled on the stove; Ray put tea bags in each of the cups and then poured the boiling water over them. He reached into the refrigerator for the milk and added a bit to his.

"Ray?" Ruby's voice was meek and barely audible from the living room.

"I'm coming with the tea." He moved into the living room and set her cup on the coffee table.

"Thank you." She reached for it with her left hand; in her right was a wrinkled and worn handkerchief she'd been using to cover her mouth. "I'm sorry to be a burden."

Ray shook his head. "I'm sorry you're not feeling well again."

"I took a dose of cough medicine about a half hour ago and I think it's beginning to help." She took a shallow sip of the tea.

"I'll have to leave in a few hours." Ray was due to relieve Ellsworth at eight o'clock. "Do you think you'll be okay by yourself?"

She nodded. "I'm feeling a bit peppier. Once I eat the soup, I'm sure I'll feel more like myself." She took another sip and then set the cup back on the coffee table. "I can always call my sister if I need anything."

Ray had been bothered about Ellsworth's seeming knowledge of his desire to move on from Schmitty's since their conversation earlier that day. Ray stayed around and had a couple of beers, at least partly to see if he could get his employee to betray a confidence, but he didn't give anything away. Besides Ruby and Bob, he didn't think anyone else knew about the Tick Tock.

Ray took a sip of his tea. It felt harsh on his empty belly. "You've never told anyone about the Tick Tock, have you?"

She shook her head and then whispered. "You asked me not to."

Ray leaned back into the chair. His back hurt a little. "The way Ellsworth was talking today made me think he knows about it."

Ruby shrugged. "I can't see how."

Ray looked at the coffee table. "You're not reading anything?"

"I've mostly been sleeping."

He nodded. He'd been lucky not to have caught any of Ruby's earlier colds and assumed he was on borrowed time in that regard. A summer cold behind the bar would be especially annoying.

Ruby cleared her throat. "What did Ellsworth say?"

"He made hints about getting out of the neighborhood. Come to think of it, he directly asked me if I'd ever considered selling the bar."

"And you said?" She wiped at her mouth with the handkerchief.

"I told him I'd thought about it. I probably shouldn't have said that." Ray sipped his tea.

They sat in silence for a few moments, which Ray took as a hopeful sign that the cough syrup was helping.

Ruby sat up on the couch. "Have you finished the Matthiessen book?"

It was sitting on Ray's nightstand. He was close to the end. Another night of Ruby's snoring and he'd be done. "Close."

"Would you mind if I started it?"

Ray shook his head. If she wanted to read that book, it was clear she didn't intend to go back to her house any time soon. Ray sighed.

"I wouldn't worry about Ellsworth." Ruby stood. "I'm going to warm up the soup. Would you like some?"

Rays' stomach was still grumbling and the tea only made it feel emptier. He stood and motioned for Ruby to sit back down. "Let me get it for you."

Ruby sat on the couch. "I'm sorry to be a burden."

"It's no bother." Ray moved towards the kitchen and sighed again. Sometimes he missed having more time to himself.

In the kitchen, he opened the container of soup into a saucepan and put it on the burner. He reached into the cupboard for the package of crackers, shoving a couple in his mouth. They were stale. He sat down again at the kitchenette. It was quiet enough to hear the flame on the stove as it warmed the soup. Ray listened to the wall clock tick loudly. Ray knew time was relative, but that didn't mean he wished to waste it.

***

235

When it became obvious that the trouble in Detroit was not going to stay isolated to the early morning hours of Sunday nor to just 12th Street, things became somewhat tense in Flint. When he arrived to open up on Monday, he found his longtime friend, Pat Maloney, waiting outside in his running cruiser.

Ray walked up to the car, tossing his nearly finished cigarette onto the pavement. "Good afternoon, Pat. Why don't you park and I'll let you in for a beer while I get cleaned up?"

Pat was normally one of Ray's most amiable cop buddies, but today he didn't crack a smile. "Not today, Ray. In fact, you ought to think about staying closed."

"Closed? Why would I do that?"

"Because if Johnson isn't going to send in federal troops, we'll have to contain things ourselves. Detroit's on fire. Flint's a powderkeg. Alcohol's a match."

The message was pretty clear to Ray. The police had no legal right to force the bars to close, but he wouldn't be able to rely on them for protection should he need it. The local television and radio news reported Flint police being on full alert. Ray was probably lucky that Maloney stopped by to warn him.

"Alright, Pat." Ray gave a single nod. "You don't have to worry about me. I'll stay closed."

"See that you do. We've got our hands full. We're tired and we're on edge." He shook his head. "Don't make it worse." Maloney drove away slowly, his hand raised in a stationary wave.

The admonition put some fear in Ray. Although it was nothing on the scale that was currently plaguing Detroit, Flint had seen a few mild skirmishes on Sunday night, and there was a firebombing just a few blocks from Schmitty's. A lot of the trouble in both cities was concentrated to looting, which Ray took to mean he had less to worry about. It didn't seem likely anyone would loot a bar when there were grocers and butchers and pharmacies within a block or two.

Still, Ray felt unsettled. He didn't quite know what to do with himself. It seemed odd to go back home. Ruby felt well enough to go to her house in the morning, so there was no impetus to go home and look after her. He figured it couldn't hurt to stick around the bar for a while and make sure the neighborhood stayed quiet.

He went to Grayson's Grocery and bought some lunch meat and bread and a bag of Better Mades, then stopped at the bakery and picked out a fresh Dutch apple pie. When he got back to Schmitty's, he remembered that it was an off day in the Majors, so there'd be no ballgame to help pass the time.

He fixed a couple of sandwiches and was finishing the second, washing it down with a bottle of Schlitz, when he heard a key in the lock of the side door.

Ellsworth opened the door and walked through it. "What gives, Boss?"

Ray swallowed a bite of his sandwich. "Maloney was waiting for me when I got here, said it'd be better if we stayed closed until things cool off."

"I hadn't thought of that." He tossed his keys on the bar and sat next to Ray.

Ray took a sip of his beer. "What are you doing here?"

"I was driving by and saw it was dark. Made me wonder what was going on. Your Rambler was out front, so it made even less sense."

Ray pointed to the meat and bread on the bar. "Fix yourself a sandwich."

Ellsworth patted his belly. "Just came from Woolworth's lunch counter." He shook a Lucky out of his pack and lit it. Stray light from the high windows illuminated a sliver of the smoke cloud. "All people could talk about was what's happening in Detroit. Whether Romney's going to be able to get federal troops in before the damage is done. People are saying there's already a hundred dead. Looting, fires, you name it."

Ray had listened to the radio all morning. He thought the trouble was a long time coming. There'd been insurrections in New York, Philadelphia, Los Angeles. The Hough riots in Cleveland the year before were close to home. Things were getting ugly all over. Detroit may have called itself the "Model City", but Ray knew it was smoke and mirrors.

Ellsworth took another drag from his cigarette. "You going to stay closed?"

Ray nodded.

"Probably the best thing." Ellsworth moved around the bar and reached into the cooler for a Stroh's. "No need to add fuel to the fire." He opened the beer.

"That's more or less what Maloney said. I didn't think much about things spreading up here until I saw him. He wasn't himself. Looked nervous." Ray reached over for Ellsworth's cigarettes. "You mind?"

Ellsworth shook his head. "Hell, I'd be real nervous. What I heard, most of the dead in Detroit were shot by police. You think those guys report for their shifts wanting to kill people?"

Ray lit the cigarette and took a deep drag. He ran his left hand over his chin. He'd forgotten to shave. "It could be days before we open. Are you fixed for cash?"

Ellsworth waved him off. "I got what I need, Boss. You want me to call Billy?"

Billy was the third bartender at Schmitty's. He wasn't due for a shift until Wednesday. Ray hoped he'd be able to open by then. "I'll take care of it."

"I could go home and get some supplies, then stay here overnight." Ellsworth took a last drag and then stubbed his cigarette out under his foot. "Guard the place."

"You think it needs guarding?"

"What could it hurt?" Ellsworth shrugged his shoulders.

It could hurt our supply of Wild Turkey, Ray thought. Ellsworth inviting a gaggle of friends in to partake of a free night at the bar didn't seem out of the realm of possibility. He pictured an alcohol and marijuana free-for-all, couples balling in the booths and the storeroom, a sort of genial indoor riot, but nearly as destructive.

Ray then thought he was being ridiculous. Ellsworth had his faults, but he wasn't a child. He stopped in to make sure everything was okay when he saw the lights weren't on. That counted for something.

He took a long drag off the Lucky. He smiled at Ellsworth. "I guess it couldn't hurt."

***

Ray stayed at Schmitty's for a few hours, drinking several beers and bullshitting with Ellsworth, who was regaling Ray with baseball stories. Ell had been a dominant high school pitcher, even winning a scholarship to Evansville College in Indiana, where he promptly flunked out after two semesters spent studying female anatomy instead of the required general education courses.

"When I was on, Ray, it felt like I couldn't do no wrong." Ellsworth sipped from his third or fourth straight Wild Turkey. He looked at the glass. "Kind of like with this here glass of Old Chicken. Neat. Clean. Didn't need to do nothing fancy. Just fastball after fastball, putting it where I wanted."

Ray nodded, although it occurred to him that Ellsworth may have had limited success at any more competitive level unless he developed strong off-speed pitches. More skilled hitters would invariably catch up with a fastball, no matter the speed, if that's all the pitcher could throw effectively. He didn't say any of that.

"Yeah, never felt so alive as on the mound." Ell finished the rest of his drink with one gulp.

Afternoon beers often made Ray sleepy, and he felt his eyelids getting heavy. His watch read half past seven, and it seemed like the

239

neighborhood was still quiet. "I should get going. Ruby's probably wondering where I am." He stood from the stool. His legs were a bit wobblier than he expected.

"I'm glad to hear you say she's feeling better."

Ray grabbed a few of the chips from the open Better Made bag on the bar and shoved them in his mouth. He'd gotten hungry again. "She told me she was going to come back to my house after clearing a few things up at home. She's bringing some hamburger that was in her icebox." He looked at his watch again, although he'd already checked it less than a minute prior. "You sure you'll be alright here?"

Ellsworth turned and looked out of the glass windowed side door. "Seems pretty quiet. I might just head home myself."

Ray patted him on the shoulder. "I think that'd be fine."

Ellsworth stood. "I'll pick up the mess we left and lock up." He stretched his arms above his head. It was easy to see how he might have been a dominant pitcher.

"Thank you."

"Don't mention it." Ellsworth moved down the bar and picked up the bread and meat, then moved towards the cooler and put them inside. He waved at Ray with the back of his hand.

"Go on, Boss. I'll see you tomorrow."

✳✳✳

When Ray got back to his house, Ruby's Catalina wasn't in front. He walked into a dark house. He looked around for a note, but didn't see anything. He opened the refrigerator, but there was no hamburger inside.

He took off his shoes and moved to the living room. He reclined on the couch. It didn't take long for the afternoon beers to catch up with Ray and he nodded off. By the time he came to, it was after five the next morning. His head was ringing, his mouth dry, his stomach angry at being so empty.

He looked around the house, but there was still no sign of Ruby. Ray thought he would try her phone at a more decent hour. He went to the kitchen and put two stale slices of Holsum White into the toaster. While he waited, he poured a glass of tap water and drank it in three large gulps, then prepped some coffee in the percolator.

The neighborhood was still asleep, which was a good sign. If the trouble in Detroit was really spilling over, Ray thought there'd at least be some activity outside. Daylight was just breaking; the days were already getting shorter.

After the coffee was finished, Ray choked down the dry toast and a half cup of the black swill his coffee pot concocted. He took a long shower, which again made him sleepy. He went to his bedroom and lay back on the mattress, thinking he'd catch a little more rest before it was an acceptable time to try and call Ruby.

He woke to his own phone ringing. Groggy, he looked at the bedside clock to see it was well past noon. He picked up the receiver.

"Hello."

"Ray? Ellsworth. Didn't catch you at a bad time, did I?"

Ray rubbed his eyes. He hadn't slept this long in years. It left him more tired than before and more than a little confused. "No, no. What's going on?"

"I just drove by the bar. Everything checked out. The radio says the Police still have emergency orders in place. Curfew, all that."

It took Ray a brief moment to remember the riots. He snapped out of it with thoughts in his mind's eye of the destruction in his hometown. "I suppose that means there's no sense in opening today."

"That's what I thought you'd say." Ellsworth sighed on the other end. "You want me to watch over things again today?"

Ray didn't have any idea what had transpired over night. It didn't make sense for him to decide before he had a fuller picture about where things stood in the city. "Don't worry about it. I'll head over there shortly."

"Why don't I meet you over there? I'll pick us up some lunch, we'll have ourselves a repeat of yesterday."

Ray had put nothing in his belly over the past eighteen hours or so but the dry toast. "How about some of that chicken from over near your place?"

"You got it, Boss."

The line was silent.

"Hey, Boss?"

Ray rubbed his chin. Two days, no shave. "Yeah?"

"Ah, nothin'. I'll see you over there."

Ray tapped the switchhook to disconnect the call and then dialed Ruby's number. He let it ring about a dozen times before hanging up. He thought about trying again, but assumed she was probably getting some rest and decided it best not to disturb her. He got dressed quickly and stumbled out into the hot noon sunshine to drive to the bar.

**

In 1943, when Ray was a teenager, riots engulfed parts of Detroit for three terrible days, blacks and whites battling each other in various spots around the city. The neighborhood of Paradise Valley sustained most of the damage, but Ray's neighborhood was several miles away and felt far removed from the fighting. Although he wasn't old enough to have developed a sense of irony, the fact that the war industry was responsible for the influx of African-American job seekers from the South struck the young Ray as confusing. America was supposed to be united to defeat the Axis, but here were citizens murdering each other in anger in his own city, burning down businesses and attacking police officers.

When asked how this could be happening, Ray's father was taciturn. He shook his head and muttered, "Nobody's no good."

Ellsworth didn't know about the '43 riots. Ray told him what he remembered. As they finished their chicken lunch, wiping the grease on the fresh, clean bar rags that hadn't been used in two days, he seemed as confused as the teenage Ray had been nearly a quarter-century before.

Ellsworth spoke with a mouthful of potato salad. "Blacks hate the whites; whites hate the blacks. Cops hate the blacks; blacks don't trust the cops. How's anything supposed to change?"

Ray shrugged. "I suppose little has."

"But shouldn't they have learned something from before?" Ellsworth fished in his pack of cigarettes, pulled one out and lit it.

"Those who don't learn from the past are doomed to repeat it." Ray took a sip from his beer. "There's no justice. There are still over a dozen unsolved murders from the earlier riots. How would you feel if one of those was a family member?"

Ellsworth shook his head. "I seen it firsthand, Ray. You think my mixed cousins get treated the same as me? Hell no they don't. My Aunt Sue's boy Robert, he's been trying for years to get hired on the line at Fisher. He's a good kid, big and strong. They've had him cleaning toilets for years." He took a drag from his cigarette. "And it ain't just black and white. I learned real quick to drop the twang if I wanted anyone to think I was something other than stupid."

Ray nodded. "This girl Mary Jo McKenna asked me to a Sadie Hawkins dance in High School. She had just moved here with her folks from Arkansas. I took so much ribbing after I said yes that I had to beg off. I still feel terrible about that."

Ellsworth smiled. "Was she stacked?"

"That's hardly the point, Ell."

He laughed loudly. "You say that, but I'll bet if she was stacked, you'd have taken her to that dance no matter what your friends said."

Ray shook his head and chuckled a little. Before he could answer, there were a series of loud bangs outside. Ray and Ellsworth met each other's glance with wide eyes. They ran to the glass windowed door to look, but nothing was visible.

Ray pointed out of the door. "It wasn't our cars." Several area fire bombings had been of unmanned vehicles.

"That sounded like a damn cannon."

"Should we go out to see?"

Ellsworth shook his head. "Let's wait a minute."

Ray felt real fear for the first time since the trouble started. He'd seen and been involved in his share of mild violence as a bar owner, but there was something unbridled about a riot that truly frightened him. Anything could happen when mob mentality took hold.

They watched for another several minutes but nothing else happened. No people were even visible from the door. It stayed quiet; no sirens wail followed and both the men calmed down.

Ellsworth headed back to his bar stool. "I'll tell you what, my heart plum stopped for what must've been a minute there."

Ray started to question the wisdom of letting Ellsworth stay at the bar without him for any length of time. "Maybe we ought to both head home."

"I'll be alright, Boss."

"I'd feel better if you left."

Ellsworth waved his hand in the air. "I got ol' Bessie if need be."

"Old Bessie?"

"My sawed-off. Some looter hears that pump action, they'll move down the block."

This made Ray even more nervous. "That's a terrible idea, Ell. I won't put you in a position where you'd need to decide between someone else's life and your own." Ray didn't mention a shotgun would be little help against a firebomb anyway. "Let's go. We'll meet up again tomorrow." Ray began to gather up their lunch trash.

"I need to go over to Ruby's and see why she hasn't been answering her phone."

Ray hadn't wanted to make too much of it, but he was getting increasingly worried about Ruby. It wasn't like her to not follow through with plans as she had the night before, or to at least check in if something changed. He'd rung her number a few times from the bar, but there was still no answer.

Ellsworth looked dejected, but helped Ray clean their mess. "I wish you'd reconsider."

"Not a chance." Ray dumped the chicken bones in the paper bag that delivered the meal. "It's not worth it. I've got insurance. There's no sense in anyone dying over this place."

"Insurance?" Ellsworth tossed a couple of beer bottles in the trashcan with a clang. "That would cover this place being destroyed in a riot?"

Before Ray could answer, there was a tap at the side door. They looked over to see Pat Maloney. Ray walked over and unlocked the deadbolt to let him in.

"You're not thinking about opening, are you Schmitty?"

Ray shook his head. "Ellsworth and I were just finishing some lunch, checking up on things."

He looked over at Ellsworth with no expression. "That's good." He reached for a pack of cigarettes in his shirt pocket, took one out and lit it. "You two hear anything recently?"

"We did. Sounded like some sort of explosions. We didn't see anything, but it sounded like it came from that way." He pointed in the vicinity of where he thought the sound had originated.

Maloney nodded. "We got a few calls, but haven't found anything." He inhaled his cigarette. "Could be nothing, but you two should think about heading out of here. There's been a few skirmishes over the last few hours. Nothing major, but I wouldn't be around here if I didn't have to."

Ellsworth threw away the rest of their trash. "We were just about to leave when you got here."

Maloney looked at Ellsworth as though he'd been sassed. Neither spoke.

Ray felt the tension. "We'll be out the door in five minutes, Paddy. Can I get you anything before we leave?"

He didn't take his eyes from Ellsworth. "No, thanks."

"No, thank you for looking out for us." Ray smiled. "Be careful out there."

Maloney smirked at Ray. It was probably as close to a smile as they'd get. "Eye's in the back of my head, Schmitty."

***

Ray stopped by Ruby's on his way home from the bar. Her car was in the garage, but she didn't answer the door. Considering the almost constant FPD patrols, Ray didn't think it was wise to walk around the house peering into windows, so he drove back to his place. Once there, he rang her phone a couple of times, but got no answer.

He knew Ruby's sister, Penny, would be able to tell him what was happening, but Ray didn't have her number. It took some sleuthing, as he didn't have her married surname at the ready, but after a few phone calls, he had Penny's number and made the call. There was no answer there either.

Ray was at a loss about what to do next. He paced around a bit, trying to calm himself down, but this wasn't like Ruby. He could feel himself begin to panic, and in moments like these, his mother's tendency toward terrible worrying grabbed hold of him. He pictured Ruby in the hospital, bruised and battered from a car accident she'd been in on her drive home. He thought maybe she'd been attacked, a victim of the racial tension, at worst gang-raped by a vicious mob. He thought perhaps she'd tried to take a bath at her house, and in her weakened state, fainted and drowned. His logical side told him to stay focused on Occam's Razor, but when his mother's side of his personality was in charge, there was no reasoning with his own brain.

He got back in the Rambler and drove to Ruby's. He grabbed a bar towel from the back seat of his car, then walked to the back of her house. He looked for a window large enough for him to crawl through, but not so hard that its replacement would be cost prohibitive, and then smashed it.

The glass stopped crashing just as the siren began to wail.

***

Ray spent Tuesday night, Wednesday night, and a chunk of Thursday in holding. The riot spillover was enough to cause a bit of a jam in the precinct, although the few times he asked around, it seemed like the majority of his fellow jailbirds were in for unrelated offenses. He was officially booked for Breaking and Entering, which was an extra annoyance seeing as how he didn't even enter Ruby's house before the police caught up to him.

Under normal circumstances, things would've gone much differently. But none of his friends on the force were available to vouch for him, and no one was able to scare up Ruby to corroborate that they knew one another and that he was only looking after her. Ray couldn't blame the police for questioning the veracity of the tale; it sounded dubious even as it left his lips. To make matters worse, he wasn't able to get his phone call in until Wednesday night, too late for Ellsworth to get to a bank and put together the cash to bail him out.

Ellsworth explained that he'd stopped in to the bar periodically, and was himself quite worried about what might have happened to Ray when he didn't hear from him for the better part of two days. He said things were fine at Schmitty's, and that there'd been some periodic disturbances according to Maloney, but nothing as bad as they'd feared. In the interim, the National Guard had moved into Detroit, quieting things considerably, and this seemed to ease some of the tension in Flint as well.

By the time his employee dropped him off at his house on Thursday afternoon, Ray was tired and dirty and even more beside himself with worry about Ruby's safety. After a long shower, Ray was fixing himself some scrambled eggs and toast when the phone rang.

"Hello?"

"Ray Schmidt?" It was a woman's voice.

"This is."

"Ray, this is Penny Wurster, Ruby's sister."

"Oh, God, Penny. I've been worried sick. Where is Ruby?"

"You're a difficult man to track down."

"It's a long story, I'm sorry. Please just tell me where Ruby is."

"She's been here in Genesee Memorial since Tuesday night. She's got TB."

It hit Ray like a ton of bricks, but it was also incredibly obvious. Although the disease had been in steep decline over the previous decade, it was still a common enough threat that Ray felt as though it should have occurred to him that it was the cause of her deep cough. "I'm on my way there."

"Very good. I'm sorry we'll meet under circumstances like these."

"Yes, of course." Ray looked at his watch. "I'll be there in about fifteen minutes."

***

Ray spent the night between the waiting room and Ruby's bedside. The doctors thought her case was manageable, but it was still early and there were often complications from the antibiotics used. It would really be at least a week before they had a firmer grasp on her prognosis.

Because she'd been staying with Ray, the doctors insisted he get a TB test, which was negative. They inoculated him before they'd let him get back to visiting Ruby.

She'd been mostly asleep since he got to the hospital, so he relied on Penny to fill in the blanks about what had happened. Ray told her about his ordeal over the past few days, and Penny said her husband's brother was an attorney and she'd be happy to have him intervene for Ray and get the matter resolved.

When Ruby awoke, her eyes lit up at the sight of Ray. She was under doctor's orders to rest her lungs and speak only when absolutely necessary, so Ray did the talking for both of them. He told her he was sorry he didn't take more attentive care; he was sorry that she was so sick in the hospital, sorry about her window, sorry he took so long to get here. She waved off each apology. Penny had brought her a pad of paper and a pencil, on which she wrote the following to Ray:

Stop it.

I love you.

How is the bar?

It didn't surprise Ray that it should take a hospital stay to precipitate their first exchange of 'I Love Yous'. He was also acutely aware there was now far more at stake and that their earlier casual stance was no longer possible.

Ray smiled at Ruby and took her hand. He told her he loved her. He thanked her for being so understanding. He said he was going to check on the bar and Ellsworth and he'd be back in the afternoon.

***

There was a police roadblock at the intersection of Hamilton and Saginaw. It took some cajoling for Ray to convince those overseeing the entrances and exits that he belonged in the neighborhood. As he crept slowly up Saginaw, the devastation was clear although not terribly widespread, except for the corner of Leith and Saginaw, which was completely leveled. But as Ray drove further north, things seemed quieter, and apart from the boarded-up windows at the grocery, the closer he got to the bar, things seemed untouched.

He turned right going east on Addison, his normal route. Addison itself was quiet, and Ray thought all of this was adding up to Schmitty's being spared, until he came to the corner where Addison dead ends into Industrial Avenue and found smoldering ruins where his bar had stood.

It felt like someone punched him in the gut. The destruction was complete and utterly senseless. Nothing else in the vicinity had been destroyed and Ray couldn't begin to guess why his bar was targeted. It had been a quiet, unassuming tavern serving the Buick City shift workers, nothing more and nothing less. Ray thought he'd been a good neighbor here.

Ray didn't know what to do with himself. He put the Rambler in park near the corner but left the engine running. There was not a person in sight, as though the neighborhood was on some sort of lockdown, although Ray couldn't imagine the curfew would start until sundown. He wasn't sure how long he sat there before Ellsworth pulled his Wildcat behind Ray and honked.

Ellsworth exited his car and walked to Ray's driver's side window. "Boss, I've been looking all over for you."

Ray hated that expression. If he'd truly looked all over, wouldn't this corner have been among the first places to try? "I can't believe it."

Ellsworth nodded. "I know what you mean. Can't make heads or tails of it myself."

Ray turned off his engine and stepped out of the Rambler. The sun was bright. Ray made a visor with his right hand to be able to look up and see Ellsworth's face. "Do you know what happened?"

He shook his head. "They won't tell me anything. I haven't seen Maloney, or I figured he'd let me know." Ellsworth began walking towards the remains of the bar.

Ray followed. "Ruby has TB."

Ellsworth stopped. "You're kidding."

Ray also hated that expression. Why on earth would that be an appropriate joke? "She's at Genesee. The doctors don't know much yet." Ray walked past Ellsworth to where the side entrance to Schmitty's once stood. "I'm not even sure what to do."

Ellsworth stood next to Ray. "I imagine the first call is to your insurance agent."

Ray looked over at Ellsworth. It seemed callous, but he was probably right. Ray needed to collect on his policy so he could make a move on the Tick Tock without losing much revenue. Ray anticipated a terrible smell, but it was surprisingly pleasant. The majority of the bar was made up of wood. The booths, the bar itself, the back bar. Its destruction by fire left behind something not dissimilar to a barbeque. "I'll call when I get home."

"Right." Ellsworth smiled. "I know it's not the right time, but maybe this was for the best."

Ray had spent a couple of days in jail, a day in the hospital, and now had been greeted by a pile of rubble where his business stood. "Tread lightly, Ell."

"I just mean there is such a thing as a blessing in disguise."

In the ensuing years, there were moments when Ray saw things Ellsworth's way. Not every day, of course. He'd never lose the feeling of that day, with Ruby so sick in the hospital, his years of hard work reduced to waste, Ellsworth standing next to him as though he'd had nothing to do with the fire. After he collected his check and bought the Tick Tock Bar, after he started making more money in one month than he used to make in six, after recovering from Ruby's death, after Ellsworth's almost predictable murder at the hands of a jealous husband, Ray would be able to see the blessings of that day.

He was alive. He was well. He had a job and a home. There were blessings.

DREW & MOLLY

Since I moved out of Kathy's, I forgot what it's like to have a woman waiting up for me when I came home. When I rolled in around three-thirty, exhausted after a pretty busy night filling in for the now permanently absent Ralph, Molly sitting awake on the couch with the stereo on low was not what I expected to find.

It was clear she was waiting for me. If she was studying, she'd be holed up in her room blasting some riot grrl band. Molly was always trying to come across a little harder than she really was. I kind of regarded her as a riot grrl-lite. I know she been playing some of my alt-country CDs with regularity; in fact, *24 Hours a Day* was what was barely audible when I walked in.

She looked up at me from the textbook splayed in her lap and smiled.

"'Smokin' 100s Alone', eh?" I laughed.

Molly rolled her eyes. "Well played." She reached onto the coffee table for her pack of Marlboro Lights and held it up. "These aren't 100s though. Now you're home, I'm not alone."

I sat in the tattered armchair closest to the couch. The halogen lamp behind the couch was the only light in the room. "What are you doing still awake?"

Molly shrugged as she lit the cigarette and then exhaled. "Couldn't sleep."

I'd been having some trouble in that department myself. Since Ralph was gone, I was picking up several extra shifts at Bob's, and Megan's impending arrival was weighing on my mind as well. "I'm hoping sheer exhaustion will hasten the arrival of Mr. Sandman tonight."

"Busy at the bar?"

I nodded. "Everyone's got a theory about what happened to Ralph."

"He's like Flint's own Amelia Earhart, if she'd been a perpetually stoned bartender." She took another drag from her cigarette.

"He was well-liked, that's for sure." My eyes had adjusted to the relative darkness in the living room. Molly and I kept things pretty clean around the apartment, which was impressive given our busy schedules. So far, I'd really liked living with her. "Except by Phil and Charlie, who'd sooner murder him than welcome him back at this point."

"I'll never forget him walking out, the look in his eyes. You know how, in a car accident, time slows down and things get all stretched out and weird? It was just like that." She shook her head.

I stood and stretched my arms over my head. I nearly caught a muscle cramp in my side, but I twisted around the other way and stopped it from taking hold. "I'd better try and get some sleep. Another double tomorrow."

Molly nodded, took a last drag from her cigarette and then put it out in an ashtray on the coffee table. She looked at me but didn't say anything.

I looked down at her. She had her hair pulled back in a clip, some of it falling out and framing her face. She was wearing a faded and torn Joy Division shirt and grey sweatpants that were baggy but still couldn't hide all her curves. I may have stared at her longer than was comfortable. It was getting harder to lie to myself about how attractive she was.

"Something on your mind?" Molly closed the book on her lap.

I shook my head. "I was thinking maybe a shower to unwind a bit before bed."

She smiled. "Is there room for two?"

✳✳✳

253

I was nearly done mopping the floor at Bob's the next afternoon when Phil came in with some supplies. He pushed through the side door with a box of paper towels and tossed it in a booth.

He was wearing a cable knit sweater minus even a jacket even though the temperature was well below freezing. "Finish what you're doing, I got the rest."

"I hadn't offered to help."

He pointed at me. "Don't you get an attitude now, too."

I smiled and kept mopping.

Phil made a couple more trips and then pulled down the stool closest to the end of the bar and sat. "Why are you all smiles? You should be pissed about the back-to-back doubles."

I hadn't even noticed I was smiling. "Can you keep a secret?"

He reached into the cooler and pulled out a bottle of Labatt. "Like you wouldn't believe, Hot Stuff."

I put the mop into the bucket and wheeled it into the side room. The floor was as clean as it was going to get. "Molly and I slept together last night."

"That's the least shocking news since Chris Farley OD'd."

I pulled the stool next to his and sat. "What's that supposed to mean?"

Phil took a sip of his beer. "Oh, don't take it the wrong way. I only mean that you two living together, young, unattached. It was bound to happen sooner or later."

"I see." I reached for the pack of Parliaments I'd set onto the bar, took one out and lit it. "It was surprising to me."

"You know how they get animals to reproduce in captivity, Drew? They put them in the same cage."

"I've heard that one before." I took a drag off the cigarette. "I'm no animal."

He slapped me on the shoulder. "Love has made you so sensitive." He took another drink from his beer. "What happens now?"

254

This was a good question, and one Drew hadn't addressed with Molly before she left for her morning class. "I'm not sure. Megan gets here tomorrow."

"The elusive Megan. I'm glad I didn't make any bets on whether she actually exists. My money would've been on 'no'." Phil took a tin of Copenhagen out of his back pocket and packed it. "Refresh my memory about this situation." He drained the rest of his beer in one long gulp.

There was a time I perversely enjoyed telling the tale of Megan's betrayal. By then it just seemed perverse. "Boy meets girl. They become stereotypical college sweethearts. Things are swell. Girl gets into medical school. Boy gets into grad school. They're moving in together. Girl misleads boy and takes an offer at a different medical school several states away. Boy comes back from class to find roommate fucking girl on the couch."

"Ouch." He put in a dip. His bottom lip swelled out from the minty tobacco. "How did you catch them? They didn't hear you come in?"

"They had one of my Al Green records turned up pretty loud." I put out my cigarette in an ashtray on the bar.

"Double ouch." Phil spit into his empty Labatt bottle. "Which record?"

"*Living For You.* What does it matter?"

Phil shook his head. "Curiosity. Sorry."

I waved off the apology. "I get it. From afar it's pretty amusing. From up close it was a head twister."

"This is why you didn't go to grad school? Why you're in Flint?"

I nodded.

Phil got up and started pulling down stools. It was nearly time to open. "This all happened almost three years ago, right?"

I started pulling down stools from the other end of the bar. "A few months shy."

"Is Molly the first woman you've slept with since this happened?" He stopped his task and looked at me.

I pulled down another couple stools before I answered. "Maybe."

"You're an idiot."

"You give Charlie a hard time for sleeping with women from the bar, but I get a hard time for the opposite?" I pulled down the last stool and then walked behind the bar.

He shrugged. "Consistency is overrated. How was it, anyway?"

It'd been so long since I had sex, I almost forgot about locker room talk. I always thought it was a weird custom. After all, are there ever really surprises in this arena? She had a vagina, a pair of breasts, and they all met up with my mouth and penis. It felt good, as it always does. There were orgasms and strange sounds and faces you don't make under other circumstances. What's to say? "It was great fun. When is it not?"

Phil smirked. "Wait till you get married."

I rolled my eyes. "You all say that sort of shit. What could be so bad?"

"You mean the weekly disappointment? Nothing at all. It's wonderful."

I felt awkward enough when pressed for details on my night with Molly, but this was getting uncomfortable. I guess I could sympathize. I worry sometimes about how I might feel about having sex with a future wife after she becomes a future mom, if I'm completely honest with myself. 'Motherfucker' is an insult for a reason. I prefer to leave this in bridges-I'll-cross-when-necessary territory though.

I was saved from having to come up with a response by Ray's arrival. He pushed through the side door and shuffled towards a stool. He was wearing a beige driver's cap that gave him an unusually jaunty look.

He took the cap off and set it on the bar. "Gentlemen." He nodded in turn at Phil and me.

I poured Ray his draft and then set it in front of him. "Real live baseball will be played in less than two weeks, Ray." Pitchers and catchers had reported for most teams the week before. I felt like a junkie who heard the year's biggest shipment of China White had arrived in port.

Ray took a sip and then nodded. "Winter's almost over."

Phil shook his head. "Baseball nerds. Drew, do you want me to get any new CDs for the jukebox?"

The last time I chose a few new discs, Charlie felt slighted and got pissed at Phil and me. I might have requested to put the new Low record in, but it wasn't exactly bar music anyway. "Nothing pressing. Why don't you ask Charlie?"

"Because everyone likes the records you choose better." Phil spit tobacco juice into his empty beer bottle.

Ray took out his pack of cigarillos and lit one. "Still no word from Ralph?"

Phil looked at his watch. "Made it through almost a half hour before hearing that asshole's name."

I understood Phil's anger, but I was more worried about Ralph than angry with him. "We've heard nothing, Ray."

Ray exhaled a cloud of smoke over the bar and then coughed a little. "Have you considered discussing the matter with the police?"

Phil shook his head. "I can't declare the cash, you know that."

"I wasn't talking about the theft. He's disappeared. You could file a report."

Phil spit into his bottle. "He walked out, Ray. Molly saw him."

Ray looked at me. "Your roommate Molly?"

Phil smiled wide. "Yeah, his roommate? Is that what you'd call her at this point, Drew? How do you think she might like that?"

All four eyes fixed on me. It looked as though Phil was lying when he said he could keep a secret. I'd have actually welcomed Butt Crack Larry into the bar at that moment. "We're not talking about me."

Ray was visibly annoyed. "Did he say anything to Molly, Drew?"

"Not to my knowledge." When Molly told me the story, I got the sense there was something she wasn't telling me, but I couldn't blame her. Everyone attached to the bar was shell-shocked by his disappearance, and it must have been doubly bad for her to be there and watch him walk out. I didn't press her. Besides, I had my own insider knowledge about Ralph's situation that I wasn't sharing.

Phil stood, picked the chew out of his lip and threw it in the trashcan. "I'm done talking about this. It's over, he's gone." He reached into the cooler for a fresh beer. He popped off the cap and then held the beer aloft. "Ralph is dead, long live Ralph."

***

Molly was asleep by the time I got home from my double on Thursday and she was gone when I woke up. We'd had no chance to talk about things before I was due to meet up with Megan for dinner. Her arrival was confusing enough, as she'd been sending me excited-sounding emails for the better part of two weeks. With things now complicated between me and Molly, I'd no idea what to think. The situation at Bob's was a blessing in disguise, as being so busy and fielding constant inquiries about Ralph was a good distraction from the mess I'd found myself in.

Normally, I had a standing lunch date with Kathy on Fridays, but I begged off this week. I told her it was because I was covering the extra shifts at the bar, which was partially true. I also didn't want to run the risk of slipping up and letting her know I was seeing Megan that evening. After nursing me back to something resembling a normal mental state following Megan's betrayal, my mom was predictably not a big fan of my ex-girlfriend. I think it hit Kathy even harder because she and Megan had been close, and it probably felt like a double betrayal. Needless to say, I wouldn't hear the end of it if she knew I'd be breaking bread with her personal antichrist.

I whiled away a few hours listening to music and dealt with my nervousness by smoking too many cigarettes. There was a time I might have viewed this visit as a chance to try and get back together with Megan. The tone of her recent emails suggested this was a possibility on her end. Until late Wednesday night, it would have been what I'd wished for over the last two and a half years. Now it was a complication.

I chose Mario's because it was close to Megan's hotel and was nicer than the average Flint restaurant. I'd never eaten there, but Charlie was always raving about it. I got there fifteen minutes early so I could familiarize myself with the surroundings and feel more comfortable before Megan arrived and made me infinitely more uncomfortable.

I ordered a Sapphire and tonic and lit a smoke. The place was nice, although I was the youngest customer by at least two decades. I could see this being something that Charlie liked about it; he was forever searching for oddball affectations that made him appear different, which explained his dedication to his eighty-nine Lincoln Town Car.

Megan was right on time. She walked through the front door, spoke to the crisp-shirted maitre de for a second, and then spotted me out of the corner of her eye. She smiled and waved, then headed over to our table.

"Drew, it's so good to finally see you." Megan gave me an extended warm hug, rubbing her right palm up and down my back.

"It's good to see you, too." I ended the embrace, but held onto her hands. "You look great." I wasn't lying. She'd cut her auburn hair into a very flattering, low-maintenance bob. Megan had a casual beauty, a natural coloring to her face that required only the vaguest hint of make-up. She was concerned that her nose was too small for her face, when in actuality, the upturned tip of it gave her even more character. She'd always seemed a bit out of my league, and it was even truer after nearly three years apart.

"Thanks for picking something near the hotel." She sat in the chair across the table.

"My co-worker Charlie is always on about this place." I spread a menu open in front of me. "How was your meeting with the McLaren folks?" I knew from her emails this was the hospital she was interviewing with.

"It was good. The program is more comprehensive than I'd anticipated. Of course, my parents are all excited at the prospect of me doing my residency close to home."

The waiter interrupted and took Megan's drink order, giving me the briefest moment to ponder my own ambivalence at the same possibility.

"How are your folks?" I was nervous, but I didn't want to chain smoke and make it obvious, so I kept my hands on the menu.

She nodded. "Dad bounced back from the bypass quickly, so that was good news. Mom's still driving me crazy on an almost daily basis even though we're six hundred miles apart." She gave a shy smile. "How's Kathy?"

For some reason, the familiarity rubbed me the wrong way. "She was a little sad when I moved out, but we still see each other pretty often."

The waiter returned with our drinks and we ordered dinner. The chitchat continued through the meal and seemed harmless enough. She told me about some of her classmates in Kansas City, including one guy who was suspected of sneaking into the anatomy lab late at night to fondle the cadavers. I caught her up on my job at the bar and amused her with stories about Phil and Charlie and Ray. I didn't say anything about Ralph. It looked like we might get through the evening without any heaviness, but Megan broke a moment of silence with a sigh that signaled a change in tone.

"Drew, I want to talk about what happened."

"It's not necessary."

"It is for me." Megan pushed her plate forward toward the middle of the table and then folded her hands in front of her.

"I've spent the last two and a half years working my way through this. It hasn't been easy." I looked at every corner of the restaurant in order to avoid Megan's eyes.

"I know. You probably won't believe me, but it hasn't been easy for me, either. I still beat myself up about it all the time." She took a sip of her Shiraz.

I waved her off. "It's over, it happened. No amount of self-recrimination could change anything."

"Have you spoken to Matt?"

My roommate and I had been incommunicado since I caught them together in East Lansing. That required me moving out of our apartment when I knew he'd be in class, and commuting from Flint for finals. It wasn't the way I wanted to wrap up my undergrad experience. "No. Have you?" This sounded as mean as I intended.

"I deserve that." She looked down.

I didn't want to have this meal in order to hurt Megan's feelings. "Look, graduation was a scary time. Moving on was daunting." I pulled a cigarette out of the pack.

"You don't have to make excuses for me."

"I understood. I was going through the same sort of thing."

Megan wouldn't meet my glance. "But you didn't fuck my best friend."

There it was. I really didn't want to talk about this. It's not as though I'm not in touch with my feelings, or that I avoid complex emotions. I'd been dealing with the hurt Megan caused since it happened. The truth is I'd had this conversation with her in the safe confines of my thoughts about a million times. No matter the subject or participants, I've always found it easiest to keep these sorts of talks there, where I can control the responses of my fellow conversant in exactly the manner I'd desire. The actual conversation was considerably more unwieldy. I didn't know what to say, even though I'd rehearsed multitudes of responses. It was entirely possible this was because I'd found myself in love with someone else. I was almost ready to tell her about Molly.

"Drew, you have every reason to hate me."

"I don't hate you. I was angry. I certainly would have preferred that you just break up with me. But I knew once you chose Kansas City over State that we had an expiration date. I'm not stupid."

"I know you're not." She paused and swallowed hard. "I don't know what else to say other than I'm sorry."

"That's nice of you, really. It means a lot to hear that."

It did do me some good to know that Megan was still hurting, too. It didn't change anything about the last two years, however. Two and a half lonely years, finding the most miniscule and sometimes absurd excuses to avoid intimacy with any woman, a bizarre, misguided exercise in proving my fidelity to someone I wasn't even with. Those days were behind me.

"I mean it. I don't know how many times I had to stop myself from calling you and telling you how sorry I am and to tell you..." Megan was cut off by an extremely ill-timed busboy who cleared our dinner plates.

"Tell me what?"

Megan looked at the ceiling with her big brown eyes and drew in a sigh through her mouth.

"I still care about you. I know I don't have any right to say that. The last two years have been so sad and lonely for me. I've missed you." She reached across the table for my hand, which I withdrew to my lap.

I felt a little bad about withdrawing my hand like that. "It can't work like this. Things have changed."

Megan bit her lower lip and looked at the table. "Maybe it was a mistake to come here." She stood, tossed her napkin on the table and moved briskly toward the door.

"Megan, wait." The waiter hadn't brought our bill yet, so I didn't know what the damage was. I panicked, pulled four twenties out of my wallet and threw them on the table. I followed her out of the restaurant and stayed behind her as she walked west on Longway, the traffic of the highway bypass overhead drowning out my shouts for her to stop. I caught up to her at the door of the hotel and put my hand on her shoulder.

"Hey." She turned to face me. I thought she might have been crying, but that could have been wishful thinking. "Let's not leave it like this. The truth is, I've wanted to hear you say you missed me for a long time. I went to sleep a lot of nights hoping that tomorrow would be the day you did. Now you're here, and you did say it, but…"

Megan pressed her right index finger to my lips. "Do I have to kiss you so that you'll shut up?"

I really wasn't finished talking. I'm not sure what would have changed if she let me say what I wanted to say. But there was something about the streetlights, the cold Flint night, the woman who wrecked me in front of me, aching to have me back that made me stop. I should have kept talking.

I nodded instead.

***

I awoke to the sound of Megan in the shower. My legs were sore and the insides of my lips were rubbed raw. I should have been happy, but instead I was having a mild panic attack in that king-sized bed. I was in rarified air, after all. I'd gone from not sleeping with anyone for well over two years to having sex with two different women within forty-eight hours of one another. I was beginning to feel like Charlie.

This was a stunning realization. I found myself wondering what Charlie might do in a similar situation. I made it a habit to not ask many questions about his sex life, but I knew he had a steady stream of new partners and little to no interest in something more meaningful. Two women within forty-eight hours was probably the norm for Charlie. The shower was still running, but I didn't know for how much longer. I had to act fast.

I wasn't thinking clearly, but what was in my head was mostly Molly. I felt as though I'd betrayed her, even though we hadn't declared any sort of mutual exclusivity. Besides, she knew Megan was coming to town and the possibility of Megan and I hooking up must have occurred to her. I began to view Molly's joining me in the shower that night as a possible manipulation, something designed to confuse me on purpose.

No matter what the situation with Molly was or might become, I couldn't face Megan. I'd rarely felt so cowardly, but the thought of seeing her walk out of the shower with wet hair and an annoying satiated smile for some reason made my heart sink. I felt stupid for having stayed with her the night before. I got dressed very quickly and quietly. I wasn't entirely sure where I was headed, I only knew I needed to be out of that room.

Once I was out of the front doors of the hotel, I felt my blood pressure return to normal and my thoughts became somewhat clearer. I got in the Prizm and started the engine. I looked up at the windows of the hotel and saw, in my mind's eye, Megan getting out of the shower, surprised I was no longer there, maybe looking around for a note I would've left behind. She'd notice my clothes were gone and wonder if I'd gone down the hall to the vending machines, but then she'd see the doorstopper wasn't in place and my shoes were gone. I wouldn't need shoes to go down the hall, she'd think. In spite of myself, I thought the mental picture of Megan looking around the room for naught was a little funny and chuckled to myself.

As I pulled out of the hotel parking lot, I started to wonder about Molly. I hoped she hadn't spent any part of the evening on the couch, waiting for me to come home as she had a couple of nights earlier. Even if she hadn't, she'd know I hadn't made it back after my dinner with Megan and would put two and two together. I didn't want to hurt Molly, but anytime someone claimed to not want to hurt someone else, I thought this was exceedingly weak. What the fuck difference did it make if I didn't intend to hurt her?

As I drove toward the apartment, my thoughts started to run away from me. I pictured Molly angry, unable to sleep, taking a kitchen knife to the clothes hanging in my closet, slicing up my favorite Arrow shirt and my Clem Snide t-shirt. I saw her taking my CDs out of the jewel boxes, snapping them between her hands, ripping up lyric sheets and cover art. I thought maybe she'd then turn her attention to my books, taking a pair of scissors to my Barthes and Cawelti and old copies of *The Baseball Research Journal.* I pictured her angry, chain smoking, drinking all my beer. I pictured her sad.

I didn't want to make Molly sad.

It was nearly ten a.m. when I pulled in front of our building. I wished it was a weekday, so Molly would be in class and I could avoid the possible confrontation that was waiting for me. But there was Molly's Cavalier, parked in her favorite spot, still covered in the rock salt dust from the storm a couple of weeks before. There was no pile of burnt clothes and shoes and CDs in front of the building, so I took that as a good sign. I walked in the front door and up the stairs, slowly, quietly. I couldn't hear anything from inside our apartment.

I unlocked the door and walked into the living room. It was still quiet except for my heart, which was audibly pounding. I could see Molly's bedroom door was still closed. As I crept closer, it was silent on the other side of that door as well. She must have still been asleep.

I took a deep breath, took off my coat and shoes and then headed for the bathroom. I turned the shower on and undressed. The room filled with steam. I wiped down the mirror over the sink and looked at my face. There were giant bags under my eyes. My hair stuck out in wild directions like a lazy man's Robert Smith. I smoothed it back with my hands and looked again at my face. It was one of those moments when I simultaneously don't know the person in the mirror and also have a moment of meta-recognition, where I see through myself or above myself or see myself as though I'm in a movie version of my own life. I don't like those moments. They feel

265

transcendental, and all of a sudden, I know why I never pursued any sort of transcendentalism and it's because that shit hurts.

I took a long shower. A hot shower. I don't normally take hot showers. A dime-store analysis would suggest I was cleansing myself of the sin, and I don't know if I'd argue the point. But I didn't expect to get any of those moments to myself, and I didn't quite know what to do with them. It felt good to be clean.

I brushed my teeth. I cleaned my tongue. I combed my hair. I put on deodorant, but sweated right through that even though Molly kept the thermostat pretty low when she slept. It was still quiet. I'd have preferred shouting. I threw on my bathrobe, a blue terry-cloth number that my Mom had bought me when I told her I was moving out and she went on a shopping spree, buying me all sorts of shit I'd had varying degrees of need for. Some of it was still at her house. But I took the robe.

I went to my bedroom. I kept a little stereo in there, a JVC mini system that I played at night when I was reading or couldn't sleep or, like the other night, when I put on *Either/Or* while Molly and I fucked. If she thought Elliott Smith was sad music to fuck to, she never said -- although I guess she'd have been right if she had. It was still in the player. I took it out and replaced it with the first disc of Neil Young's *Decade* because for some reason, I really wanted to hear "Broken Arrow". I lay back on the bed, looking at the ceiling. I'd hit repeat on the track a couple of times and it was on its third or fourth play when Molly opened my bedroom door sans knock.

She looked tired and annoyed. "Can you give this song a rest?"

I leaned over and hit the power button. "Sorry."

"Don't be sorry. That only makes it worse."

I sat up on the bed. "I didn't mean to wake you."

"I've been awake."

"Oh." I wondered why she hadn't come out of her room when I got home. "What are you getting into today?"

She shook her head. "Don't, Drew."

"Don't what?"

266

"It's my fault as much as yours. I should have known better. You've been hung up on Megan forever. In the back of my mind, I probably knew sleeping together would only confuse things between us."

It almost sounded as though Molly was letting me off the hook, which I didn't think I deserved. "I'm not confused."

Molly put her hands on her hips and tilted her head. She looked beautiful. "What's that mean?"

"I'm here, aren't I?"

"You weren't last night Drew, when it mattered."

That felt a little bit more like what I deserved. I sort of wanted her to keep it coming. "It was a mistake, staying with Megan. I'm not in love with her."

Molly nodded. "You don't have to explain. You and I shouldn't complicate things. We're fine as roommates and friends."

I sat up all the way and put my feet on the floor. I'd been preparing for a fight with Molly, for anger and recriminations. Her casual tone was disarming. She sounded ready to give up. Maybe I'd overestimated the seriousness of her feelings for me.

I shrugged. "If that's what you think is best."

"I can't afford to find a new roommate."

I didn't want to move back to Kathy's, but I also didn't want to give up on something bigger with Molly. Like my dad used to tell me though, actions speak louder than words. If I'd really wanted something with Molly, then I shouldn't have spent the night with Megan.

I found Molly's pragmatism a little depressing. I was ready to be shouted at, to have things thrown at me. In a way, I'd have preferred the pile of clothes and CDs I'd envisioned on the way over rather than this practical and completely unromantic version. Maybe I'd overestimated the seriousness of my feelings for her.

I reached over and turned the stereo back on. I pressed play and filled the room with "Broken Arrow" again. It'd be forever linked with this moment.

Molly nodded and forced a weary smile. "I guess that's my cue." She turned on her heel and left the room, clicking the door shut behind her.

***

When I pulled up in front of the bar that afternoon, Phil's SUV was already out front.

I unlocked the side door and entered. Phil was mopping the floor.

He looked up, confusion all over his expression. "What are you doing here?"

"I've only worked Saturday afternoons for eighteen months." I did the math in my head. "Seventy-two straight, give or take."

Phil still looked confused. "I thought we decided I'd cover Saturday afternoon until we got someone new so you could have back-to-back days off."

I had no recollection of any such discussion. "Are you sure that conversation didn't take place entirely in your head?"

"Of course I'm not." He put the mop back into the bucket. "If I'm not supposed to be here, then you won't mind if I stop cleaning the floor for your shift?"

I shook my head and then made a show of looking at my watch. "I'm way ahead of schedule now." I sat in the closest booth and took out a cigarette.

Phil sat across from me. "Mind if I join you?"

I handed him a cigarette. "Since when are you smoking?"

"Since this situation here is fucked." He grabbed my lighter and lit the cigarette. "This place is more trouble than it's worth."

I waved him off. "This is an aberration. We'll get someone in here."

Phil tapped the smoke in the ashtray on the table. He'd already cleaned them. "What about that friend of yours? Adam?"

"Aaron?" I took a drag. "He's been banned for like a year. I haven't spoken with him in about as long. Last I heard, he was in Detroit, working the door at the Magic Stick."

"He's banned? Why don't I remember this?"

I shrugged. "It was a long time coming. Ralph and Charlie were fed up with him. I think they let him overstay because they didn't want to offend me, but I didn't give a fuck at the end."

"So what did he do?"

I took another drag from my cigarette. "I wasn't here, but what Ralph told me is he was up to his usual bullshit, getting way too drunk and handsy on a couple of women. So Ralph tossed him, and he started freaking out about finishing his beer, moving like he was going to take it out of the bar with him. Ralph came around and went to grab it from him, and Aaron dumped it on him. Ralph said he wrapped him up in a bear hug and threw him out onto the street."

Phil shook his head. "You and Aaron go back?"

I nodded. "Middle school."

Phil's eyes went wide. "Speaking of going back, I almost forgot you were getting together with your ex last night. What happened?"

I took a deep breath. I was sort of hoping Phil wouldn't ask. I hadn't fully digested the sequence of events of the previous eighteen hours. "I spent the night with her." I looked down at my shoes.

"Why the long face? You've been hung up on this girl for how long?"

"I don't want Megan anymore."

"Obviously. She wouldn't have slept with you unless she sensed that. That's how it works." Phil took a last drag from the cigarette and put it out in the ashtray.

"I want Molly."

269

Phil shook his head. "You really are an idiot."

"I know."

Phil stood. "That's alright, it takes one to know one."

I thought that comeback was a bit of an anachronism. "Sounds like you're talking about something else."

He nodded. "I think I'm about done with this place."

"What are you talking about?"

Phil's face turned lightly red. "I'm talking about being too old for this shit. I've got a wife and kid at home. I can't be covering a bunch of shifts in here, running around when I should be at home with my family."

I'd never heard him say anything resembling this. I waved him off. "It's not the normal state of affairs. Ralph walked off with no warning. We'll find someone soon."

He shook his head. "It's more than that." He sat in the booth. "Eight years of this. Running from the tax collectors, from ASCAP, BMI. I'm paying for my attorney's house up North. It's not worth it anymore."

I wanted to point out he could run the business in a more legitimate fashion and bypass the attorney's fees, but it wasn't the time for that discussion. "You're just frustrated, and I understand. You lost your most popular bartender with no warning. He even grabbed the cash out of the till on his way out."

"Straw and camel, Drew. Straw and camel. It's time to grow up, time to admit Flint's fucked and one little bar that brings the cool kids downtown isn't ever going to stem the tide."

I don't know why I was trying to talk Phil off this ledge. If I was to be objective, he was absolutely right; Flint was fucked. It didn't matter how much the powers-that-be wanted to clean up downtown because pretty facades and freshly paved streets wouldn't make any difference if there were no businesses. Maybe some adventurous younger people would continue to rehab houses in Carriage Town, or move into one of the lofts in the Republic Bank Building if they ever complete that project. That would be fine for a few years. Eventually, those same adventurous younger people will get a little older and marry and have children, and there's zero chance of the same sense of adventure applying to sending their kids to Flint Community Schools. Talk was talk and action was action. People would forever talk about the potential for places like Flint to bounce back and reinvent themselves after post industrialization. The fact was that if it didn't happen in the previous decade, when things were swinging and cash was flowing and even a place like Cleveland could be called "Comeback City," then it was too fucking late for Flint.

"I don't blame you for getting down, Phil. At all." I took a last drag off the cigarette and put it out. "What are you thinking about?"

He shrugged. "Charlie's made entreaties. I'd sell him the inventory and lease the space, but I'd still own the building."

I nodded. It was hard enough to work with Charlie. I wasn't sure I could work for him.

Phil stood again. "I'm just thinking out loud. Don't freak out just yet."

"I'm not freaking out." I looked at my watch. "I need to finish getting the place ready."

"I'll get out of your way." Phil pointed at my pack of Parliaments. "One for the road?"

"Be my guest."

He took one out of the pack and lit it with a deep drag. "I'll leave you with one last thought." He pointed at me. "Do you want a wife and kids?"

I nodded. "Someday."

"Do you think Charlie does? Or Ralph?"

I knew Ralph's stance on having a family explicitly, and Charlie's was obvious from the way he treated nearly every woman who crossed his path. "I guess not."

"Then don't be like Charlie and Ralph."

Phil turned and walked out of the bar without saying goodbye.

✳✳✳

Later that afternoon I was sitting on the stool at the end of the bar, half-listening to Kirby and Kent trudge through yet another argument about George W. Bush. They'd gone at it pretty good in the aftermath of the election, but now that it had been decided a couple of months earlier by the Supreme Court, they'd turned to disagreements about what effect the new administration might have on foreign policy and economics.

Kent spoke quietly. "If you think those air strikes on Iraq a few weeks ago were the last, you're kidding yourself."

Kirby smiled knowingly. "Clinton bombed the shit out of Saddam quite regularly."

Kent shook his head. "Not like that. And not so close to Baghdad. Look, Saddam tried to kill W's dad. It's personal. He'll find some reason to go in there and get him out of power."

"And if Saddam lets weapons inspectors in?"

Kent laughed. "Never gonna happen. Saddam can't let his enemies know he's got no nukes. They'd run right over him."

I may have thought Kent was making a surprising amount of sense, but I adhered fairly closely to keeping all political and religious discussions out of the bar. The only reason I didn't interrupt this argument was because the bar was otherwise empty and I was distracted.

Kent was haranguing Kirby about the hawkishness of both Vice President Cheney and Secretary of Defense Rumsfeld when the front door opened and Megan walked in.

I'd almost forgotten about her.

She stormed up to me. "What the fuck, Drew?" Her tone was exasperated.

I wondered how often Charlie received angry visits such as this one. "Hi Megan."

"Hi?" She looked at Kirby and Kent. "Can we talk more privately?"

Kirby and Kent looked at me quizzically. This was certainly one way to shut them up, although I'd have preferred to hear Kent talk about Ashcroft losing the Senate election to a dead guy for the fiftieth time.

I pointed at one of the booths on the other side of the bar. "That's as private as it's likely to get." I stood and followed Megan.

We both sat. Megan pointed at me. "You've got a lot of nerve running out like that without a word. I've been wracking my brain trying to figure out what must be going through yours."

"Last night was a mistake."

"You're telling me. I should've known you hadn't matured, working in this shithole hanging around with a bunch of losers, going nowhere."

Under other circumstances, I might have pointed out that her actions were at least partially responsible for my present situation. But I was through blaming her. "I shouldn't have left like that. I'm sorry."

She huffed. "I thought I was really going to have to work to get that out of you."

I took the pack of Parliaments from my shirt pocket and lit one. "Aside from how inconsiderate I was, why does it make any difference?"

She shook her head. "Why do you think I was interviewing at McLaren, Drew? Do you think it's a dream of mine to live in Flint?"

I truly hadn't considered the possibility that Megan wanted to reconnect with me. A few months prior, I would have obsessed over the very possibility. By then, it made no difference. Even if I couldn't have Molly, I knew I no longer wanted Megan. "Why didn't you say something?"

"I shouldn't have to."

That was just like Megan, to expect me to read her mind even though we'd barely spoken for the better part of three years. "I didn't mean to lead you on." I took a drag of the cigarette. "The truth is, I'm in love with someone else."

"That's a funny way to show it, sleeping with me."

Cher's voice rang in my ear, singing 'If I could turn back time'. That was unpleasant. I shook my head. "And maybe it was a shitty thing to do, for you to show up here with all these expectations I don't even know about and then throw yourself at me."

Megan's eyes were wide. "I threw myself at you?"

I looked at the ceiling. I'd have really preferred to have a similar fight with Molly. I had no passion for this discussion. I wanted it to be over. "What do you want, Megan? Why did you come here?"

She grabbed her purse and stood. "I wanted you to know you can't just treat me like that. There are repercussions. I'm not some piece of trash you take home from this bar."

I could've pointed out I'd never taken a woman home from this bar, trash or otherwise. I could've pointed out the hurt she visited on me was twenty-fold what I'd done to her. I could've pointed out it was actually somewhat pathetic that she'd taken the trouble to ask around an unfamiliar city for the name and location of this bar and then shown up throwing accusations around, acting like a spurned girlfriend. I could've pointed out that I'd probably never lose the image of my roommate pounding her from behind on my couch, and I hated her for it, and that I'd never again over-romanticize a single moment from our relationship.

I took another drag from my cigarette. "And what repercussions are those?"

"You'll never see me again."

In spite of my best efforts, the corners of my lips fought to turn up in a slight smile.

I stopped fighting it and grinned widely. "Is that all?"

***

I spent most of the rest of the afternoon trying to deflect Kirby and Kent calling me "Scarface" or "The New Charlie", and trying to get Molly on the phone.

She wasn't answering.

I didn't know what I'd say if she did -- which was strange. It was exactly the sort of conversation I'd have in my head over and over; one I'd rehearse and then be perplexed when the other participant said something that was off the script I'd written.

I probably should have been offended or at least annoyed that my mistreatment of Megan was such a resounding hit with Kirby and Kent, but the truth was I found it funny too. I hadn't set out for any sort of revenge, which made the outcome somehow more satisfying. The two of them settled into a drunken reminiscence of their other favorite moments featuring me behind the bar, as though I was a fading rock star coming to the end of a recording contract. Maybe the times when you can actually feel things change, when the ground seems to move beneath your feet, are exceedingly rare. Maybe you're lucky to be awake during those moments, or maybe that same awareness is a curse.

I rang the phone in our apartment one more time.

After all, transcendentalism hurts.

RALPH & BETH

When Beth told me she was pregnant, I honestly felt a switch turn in my brain. That's not an exaggeration or hyperbole; an honest-to-God switch flipped. Click. And I wish I could say it flipped to something positive, that all of a sudden, I grew up and knew I had to be responsible and turn over a new leaf for this person who I'd made. That wasn't the switch that flipped.

I hadn't told anybody about the baby. Nobody at the bar even knew that Beth and I had stayed involved after Phil dressed me down for it almost two years earlier. It wasn't a real relationship after all; Beth bought weed from me to sell to some friends, and when she'd pick up, we'd get down. There was no guarantee of exclusivity. No dates, no dinners, no movies. Just the pot and the fucking. She'd told me she was on the pill. Maybe she really was, I don't know, and it doesn't matter even a little bit at this point. What was that old joke Steven Wright used to tell about his girlfriend being on like eight types of birth control and getting pregnant anyway and the baby coming out wearing armor? Oh well. I couldn't ask anyone because maybe they'd start wondering why I was asking questions about pregnancy and babies and figure out what I hadn't told anyone. It was too much.

The pressure was getting to me and I needed someone to confide in. I hadn't cultivated any real close friendships recently; most of my friends were of the party buddy sort. Although I didn't spend much time with him outside of the bar, I thought Drew was a genuine person, something Bob's was often lacking. Once he started working at the bar, he also revealed himself to be reliable, even if he was a little prissy. We'd chatted from time to time and I could trust him, at least more than most of the people around me.

I'd come in a little early on a Tuesday to relieve Drew from behind the bar because I figured it'd be empty. It was.

I put a couple of singles in the jukebox and tried to amuse myself with some tunes. I was still a little cloudy from an afternoon of bong hits. I wasn't even all that sure what I was playing.

Drew sat on a stool on the other side of the bar and I fetched him his shift beer. A pint of Anchor. I didn't need to ask.

We chitchatted a bit. He told me that Butt Crack Larry had been in for a couple of drafts earlier in the day. Drew mentioned that he appeared to have bathed that day, as his stench was a little less oppressive than normal, but his hair still seemed weighed down with Crisco. We all wished that Larry would do something worthy of getting himself banned from the bar, but as annoying as he was, he was also mild-mannered.

I poured myself a pint glass of ice water and stood across the bar from Drew.

"You look like something's on your mind, Ralph."

I nodded. I told him all about Beth and the pregnancy, our years of clandestinely hooking up, even my buying large quantities of weed from The Man for re-sale, which I figured he already knew since it wasn't a very well-kept secret.

Drew took a sip from his draft and set the glass down on the bar. "Are you excited?"

I thought it should have been obvious just from the context that I wasn't. I didn't want to be anyone's dad. "No. Of course I'm not."

Drew nodded. "Do you have feelings for Beth?"

"I'm sorry?"

He looked confused. "You said you and Beth have been hooking up for a long time. You must have some sort of feelings about her, right? Why else continue with your arrangement?"

What Beth and I had was not about feelings, it was about convenience. We had uniformly outstanding sex, although I'd always attributed most of that to marijuana's aphrodisiacal properties. "I don't hate her or anything."

"That's real warm, Ralph." Drew shook out a Parliament from his pack and lit it. "Can you see yourself in a relationship with her?"

Drew was asking a lot of questions I hadn't bothered asking myself. It was hard for me to envision anything serious with a woman who I'd never even taken to dinner or a movie, who'd never met my parents nor I hers. "Our relationship is going to change whether I like it or not."

"That's putting it mildly." Drew took a drag from his cigarette. "I guess I'm more than a little confused, though. You haven't really been dating anyone for years, which means you and Beth are exclusive."

Phil and Ray had effectively scared me off of dating any customers and I didn't have the sort of social life outside of the bar that lent itself to meeting potential dating partners. "I don't know whether or not Beth sees other people."

The jukebox flipped over to the initial guitar chimes of Radiohead's "No Surprises". Apropos, although I didn't remember choosing that song.

Drew fixed me with a sideways glance. "Then how does she know the baby is yours?"

I shrugged but didn't answer.

"Let me ask you this," He pointed at me with his cigarette. "Has she ever said she loves you?"

I shrugged again. I honestly couldn't remember.

※※※

Beth stepped over my legs, which were stretched out on the coffee table and sat next to me on the couch. She'd spent a chunk of her afternoon cleaning my apartment. It was literally cleaner than it had been in years. "The bathroom was the worst. I don't know how you live like that."

I shrugged. I looked at Beth. She was cute: her brown hair in pigtails, her chubby cheeks with one single chicken pockmark just enough of a flaw to give her character. It wasn't a stretch to say I was attracted to her; after all, she and I had sex about a million times. Even if it had been casual, if there was nothing physical between us, I'd have given up long ago.

I knew the bathroom was gross and I was grateful she'd cleaned it. "You get used to it, I guess." I wanted a clove, but I wasn't going to light up around Beth. "You didn't have to do all that."

"I know." She put her head on my shoulder. This sort of intimacy was usually reserved for the tenderest of our post-coital moments, but all the old rules were out the window as Beth's pregnancy progressed. "I think it's hormonal. Nesting."

I liked Beth, and I was beginning to feel more comfortable around her, but the situation was still new and strange. "How many kids do you think have parents who met when their dads sold their moms some high-grade marijuana?"

Beth lifted her head and punched me in the arm. "Don't be an asshole."

It was a serious question. I wasn't trying to provoke her, so I dropped it. "Tell me more about your parents' house."

It felt weird to be doing so much getting-to-know-you sort of talk with Beth considering how long we'd known each other, at least biblically. But I'd found myself swept up in her desire to make an effort at a relationship in anticipation of being parents together. In a way, it felt like the least I could do.

Beth smiled. "I guess it's pretty big, although it wasn't the biggest house I knew growing up. It's on a cul-de-sac: all brick, four floors, pretty intense landscaping out front."

I was a little surprised to find out that her dad owns Michigan Luggage and Travel, a small chain with ten or so stores scattered around the Southeastern and Central parts of the state. Beth didn't carry herself like a rich girl. It was a family business, handed down from his dad, although Beth had chosen not to enter it.

I leaned back on the couch and put my hands behind my neck. "Your folks are gonna hate me, aren't they?"

Beth shook her head. "They already think I'm weird. Dad hates that I'm a social worker; he gets scared all the time about some of the situations the office puts us in. Besides, they're so excited about the baby, and you're the father, so they're actually going to love you. I think they believe having the baby means I'll quit my job."

I wasn't convinced. I felt out of my element just discussing this Grand Blanc mini mansion. In addition, I wasn't sure how I felt about raising a kid on a drug dealers' income. "Do you want to quit your job?"

She looked at me and smiled. "There's plenty of time to talk about what happens next." She stood and grabbed her dusting rag from the coffee table. "Just be ready for my dad. He can be a little enthusiastic."

I guess that made one of us.

***

It hit me when I was asleep. To be more precise, it was in that nether region between sleep and wakefulness, when I'd finally gotten to lie down after working a double on a Monday. I'm not sure what I was thinking of, but predictably, I'd been having a lot of trouble falling asleep since Beth had sprung that baby shit on me. I'd spend an hour or two or more spinning over various scenarios in my head, running through permutations and calculations and things like the effects of marijuana on the quality of my sperm.

About a week earlier, The Man informed me that he'd be going on another lengthy vacation, this time to the Bahamas, and asked if I'd be willing to help him with some aspects of his business that would need attending to while he was gone. At the time, all I could think was how wonderful it'd be to hightail it off to some island myself. He'd done this a few times over the years and entrusted me to make a couple of pick-ups and drop-offs while he was gone. I half-listened to the details, knowing he'd give them to me again closer to his trip.

I sat up in bed, remembering how much cash was involved during The Man's vacations. It wasn't the sort of money I could retire on, but it'd certainly ferry me away from Flint and into some sort of alternate reality that was far removed from my present situation. I wasn't entirely awake, and I may have been taking some of my nerve from my drowsy state, but I was starting to feel as though I needed to consider some different plans of action. I got up out of bed and searched through a few drawers in the kitchen trying to find a notepad I remembered buying a few months prior. Maybe it was a year. At any rate, I couldn't find it, but I did find a pen and a weeks-old copy of the *Journal*, so I started scribbling some notes and numbers in the margins in the Sports section. I wasn't sure any of it would make sense later or if I'd have the courage to do what I was writing about, but getting the thoughts out of my head and onto paper made them feel more real somehow. Beth was real and the baby was real, and this opportunity was real. I was tired of feeling like a spectator in my own life. It felt like a good time to change roles.

***

Drew's roommate Molly had commandeered me on a slow Wednesday near closing. I wondered if maybe Drew had spilled my beans, but I figured he could keep a secret and she wasn't acting funny apart from peppering me with questions about Drew, who she was clearly in love with.

I poured a pitcher for a couple of UM-Flint kids at the end of the bar who had presented me with pretty lousy fake ID's. It was too slow to throw them out, but I kept an eye on their intake to make sure they remained in some semblance of control. I could rely on Charlie to toss them from the bar if they ever tried to come back. I took their money and headed back to the other end of the bar where Molly was sitting.

Molly looked good. When she first started coming into the bar, I thought she was someone I could potentially date, but I was almost sure Charlie had slipped his tentacles around her, so that was that. It wasn't an ethical stance; I just wasn't about to go where Charlie had been. Ever.

The UM kids moved to the jukebox and punched up a few tunes. "The Lost Art of Keeping a Secret" from the most recent Queens of the Stone Age record filled the bar. I smirked and shook my head.

I pointed at Molly's pint glass, which was nearly empty. "Ready for another?"

She shook her head. "Not just yet." Molly gestured with her head at the jukebox. "All the goddamned dude rock in this place."

I shrugged. "Just be glad I didn't get in there and play of bunch of Rush."

Molly laughed. "Geddy Lee kind of sings like a girl. It'd be better than this dick rock."

It wasn't like her to complain. I'd found her to be an extremely laid-back, roll-with-the-punches sort. As low-maintenance as any woman I'd known. I'm not sure why Drew hadn't hooked up with her yet, but then I thought maybe he also knew about her and Charlie.

I sat on the stool at the end of the bar and shook a Sampoerna out of the pack. "Why don't you just tell Drew how you feel about him?"

"We live together. It's complicated. What if he doesn't feel the same way? How could we stay in the same apartment together? It'd be awkward." She took the last drink from her pint glass and set it on the bar. "Besides, he's in love with his ex-girlfriend."

The college girlfriend who broke Drew's heart before heading off to medical school was infamous. To hear Drew tell the story, which he generally did for comedic effect, it sounded like he was completely over it. However, he didn't date much if he dated at all, so it was possible that he wasn't. "Have you thought about making him jealous?"

She shook her head and then pushed her empty pint glass across the bar. "This isn't high school."

I took a shallow drag from my clove and then got up to bring Molly another bottle of Sam Adams. I brought it back and put it in front of her. "That one's on me."

"Thanks, Ralph." She poured the bottle into the pint glass in front of her. "You know she's coming to visit, right?"

"His ex?"

She nodded.

"Is she staying with you?"

"No, she's interviewing at a hospital. They're putting her up in a hotel."

I imagined Molly was grateful that their reunion sex would happen somewhere other than the apartment she shared with Drew. "That's good."

Molly put her head in her hands and rubbed her eyes. "I'm so stupid. I can't believe I got myself into this situation."

"We all do stupid things."

She looked at me through clasped fingers over her face. "What do you mean?"

I looked down at the UM-Flint kids at the other end of the bar. I couldn't hear what they were saying over The Dismemberment Plan on the jukebox, so I assumed they couldn't hear us either. "I'm gonna be a dad."

∗∗∗

Beth's dad insisted I call him Carl. Her mom was demure. The house was easily the biggest I'd ever been in, and the dining room, in which we sat, was nearly the size of the entire first floor of my childhood

283

home. They'd served us a gut-busting meal of filet, roasted potatoes, giant salads and a coconut cake. We were on our third bottle of wine, and each one tasted more expensive than the last, and all of them were worth more than I probably made in an above-average night at the bar.

Carl peppered me with questions about my schooling, my years at Michigan Electrical Supply, the bar, my family. I rolled with the punches and did my best to keep a smile on my face; after all, his curiosity was perfectly understandable considering I was now inexorably intertwined with his family.

Years ago, my dad taught me to look at a woman's mom if I wanted a sense of what a potential wife might look like as the years passed. This was not an encouraging thought on this particular night. Beth's mom was her height, which is to say on the short side of average, and they had the same rounded face and button nose. Whereas Beth was not thin, her mom had full-on blown up. One can assume having children to be at least partially responsible for the body change, and Beth's mom was, well, fat. Not in a pleasantly plump way, either. She was gross.

Carl was telling me all about his business, giving me a crash course in Tumi and Hartmann, complaining about a couple of his local store managers. Beth and her mom went to the kitchen to make more coffee and fix a Rusty Nail for Carl. When they left, he moved to the chair closest to me, where Beth had been sitting.

He smiled wide at me. His teeth were preternaturally white. He had a more casual Blake Carrington thing going on, dressed in crisp tan slacks and a thin Merino argyle sweater. I got the sense he may not have owned a pair of jeans. "Have you ever thought about retail work before, Ralph?"

The truth is I rarely thought about any work other than what I did. "I worked at a Kohl's for a couple years in High School."

He nodded. "Did you find the work enjoyable?"

I didn't remember all that much about it, apart from people shouting at me about being out of a size XXL in a particular sweater or complaining that there weren't enough registers open. Maybe

Tully deserved more sympathy, come to think of it. "I enjoyed interacting with customers, helping people."

"It's what I love too. Ralph, you'd be amazed at how wonderful it is to sell people luggage. They are excited to plan trips, vacations, send their children to college. It isn't like other retail businesses. People are energized when they shop at Michigan Luggage and Travel."

I nodded. I felt like he was trying to get me to invest in the company. "That sounds great, Mr. Davis."

"I thought I told you to call me Carl." He gave a fake laugh that was so rehearsed it nearly sounded real. "And it is great, Ralph." He looked at me and waited for a response.

I swallowed hard. "Mm-hm."

He slapped me on the knee and then stood. "I don't want to seem like I'm pressuring you, Ralph, but I think you might benefit from a change in direction. What do you think?"

I couldn't have agreed more. "I've thought it might be time for something new."

Carl nodded and then walked back towards his seat at the head of the table, underneath a giant portrait of a steam ship at port, in front of a well-appointed buffet that had to have been generations old. He sat and folded his hands in front of him. "I'm looking for someone I can trust, someone who'll have a sense of ownership. Someone who cares about the store. It may benefit both of us, Ralph, if you are that person."

I was sure I was not the person he was looking for. He'd be sure if he knew me. "I think it's something worth discussing further."

He smiled. "That's smart. Don't commit yourself without the details." He unfolded his hands and put them behind his neck. "I like you, Ralph."

I was saved from having to concoct a response as Beth and her mom came back into the room. They each carried a sterling silver tray, Beth's held a couple of coffee cups and a carafe, her mom's a single rock's glass which she placed in front of Carl. I wasn't sure why the drink needed to be carried in on a tray, but I didn't bother to ask.

I sort of wished Beth had allowed me to do some bong hits before we came. She was pretty firmly against it though.

Beth put a coffee cup in front of me and then leaned over in front of me and poured some in. It was a little weird to have her serve me this way. I hoped it was a show for her parents. She smiled at me and gave me a sly wink. Her hormones were wreaking havoc with her sex drive, and she was in pretty constant demand of intercourse. I wasn't exactly complaining, although I thought I might feel a little differently once the pregnancy started to show.

Beth sat next to me and her mom sat next to her dad. We sipped our drinks in silence for a moment before Carl spoke.

"Now that you're both back, we wanted to share some news with the two of you." Carl reached out for his wife's hand.

I wondered if Carl still had sex with this woman, or if he had a secretary or some store manager or whatever on the side. It seemed almost certain to me. I'd never say that to Beth, though.

Beth's mom smiled widely. "The Putnams are moving to Florida and we put a bid in on their house for you."

Beth screamed and her mom stood and screamed in response. It was a big dining room, but the combined decibel level was still sufficient to hurt my ears and make me wince.

My ears were still ringing, but it was quiet enough in my head to know it was time to wrest control of this situation.

***

A couple of days after The Man had left on his vacation, I stood in front of my linen closet looking at the ten pounds of marijuana he'd left with me. It made me nervous. He must have had some sort of airtight sealing apparatus, because it didn't smell up the house or anything like that, but it was a lot of weight just the same.

I wondered if he gave even a passing thought to my trustworthiness. I'd never been late with a payment or shorted him a cent in the two plus years we'd done business together. It struck me that this was the brilliance of the move; had it been a planned long con, maybe he'd have seen through me and never provided this opportunity. At the same time, my usual monthly delivery was only a half-pound. I sort of wondered why he didn't trust any of his other distributors more than he did me.

There was a knock at the door. I slammed the closet shut and bounded down the stairs. Tully. It was just like him to be early. Our appointment wasn't for another hour. I opened the door and let him in.

"Hey, Ralph." He shook some snow off his coat. "It's really coming down."

I hadn't realized it was snowing. I looked out the window and noticed that my Explorer was covered with at least two inches of the white stuff. The bar would probably be slow tonight. I wouldn't need to worry about tips much longer. "Then take your shoes off." I turned around and sat on the couch.

Tully joined me in the living room after getting his coat and boots off. "This is right around the time I get tired of winter every year." He was still dressed in the maroon polo he wore as a uniform at the greeting cards store in the mall. Although he bellyached to anyone who'd listen about still hating that job, and the Beanie Babies craze had only grown since it first became the bane of his existence, I think he'd settled into a weed-induced stasis.

I disliked it when people complain about things over which they have no control, and I had little to no use for just about anything that came out of Tully's mouth for quite some time. He may have thought we were still friends, but I viewed ours as a business relationship and had for years. I gave a guttural acknowledgement that was meant to put an end to the discussion of the weather.

Tully pulled a pack of Winston's out of his front jeans pocket and lit one. A stray beam of sunlight caught the cloud of his exhale. "So, are you going to tell me why you have so much extra to unload today?"

"I'm not." Although it had been over a week since my last after hours, I hadn't bothered to pick up the living room at all. There was a stack of photo prints on the coffee table. I picked them up and started leafing through. I didn't recognize anyone. "Did you get the money?"

Tully reached into his other pants pocket and pulled out a white envelope. "Big bills, just like you asked." He slapped it on the table. "C'mon, man, just tell me what's going on. That's three thousand dollars I just put down on the table. It's gotta be worth something."

"It's worth the half a pound of high-grade marijuana you'll get in return." I was selling Tully my monthly allowance at a small profit in order to speed things along. Time was of the essence, although I suppose it almost always is. But I needed a head start.

"Whatever." He took another drag from his Winston. "Do you have any beer in the fridge?"

I didn't know. "Look for yourself."

He got up and went to the kitchen. I hated selling the half-pound to Tully. There was something about giving him a two-thousand-dollar discount that made me want to punch myself in the balls.

Tully came back to the living room with a bottle of Sierra Nevada Celebration Ale that had been in the refrigerator since well before Christmas. "Thanks for the beer."

"Thanks for getting me one."

He sat on the couch and shrugged. "You know who I saw coming out of the maternity store yesterday?"

I had an inkling. My heart sped up. "How could I?"

"Beth Death."

"Is that right?" It was cold in the apartment, but that didn't stop me from sweating.

"Yep. Big bag of what I assume was clothes. I also assumed they were for her. Why would you buy a giant bag of maternity clothes for someone other than yourself?" He looked over at me, waiting for a response.

"What?" I reached for the stack of photos. I looked down to see pictures of someone's office Christmas party. It looked like the workers were being forced into seasonal joyousness, all strained smiles and Santa hats.

"You used to bang Beth Death, didn't you?"

"So the fuck what?" I put the pictures back. They fell off the table in a heap on the dirty rug.

"It's just funny, that's all."

"You need to put that bottle in your mouth before you say anything else." I concentrated on stopping my hands from shaking.

Tully took a sip from the beer. "I don't see what you're getting so pissed about." He stubbed out his cigarette in the overfull ashtray on the coffee table. "Unless that's your baby." He smirked.

I stood and moved toward him. "I'm pretty sure I told you to shut the fuck up, Tully."

He put his hands up in front of him. "Calm down, man. Let me just get my weed and get out of your hair."

I had a thought. As long as I was burning bridges, adding one more didn't seem to make much of a difference. I reached down and picked up the white envelope from the coffee table. "You're not getting any weed today. Get out, and feel lucky that I didn't fuck you up."

He stood and then moved a couple of steps away. "What the fuck are you talking about, Ralph? This isn't like you." He was trembling. "I didn't mean anything about Beth. Your secret's safe with me."

"Keep fucking talking, you piece of shit, and your luck's bound to run out quickly." I was calm. I could tell he was scared.

"That's my rent, my car payment, all my bills right there." He pointed at the envelope, which by then was in my pocket.

"Your rent, your car payment." I smiled. "Your problem."

"This is fucked up. This isn't you."

He was right about that. But the new me was all about seizing opportunities wherever they might arise. I nodded and then made a show of looking at my arms and legs. "Looks an awful lot like me." I went to the breezeway and picked up Tully's coat and boots. I brought them back into the living room and slowly set them down in front of him.

"It's cold out there, I'll tell you. I get really tired of winter right about now. But then, I'm tired of all sorts of things."

He slipped on his boots, not bothering to tie them, then stood and fumbled with the sleeves of his coat before getting it most of the way on. "This isn't over, Ralph." His voice was shaky. He turned to leave.

Add Tully's three grand to the fifty I'd be picking up the next day, and this was turning into the greatest opportunity I was likely to ever get. I also no longer felt like punching myself in the balls.

Tully pulled open the front door and stormed out, not bothering to shut it behind him. A cold wind and some snowflakes pushed their way in. I went to the door and considered calling after him. Something about Beanie Babies or finishing his beer. I figured I'd let him have the last word instead.

***

Drew came in through the side door of the bar. Even though it was his afternoon off and he wasn't due to relieve me for several hours, I wasn't surprised to see him.

"You told Molly?" His voice wasn't as incredulous as I might have expected.

"Yeah, well, I thought it'd be nice for you to have someone to talk with about it."

He took off his coat and tossed it into one of the booths, and then went to the other end of the bar to help pull down stools, shaking his head. "I'm just surprised is all."

I wondered if he'd be surprised to hear everything Molly was telling me when she was here the other night, but I bit my tongue. Playing matchmaker was not my strong suit. "Honestly, it's been a relief."

Drew pulled down the last stool and sat on it, close to the end of the bar. "I'll bet."

"You don't get enough of this place? You'll have to be back before you know it." In fact, I'd be heading straight from the bar to make the big delivery for The Man. The ten pounds was under a blanket in the back of the Explorer. It made me nervous.

"I'm here now. I can work the double if you wanted to take the afternoon to clear your head." Drew took a pack of Parliaments out of his pocket and set them on the bar.

It was an intriguing offer. "Let's have a beer and I'll think about it."

Drew nodded, and then lit one of his cigarettes with a Bic someone had left on the bar.

I moved to the taps and pulled a couple of Anchor Steam drafts. I brought them back to where Drew was sitting and sat on the stool at the end of the bar. "Cheers." I held out my glass.

Drew met it with a clink from his. He took a small sip. "I don't mean to pry, Ralph, but is it weird not to have Ray come down in the afternoons?"

In the old days, Ray would be due to come ambling in from upstairs. I was used to him not coming down, but obviously Drew was accustomed to the opposite. I knew he and Ray had gotten close since he started working here. I wasn't jealous; it was nice for Ray to have Drew helping to look out for him. It had been years since Ray and I had our falling out. I'd tried periodically to send along peace offerings: Christmas cards, a gift certificate to the book store near his birthday, copies of *Baseball Weekly* that people had left behind at the bar. Ray wasn't the forgive-and-forget type. "It breaks my heart that he's not here."

"I hope I'm not talking out of school, but I asked him about it. Last spring, when he and I went to Comerica." He took a drag from his Parliament and exhaled.

I wasn't sure how to react. Normally, I'd see this as a sort of invasion of my privacy, but Drew wasn't the gossipy sort. "What made you do that?"

He shrugged. "I guess I wondered if he was hurt, too. I knew you were pals before I started. Plus, Charlie told me you used to run errands for him before he and I took over. Ray's prideful and all, but I couldn't imagine what would cause that sort of reaction from him."

I took a sip from my beer. "Can I get one of those Parliaments?"

Drew slid the pack across the bar. "You don't have to talk about this if you don't want to."

I shook one out of the pack and lit it. I rarely smoked anything other than pot and the cloves. It tasted stale. "Ray hates drugs."

"Okay."

"He caught me smoking up one afternoon when he came down. He gave me a big speech. Then I started selling, and he put two and two together after a couple of people stopped in and left without having a drink."

Drew had a puzzled look on his face as he took a big drink from his beer. He put the glass down. "It makes sense if you think about it. Ray was too old to be a hippie. He's no conservative, but he's a vet. Weed equates to the counterculture for him. That's the type of stuff that hurt his business for a long time. It was like an entire generation of people who skipped over bar culture."

I shook my head. "I'm not sure." I took another drag from the Parliament, which didn't taste any better. "I think it's more about loyalty to Phil, not wanting him to get in trouble."

"But he knows all about how Phil runs this place. He could get into plenty of trouble for that."

I'd been behind the bar for various visits from representatives from ASCAP, BMI, the IRS, and the city over the years. The wolves were never far from Phil's door. Only a few friends in the right places and attorney's fees to choke a pig kept him in business. "Yeah, but that would be trouble Phil invited rather than had foisted on him." I took a drink of beer. "Ray hated the guy you replaced for similar reasons."

"Doug?"

I nodded.

"No one seems to have anything nice to say about that guy."

I smiled. "He was a fuck-up. And not in the Charlie or me sense. He was forever calling off. And he was a generally shitty bartender." I took one last hit from the cigarette and then stubbed it out, half-smoked, in an empty black plastic ashtray on the bar. "Let me ask you something, Drew."

"Fire away."

"Are you still in love with this place?"

He thought for a minute. "2000 was the first year I didn't file a tax return. I'm not sure I can do that again."

I sipped my beer. "I know what you mean."

"Charlie and I don't get along very well anymore."

I chuckled a little. "He's just jealous because customers like you better."

Drew smiled. "You think?"

"Don't get a big head. It's not winning a hotly contested matchup to be better liked than Charlie."

"No offense, but I like hanging out with Ray."

293

I waved my hands. "None taken. I already told you I miss him all the time." I turned the pint glass around in my hands. It would be nice to take the afternoon off, especially with the payload in my car. "Thanks for offering to stay today. I think I'll take you up on it." I stood and finished my pint with a couple of large gulps.

"Happy to do it." Drew stood and walked behind the bar. "I brought some singles. Are we low?"

I nodded. "Only about ten in the register." I grabbed my coat off of the back bar and put it on. "Hey, Drew?"

He looked up from the register where he was trading out the bills.

"Do you feel like you're stuck here? In Flint, at Bob's?"

He shrugged. "Sometimes. I assume a stiff breeze will push me along sooner or later."

I smiled. I almost told him that he was impervious to just such a wind in the form of his roommate, but I had enough on my mind.

"Just don't forget you've got legs and feet. You can make your own luck." I gave an exaggerated salute and left through the side door to my waiting vehicle and its trunk full of luck.

✳✳✳

By Friday, the bulk of the snow had been cleared and as a consequence, it was the busiest night I'd had since Christmas. They were three deep at the bar, the jukebox hadn't quit, and even though it was only about twenty degrees that night, it felt like ninety inside Bob's.

I'd made The Man's drop the night before. I think I would've been nervous even without the endgame in mind, so it's hard to know what made me shake and sweat. I really hadn't stopped since then. The fifty thousand dollars sat in my linen closet inside a battered old Hartmann duffle I inherited when my grandpa died. It sort of felt like I should carry it in one of those aluminum Zero

Halliburton attaches that drug dealers use in the movies, but this was the real world. The duffle would suffice.

Although I'd had a few days to plot things out, I was no closer to choosing a destination than I had been when I decided on the plan. I considered lots of possibilities, places no one would think to look or cities that didn't seem attractive to people living under more normal circumstances, but something about Drew and his talk of breezes was stuck in my head. I figured I'd get in my Explorer early Saturday morning and go where the wind seemed to be blowing me.

I was almost caught up washing glasses when a skinny brunette summoned me at the far end of the bar.

She smiled at me. She had the sort of white and straight teeth that can only be the result of orthodontia. "Charlie's not working tonight?"

I shook my head. "He'll be here tomorrow. Can I get you a drink?"

She thought for a moment. "Grey Goose and Tonic, no lime?"

I nodded and then turned to make the drink. While I poured, I overheard a couple of the lawyers arguing over last November's presidential election. I'd hoped the inauguration a few weeks prior would've put an end to all the contentiousness. I didn't even care all that much, and certainly hadn't bothered to vote. I thought about reminding these two that the bar was no place to discuss politics or religion, but something made me hurry back to that brunette.

I handed her the drink. "Why do you look familiar?"

She shrugged. "I'm not sure we've met. I've been out of town for a while."

"I see." I wasn't convinced. "The drink is four bucks."

She handed me a five. "You still don't take credit cards in this place, huh?"

I shook my head. "It's like traveling back in time."

She raised her eyebrows. "In more ways than one." She took a sip of the drink.

"Can I give Charlie a message for you?"

"Oh no. In fact, I was actively avoiding him, truth be told."

A conquest. As the years progressed and Charlie refused to curtail his tomcatting bartender routine, it was surprising the bar still had any female customers. "I guess time doesn't heal all wounds."

She smiled. "We can only hope that it wounds all heals."

I laughed. "I like that."

She extended her hand. "I'm Cindy. It's nice meeting you."

"Ralph." I shook her hand. She had the tiniest wrist I'd ever seen.

She gestured with her head at the corner of the bar near one of the TVs. "I'll be right over there if you get a moment to chat, Ralph."

Over the years, it had gotten easier to deflect flirtation with tact. Phil and Ray had successfully pounded it into me to toe that company line, even if Charlie wouldn't. It meant I probably pulled down double his tips and had far fewer enemies, so in the end, their reasoning had been sound. "It's pretty busy tonight, but I'll do my best."

She tongued the drink stirrer. "You'd better."

I wouldn't miss this nonsense when I was gone. As I headed down the bar to take an order from a tall guy in a Steely Dan shirt that I wasn't sure was ironic, I thought I spotted Tully near the jukebox. It was probably the twentieth time I could've sworn I'd seen him. I wasn't afraid of him showing up except for the distraction it'd cause. In reality, he was probably too scared to do anything other than slash my tires or something like that.

I fetched Steely Dan a pitcher of Stroh's, which meant the shirt was not genuine. Mystery solved. As I headed back down the bar, I saw that Molly had nudged her way through and was waving at me. I smiled at her. "Just getting off work?"

She looked down at her Hamilton's shirt. "Can you smell me?"

I shook my head. "Roses."

"Alright, Princess. How about a beer?"

"Sam?"

She nodded.

I moved toward the cooler to grab her beer when I heard the phone ring. I grabbed her beer and picked up the receiver with one motion. "Bob's."

"Ralph?"

It was a fairly poor connection, but I recognized the voice of The Man. "Yeah."

"All go swell yesterday?"

"Nothing to worry about."

"Great. Sorry if it seems like I'm checking up on you."

Even under the best of circumstances, I don't think he owed me an apology. "Not at all."

"While I've got you, I'll let you know I'll be back early. The weather is for shit down here. Rainiest February in a century. Just my luck."

My heart started pounding. The head start I'd planned on was evaporating. "Sorry to hear that. When are you leaving?"

"Monday."

Fuck. Fuckfuckfuck. The screams in my head were almost enough to drown out the Grandaddy pouring out of the jukebox. "Right on. Look, dude, I'm pretty slammed in here."

"Say no more. Thanks again. I'll talk to you Monday."

I could feel sweat forming on my brow. "Right on."

I looked down at the bottle of Sam Adams in my left hand and remembered I needed to deliver it to Molly. I hung up the phone and walked over towards her, twisted off the cap and tossed it towards the trashcan. I missed. "Here you go. On me."

"Thanks." She took a sip. "Are you alright? You look a little green around the gills."

297

My head was spinning. I felt like I needed to sit down. I needed time to think. I started to wonder if I should just scrap the whole plan, give The Man his money like he was expecting. Stay in Flint. Have this baby, marry Beth. Get a real job.

Molly poked my hand from across the bar. "Ralph? Seriously, are you okay?"

Originally, I would've had three weeks to get where I was going before The Man would know the money was gone. Now it would be about three days. Fuck it, I thought. Three days is plenty.

I nodded at Molly. Then I turned around to the cash register, opened it up, and pulled out the cash. The busy night made for a nice addition to the tally.

Molly watched me with her mouth open but didn't say anything. Circumstances reversed, I'm not sure I could've come up with anything myself. It must've been a sight. I smiled at her. "Just tell him you love him."

I didn't feel like wasting another minute in that bar. I'd lost enough time. I didn't want to keep looking over my shoulder for Tully. I didn't want any more googly eyes from that creepy Cindy.

Molly opened her mouth to say something but nothing came out. A customer a few stools over called out for me, waving a twenty. I always hated that. I'm not a whore.

I'm a thief.

I didn't bother with my coat. I pushed through a few people and then out the side door. I can't know what they were thinking, or what Molly must've thought. I figured she'd pick up the phone and get Drew down to cover the bar quickly. Most of the crowd wouldn't even know what happened.

On the street, it was cold. The cars were packed onto the block, black tires on sooty snow. At that moment, I couldn't imagine missing this alley or Saginaw Street or the Flint River. I knew I wouldn't miss the people in that bar, trying too hard to impress one another in such an unimpressive place, fooling themselves into thinking they were part of some miraculous urban renaissance, and that they were better people for reclaiming what their parents had abandoned.

Bob Dylan said you've gotta serve somebody. Maybe that's true. As I got behind the wheel of the Explorer and then sped away from the bar, I only knew I was glad to no longer serve those nobodies.

***

For obvious reasons, I can't tell you where I ran away to. It's best for all involved. I highly doubt The Man ever killed anyone or had anyone killed, but I don't want him to start with me.

Sometimes I wish I had a way to get in contact with Drew or Molly or, hell, even Tully. I hope he doesn't have any hard feelings, although I suppose that's not practical. I wish I could've had the chance to make things right with Ray. I don't want Ray to hate me. I imagine Phil and Charlie are mighty pissed, will probably never forgive me, although the amount I took from the bar that Friday sure does pale in comparison to what The Man was missing.

And, of course, Beth. Maybe you won't believe this, but leaving her behind was hardest of all. I don't even know if she had a boy or a girl. For all I know, she had an abortion or a miscarriage. It gets to me. I didn't have it in me, couldn't envision myself in the role. It's better for everyone this way. I wasn't cut out to raise a child or marry, at least not as long as I stayed in Flint.

I can tell you that I'm not lonely. I got my shit together; well, at least as much as someone like me could ever hope to get their shit together. I put the money to good use and settled down. I have a real job, real friends. Maybe someday a family. It's funny that I had to run away and change my name and my clothes and my hair and invent a whole new life before I finally felt like I had some control. Maybe you're not even rooting for a happy ending, I don't know. It's not entirely happy anyway. As good as things are, I'll never lose the eyes in the back of my head that always stay open should The Man ever decide to track me down.

The weirdest moment had to be filing my first tax return under my new name. I looked back over those years at Bob's, hiding all that money from Uncle Sam. Living off the grid, so to speak, always waiting for the other shoe to drop, be it at the bar or from the cops. Every envelope from the city or the IRS or with some attorney's name in the return address made my heart sink into my gut, and I sure don't miss that. You probably think running away was weak, and in a way, I guess you'd be right. But it also took more strength than I ever thought I had. I imagined a new life for myself, saw my chance and took it.

Could you do that? Would you?

CHARLIE & BOB'S

Last night I took home this girl Misty from the bar. Craziest lay I've had in I don't know how long. We were on the bed, which doesn't sound crazy. But I don't have a headboard, and the bed is pushed up against the east wall of the bedroom. She's on top, grinding away, and as she starts getting closer to what I assume was her orgasm—who the hell ever really knows—she starts banging her head against the wall with each thrust. Doesn't even seem to notice. She's humping and pumping and making those "I'm cumming" noises, and I'm trying not to laugh because she's pounding her head against the wall like some kind of fucking animal that's trying to kill itself.

Later that afternoon, after treating Misty to a morning lay and then sending her along, I was cleaning the bar and thinking a lot about Timothy McVeigh. The feds had just put him to death a couple of days earlier, and there was a copy of the *Journal* on the bar with that headline. Here was a guy a few years younger than me, someone with the courage of his convictions, ready to fight and die for what he believed in. He never apologized, showed no remorse, regarded himself as a soldier, a necessary sacrifice in the war against totalitarianism. I hadn't even bothered to vote. I'm not suggesting any sort of respect for McVeigh's actions; killing innocent people and babies seems pretty cowardly to me. I think it was more about the belief in something, the willingness to see past himself and even his own suffering and death that moved me. It wasn't like he was pounding his head against the wall like some fucking animal that's trying to kill itself.

After the upheaval left in the wake of Ralph's unexplained departure, things had finally settled down in the bar. We'd brought on two replacements, Kenny and Eddie, a couple of long-time customers who we know and trust. Something hit my ear funny about having too many "e" sounds behind the bar, three when you consider no one ever calls me Charles or Chuck, but it was a small sacrifice to get Phil to stop whining about having to work. He was back to being Phil the unfriendly ghost owner who only comes around once a week to have his fan club kiss the ring, and I made sure I didn't work that night.

It felt like a million years ago that Phil and I were at Schneeberger Honda. Things were different then. Even though he was a salesperson and I was the lowly paean who cleaned the cars, I never felt like he treated me as though I were beneath him. When he brought me aboard with him to buy Bob's, it was a high time. My share may have only amounted to fifteen percent, but it felt like we were equals.

When Colleen and I split, the dynamic changed. He had an opinion about every little thing I did in the bar, and sometimes outside of it. I felt his judgment all the time, and it didn't take me long to resent it. He didn't want me taking women home from the bar, he wanted me to be nicer to customers and suppliers, he wanted me to stop inviting customers to card games.

Eventually, I just wanted Phil gone.

For years, I'd been living like a pauper, squirreling away cash, never spending a dime of any gambling winnings. I knew Phil was getting tired of owning the bar, and Pam had been putting a lot of pressure on him to have a second kid. Once Ralph left, I noticed an even bigger shift in his attitude, although he never said anything to me about it. Once Kenny and Eddie were trained and ready to cover shifts on their own, I thought maybe Phil's mood might improve, but it hadn't.

I felt like the opportunity I'd waited, saved, and planned for, was now.

I finished pulling down the stools and unlocked the doors just in time for Ray to come in. Even though the weather had finally warmed up for good, Ray still seemed to be moving a little slow. I didn't pester him about how he was feeling, especially because his mind was as sharp as ever. If he wanted to let me know something was bothering him, I figured he'd do it with no provocation.

I poured him a Stroh's, he lit a cigarillo, and we chatted about the previous night's Tigers' game. It was an ugly loss, by ten runs, at home to the lowly Pirates. Although Comerica Park was only in its second year, the place was half empty.

I poured a pint glass of water. "This owner needs to sell the team. They've been terrible since he bought them."

Ray shrugged. "He's brought success to the Red Wings."

"It's weird, I'll grant you. But the results speak for themselves."

Ray tapped his mini cigar in an ashtray. "He has the resources."

I smiled. "Pizza money."

"It's still green."

"But covered in sauce." I laughed.

Ray shook his head and smirked a little. It took a lot to make Ray laugh at anything. This was about as close as he came. "It's been almost a decade since Ilitch bought the team. Maybe you're right. A change in ownership might bring about a reversal of fortune."

"You know what else could use a change in ownership?" I looked around the bar. "This place."

"The bar is doing better than the Tigers."

I laughed. "That's true. But ownership is equally disinterested here."

"Charlie." Ray looked directly at me. "This is a conversation for you and Phil, not you and me."

I took a sip of water. "Is Phil looking for a buyer?"

Ray took a drag from his cigarillo. "You should know after all these years that I wouldn't betray Phil's confidence in me."

That didn't sound like a no. In fact, if the answer were no, it seemed to me Ray would have just said it rather than do a dance about confidentiality, like he was Phil's priest. "I'm not looking for you to talk out of school. I just want your thoughts."

"My thoughts are that I have no idea what makes you happy, Charlie."

It wasn't like Ray to be this direct, except maybe about his disapproval of me sleeping with female customers. "What makes anyone happy?"

"That's not an answer."

I took a sip of water. This wasn't a question I gave a lot of thought to. "I don't know, Ray."

"Then why do you think owning the bar will make you happy? Because there'd be no one to criticize you?" He took another shallow drag from his cigarillo. "When Colleen left and you started sleeping with anything that moved, I assumed it was a phase and you'd get past it. It's been five years, Charlie."

I had to admit, there was a certain amount of autopilot involved in the constant stream of conquests. "I just haven't met the right person."

Ray waved me off. "You're not with any of them long enough to make that determination."

"You never married and you're perfectly happy. You're free. You owned your own business, no one looking over your shoulder, telling you how to run things or how to behave."

Ray looked at me sideways and then took a long, deliberate drag from his cigarillo. "Freedom is often lonely."

***

A few nights later, I was having a conversation with Walt, who had been the drummer for God, I Love Pie! until they moved to Chicago en masse and didn't bother to tell him. He was keeping time for a couple of go nowhere local punk bands and working at the Hardee's all the way over in Owosso, which explained why he smelled like a giant French fry every time he came into the bar.

It was pretty slow; there was a couple in their mid-twenties groping each other while they picked out a bunch of White Stripes songs on the jukebox, and three Knight-Ridge lawyers who hadn't bothered to go home after work and were predictably sloshed as a consequence. Walt and I had one end of the bar to ourselves and no one eavesdropping, so I thought it was as good a time as any to see if he might be my partner in fake crime.

I outlined the plan to him and he was receptive, although he wanted two hundred dollars up front and three hundred more after the job. I thought that was reasonable, and I wasn't worried about him running out with the advance. Even if he did, all I had to do was drive way the far fuck east, order up one of those biscuit sandwiches for breakfast and I'd have found ol' Wally.

I looked down at the other end of the bar to make sure no one needed anything and then looked back at Walt. "Not a word to anyone. Not before, not after. No one."

"I got it, Charlie. You don't have to worry about me." He took a drag from his cigarette. He was wearing a ratty black Kangol that might have been in fashion when he bought it, and a pair of worn eyeglasses with out-of-fasion frames. He was edging toward the gutter part of gutter punk. "I know how to keep my mouth shut."

"That's good." I smiled. "Maybe I'll let you play that payday at one of my Tuesday games."

He shook his head. "I'm no good at poker."

That was the idea. "Well, either way, I'm glad to have you aboard." I held out my hand for him to shake.

He gripped it with a greasy palm and shook. "It's cool. It's a smart idea."

I didn't need a fuck-up like Walt to tell me what I already knew. The side door opened and a couple of acceptable-looking women tentatively stepped inside. Newbies, one tall and blonde, the other on the short side and brunette. I already liked the brunette.

I smiled at Walt. "Feel like partying tonight?" I gestured with my head at the newcomers.

Walt craned around in his seat to look, like a fucking idiot. "Those two?" He shook his head. "I got a girlfriend, Charlie."

I shrugged. "Where is she?"

The women walked up to the bar. I gave them an almost imperceptible smile. The jukebox shifted over to a song from that new Shins record Drew put on the box this week. I wasn't sure how he'd heard about that album before I did, and it pissed me off. "Hello, ladies." I spun cocktail napkins down in front of each of them. "What can I get for you?"

They looked at each other and then at the chalkboard behind the bar. They were each in their mid-twenties and had an unimaginative suburban look to them; they wore too much makeup and clothes that were last year's closeouts.

The blonde spoke first. "I've never heard of most of these beers."

"Then just get a Captain and diet, Mindy."

They might just have driven all the way in from Otisville. "Why don't I give you a minute to decide?"

They nodded and I headed back down the bar to try and talk Walt into hanging around, girlfriend or no. I leaned in close to him in spite of the grease smell. "This one's almost too easy, Walt." I pointed at him. "You're in."

"C'mon, Charlie. My girl's expecting me."

I looked back at the suburban girls. They were still staring at the chalkboard, not speaking. I looked back at Walt and shrugged. "I thought you said I could trust you."

"You can trust me." He shook his head. "Just don't make me do this."

The jukebox turned over to a song from that New Pornographers record. Another Drew pick. Neko Case was a whore anyway. "Make you?" I smiled. "I'm not going to make you do anything." I shook out a Red from my pack and lit it. "I just worry, you know? A guy will tell his girlfriend just about anything. It's like Springsteen sings in 'Atlantic City', right?"

Walt's eyes went wide. "Everything dies?"

The brunette was waving at me; they were ready to place their orders. I hadn't meant to scare Walt; I only wanted to point out the narrator in that song is telling his old lady all about how he's going to off someone even before he does the deed. But once I saw he was afraid of me, I figured I'd just go with it.

I gave the brunette the 'one moment' gesture and then turned to look at Walt. "And no matter what the Boss says, everything that dies don't ever come back, Walt."

***

I wanted to be sure to put a few weeks in between deciding on a plan with Walt and the actual deed. This way, on the off chance anyone saw the two of us talking and something went wrong and people starting putting two and two together, there might be enough plausible deniability. Of course, if Walt couldn't keep his mouth shut, none of that would matter anyway. I was getting more nervous the closer it got to that Saturday.

The Wednesday prior, I was relieving Drew. He had a pretty full bar for a weekday evening at eight, and his tip jar looked about as full as mine on a closing shift during the week.

I put my backpack on the back bar and went over to refill the sinks. Drew was standing at the other end of the bar talking to a few customers I didn't recognize. He seemed to be pretty familiar with them.

The sink had no backlog of glasses; Drew must have washed them all shortly before I showed. Sometimes it felt like his doing everything right was a sort of dig at me. He looked down the bar at me and gave me a little wave in greeting.

I nodded at him. "Drew."

He walked over to me. The jukebox was playing "Once Around the Block." It made me feel a little better because I'd chosen the Badly Drawn Boy record. Knowing Drew, I thought it was possible he'd played the song purposefully before I got there as a peace offering.

"Hey, Charlie. Wanted to let you know the Nut Man wasn't in today."

"I looked down at the rack where we displayed the selection of nuts. It was nearly empty. Only a few packs of sorry-looking mixed nuts remained. "Were you here on time?" This was a stupid question.

"Yeah, I was here."

A booth full of customers got up to leave. One of the guys from the table came over to say good night to Drew. He didn't even acknowledge me.

I turned on the water in the sink full blast. Drew's popularity was getting on my nerves. I thought once Ralph was out of the picture, I might pick up some of his more faithful customers, but it was obvious they were coming in when Drew was working instead.

I ran my hands under the water to test the temperature. "So I've got no nuts to sell tonight?"

Drew shrugged. "I could go to the store and pick something up if you want."

What a fucking goody-goody. I assumed what he really wanted to do was run home to that roommate with the big tits who I banged awhile back. "Don't bother."

"It's no bother, Charlie."

I really didn't want to feel like I owed Drew any favors. Besides, Bob's customers were peculiar. If we had a bunch of Planter's nuts on the rack, people would complain that they weren't the brand they were used to, even though nuts were nuts as far as I was concerned. "It's fine. We've got Better Mades. People can just deal."

"Alright, well I'll just clean out the tip jar and sell some singles back to the register. It's a little low."

He grabbed the pitcher that held his tips and emptied it onto the back bar. It was pretty full. He started sorting bills. He'd been busy enough to already sell back some singles throughout the afternoon, as there were a couple of tens and a twenty already in his jar. I didn't want to stare, but by my estimation, he had well over a hundred bucks in there. I averaged about twenty on an afternoon shift.

I tested the water temperature again. It was warm enough. I plugged up the sink and added detergent. "Hey, Drew. How's Molly anyway? Haven't seen her in a while."

Drew stopped counting bills. He looked a little confused by my question. "She's alright." He looked back down at the money in front of him and then to me. "You know, that reminds me. A woman was in here earlier asking after you."

That narrowed it down. "She leave a name or a number?"

He shook his head. "She said she'd come back some other time. She was like five-six or seven, really thin, dark hair. Smartly dressed. If I didn't know better, I'd have thought she was from Knight-Ridge."

I nodded. If he'd said she wore braces, I'd have thought he was describing Cindy. That couldn't be anyway. Last I'd heard about her was she was in L.A., working publicity or something like that. "Next time, get a name."

Drew narrowed his eyes. "I asked, she refused."

"You didn't check her I.D.?"

He shrugged. "She didn't look that young."

Still, it didn't take a genius to ask for a driver's license. Although, if she didn't look that young, then I figured it couldn't be Cindy.

Drew finished counting out his tips, then put a stack of singles in the register and pulled out four twenties. That meant he was well over a hundred in tips for the shift. What a little kiss-ass.

He put the bills in the front pocket of his jeans. "Alright, I'm gonna head down the road." He smiled. "Have a good night."

Since Ray had asked, I kept thinking about what it is that makes me happy. I still wasn't sure I had a good answer, which was more than a little troubling. It might be a cliché to say misery loves company, but clichés often exist for very good reasons. It might be time to admit I was miserable.

I nodded and smiled. "You too, Drew." I laughed. "That rhymed. Be sure and tell Molly I said 'Hey'."

***

Of course it was my luck that the night I planned to have Walt come back would be the slowest Saturday in months. I wasn't sure what was keeping people away; the Fourth was Wednesday, so I couldn't imagine there were still people throwing barbeques. It was too far from the start of fall semester for younger customers to be busy with back-to-school tasks. There weren't any big parties that I was aware of. Whatever was behind it, there was only about four hundred in the register, barely enough to cover the balance of what I'd promised Walt.

There were a few dudes near the jukebox who'd pumped it full of Radiohead songs for most of the night. It was getting on my nerves. I was already a little bit on edge, and I didn't need their keening, paranoid songs making it worse. I didn't skip any tracks, no matter how tired I'd gotten of "Optimistic", because I didn't want to cost myself any more tips.

The bar was sparsely populated. Scott the Mailman had been drowning his sorrows most of the night, the Walshes and the Timmons were nursing a second pitcher of Leinenkugel's between them. Under normal circumstances, I might be making a play for a lonely drinker like the short blonde at the other end of the bar, but I'd barely spoken to her. I'd resigned myself to anxiously waiting for Walt until my old poker buddy, Scratch Barnett, walked in the side door.

I hadn't seen Scratch in at least two years. I knew he'd had a rough patch with junk; he'd been in and out of rehab, divorced, living at his mom's. I was frankly a little taken aback to see him in the bar. I always figured this sort of place was terra incognita for a junkie trying to go straight.

He beamed when he saw me. "Snarly." His voice boomed. Every head in the bar turned to see where the booming voice originated.

No one had called me Snarly in a long time, at least to my face. I came around the bar and wrapped him up in a bear hug. "How've you been, Scratch?"

He stepped back and tried to smile. "Hangin' in, man. You?"

I nodded and took him in. He wasn't as gaunt as I expected, in fact, he'd probably added twenty or thirty pounds to what had already been a chunky frame. Maybe he'd fallen into that post-rehab addiction to sweets you hear some junkies struggle with. He still kept his beard, although it was graying around his jowls, and he'd lost quite a bit of hair. At least he was still kicking, which was better than most would've predicted for quite a while. "I'm doing alright. Same as ever."

Scratch sat on a stool and I walked behind the bar. I took the Reds from my shirt pocket and lit one. "What're you drinking tonight?"

"Bud Light, Miller Lite, whichever's closer."

I wasn't one to pry, but if he's trying to stay clean, those seemed like a good choice. I walked over to the cooler and grabbed a bottle of Bud Light, opened it and put it in front of him. "On me."

He lifted the bottle. "Thanks, Charlie. Shit, it's good to see you."

The jukebox switched over to "Station to Station." Fucking Phil always insisted on having at least one Bowie disc in there, and was forever switching them around. Now I had to put up with ten-plus minutes of this boring, plodding mess.

"You know what, let me join you." I went back to the coolers and opened a bottle of Sam Adams. I held out the bottle and Scratch clinked it with his.

Scratch took a tentative sip. "You got a regular game going these days?"

He was asking at just the right time. Tuesdays had coalesced around a group of flush players and was going well every week. I nodded. "Tuesdays."

"You got room?"

I guessed there was no rule against gambling in Narcotics Anonymous. "Sure. Two hundred to sit."

Scratch nodded. "I can do that. Anyone I know there?"

I thought for a second, trying to recall if Scratch's tenure overlapped with anyone in my current game. "Ed Leach? Tall skinny dude from Ypsi?"

Scratch shook his head.

"Danny Castorena? Fat Italian dude in his forties? Always wears a vest."

He shrugged. "That sort of rings a bell. My memory isn't what it used to be."

I imagined that wasn't all that had suffered. "It doesn't matter. It's a good group. No chumps, competitive games. Winner has walked out with close to a dime here and there."

He looked a little surprised. "Not bad. I'd hate to walk in and be the donator."

I shook my head. Scratch had skill, at least back in the day. "No guarantees, but I think you could hang. You want in?"

"Thanks for asking, Charlie. I think I'd like that." He took another small sip of his beer.

It felt good to reconnect with an old friend. It was a little hard not to press for details about what Scratch had been through with the dope and the divorce, but I assumed if he wanted to talk about any of it, he'd speak up. He hung around for a while, sipping on a couple of beers, but for some reason, his presence got my guard down and I must have had six or seven and was feeling a little loose by midnight.

When Walt charged in through the side door, wearing a ski mask and a black trench coat, I'd totally forgotten about the plan.

Walt stormed up to the bar, hand inside his pocket just like we talked about. "Let's make this quick." His voice was calm but firm.

All conversation in the bar stopped. The only sound was Pavement on the jukebox, Stephen Malkmus repeating "Fight this generation" over and over again. I still have no idea what he meant by that. Which generation? Why does he assume I know which one he's referring to? Why should I fight them?

Walt looked at me with wide eyes behind the black ski mask. I could tell he was scared, and oddly, even though it had been my idea, I was too.

I held my hands out and got into character. "Take it easy, man. We don't want any trouble."

Walt's voice broke as he talked. "Just get the money."

I turned around toward the cash register, opened it and started to take out the bills. I heard a scuffling behind me and looked just in time to see Scratch moving to put Walt in a headlock.

"Don't give this lowlife a fucking thing, Charlie." Scratch had a pretty firm grasp on Walt, arms over his head in a Full Nelson. Scratch always was pretty strong.

I panicked. Before I had a chance to think, I almost ran around the bar and started pounding on Scratch to get him to release Walt, but that would've been potentially disastrous. Thankfully, I stopped myself and looked down at the bills in my hands. I didn't have any idea what to do with them in that moment. I looked up at Walt and Scratch, still tussling ten feet away, and then back down at the bills.

"Let him go, Scratch."

Scratch and Walt both stopped struggling and looked at me with confusion in their eyes.

Walt didn't loosen his grip. "What? I'm not letting this asshole go."

I looked down again at the money. I peered around quickly for somewhere to set it down, but I didn't want it to be unsecured. I quickly stuffed it in my pockets. Phil's money. Not mine. "We don't need the cops filing a report. It's bad for business, ends up in the papers."

Scratch shook his head.

"I said let him the fuck go." I pointed at the two of them.

Walt's eyes had a pleading look in them. Scratch had him completely overpowered.

Scratch lifted his arms up and Walt scurried out of his grip. Walt turned to run so fast that he lost his footing and sprawled out on the bar floor, scrambling around to get back to his feet. A couple of people in the booth closest to him started chuckling. He finally got up and moved out of the door quickly but deliberately. I wondered to myself if he'd worn his work shoes, coated with grease. He probably did.

"What the fuck, Scratch? You don't need to put yourself in harm's way like that."

He shook his head. "I didn't see a gun. He was just a punk."

Although I'd lost out on the take from the register, it wasn't really the point. This incident might still work to scare Phil even if it wasn't a full-on robbery. I thought it would be hilarious if Walt were to come around and try and collect the second half of what I'd promised him. Maybe I could still salvage something positive out of the situation.

I addressed the bar as a whole. Apart from shouting out "Last call for alcohol" to a collective groan, I'm not sure I'd ever done this before. "It's all over. Thanks for remaining calm. Everyone gets a round on the house."

I went behind the bar and grabbed my cigarettes. I lit one and took a deep drag. Scratch sat on his stool, still shaking his head. I was lucky. I was lucky this situation hadn't gone worse. I was lucky to have someone like Scratch looking after me and the bar at that moment; after all, he didn't know the whole robbery was a fake. I was lucky to have a job in a place like Bob's, where the worst thing that happened on any given night is that I had to listen to ten minutes of "Station to Station", which was actually a pretty good song anyway. I was lucky I hadn't turned into some sort of Flint version of Timothy McVeigh.

I knew I was lucky. But it'd never be enough.

PHIL & MOLLY & KATHY & DREW & CHARLIE

PHIL

I'd had feelers out, looking for buyers, for several months before I had any serious action. There were some nibbles, sure; I even got a call from my old boss at Schneeberger Honda, Gary Danko, who was looking to invest an inheritance from a wealthy aunt. I'd be goddamned if I was selling that gutless prick a bag of goat shit.

I didn't have any direct contact with the prospective buyer for weeks. She kept all communication through her attorney, Joanne Black, who until last year, had been at Knight-Ridge but struck out on her own after she didn't make partner quickly enough for her taste. I didn't blame her. That firm was a real sausage party and she had balls. Joanne called me and said the buyer, who she still hadn't identified, wanted to meet for lunch. Joanne said she'd be there as well, and I should bring along my lawyer if I wanted. I brought Ray instead.

We sat in a booth at Hamilton's for twenty minutes before the two of them showed. We introduced each other all around and Joanne gave me what I thought was an askance glance when I introduced Ray. The buyer and Joanne sat on one side of the booth, Ray and I at the other. She was young, on the tall side, very thin. Very attractive. I don't know what sort of person I expected to eventually buy my bar, but this wasn't it. She was dressed to match Joanne's power suit, which is a term I hate but I don't know what else one would call it. And they did exude a sort of power. And she was serious.

They had papers at the ready. The money appeared to be there. It was a serious offer, about ten percent more than I'd have been willing to settle for. I wanted to eat some lunch and get to know one another. It was like giving up my baby, no matter how ready I may have been to see him go, and I wanted to know her plans, her thoughts. If she'd send him to boarding school, take him on nice vacations.

Drew's roommate Molly brought us drinks and took our orders. For whatever reason, it made me feel more at ease to have her there. I could see why Drew had transferred being hung up on that med school ex of his to Molly. She was warm and smart and quick-witted and pretty. I can't say exactly what he was thinking, but it had to be torture living with someone you were in love with and not be able to be with them. But if there's one thing I'd learned about Drew, torturing himself was something he did extremely well.

We ate some steaks and chicken and salads, bread, baked potatoes, rice. Ray showed more of an appetite than I might have predicted, which I thought was a good thing. Pam was going to be happy. She was tired of hearing me complain. The deal between she and I was that we would start trying for baby number two as soon as the check cleared. I thought that was fair, and I might have even been a little excited about it if I was being honest.

I couldn't pull the trigger at that moment. I wasn't saying no, but I wasn't ready. I suppose subconsciously it was exactly why I brought Ray instead of my lawyer. But I'd been selling houses long enough to know what to look for, and everything was in order as far as I could tell. I just wanted to buy time. It's one of those things, I guess. Being careful what you wish for was part of it, but also there was a sense of panic that was setting in when reality hit. It's like graduating high school: you look forward to it for so long, but when it's actually getting ready to happen, there are waves of nostalgia and anxiety about what comes next. Uncertainty. Inevitability. Change. Growing up. Whatever.

I told them I wanted a few days to look things over and make sure there was nothing that needed touching up and renegotiated. They said they understood. The buyer said she had something a little touchy to discuss and it wasn't the sort of thing she felt could be written into any of the contracts. I told her to go ahead and ask.

She wanted to make sure Charlie was still at the bar before she took possession. She wanted to be the one to fire him.

***

MOLLY

It was difficult not to give in and crawl into bed with Drew most nights. I'm not sure I even know what was stopping me. Pride. Some semblance of anger. It was true that something about the way I felt changed when he didn't come home that night, but he had been beating himself up about it far worse than I ever could. Neither of us even mentioned moving out at any point. There must have been a reason for that.

We'd kept it casual for months, chatting cordially, never too deep, not usually about anything of substance. But when I came home from work that Tuesday after waiting on Phil and Ray and those two women at Hamilton's, it seemed like there was something bigger to discuss.

I waited up for him. He was closing the bar, as he always did on Tuesdays. I knew Phil drank there that night, too. His one night of the week. Drew often came home somewhat tipsy himself. When Phil was there, a lot of his old friends came out and it was a pretty fun atmosphere in the bar. I'd hung out on those nights a few times. Those were nights it was particularly hard not to show Drew I'd forgiven him.

I only had one-third term summer class left. I'd be graduating in two weeks. August twenty-fifth. It was a long, hard road but it was almost over. I'd had Senior-itis for at least the last two years. I wasn't at all sure about my next move. But I'd have that paper. There had been times I didn't think that was possible.

I heard Drew's key in the lock and sat up. I used the remote to turn the stereo down. Drew had nice things. I was listening to some old Kinks record Drew liked. It was hot in the apartment. It had

318

gotten up well over ninety that day, maybe even cracked one hundred, but I tended to ignore temperature readings on days like that. It only makes it worse to have evidence of how miserable it is. When it gets that hot, there's only so much the ancient wall unit air conditioner in the living room can do about it. I'd thought about opening the windows once the sun went down, but it was so humid out I thought it best to keep the stickiness outside. My hair was frizzy enough as it was. He walked in. It was dark, but I could see he looked tired.

He smiled at me. "What are you doing up?"

I shrugged. "I wanted to talk to you."

He threw his keys on the kitchen table. "Sounds like a conversation that could be accompanied by a beer. You up for one?"

I nodded.

He went into the kitchen and returned with a couple of bottles of Pilsner Urquell. I thought it was a good choice for a hot night.

He handed me one of the beers and sat at the other end of the couch. "What did you want to talk about?"

I reached onto the coffee table for my Marlboro Lights, took one out of the pack and lit it. "I had a weird table at Hamilton's for lunch today. It was Phil and Ray and these two women I didn't recognize."

Drew sipped his beer. "Like a double date?"

I unexpectedly laughed, which caused it to come out more as a snort. I held my hand up in front of my face. "Goddamnit." I smiled. "More like a business meeting."

"Good. Ray's really picky." He smiled.

"Be serious. Do you know what it could've been about?"

Drew reached into his shirt pocket and pulled out his pack of Parliaments and lit one. He took a deep drag. "Phil didn't say anything tonight. He might have been in a bit of a weird mood, now that I think about it, though."

I took a drag and exhaled through my nose. Drew told me once that it turned him on a little. I wondered if it still did. "How do you mean?"

"I don't know. He's usually in a good mood on Tuesdays, but there was something a little sad about him. Quieter than normal. He also doesn't usually play anything on the jukebox, and tonight he was dumping money in it all night. Webb Pierce, George Jones, Ray Price. All the classic stuff he keeps in there just to piss Charlie off."

I liked the idea of anyone doing something just to piss Charlie off. "Do you think he could be selling the place?"

Drew shrugged while he took a drag from his cigarette. "He was all about it in March, after Ralph left. He hadn't really said anything more to me since then."

"But then there was the robbery."

He nodded. "That's true."

I took a big sip from the beer. It tasted good. Cold. "What would you do if he sold the bar?"

Drew scratched his scalp. "I've been thinking about going back to school. My mom's selling the house, moving to Florida. My grandmother's not getting any younger. I think my mom wants to spend some time with my grandma while she's still got it together. There's less keeping me in Flint."

He didn't have to say that included me. "You never mentioned any of that."

He gave me a flat smile. "I know, but we haven't been talking in depth about anything for a little while now."

I looked at the floor, my toes. The nails were painted. Red. I don't remember the last time I painted them. "I know. It's my fault."

Drew waved me off. "That's ridiculous."

I shook my head, took a last drag from the cigarette and leaned over to put it out in the ashtray on the coffee table, not bothering to clutch my t-shirt as I stretched. "We don't have to talk about it. I don't even want to. I just want to go to bed with you tonight."

He tried in vain to not crack a smile. He took another drag from his cigarette. I think he was trying to look cool. The smile grew wider and betrayed him.

"Everything's going to change. You know that, right?"

He put his cigarette out. The cherry still burned a little in the ashtray. Hot. It glowed. "I want it to change. All of it."

I got up, walked over to him, and straddled his lap. I put my mouth on his. "I'm really sorry about the past few months."

Drew shook his head. "No talking." He kissed me, then pulled away and smiled, his hands on my back and his eyes on mine. "Action."

✳✳✳

KATHY

In the years since Roger died, any time I thought seriously about selling the house, waves of panic would come over me as I envisioned meeting realtors, filling out paperwork, packing, moving. Then I'd see, in my mind's eye, the next family living in our space, putting their things in our cupboards, mowing our lawn, walking up and down our stairs. It was too much to face.

The reality was completely different. As it actually happens, the panic was replaced by excitement. The fear was replaced by eagerness. Instead of being troubled by the visualization of a new family living in the house, it was satisfying to me that a young family would build their life here. It had served the Nemec family well. It was time to pass it along.

Jeff had brought his wife and kids from Atlanta to say goodbye to the house, which I thought was touching. Kevin said he didn't have the time to come in from Arizona, which I really took as confirmation he didn't feel the same emotional connection to the home. Drew had been pushing me to make the move for years. It wasn't in a negative way; I never got the sense he was trying to get rid of me. Even though Drew hadn't made any substantive changes in his life--he was still single, still a bartender, still not back in school—I didn't worry so much about leaving him as I might have a year or two prior. He was more at peace, as though he'd finally moved past the heartbreak caused by that terrible Megan person. I knew he'd be fine.

I wasn't as sure about my sister. Rose had what seemed like a full enough life, between her job and her friends and vacations. But as the moving date drew closer, I began to get more of a sense of how much Rose depended on me.

She was helping me box up the living room. I'd have about one-third the square footage in my condo in Titusville. Lots of things acquired over the thirty-plus years of living in this house wouldn't make the trip.

Rose held up a small music box in her hand. It was wood with a brass cast of the *Arc de Triomphe*. Roger had bought it for me on our honeymoon. She held it up for me to see. "Staying or going?" This had become our shorthand as we packed everything up. If the item was staying, it went into a box for donation, unless Rose or one of the boys wanted it. If it was going, I was taking it to Florida.

The music box was one of those objects I hardly took notice of anymore, having been on the shelf for so long, just blending in. I'd probably dusted it a million times, passing over it without much thought. The brass needed cleaning. I couldn't even remember what tune the little pieces of metal inside plinked out. "Staying."

She nodded and put it in a plastic bin with the other items going to Goodwill.

"Rose, are you alright?"

She shrugged, picked up a small vase and held it up. "Staying or going?"

"Staying." She had to know leaving her behind was one of the hardest parts about the move, but she also should have understood that I needed a change, and our mother had stayed down south by herself long enough. "Can we just slow down a minute?"

"This has to get done, Kathy." She grabbed the first in a series of Avon beer steins I'd bought for Roger in the seventies. They were ugly, garish, but he liked them and I'd never bothered to get rid of them. "What about these?"

I walked over to her, took the stein from her hands and put it back on the shelf. "Why don't we take a break and go out for lunch?"

"You don't have to baby me." She picked the stein back up and looked at me for an answer.

"Staying."

She looked it over. "I think these might be worth money."

"You can keep them if you want."

"I don't think they'd work in my living room." She put the first of them into the plastic bin.

"You could sell them on eBay." Drew had mentioned setting up an account to make a few extra dollars on some of the things I wasn't taking with me.

She picked up the second of the steins and put it in the bin. "It's not worth the trouble."

I stood over Rose, but she kept picking up the steins and putting them in the bin. I was hungry, but I also wanted to shake her out of this mood. It wasn't healthy. I reached for her hand. "Rose, let's go to lunch."

She withdrew her hand to her lap. "I need you more than Mom does."

I sighed. It was just like Rose to make everything about her. "You'll visit. We'll go to the beach."

"And what will you do for the Holidays? Your boys are scattered. You'll go to Atlanta or Phoenix. You won't come to Michigan." She looked at me and blinked. It looked like she might be trying to force tears to her eyes. My sister did more drinking with

323

her friends than spending time with family at Christmas. "It won't be the same."

I sat on the couch. "Things are going to be different. But I've held onto this house long enough. It's time to let the past go. I'm sure you can understand that."

She nodded and wiped at her eyes with the back of her right hand. "I know. I guess I just feel like Flint is where the Lynches are supposed to be. It's always been sort of a member of our family. Everyone's gone or leaving, abandoning this place and me. What are we without Flint?"

I'd felt like Flint had shaken us all off like fleas many years ago. My boys scattered because they understood they couldn't make a life here, and I knew it wouldn't be much longer until Drew learned that as well. I did admire him for trying. The people at that bar saw value in their hometown where others saw none, and it made me love him even more. It was certainly of more worth than Rose's lip service. Either way, it seemed like a done deal. The jobs would never return. Things would only get worse. Maybe Rose was right about Flint being family, but that didn't make it any easier to watch your loved one deteriorate, wither, shrivel, and inevitably die. That's probably why those visions of panic that used to accompany my thoughts of moving away never materialized. I was glad to go.

I stood from the couch and smiled at my sister. "I'm ready for lunch. I'm starving."

She stuck out her bottom lip in an exaggerated pout.

I reached out my hand. My sister needed to decide for herself, and I knew she would in time. "Staying or going?"

***

DREW

It might not sound like much to say there was a spring in my step, but I really did feel bouncy. Lighter. Nothing could get me down. Even Charlie's continued efforts to give me a hard time about nothing didn't give me pause any longer. He didn't like me. That was clear. But Ralph told me long before it was mostly jealousy, and I knew he was right.

It was a relief that the weather broke and the temperature returned to something more normal. It almost felt cool out. It made for a nice morning on that Saturday, a cool breeze coming in through my open window with Molly in my bed, where she'd been almost continuously since the week before. It was great. We couldn't get enough of each other.

That morning, we'd made the first steps toward a substantive discussion of where we were headed and a tentative plan for the immediate future. Once I told her I wanted to go back to graduate school, she was convinced that was the smart move. But it was August, and far too late to apply for any programs that began in the fall, so we'd have a full year to play with. August 2001 to August 2002. We talked about hanging out in Flint, her taking a breather after finishing school, but if Phil was selling the bar, I didn't know how realistic it was. I wasn't excited about the possibility of returning to the video store. We talked about traveling to Europe on the cheap, but I was a little more scared about doing that than Molly. We thought we could relocate to New York or Chicago or San Francisco for a year, get crappy jobs and enjoy city life before joining the real world. I suggested we could travel around the U.S. seeing major league ballparks, and to her credit, Molly didn't immediately veto the idea. It was all exciting. Every possibility seemed real, and the possibilities were innumerable.

It felt great to open the windows at Bob's and air it out as I cleaned. It seemed like Kenny had a pretty busy Friday night, which was good. He'd been doing well as of late, although I wasn't as sure about Eddie. But Charlie had the right idea to hire two newbies at the same time. That way, if one of them didn't work out, we were still fully staffed. At this point, the smart money was on Kenny.

I put a couple of dollars in the jukebox and played several songs from the new Clem Snide record. I'd put that one in a couple of months earlier and no one but me seemed to be playing it. If I artificially pumped up its plays, then maybe it could stay and get a chance to catch on. I wasn't sure why it mattered so much to me. I just thought they were a cool band.

Even the Pine-Sol smelled nice that day, and it dissipated quickly with the wind pouring in the windows. I found myself wondering about Phil, in between daydreams about Molly. It seemed like he'd calmed down once Kenny and Eddie were in place, but he had been so serious about selling the place and moving on just a few months ago, even if he never mentioned it again. The lunch Molly told me about would have seemed curious even without my prior knowledge.

After I pulled down the stools and propped open the doors, Ray came ambling in and sat on his regular stool. I hadn't seen him since Molly told me he'd been with Phil at Hamilton's, which wasn't all that strange given the heat. Ray sometimes stayed in his apartment when the mercury climbed high. I didn't want to pester him, or make him feel like I was trying to get him to betray a confidence, but it would be easier for Molly and I to decide on our immediate course of action if I knew Phil's plan.

"Hi, Ray." I moved to the taps to pour Ray a pint.

"Drew, good afternoon." Ray unwrapped a fresh pack of cigarillos.

"Quite a change in temperature." I nodded toward the open door.

He nodded. "It's refreshing."

I brought him his beer just as he was lighting a mini cigar.

I looked at my watch. "Tigers and Royals in an hour."

"Two teams going nowhere."

It had been another frustrating season for my beloved Kitties. General Manager Randy Smith seemed intent on turning over the roster yet again. He'd made more trades during the five seasons of his tenure than most teams make in two decades. He had a strange habit of trading the same players over and over, acquiring and then trading catcher Brad Ausmus five times over the course of a few years. There were few constants, except for the losing.

"I'd almost rather be a Royals fan right now." I laughed. "I think Randy Smith is in his office right now trying to figure out how he can reacquire Doug Brocail for the fourth time."

Ray smiled. "The Yankees were locked in a similar constant state of flux for several years in the eighties, don't forget."

Ray's Yanks were cruising that year, mostly due to some great starting pitching. "Please don't compare the Tigers and Yankees. Besides, when they were bad, they always had Mattingly, at least."

He shrugged. "I was only trying to help you see a bright side."

There was no bright side to the lineup of stiffs the Tigers were trotting out at this point in the season. Their best pitcher was a thirty-five-year-old knuckleballer who had never won more than nine games in a season before that year. "Bright side? Maybe Jeff Weaver, although they'll probably trade him soon. Randy doesn't like anyone to get too comfortable."

Ray took a sip of his beer. "Did anything exciting happen around here while I stayed out of the heat?"

"I was about to ask you the same thing." I poured myself a pint glass of ice water. I needed to rehydrate.

Ray looked confused. "I'm not following."

I sat on the stool at the end of the bar and took out a cigarette from my pack. "Maybe a big lunch? Tuesday? Hamilton's?"

"Molly told you." He took a small drag from his cigar.

I nodded. "Phil should've chosen a place where I have no spies if he wanted it to remain secret."

"He hasn't signed any papers. He has concerns."

My eyes went wide. "So he is selling?"

Ray furrowed his brow. "I thought you knew. Phil said he told you months ago."

327

"He told me he wanted to sell, not that he had a buyer lined up."

Ray put his hand to his forehead. "I'm sorry. You shouldn't have found out this way."

I shrugged. "What's the difference? I'm just glad to know." I dragged on my cigarette. "Has anyone told Charlie?"

Ray shook his head. "Phil doesn't want to tell him until he's sure it's happening."

"What's the holdup?"

Ray tapped his cigar in the ashtray. "He's selling the whole building and wants to make sure I have a place to live."

I nodded. I knew Ray lived upstairs rent free, an arrangement I wouldn't figure a new owner wanted to continue. "How do you feel about it?"

"I want Phil to do what's best for him and his family. He's getting a fair price. The time seems right." Ray put his hand to his forehead for the second time.

"You alright?"

He nodded. "Just these little headaches I've been getting since this morning." He looked at his cigar. "I don't think this is helping." He stubbed it out in the ashtray.

"Thanks for being honest about Phil selling."

Ray chuckled a little. "It was purely an accident."

I wouldn't want to be there when Phil told Charlie. He was liable to lose it in any number of different ways. Crying. Screaming. Punching. It was hard to predict.

I took a big drink from the glass of water. I was thirsty. "I almost forgot. Who's the buyer anyway?"

"A young woman named Cindy Glaser."

I shrugged. "Doesn't ring a bell."

***

CHARLIE

I canceled my game and went to the bar on a Tuesday for the first time in I-don't-know how long. At least a year. It had been considerably longer than that since I enjoyed watching a bunch of Phil's fat married friends kiss his ass, and come to think of it, I'm not sure I ever really did. But it did get worse as they all got older, fatter, sorrier, and breed-ier. It was a gross display.

When I walked in, I made eye contact with Drew and could tell he was surprised to see me. He was at the sink washing glasses.

I walked up to him. "What's up, Drew?"

He nodded at me but didn't pull his hands out of the sink. "Weird to see you here on a Tuesday."

That was a brilliant observation, and I was sure it wouldn't be the last time I heard it that night. I got a weird feeling from Drew since the foiled robbery, almost as if he knew something. It was probably nothing. It seemed like the official narrative had coalesced, and people mostly felt sympathy for me. Everyone wanted to suck Scratch's dick for being the savior. I could've pointed out that he was a fucking junkie who beat up his ex-wife, but I let him have his moment. Who knew how many more he'd get.

I smiled at Drew. "How's Molly?"

Drew finished washing and wiped his hands on a bar towel hung around the belt loop of his jeans. "Great. She graduates Saturday."

I wondered if she ever told her new boyfriend that she nearly minored in slobbering on my knob. "Good for her. Be sure and tell her I said congratulations."

"Thanks. I will."

"I'll take a Sam when you get a second." I headed over to the end of the bar where Phil was surrounded by several of his flunkeys.

Phil smiled wide. "Charlie Tracey. As I live and breathe. What brings you out on a Tuesday night?"

I was trying to figure out if the rumors I'd been hearing about Phil selling the bar were true, but I wasn't ready to come out and say it. A couple of his friends shook my hand and slapped me on the back. I used to hang out with this group weekly. They seemed genuinely happy to see me.

Drew handed me the beer across the bar. "On me."

I nodded and then reached for it and took a sip. I looked at Phil. "It's been too long since I did a Tuesday with you guys."

He smiled. "I agree. We were just talking about the latest big news."

My heart raced. "What's that?"

He finished a bottle of Labatt and tossed it in the trashcan behind the bar with a clang. "You remember Beth Davis?"

"Beth Death?" I took a sip of my beer.

"That's her."

"Sure I do." Beth was a sort of goth hippie who used to hang around the bar trying to get on any available bartender. I'd fucked her three or four times years ago, and then Doug had a little thing with her. I was pretty sure Ralph was the last in that line. Maybe Drew would've thrown her the high hard one if he had any balls. She was pretty pliable in the sack, as I recalled. Might've done him some good. "Haven't seen her in here in forever."

Phil chuckled. "That's because she got herself knocked up."

I nodded. "That'll do it."

"Yeah. Beth Death is a proud mama to a bouncing baby boy."

I wasn't sure why this was the big news of the day, and it wasn't at all what I came down to talk about. "Good for her. I hope she's happy."

Phil reached into the cooler closest to the end of the bar and served himself another bottle of beer. He could really put it away on Tuesdays. "You're not curious about who the dad might be?"

I took a sip of my Sam Adams and shrugged. "I know it isn't me. I haven't touched that broad in years."

Phil shook his head. "It's Ralph."

If I'd had beer in my mouth, I may have done a spit take. "Ralph? Our Ralph?"

"Former bartender and thief of my money Ralph. One and the same." Phil held his beer aloft and called out to his friends. "To Ralph."

They all laughed and exchanged clinks of their bottles and glasses, hoots and hollers.

It certainly made more sense what Ralph was running from. "Who told you about this?"

Phil pointed at one of his friends, a tall guy with brown hair in a suit. They all looked sort of the same. "Conners does some books for Beth's dad at the luggage store."

I took a sip of my beer and then nodded. "Do they have any idea where he ran off to?"

Phil shrugged. "He didn't leave them a forwarding address. What can I tell you?"

By my math, that meant Ralph must have been clandestinely carrying on with Beth for a couple of years, give or take, unless it was a one-shot past the goalie kind of thing. Somehow, I doubted that because Ralph didn't seem to do much dating. So either he was some sort of stoned monk or he and Beth were regularly fucking. It made me think I didn't pay enough attention to what was happening around me. "What did she name him?"

Phil swallowed the sip of beer he'd taken. "Rasputin."

I furrowed my brow. "Seriously?"

Phil slapped me on the back, hard. "Jesus, Charlie. You have a finely developed sense of irony. No, she didn't name him Rasputin."

I shook my head. I used to think it was funny when Phil would bust my balls, but we were too old for that shit now. "We haven't had a chance to talk since the robbery."

He shrugged. "What's to talk about? It was over a month ago. I got over it. You and Scratch broke it up. It could have been worse."

It could've been better, too. "I just wanted to be sure there were no lingering effects on your psyche." You'd think maybe he'd be concerned about the same thing on my end, seeing as how I'd had a non-existent gun pointed at me.

Phil took a sip of his beer. "What are you saying?"

I steeled myself up. "I'm hearing rumors that the bar is for sale."

Phil looked down his nose at me and considered my expression for what felt like a minute. He might have been a little drunk. "Where'd you hear that?"

I found it curious that no one simply answered in the negative when faced with this question. "Around."

"Why didn't you ask me?"

I put my beer on the bar and my hands in my pockets. "I am asking you."

Phil cleared his throat. "The bar is for sale."

I could feel my fists clench inside my jeans pockets. I tried to calm down. Maybe Phil didn't think there'd be any way I could afford a legitimate bid, but he had no idea how much I'd saved over the years. On the positive side, I assumed my plan with Walt had at least some of the intended effect. "I want to buy it."

"Charlie, this isn't a good time to discuss it."

Drew came back to our end of the bar to take a couple of drink orders from Phil's buddies. He was probably cleaning up in tips.

I took a five out of my pocket and waved it at Drew. "Can I get singles?"

He nodded and went to the register, counted out the bills and handed them to me. "Pretty crazy about Ralph and Beth, huh?"

One brilliant observation after another. I leaned in, "Did you know Phil was selling?"

He shrugged. "Not for sure."

I shook my head. Phil had trusted this dipshit mama's boy enough to tell him the bar was for sale, but he didn't tell me. I'd intended to take the singles and play some tunes on the jukebox. Instead, I put them in my pocket and headed for the side door. I pushed it open without saying goodbye to anyone.

As I headed for my car, I was fuming. Ray knew. Drew must have had a conversation about it with Phil at some point. It was a kick in the face that Phil felt like he couldn't talk to me about his plans. Eight years. I put up the money to help Phil buy this fucking dump eight years before. I broke my back and sold my soul to a steady stream of suburban assholes who thought it was cool to slum it downtown when I lived it and I breathed it. I had my keys in my fist as I passed by Phil's Explorer. I hesitated for a moment, considering running one over the shiny paint when I heard footsteps behind me.

"Come up off your cash, faggot."

I turned around to see a skinny black kid, probably about fourteen, standing in front of me, shaking. "Or what, slick?"

"Or this." He pulled a dull-looking twenty-two from his shorts pocket and grinned.

"You know you got a girl's gun?" I reached into my pocket for the five singles Drew had given me. The rest of my cash was in my right sock.

He grabbed at the money. "Takes a faggot to know a girl's gun." He grabbed the bills, dropping one. "This all you got?"

I pointed my head at the bar. "I left the rest in there." I smiled and pointed at the door. "Go on in."

***

MOLLY

333

I hadn't spoken to my mother in at least six months. It wouldn't have made any difference to me if Drew and I left town without me even bothering to tell her, but for whatever reason, he wanted to meet her. An annoyingly traditional approach to a completely non-traditional relationship. But I loved him and if he wanted to meet her, I was happy to oblige. I thought maybe an hour or two in her presence would clear up the nature of our conflict. That doesn't mean I wanted a fight.

We invited her to lunch. Drew suggested our apartment, but even if we were only going to be in town for a couple weeks, I still didn't want her to know exactly where I was living.

On the way to the restaurant, Drew was playing that new Clem Snide CD yet again. Truth be told, it was growing on me. The guy was singing about some girl, his Joan Jett of Arc.

I tossed a half-smoked cigarette out of the car window. "This song's pretty dirty."

Drew turned and smiled at me and then put his eyes back on the road. "Is it turning you on?"

I was pretty sure it was all about losing your virginity, teenager sex. I shook my head. "No."

He shrugged. "Too bad." He pulled the car into the parking lot of the Bennigan's where my mom insisted on meeting us. Drew and I made it a habit to never eat in chain restaurants, but he didn't complain at all when I told him where we were going.

He swung the car into a parking space near the back, even though there were about a dozen spots closer to the door. "Here we are." He smiled and killed the engine. "Applebee's."

I shook my head. "Bennigan's."

He feigned confusion. "This isn't Chili's?"

I rolled my eyes. He played this game frequently, pretending to get things wrong and acting confused when he was corrected. It was cute. He was cute. I made myself want to barf with how cute we were. "It's Friday's. Let's just go in and get this over with. If we wait too long, she'll have time to down another Long Island."

Drew got out of the car and I followed. He had dressed nice but not up: a short-sleeved cotton shirt with a collar, nice jeans, Top Siders. He waited for me to catch up, and we held hands as we walked into the overly air-conditioned restaurant.

Drew winced. "I should've worn a fucking jacket. What is it with these places? Goddamned Ruby Tuesday."

That one made me laugh. The hostess smiled widely as she greeted us. We told her we were joining my mom, and she directed us to a booth near the bar, in the smoking section.

She looked terrible. She was wearing a tank top, which revealed too thin arms, skin hanging down badly. She must have lost twenty pounds when what she'd needed was to gain ten. She stood and made a show of giving me what would appear a warm, long hug.

I broke it off and stepped back. "Mom, this is Drew."

She smiled. She'd lost a bicuspid. I thought it might have been possible that the asshole knocked it out. "Aren't you a handsome one?"

"Mom."

She looked at me. "Well, he is. I'm just stating the obvious."

"It's nice meeting you, Mrs. Caldwell."

"And manners, too." She motioned to the booth. "Please, let's sit." She looked at Drew. "You call me Peg, alright?"

Drew nodded. "Sure."

My mom spread the menu open in front of her. She had a Long Island in front of her, half gone. "How is school, Molly?"

"I'm graduating Saturday."

She looked up at me, wide-eyed. "Why hadn't you told me?"

I shrugged.

She looked at Drew. "You must be proud of your little woman."

Drew looked mildly confused, probably unsure of how to react to my mom's choice of terminology. "Molly's worked really hard."

She kept her eyes on him, almost flirtatiously. It was something she'd done with several of my boyfriends. I was still convinced she'd given Tommy Doucette, my junior homecoming date, a blowjob while I finished getting ready. "Are you educated, Andrew?"

He nodded. "I finished my bachelor's at Michigan State a few years ago."

She smiled. The hole where her tooth should have been turned my stomach. "Your mom must be so proud."

I didn't give Drew a chance to answer. "How's work, Mom?"

She waved me off. "A job's a job, you know that."

My mom had been a waitress since she dropped out in tenth grade. She rarely worked anywhere longer than a year, as she'd get too drunk one day after her shift, make a scene and move along. One after the other after the other. "I know, Mom."

Our waitress came to the table for drink orders. Drew ordered an appetizer. He told her something about bringing us a plate of your finest fried cheese, which no one but me seemed to think was funny. I loved him.

My mom picked up the pack of Virginia Slims she had on the table, took one out and lit it. "What are your plans after graduation?"

It must have stuck Drew strange to hear a parent and child have to catch up on each other's lives in this fashion. He and his mother saw each other two or three times a week. She was very nice and seemed to like me. It can be hard to tell sometimes, mothers and sons are often connected in a way that mothers and daughters aren't. I didn't like to think too much about it. I purposefully forgot most of the Freud I'd learned.

At any rate, I certainly wasn't going to tell my mother anything about the check Drew's mom had just given him. She'd split the proceeds from selling their house between him and his brothers. $115, 834. The number was burned in my brain.

336

I took out my own cigarette and lit it. "We're going to put our things in storage and travel for a while. Drew's going to start graduate school in the fall."

She exhaled a hit of her cigarette and took a large sip of her drink. "How exciting." She looked at Drew. "Where are you going to travel to?"

Drew looked at me as if wondering whether he should answer. "We're going to visit my brothers in Phoenix and Atlanta. But first we're going to see some of the east coast, Boston, Philadelphia. We'll start in New York."

She nodded. "That sounds nice. You're leaving when?"

The waitress came back with our drinks. Another Long Island for my mom, a couple of Sam Adams for Drew and I.

I took a sip of my beer. "We leave two weeks after graduation."

She held up her drink. "Well, here's congratulations to you on your degree and safe travels to you both." She looked like she might cry.

Drew and I held up our beers and clinked glasses with my mom. She turned her glass up and drained half of it in one gulp.

"Take it easy, Mom."

She glared at me. "You know, Bruce warned me you'd hightail it out of here at the first opportunity."

I cringed at the mention of my mom's boyfriend, a low-life layabout who claimed disability from GM and spent most days drunk on the couch watching Lifetime movies. "You expected me to hang around in Flint? How do you make a life here exactly?"

She pointed her cigarette at Drew. "Watch out for this one. She tried her damndest to steal my man right from under my nose."

She must have had a couple of drinks before heading to the restaurant.

Drew didn't skip a beat. "Is that exactly how it happened, Peg?"

I'd told Drew all about Bruce climbing into my bed one night, me nearly scratching his eyes out before he'd get off of me. How I'd had to scramble to find an apartment, struggle even more to pay for school. I wasn't happy to be sitting in that booth, but at least Drew would never again question my relationship with my mother.

She stubbed out her cigarette. "I'm not sure I know what you mean."

He shrugged. "I mean, I highly doubt she was trying to steal him from you."

She fixed a glare on Drew. Her flirtation stage had clearly passed. "Wrapped around her finger. I shouldn't be surprised. She flashes her tits at a boy and it's all over."

Drew drained his beer. "I'm not a boy. And I'm not wrapped around anyone's finger."

"Drew. Mom. Can we just stop this?"

My mom drank the rest of her Long Island in another long gulp. "Stop what? I just thought this one should know what he's getting himself into." She lit another cigarette and blew smoke all over. "Has she told you I had to drive her to get an abortion in High School? Bet she hasn't."

I had. "Mom, stop this."

"What about the time I caught her in bed with a nigger from her school? She tell you all about that? She was fifteen years old. Fifteen, fucking a goddamned nigger in my fucking house."

People in the booths near ours were craning their necks to get a look at what was happening.

Drew pulled out his wallet and dropped a couple of twenties. "I think we should go."

She grabbed for the bills but missed, then flicked them with her forefinger back at Drew. "I don't need your money."

He looked at my mother with a mixture of sympathy and disdain. I'm not sure I ever saw someone give a look that said more. I loved him.

He put the bills back in his pocket. "Suit yourself." He stood and motioned for me to follow. "There's a lot I could say right now that I'll keep to myself. I would tell you to not worry about your daughter, that I love her and care for her and that what happened before we met isn't any of my business. Somehow, I don't think any of that would make any difference, so I'll just say I'm glad to have met you and good-bye."

I stubbed my cigarette out in the ashtray. "Bye, Mom."

We turned to leave. Drew took my hand. I loved him.

As we walked out, my mother shouted at our backs. "Have fun in New fucking York. Don't think twice about what you're leaving behind."

Her voice trailed off and faded as we walked through the first set of doors and faded to nothing as we made it outside. I took a deep breath and said a silent thank you to Drew. I held his hand tight as we walked through the parking lot, past the Toyotas and the Fords and the Pontiacs. I thought about how I really hated cars. I wanted to live somewhere you didn't need one. Somewhere big enough that you faded in most places, big crowds, always moving, so that the only people who mattered were the ones you love, the ones you choose.

Those we don't choose, the ones who don't matter, could just trail off. Fade.

☆☆☆

PHIL

Pam held her legs up in that way women do when they're trying to keep the semen inside. One of the best things about trying to get pregnant was the frequency of the sex, but also its mission. You spend so much of your life in avoidance of pregnancy, in worry, wrapped up and medicated and scared, that when you're doing the opposite, it's freeing. Uninhibited. Sexy as hell.

When I came home and told her I'd signed the papers, she jumped me and we had sex right there in the front hall. I could be wrong, but I wondered if it might have been a one-shot deal, and those little swimmers weren't finding their way to create Franklin child number two as she lay there.

She laughed. "This tile is fucking cold."

"Are you sure Nate's asleep?"

She nodded and adjusted her grip on her legs, pulling them tighter. "He was five minutes ago."

I stood and put my boxers on. "I'm going to go check."

I crept up the stairs and peaked into Nate's room. He was on his side in his bed, right thumb in his mouth. He was gorgeous. I pulled the door shut until it made a quiet click.

I walked back down the stairs and sat on the bottom step, my bare feet six inches from Pam's head. She did her best to turn around and look at me, her movement limited by her position. She smiled at me.

I'm glad she didn't give me a minute to think things through. I might have hesitated. I might have thought twice. I might have tried one last time to cling onto the old life for just a bit longer, the one in which I owned a bar, the one in which we had one child, the one in which I kept deluding myself I was part of some big movement that would save my hometown, the one in which I watched an old friend slowly destroy himself, an even older friend whither in a lonely apartment in a shitty neighborhood. I was glad to not be clinging to anything anymore. It would be a new life now, a new time.

Pam wiggled her butt, I guess in an effort to keep it off the cold tile. "When does Ray move?"

"A week from Tuesday. The eleventh." We'd found a good retirement community in Burton where his VA benefits would help defray the costs. I felt bad about it and apologized several times, but Ray just told me it was fine and he probably should've been in a place like it a few years before and he was grateful he got to stay in the apartments for as long as he did. I promised to visit all the time and bring Nate, and he said he'd like that. And I meant it.

She nodded. "I know that was hard."

"He's so nice."

"And Charlie?"

It would be happening any minute. I agreed to let the buyer inform Charlie. Maybe I shouldn't have done that, I don't know. But it got hard to give a fuck about someone who proved, time and time and time again, that he didn't give a fuck about you. There'd be no time again this time. It was a new time.

"Charlie's not so nice."

She wiggled again. Her ass made a small slapping sound against the tile. "Has it been five minutes?"

I hadn't been keeping track. I looked at my watch, the same one I'd bought when I worked at Schneeberger Honda, the cheapest Rolex. I'd bought it so I could look the part, walk the walk. I kind of wanted to buy a new one, something simpler. It was a new time. I nodded at Pam, still bunched up on the floor, trying to make our baby. "Yes. Five minutes."

⁂

CHARLIE

I was finishing washing some glasses from the after-work rush, if it can really be called that these days. It was quiet, the Tigers pregame show on the televisions, just a couple of guys finishing a pitcher at one end of the bar, the slow hours before ten o'clock hit and things picked back up. The side door opened. The light was shining in through the glass so I couldn't see the face of the woman who was walking in. She was nicely shaped, though, that's for sure. Not too tall but still statuesque, nice hips, smartly dressed. If a silhouette were ever enough to give me an erection, this would've been the one.

She walked up to the bar and sat on a stool. I blinked once, twice. I wasn't sure what I saw.

"Cindy?"

She smiled; her teeth were perfect and white. "Hi, Charlie."

My heart pounded in my chest. I hadn't seen her since that scene in my apartment, where I purposefully invited her over, told her to walk in, that I'd be in the shower, and was instead balls-deep in this sure thing redhead with big tits who I could always call upon in a time of need. Charlene. I wondered what Charlene was up to. Cindy had freaked, screaming and vowing revenge again, but I figured canceling that bet was a once-in-a-lifetime stroke of genius on her part and there was no way she'd ever be able to get over on me like that again. As the months piled up and turned into years, I'd more or less forgotten about her, except for those occasions when I called up her memory if I needed a solid masturbation fantasy. No matter what else, Cindy had always remained a top three fuck. Maybe top two. Shit, she might have been the best I ever had.

I reached into my pack of Reds, pulled one out and lit it. "Been a long time."

She nodded but didn't say anything.

"You know you're banned from this place, right?"

She smiled and shrugged. "I think you can make an exception for one beer. Just this one time. Can't you?"

I looked her up and down. She was amazing. She'd matured and filled out, her earlier boniness replaced with curves, her once too short hair grown out to her shoulders, shimmering. The very thought of getting her back in bed looking like that but fucking like she used to was enough to fill my boxer briefs with pre-cum. "A Stroh's for old time's sake?"

She nodded and reached into her small clutch for a pack of Benson and Hedge's 100s. She shook one out and lit it.

I moved to the taps and poured her beer, and then set it on a cocktail napkin in front of her. "On me."

She smiled and took a sip. She got up and went to the jukebox and slid a couple of singles in. She filed through the discs for a few minutes and then looked over her shoulder at me.

"You took out that Liz Phair CD I always used to play?"

I nodded. "It fell out of fashion."

"I'll have to get it back in there."

I had no idea what she meant by that, so I ignored her.

She punched up some numbers and a song from the newest PJ Harvey album filled the space. It made sense Cindy would regard PJ Harvey as a suitable replacement for Liz Phair. She punched in a couple more tunes and came back to the bar.

She took a drag from her cigarette. "Do you like this record?"

I shrugged and exhaled a drag from my Red. "She's okay."

"I love it. 'The Whores Hustle and Hustlers Whore' was like my song of the year."

The only reason the disc was even in the jukebox was because there were always female customers who'd complain if there weren't enough women artists available to play. I personally could give a fuck and would just as soon have an all-dude selection. It all sounded like caterwauling to me. "So, how've you been?"

She took another sip from the pint. "Wonderful. Best day of my life."

I was beginning to wonder if she'd be willing to turn it into the best night, too. "Oh yeah? Why's that?"

She smiled. "I bought a bar."

I took another drag. "Is that right?"

She nodded and then started laughing uncontrollably. "I can't do this anymore." She laughed some more and then took a deep breath and tried to collect herself. "I've waited so long, I thought I could pull it off, but fuck it." She put her cigarette out. "You're fired, Charlie. You don't work here anymore."

I didn't think she seemed like she was high when she came in, but between the giggling and the nonsense coming out of her mouth, I wasn't so sure anymore. "This is stupid. I don't know what your deal is, but I'm not in the mood."

She put her hand to her mouth to stifle another giggle. "My deal is I own this bar as of today, Charlie. I paid your friend Phil a shit-ton of money for this building, and part of the deal was that I get to be the one to come down here and send your blanket ass packing."

I didn't remember ever telling her I was one-quarter Menominee. "This isn't true."

She nodded. "Oh, it's true. Maybe they'll welcome you back on the rez, Chief."

I started shaking. "I'm calling Phil."

She turned her head sideways. "That's cute. Go ahead."

I used the jukebox knob by the sink to kill the volume, and then turned around and grabbed the receiver off the cradle. I could barely see the numbers and my fingers trembled as I tried to press the buttons. It rang a few times before Pam answered.

"Put Phil on the phone."

"Charlie, Phil's not here."

I hadn't spoken to Pam on the phone in years. I wasn't sure how she'd recognized my voice. I walked closer to Cindy, pulling the phone cord taught. "Well, maybe you can clear something up. There's a syphilitic goat here who claims she bought Bob's from Phil today."

I could hear Pam breathing on the other end, Nate babbling in the background. "Pam?"

She sighed. "It's true."

I could feel my nostrils flare, my pulse quicken, the tips of my ears turn red. I took measured heavy breaths. "Tell Phil he's fucking dead when I see him."

"Charlie—"

344

I slammed the phone down before Pam could say more.

Cindy's smile was gone. "Charlie, calm down. Take a shot of Bushmill's and come sit by me." She patted the stool next to her.

"I'm perfectly calm." I shook out a cigarette and lit it. "None of this matters. You're all conveniently forgetting I own fifteen percent. Phil can't sell without my approval."

She looked at me as though I were a child. "Is your name on a single piece of paper associated with this place?"

It wasn't. I took a long slow drag and then walked to the back bar and grabbed two shot glasses and the bottle of Bushmill's. "Join me?"

Cindy nodded. I poured the shots and we drank them with a flick of the wrist. I poured a second for each of us and then took a drag from my Red.

Cindy drank hers and winced. "Feel better?"

I took my shot. It burned. I hated Bushmill's. I don't know why I drank what she suggested. "No."

She took a sip of her beer. "I warned you Charlie. I told you no one treats me the way you did. You chose not to believe me, even after I fucked up your football bet. You still treated me like trash."

I took a last drag from my cigarette and put it out in the ashtray. The two dudes at the end of the bar got up to leave. I was alone with Cindy. I thought about putting my hands around her throat, watching her eyes pop out. "How did you get the money?"

"I whored."

I furrowed my brow. "What do you mean?"

"I mean, I fucked men for money. I moved to Los Angeles. There are a lot of rich men there, men who like to pay to fuck young girls in the pussy and the ass, watch them eat each other's pussies, maybe make some movies about it, I don't know if they're real, I never went to a video store to check. I just made the money. Getting fucked, sucking cock. You know better than anyone how much I love to do all of it. It doesn't matter who, really, a cock is a cock. The useless skin attached to it doesn't concern me much."

I looked around the bar, the bar I'd helped build into what it was, the bar I'd sweated for and broke my back in and tried to turn into something that gave people a place to be themselves, a place to rise above the shit that Flint was becoming. Had become. "I could kill you."

"You could." She smiled. "If I weren't already dead." She reached into her purse and took out a single key. She got up and turned the lock on the front door, then moved down the bar and turned the lock on the side door.

"Looks like we're closed for the night." She smiled, and then sat on the stool. "Are you just going to stare, or are you going to fuck me?"

***

DREW

Just as I'd thought, it was a good thing Charlie had hired two bartenders instead of one, because trying to cover extra shifts while packing and moving our things into storage and saying good-bye to my mom and all the rest would've been near impossible if I had to cover half of Charlie's shifts. No one had seen him or heard from him since he was told he was out of a job. I may not have liked him very much, but it's not like I wanted anything bad to happen to him.

It was my second-to-last Saturday in the bar. I'd told Cindy, the new owner, that I'd be happy to work out two weeks' notice, but that Molly and I had non-refundable tickets to New York, and that I'd need to be finished before that flight. She was nice enough about it, told me she understood and that she'd heard I was a good bartender and popular and I'd be welcomed back if I ever decided to return.

It's funny how your mind works when things are coming to an end. You keep thinking how everything is the last time you'll be doing it. This is the last time I'll drive to the Farmer Jack. This is the last Mass I'll attend at Holy Family. This is the last time Molly and I will fuck each other in this apartment. Everything, no matter how mundane, becomes poignant, even if it's a disagreeable task.

This was the second-to-last Saturday I'd empty these overflowing trashcans. The second-to-last time I'd try and clean these never-clean bathrooms. The second-to-last last time I'd scrub at spilled beer with this smelly mop. The second-to-last time I'd pull down these stools, and the second-to-last time I'd open the door in time for Ray to spend some time with me at Bob's.

Ray smiled as he walked in the door. It seems odd, but he actually seemed happier once Phil sold the bar and he found out he'd be moving to the home in Burton. Maybe he was excited to be around people his own age. Maybe he was tired of living all alone up there over the bar.

"Hey there, Ray."

He sat on his stool and took the cigarillos from his shirt pocket. "Good to see you, Drew."

I went to the taps to pour him a Stroh's. I watched the beer fill the glass, golden and cold. I reached for a second glass and poured myself one. I brought them back to the end of the bar and sat.

Ray accepted his and smiled. "Nice of you to join me."

I took a sip and shrugged. "What are they going to do, fire me?"

He laughed. "I missed you last Saturday."

"Molly's graduation."

"That's right. Please be sure you pass along my congratulations. College graduation is a real achievement."

I nodded. "Especially the way she had to do it. She's something else."

"I'm glad you're happy."

347

I took out my Parliaments, shook one out and lit it. "How goes your moving prep?"

"I'm surrounded by boxes. It makes it simultaneously easier and harder to know it will be my last move."

I'd been so wrapped up in all my lasts that I hadn't even thought of that. I struggled for a response that didn't sound morbid or maudlin. "Phil says the place is real nice."

Ray nodded. "It is. It's long overdue, frankly. I'm not sure how I'd have survived up there without all of you helping me, and I knew it couldn't continue forever. You have your own lives to lead. It's time."

"I was happy to do it." I sipped my Stroh's.

"Have you heard from Charlie?"

I shook my head. "No one has."

"It's too bad, but it's hard not to see how he might have had it coming."

I couldn't imagine Charlie's behavior would have been tolerated anywhere except Bob's for too terribly long. "I wonder what he'll do."

"He'll survive."

I got up to turn the televisions on. "I don't think your Yanks are the national game today. Seattle at Orioles."

Ray nodded. "Of course they want Ichiro on the broadcast whenever possible."

I walked back to my stool and sat. "Who'd have thought Barry Bonds would have fifty-seven homers at this point and still be the second biggest story in baseball?"

"Fifty-seven?"

I nodded. "He hit one against the Rockies last night."

"It's unreal."

Ray and I had talked plenty about the increase in home runs, the causes and the reasons. I thought it was obvious players were on steroids, and there were many whispers about exactly that, but Ray thought it had more to do with a lack of quality pitching. I suppose we were both right to some degree.

I paused for a moment and thought about this being the second-to-last time Ray and I would sit here talking about Ichiro and Barry Bonds.

Ray and I chatted about a few things over the next hour or so; I told him about the trip Molly and I were getting ready to begin, how my mom's generosity was funding the whole thing but there'd still be plenty left over to help Molly and I get settled when I started school in the fall. We talked about the programs I was thinking of applying to, my prep for the GRE. We talked about Ray's hesitance to part with many of his favorite books, even though he wouldn't be able to keep them all in his new home. He told me a couple of stories about his old bar, the shift bar he owned before the Tick Tock, and his old employee, Ellsworth.

Eventually, a few more customers filtered in and the bar livened up. Saturday afternoons could be unpredictable that way. Sometimes, I'd have hours to spend shooting the shit with Ray. Kirby and Kent came in and kept Ray company. They loved talking with him, having him school them on whatever nonsense disagreement they might be having, knowing he was always right. I moved around, fielding lots of questions from customers about the sale of Bob's; would it be closing? Was the new owner going to remodel? Would there be a kitchen? I didn't really know most of the answers, but I assumed anyone who bought it did so with the idea of keeping Bob's exactly as it was.

Several customers had caught wind of my impending departure, so in addition to the questions about the bar, I was giving answers about my plans post-Flint. No, Molly and I weren't engaged. Yes, it was a possibility. No, I hadn't been accepted into any graduate schools yet. Yes, we'd be visiting family in Phoenix and Atlanta. Yes, we planned on doing all the touristy things in New York, Nashville, Memphis.

Things slowed down after three o'clock. I sat on the stool at the end of the bar and lit a cigarette. Ray sat next to Kirby. He'd been quiet for a while, nursing the same beer for at least the last hour. Kirby and Kent were discussing barbeque plans for Labor Day. It occurred to me that since my mom had moved, I wouldn't have a plan for that day. Kirby was lecturing on his favorite marinades, and I was spacing out a little, taking a breather from what had been a couple of unexpectedly busy hours.

I looked over at Ray to ask him a question, I'm not sure what. He'd been quiet, I remember thinking maybe he was bored, tired of hearing Kent and Kirby prattle on about nothing, disengaged with the listless Tigers and Blue Jays game that was on the televisions. I watched his face, looking like he was getting ready to speak, looking right at me. Behind his eyes, it looked as though a switch had been turned, the light behind his eyes instantly changed, gone, snuffed. His jaw went slack, his eyes still open; he slumped to his right, resting on Kent's shoulder.

Kent turned to see what was happening, feeling the full weight of Ray against him. He shook his shoulder, causing Ray to slump further, and then moved to wrap his arms around him to prevent him from falling off the stool.

Of course, I'd never seen anyone have a stroke before that moment, but somehow I knew that's exactly what had happened. It all happened in the blink of an eye; Ray slumped, Kent turned and caught him, I stood to help prop him up, Kirby jumped off his stool to offer his help.

Kirby kept his right hand on Ray's back. "Why don't we move him to the booth so he won't fall?"

Without agreeing verbally, Kent and I lifted Ray from the stool and moved him to a seated position in the closest booth. He offered no help or resistance. His was a dead weight. Once in the booth, he remained upright somehow, staring off in the distance, and I couldn't help but think he was already gone.

I moved behind the bar, telling Kirby and Kent I was going to call 911. I grabbed the phone and punched in those digits for the first time in my life. I spoke calmly and quickly, describing Ray's condition, our location, answering a question or two, hanging up. I knew it was important to remain clam, and I was grateful that Kent and Kirby were also keeping it together, glad I wasn't alone and that familiar faces surrounded Ray, hoping he took some comfort in it.

I went back to the booth. There was no change in Ray's condition, which I supposed meant it hadn't gotten worse. Kent and Kirby discussed what they might do to help him, but I explained it was pretty clear Ray had a stroke and I didn't think there was anything we could do. I rubbed Ray's back and told him to hang in there, that I'd called an ambulance and it would be there soon.

The sirens followed admirably quickly. The technicians were efficient and impressive, and Ray was strapped in and hauled out in what must have been less than two minutes. Once the ambulance pulled away, Kent, Kirby, and I sat in a stunned silence, unsure of exactly what to do next.

Kent shook his head. "It was a good thing I was sitting there, or he'd have fallen right to the floor."

Kirby put his arm around his friend. "I've never seen anything like that."

I swallowed hard. "I don't hope to ever again."

Kent and Kirby talked about driving to the hospital, but they'd had more than a few beers and I told them I didn't think it was a good idea at the moment, that they should take a little while and sober up. Besides, I didn't think any doctor would have real answers about Ray's condition anytime soon, and that they could either wait in the bar or in the hospital, and wouldn't they be more comfortable in the bar? They agreed and we sat back in our stools, still shaking our heads and not knowing what to say or do or how to process what had just happened.

As my thoughts slowed and became clearer, I rose with a start. I ran to the phone and punched in Phil's number. He answered in two rings.

"Phil, it's Drew."

"Hey now, why're you calling me from the bar on a Saturday? I don't care if you're out of lemons."

"It's Ray. He had a stroke. An ambulance just took him to McLaren."

"In the bar?"

"Yes. Just a few minutes ago."

"Fuck." He took the phone away from his mouth and shouted. "Fuck. Fuck." He brought the receiver back. "You're sure it was a stroke?"

The image of the life leaving Ray's face would never leave my mind. "As sure as I can be."

"Okay, okay." I could hear Phil's thoughts getting away from him. "I'm going over there right now. I'll call you as soon as I know anything. What time is it?"

I looked at my watch. "A few minutes after four."

"Okay." He paused. "Okay." He didn't hang up. "Drew?"

"Yeah?"

"I'm glad you were there for him."

We said our quick good-byes and disconnected. I'd done my best to remain stoic, but that did it. I'd tried to think positively, but in that moment, I knew Ray was gone and that he'd died alone, living in an apartment above a bar in a shitty neighborhood, all alone, surrounded by boxes, waiting to go to an old-folks' home where he'd wait to die. I knew Ray thought he'd found love in his life, only to lose it. Ray had friends and a business and family, and for what? To have a massive stroke, slumped over on the shoulder of an acquaintance, someone who probably wouldn't make a list of top one hundred people Ray'd known, literally dozens of people with whom he'd been closer, the only thing stopping his head from smashing onto the concrete floor was the arm of some nitwit who mattered not a wit. It started to piss me off even more than it made me sad. Ray living upstairs, relying on me to bring him bread and eggs, some dumb kid the only thing between him and starvation. An entire life, days and nights and mornings and evenings, springs and summers and winters and Ray was somebody's baby once, he was an infant, and a college student with a life of possibilities in front of him and a mom and a dad and for what? To die alone, all alone, in this stupid fucking bar, this stupid fucking bar, in godforsaken Flint, and he was right, Ray was right, I needed to commit. I needed to commit.

***

CHARLIE

I hadn't answered my phone for days. I'm not exactly sure how many. Most of that time I'd been rolling around in bed with Cindy, day blending into night, one day into the next, time stretching out and contracting and snapping back in on itself, Cindy and me fucking in positions I'd never even tried before. She punched me in the face. I called her a lot of names. I'd done a lot in the past with all sorts of women. It all led to this. It didn't matter if I never fucked again or if I died. I kind of wanted to die.

No one bothered to leave a message or knock on my door. It was just as well. I didn't want to see anyone or be seen by anyone. Cindy didn't count, after all. She was dead, remember?

Can't no ghost see you.

When the phone rang on a Saturday in the evening sometime, I only know it was evening because it was September and the sun was setting earlier, it was another call I didn't pick up. The answering machine beeped and I expected to hear the dial tone meaning someone had hung up, someone didn't want to bother. Cindy was asleep next to me. We'd been fucking for four hours straight. Crazy shit. She cried a little. That felt good. Instead of the dial tone, I heard a voice and sat up. It was Phil. Fucking Phil. I wanted to get up and rip the machine out of the wall, throw it, smash it, stomp on it. Instead I listened.

Ray. Stroke. Bob's. McLaren. Died.

I picked up. Phil was crying. He told me Ray was dead. He'd had a stroke in the bar that day. There wasn't anything that could be done. He said he was sorry that things went the way they did. He was sorry. He was sorry about Ray.

I told him I was sorry about Ray, too. I told him to get bent. Really, that's what I said. I don't know where that came from. Get bent. I said you treated me like half a fag. You treated that full-on fag Drew better than you treated me. I said how could you do that.

He said he didn't call me to fight. He called to tell me about Ray. He said if we didn't have anything else constructive to say to each other that he was going to hang up.

I said hang up, shove the phone up your ass, either way it makes no difference to me. I hope you get cancer, I said. I hope it eats out your insides. Cancer. I hope you join Ray real soon, to treat me that way. Fuck you, Phil. Fuck your mother. I hung up.

I went back into the bedroom. Cindy was still asleep. I took my underwear off and played with my cock a little, smacked it against my leg, trying to get it hard. My nuts were drained. It'd be nothing but a dry heave. I had little friction burn up and down my shaft. It hurt. I went over to the bed and turned Cindy on her stomach. I smacked my dick on her ass. I reached onto the nightstand for the lube, poured it on my cock, smacked it on her ass again. It hurt. It hurt. I hurt. Cindy woke up, smiled, put her mouth on my dick. It hurt.

I hurt.

***

DREW

I opened the door. Phil was already inside.

"Hi, Drew." He walked over and gave me a hug.

I gripped him back, tight.

Phil broke away and moved back towards the box he'd been looking through. "I thought this was going to be hard, but I was wrong." He shook his head. His voice cracked. "It's impossible. I can't do this."

Just as Ray had told me, his entire apartment had been boxed up. He'd been meticulous in his packing; every box was labeled, every item inside catalogued on a note card taped to the side of the box. Phil said it was hard, but in a practical sense, it seemed like it'd be pretty easy to me.

I sat on Ray's couch. It was one of those wood models with thin cushions that were in a huge number of off-campus apartments in East Lansing. I wasn't sure where one even bought a couch like that. I'd never seen one in any store anywhere, ever. "I'm not sure I'm going to be any real help here, Phil. Molly and I just finished putting our stuff in storage. We're leaving Monday."

"I know." He sat next to me. "I wasn't expecting you to take anything with you, really. But Ray specified no memorial service, and I wanted to honor that, but I also wanted some sort of community, you know? I don't think I'm explaining myself very well."

I waved him off. "I understand. Did you reach out to Charlie?"

He nodded. "Charlie's gone."

"Where'd he go?"

He pointed at his head, made a circular motion with his index finger.

"I suppose that wasn't a long journey."

Phil laughed. "I did my best with him. For a long time, longer than most people would've."

"Of course."

Phil looked down into the box for a few seconds and then back up at me. "You know I'm proud of you, right?"

I didn't know exactly what he meant by saying that, but I'm not sure it's ever not nice to hear those words. "Thanks."

"I mean it. Everyone else we know, Drew, it's all excuses. My mom didn't love me. My dad died. My girlfriend left me. I'm too short, too slow, too old. You're not like that. And you found a woman who's just like you in that regard."

I took out a cigarette and lit it, offered one to Phil. He nodded, slid one out of the pack and used my Bic to light his. We smoked in silence for a moment, ashes on the floor.

I looked in front of me at the boxes. There were several that were labeled books, author's names and titles written on cards on the side. I thought about how long that must have taken Ray, writing down the names and writers of hundreds and hundreds of books, placing them in the box, one after the other after the other, over and over. It seemed to me that he had to have started the process long before he got the news of his impending move; I got up, looked closer, and noticed there was some yellowing around the edges of the note cards, the tape holding the boxes closed was curling at the ends. These boxes made the move from Ray's house. He'd never opened them.

I looked over at Phil. "Have you been in the bedroom yet?"

He shook his head.

I walked in between the boxes towards where Ray slept. The bed was made, a thin, worn quilt covering the double mattress. Next to the bed was an open box, this one only half-filled. I sat on the bed, catching a spring in my ass crack, moving to the left and catching a different one on my cheek. I moved off the bed and sat on the floor next to the box, Indian style.

Inside, there was a couple of old issues of *Time*, one from JFK's funeral, one from after the Tet Offensive. There were a couple of worn paperbacks, titles and authors I didn't recognize. There was a program from the game at Comerica I'd taken Ray to last season, Sunday May 14, 2000, Detroit Tigers vs. New York Yankees. I smiled at that, brought it out of the box, set it down next to my leg.

I dug through some other odds and ends until I came across a framed photo at the bottom. A woman, in her early twenties or maybe late teens, posed, hairstyle from the late forties or early fifties.

Miriam.

Ray kept a framed photo of his first love with him, this close to where he slept, for fifty years. I thought this photo must have made the trip with him to basic training, then on a transport plane to Korea, Ray not knowing if he'd live or die, then maybe a steamship home, New York then Detroit, the photo in his bag, probably in the pages of a book, because to look at it then, in 2001 in Ray's bedroom, it looked like it'd never been creased, didn't have a wrinkle or water damage. I saw Ray keeping this photo in his bar, first in Schmitty's and then the Tick Tock, somewhere hidden in a drawer on the back bar, always there to remind him what she looked like, just in case that was the day she saw the error of her ways and returned, that was the day she knew their differences weren't so great they couldn't be overcome. I saw it in his house, when other women would enter, Ray lying and saying it was a cousin or a sister, or telling the truth and saying it was Miriam, his first love. He told the truth to Ruby. I'll bet he told the truth to Ruby.

Phil walked into the bedroom and sat on the bed. "Jesus, the springs on this thing."

I smiled.

He pointed at the photo. "Who's that?"

"It has to be Miriam."

Phil furrowed his brow. "Miriam?"

"Ray never told you about Miriam?"

He shook his head.

At first, I thought Phil was confused or had forgotten, because it didn't seem possible Ray hadn't told him about Miriam. Then it occurred to me Ray only told each of us what he thought we needed to hear, those things that might teach us something or guide us from the mistakes he'd made, the pitfalls he didn't escape. Phil had known Ray for far longer than I had, but he'd never mentioned Miriam because Phil didn't need to know about having your heart broken. He'd had different stories for Phil, for Charlie and Ralph.

I looked down at the photo. Miriam looked back. She wore a sundress, a flowered pattern. She'd looked at Ray with the same eyes, the same expression, almost but not quite a smile, for fifty years.

Phil poked me in the arm. "Drew, who's Miriam?"

Ray only told us what we needed to hear.

I looked down at my cigarette. I'd forgotten about it. It had burned out. "It's not important."

He shrugged. "Where are you and Molly off to first?"
"We fly into New York Monday night."

"That's cool. Where are you staying?"

"The Chelsea Hotel."

Phil smiled. "Of course. September in New York. Not quite autumn. But still nice. Then what?"

I'd learned my lesson. Ray had told me what I needed to hear, and showed me what I needed to see. We don't get a second chance at this life. I'd bought the ring. We'd go to the tip of Manhattan, Bowling Green, Battery Park. With Lady Liberty over my shoulder, I'd put it on her finger.

I would commit. I will commit.

ACKNOWLEDGEMENTS

My most sincere gratitude and deepest thanks belong to everyone who believed in me. Some of these people I will mention in the following paragraphs.

To any and all staff at Cleveland Clinic Akron General Hospital and Cleveland Clinic Rehabilitation Hospital who had a literal hand in saving my life, I'm only writing this because you are good at your job.

The staff at Unsolicited Press, especially my kind and generous editor Summer Stewart. Thank you for your understanding and dedication and advocacy. You were crucial to my spirit when I most needed it.

My NEOMFA friend and compatriot Michael Goroff, who may have grown too big for Akron, but will never grow too big to have a place in my heart.

My NEOMFA instructors, thesis committee members and all-around supportivest of the supportive, in no particular order: David Giffels, Christopher Barzak, Eric Wasserman, Mary Biddinger, Robert Pope and Imad Rahman. Thank you all for your wisdom, advice and kindnesses both professional and extra-professional.

To everyone who ever helped make Joe's Bar a special place, but especially Frank Phillips, Keith Kennell and the late Bob Best. Thank you for recognizing I'm special. You're all special.

My old Chicago friend Dana Landis; without your encouragement to turn what was a manuscript into a book, no one would hold this in their hands. You gave me courage.

Speaking of Chicago, I don't really know how to express my thanks to Joe Popa. I knew when you agreed to design the cover that it would be gorgeous, but good lord. Sometimes I just stare at it. Thank you, and thank you for being my friend for so many years.

Still speaking of Chicago, my friends Davids Wilson and Garland (and the aforementioned) helped me turn into the sort of person who would someday write a book. I love Chicago, but really it just means I love the people I know from having lived there.

To my old editors Jeff Niesel (Cleveland Scene) and Mark Redfern (Under the Radar). It took discipline and dedication to please each of you, and you were each crucial to my development as a writer. Maybe someday one or both of you will publish a career retrospective that I will write about some band only I like.

To my oldest and best friend Don Duerr, who read this entire thing as I was writing it and offered wise thoughts and kind words and the sort of encouragement only possible from someone who loves you and believes in you. I also love you and I believe in you, even though life is pretty stupid.

And to my family. When I started writing this novel, there were only two of us. We've doubled in size, but somehow there is still more than enough love to go around. To Alison, thank you for thinking of me as a writer, and to Augie and Elliott, watching you grow has been wonderful and frustrating and amazing and funny as hell. My family.

ABOUT THE AUTHOR

Chris Drabick is a former rock music journalist whose fiction has appeared in *Cease, Cows, Midwestern Gothic, After the Pause* and *Great Lakes Review*, and non-fiction in *BULL* and *Stoneboat*, among others. He is a graduate of the NEOMFA, the northeast Ohio consortial program. He teaches English at the University of Akron in Ohio, where he lives with his wife Alison and their sons, Augie and Elliott.

ABOUT THE PRESS

Unsolicited Press is a small publisher in Portland, Oregon. The press seeks to produce art, not commodity, from emerging and award-winning authors. Dedicated toward equality in publishing, Unsolicited Press publishes an equal number of men and women each year.

Learn more at unsolicitedpress.com and connect with the press on Twitter and Instagram (@unsolicitedpress).

Made in the USA
Monee, IL
20 December 2022

22869766R00215